Chapter 1

The ancients got it right—true identity resides in one's calling, one's mission, and nothing is more tragic than to turn from that calling and drift into any of its laborious and empty alternatives.

I was convinced I heard my calling at age 8 on a 3rd grade class trip from a New Jersey suburb to New York City's Radio City Music Hall where I got lost in a contortionist's performance. It was the first time I experienced a world wracked with tension dissolve so thoroughly by the magic of a body in motion, the contortionist's every twisted gesture, more powerful than any thought, pulling me into a world outside every suffocation.

He closed his act by folding himself up in a box, two assistants coming out and carrying the box offstage, the contortionist then returning to center stage to bow to my rapturous applause. After leaving the stage, up came loud music as a dance troupe, *The Rockettes*, long-legged ladies with wide smiles, hands on hips, legs alternately kicking up in the air, entering sideways stage left with foot-stomping precision in a uniform line.

The next day I go to the library and check out a book on contortionism and begin practicing. A week later I check out a book on tightrope walking, and there in the introduction is the consummate encouragement: the writer explained that the most difficult balancing act in the

3

world is walking, and that if you had learned to walk, you could learn the tightrope. I try for four days to tighten a close-line rope between two trees to practice, but I can't get the rope tight enough to stabilize it, to stop it from wobbling and sinking, and go back to the contortionist book.

Because of my young, pliable tendons and ligaments, I become a fairly accomplished contortionist by age 10, but the kids in the park whom I thought I could impress with this skill only poked fun at me: "Look at the double-jointed freak!" "Yeah…Hey, rubber-boy!—show us how you stick your head up your ass!"—their laughter like razors shredding my insides. I begin more and more to keep to myself, becoming as invisible as I can, never responding in any way to their jeers and insults, always walking away. In Junior High School I would sneak into the gym while they were outside playing any number of sports, mastering the gymnastic rings that had been gifted to the school but never used, stretching and strengthening my emaciated body, and once during mid-flight in attempting a flying double dislocate I take a fall head first into a hard-wood floor. When my mother picks me up from the nurse's office and we walk out into the hall to return home, I can hear snickering in the background. By age 13 I developed what I considered a spectacular act:

With the help of my 9-year-old sister-assistant Sarah, I dig a 10x10x4 foot hole and fill it with 4 fully-inflated car-tire inner-tubes, stabilizing the base with dirt, and then laying an old mattress I had found at a dump site on top, filling in and packing the edges of the mattress with more dirt, and then covering it with dry leaves. Climbing a two-story height of our back yard cherry tree through a clearing I had pruned for my descent, I stand up on a board I had nailed between two branches, my arms and head held high. Then lowering my arms to my sides and bending my knees, I leap out into space in a swan dive, and at the arc of my leap I bend my head

4

inward and turn my body over mid-flight into a fetal position, landing on my back, my body bouncing up into the air in an inertia-rest-but-moving slow-motion with outstretched arms over to solid ground where with bent knees I land squarely on my feet to receive Sarah's applause.

At age 14, amidst the beginning of a serious alcohol and barbiturate addiction, I learn from my aunt Leonce that the Vaun Brothers Circus would be playing at a field just outside of downtown Philadelphia where she lived and where I was born. I took this as a sign to heed my calling. I had already envisioned my act, and I would call it ETERNITY MAN. Much like men of the past who had dived into a tub of water from a two-story height, I would jump from the same height, maybe higher, with no tub of water to break my fall, just a big lime circle on what appears to be hard ground with the word ETERNITY printed with lime across the center. But under artificial turf there is a large, inflated rubber pad designed to deflate on impact and then automatically inflate while I lay there motionless in the lime-dust, my apparently dead body beginning to appear as the dust settles. And then an old restored ambulance (my home while on the road) with siren on races out to the field, two men in paramedic whites jumping out with a stretcher, placing my body on it and then hurriedly sliding it into the ambulance, and then racing off the field through an exit and disappearing behind the large tent. And after 30 seconds—some of the audience mumbling and others still stunned in shocked silence—the ambulance reappears from the rear exit and moves out to the center of the field, and I jump out the back door with hands held high in the air to thunderous applause.

I prepared for the journey, packing one change of clothes, opting to leave behind my stack of comic books, especially my prized collection of "Tales from the Crypt" they had stopped printing when I was age 9 and "Challengers of the Unknown", and instead take the only book that had ever interested me, gifted to me by my aunt Leonce (*The Complete Works of Edgar Allen Poe*), four peanut-butter sandwiches and a handful of pocket change. I figured once I arrived at the circus I would explain to the owner about the years I had dedicated to my dream and the skills I had developed without any encouragement, the act I was looking forward to developing, and that I was willing to drive spikes, pull tents, shovel animal dung and whatever else it took just to be a part of circus life, that I wasn't concerned with pay, that there simply was no other place for me in this world. It was the truth and I believed he would hear it and not turn me away.

It took all day and all night to get to the circus grounds the next morning, but when I arrived all I found was an empty field with wisps of a shifting wind kicking litter around.

I returned home and drifted back into getting stoned on glue, alcohol and barbiturates. Three years later, nodding out on heroin with my best friend Kris, I was offering up yet another lament on how I had abandoned my true calling. Kris was half listening with eyes closed in a nod while scratching an itch at his ankle: "Let it go, Sam…the circus is always in town."

**********

I was born on August 5, 1947 in Philadelphia, a city whose only claim to fame in modern times was that it took a referendum to get a statue of Rocky, a cinematically generated Great White Hope, removed from the front steps of City Hall. Because of a genetically deformed chest, sunken so low it almost touched my back, radically impairing my breathing, along with a compromised immune system that wasn't holding up to an attack of pneumonia, I wasn't expected to live very long. I was still in an incubator after 8 days, and in anticipation of my death

6

my parents called in a priest to baptize me and receive last rites. But I didn't die, and was eventually taken home.

The first birth certificate my mother received had the wrong date on it—August 13, obviously processed on the day the priest baptized me. She complained and got a certificate with my real birth date, but kept the first one. Three years later my father was changing our names (the local loan shark he was indebted to was pressing him with threats, and not being able to come up with the money, he packed us up and moved to the far side of New Jersey, legally changing our names from O'Brien to Jones. He reasoned that even if the loan shark discovered what the name change was, to find a Jones would be like finding a needle in a hay stack). When my name was being changed the records office had me listed as being born on August 13, but my mother once again complained that it was the 5th, and that she could produce the document. But the clerk insisted on the date that was logged in the big, black registrar book. Dad changed my first name to Sam.

*********

At age 17 heroin became my exclusive drug of choice, and on  particular night I was settling into my ritual, sitting in an old dusty, dark green over-stuffed a t-deco armchair in the middle of an otherwise vacant living room of a run-down mansion, zor. g out on a television placed three feet in front of me on a stool, getting ready to shoot up. My brother Tommy and a crime-partner had gone into New York, 20 miles from where we lived in a New Jersey suburb. He left me with plenty of dope, seven bags. All I needed was one, and I s ot it up. While the TV droned on, its pale light flickering off nicotine-stained walls and ceiling, i occurred to me that

7

because there was no valid record of my actual birth, and my real name was long gone, I officially didn't exist. And then a strange sensation overcame me, a feeling of everything falling away—the walls and everything beyond. Even the chattering from the TV became a distant, hardly audible hum. And then a thought crept into my mind: *Why not shoot up the other 6 bags?* That would kill me, no doubt, but *that* thought never entered my mind. I cooked up the heroin and drew up the liquid, tying my arm up with a belt, and when I pushed the needle under the skin, puncturing a vein, blood gushed up into the eyedropper, commingling in soft patterns in the liquid, and then, looking back up into the fuzzy glow of the TV tube, I squeezed it all in.

I can't remember pulling the needle out of my arm. I went unconscious for a long time. But I didn't die. It wasn't possible, but there I was—eyes and mouth wide open, my vomit-smeared face stuck to the floor like silly putty. I had no idea how much time had passed. I just lay there on the floor in a fetal position for a moment, and then reaching up and grabbing on to the arm of the chair, I pull myself up from the floor and fall back into the chair. After a few minutes of staring into the TV it occurred to me that perhaps I had died, that there had been a burial and that I was now in a purgatorial continuance field outside time and eternity, and that the movement into this place is true for every person who hadn't properly arrived. No matter what age a person dies prematurely, everything picks up where it left off and goes on and on, regardless how many times one dies, until one's life is finished where it was destined to end from the beginning.

I obsessed on this theme for a couple of weeks—I couldn't kick it, and my speculations got more elaborate every time I found a space to be alone in a heroin nod for long periods of time. I recall how at one point I was seized by the thought that parallel universes might exist where our universe is not only duplicated endlessly, existing simultaneously and in

8

perfect harmony with those endless universes, but that our experiences are not precisely replicated, that there are endless nuances, and even radical departures from what we experience in the now of our lives in this or any other parallel universe, even, as in my case, a death of self, and this is true even to the degree of experiencing in some context what every person has experienced from the dawn of time, which, in the end, makes us totally complete as empathic entities in the eternal now of parallel universes, for we in this universe are in no way separate from the experiences of our replicated selves in these parallel universes except in a necessary limiting/filtering consciousness that optimally sustains endless motivations that make life meaningful. And then one night my friend Kris was excited about Frank Sinatra appearing in New York, insisting we had to go to the concert. It would be another facet to the intricate bonding process Kris and I would go through as best friends since age 13, for there was a DJ, Jonathon Swartz, on New York's most popular rock station who played an hour of Sinatra every night at 6:00, and Kris and I made it a point to get stoned at precisely that time and do sing-alongs with Old Blue Eyes. But I had distinctly remembered Sinatra dying in a car crash years before. *This* was a slip in the purgatorial matrix, which drove me deeper into the obsession that I had died. I began to suspect that not only had I died the night I overdosed, but many times before, beginning with my death a few days after birth. I thought back to what a passionately religious young nun with a thick Irish accent who preferred playing her guitar and singing songs to teaching math had told us students when I was 10. She would always at some point steal some time to sneak in one of her own strange theological observations, defying a rigid mother superior who would never permit her to teach a religion class:

"There is this Russian Orthodox village where mourners at funerals walk through the streets for three days chanting 'Eternal Memory, Eternal Memory' over and over. They say nothing else. This is a reminder that every second of our lives—past, present and future—has always existed in God's memory, long before we were born. When an infant dies, the completeness of his life still exists in God's memory, and God's memory is more real than reality. Our real freedom is not about our willful ways outside of God's love, but the moment where with true competence we choose to be with him or far from him. He never decides this for us. All of the complexity of a life's journey takes us to that place where we will simply answer 'yes' or 'no', the only place where the meaning of our lives can unfold. In any case, there is no judgment, for in God's memory we freely mingle inside each other's experiences throughout all of history in the transparency of God's crystal sea, where it would be absurd to accuse another of anything, for all of our experiences are equally shared in the singular experience of God's love for us. It is only there that we can process our lives, and what the Church means when it says we all sinned in Adam."


This thought of an emasculated death poked fun at my laments. Death spawns urgent themes, keeping us active inside the great game of *Beat the Clock*, and to rob it of its sting would kill every sense of urgency in any serious search for meaning: no death means no incentive to defeat it, which means no immortality projects, the *raison d'etre* of our addiction to progress, what makes possible civilizations in our obsessive development of ever-advancing technologies in defiance of death. There would be no passionate race in medical science to defeat a degenerative gene, and no fear of being executed for a crime, for with a prayer for forgiveness off to eternal bliss we would go, and if we in the marrow of our bones committed to a rarefied realm of unrelenting rebellion, a realm of transcendent cyclical violence, then off to hell to share in Lucifer's willful delight. Even if death were an illusion absent a God that grants an eternal life of self-consciousness, that we somehow in death degenerate and dissipate into and coalesce with some inexplicable energy source greater than ours, a source where we might be left with some form of diminished self-awareness, and in that union becoming greater than we were when trapped in our bodies, we would still have no choice: we would still have to conjure and engage in meaningful battles with an imagined death to defeat the degenerative gene's rabid attack on our bodies that harbor a genetically-induced fear of annihilation of our radical sense of unique self-consciousness, or at least stave it off long enough to develop better weapons against it. But a Godhead that grants immortality with a guaranteed survival of unique self-consciousness in a state of eternal bliss would leave us with nothing to fight for—for our only real meaning would be a depth-oriented longing for this perfection of self-actualization in the afterlife, a realm desired far more than the absurdity of mulling around inside a painful life in transit. For if the finality of a decision for or against a God is the only realm of meaning as the crazed nun insisted, how could I with integrity long for actions generated by a fear of death, a death I would have to *willfully imagine* to generate the fear that makes those actions meaningful? That would be absurd and pathetic.

Before death's demotion, in my subconscious even the preparation for a heroin injection was a lofty ritual: I was nothing less than a high priest of many dark inner-sanctums (mostly inner-city basements), with running nose, muscle cramps and spasms, meticulously assembling a makeshift syringe out of an eye dropper, baby pacifier, elastic band and a needle, adding water to white powder in a bottle cap, and with fire carefully bringing the mixture to a boil with a sizzle that teases the temples more than any delectable cuisine, and then drawing up the precious liquid in the syringe, tying up my arm and tapping at its taut flesh, calling out a vein rich in potential to carry the alchemical substance on a bloodline to my brain for the ultimate, perhaps final, transformation. But that ritual absent a dance at death's door became empty, the heroin just another item in a panoply of pain reliefs.

Not too long after moving into this obsessive thinking I let it go. Nothing is as maddening as having nothing to be mad about.

*********

My sister Catherine possessed stunning beauty that mirrored our mom's, who resembled Elizabeth Taylor in looks with that perfectly-concealed frailty protected by enormous strength of will and flawless acting skills developed since childhood. In fact, our mom's maiden name was Taylor, and when persons found this out, they would always ask if she was related to the star. And it is fitting that Catherine later in life was terrified of the film *Who's Afraid of Virginia Woolf?*, which in a certain sense was a clue to why later in life Catherine's demoralized and vengeful lesbian lover, a George to Catherine's Martha, would methodically, and at great expense, arrange for Catherine to die a prolonged and painful death in the dreadful home of a poorly paid heroin addict after Catherine's failed suicide attempt left her severely incapacitated. Catherine had one evening in a conscience-stricken mode concluded that suicide was the only action that could redeem her in her lover's bitter eyes, and so she drank a quart bottle of a methadone-based pain cocktail. Not long before her suicide attempt Catherine had made this drunken observation:

"Sam, I know why dad wouldn't spend any time with you, why he wouldn't look at you, why he just stayed away from you unless he was beating up on you. You know how beautiful mom was, especially her long black hair and her purple-blue eyes, and how men so easily fell to their knees in her presence. Tommy and I had her hair and eyes, and that more than anything represented for dad the beautiful, because for him mom was beauty itself. And because your hair was flaming red, like his was as a child, he saw in you himself, and he saw himself as the embodiment of what is ugly and unredeemable. How precisely your sunken chest mirrored his soul, as if you were empty inside, a collapsed heart and soul."

*********

When I was 14 and Catherine 12, the whole family was lounging around in the living room watching television. Dad got up and walked out. He was gone for a while, and then Catherine got up and walked out. The barbiturates and alcohol swimming around in my brain distanced me from the commotion when Catherine appeared at the dining room entrance to the living room with a grimace, anxiously motioning mom with a flailing arm to hurry. My brother, lying next to me on the floor with his head propped up in hand blithely commented: "She's probably havin' her first period."

My eyes stayed fixed on the colorful images dancing around on the tube. It turned out that dad had gotten up and went down into the basement, and with some rope hung himself from a pipe. Catherine's instincts, enmeshed in her assigned role as surrogate wife (although mom was more the sad voluptuous nymph and Catherine the broken-hearted warrior maiden), had picked up that something was wrong, and going to the basement and finding dad hanging from a pipe,

13

she ran and got a kitchen knife and cut him down. Inevitably, whenever Catherine and I got together to get drunk and hash over the torments of her life, she would come back to that moment and say it was her only regret.

It was a curious event, though. Dad, a dirt-poor Irish boy who had grown up in an isolated, rocky inlet fishing community in Newfoundland, Canada, never expressed to anyone any regrets about anything. Life for him was something you grabbed, held on to and twisted till every drop of blood dripped from it into an empty tomb of desire. His favorite phrase was "The only crime is getting caught." I figured that moment in the living room, prior to lifting himself up from the sofa, was a rare, unrepeatable moment. It probably all came to him in one very quiet illumination, all that he had done, all that he had inflicted, all that he was incapable of touching and staying with. And from there he just moved into his death. And after his reprieve he returned to where he had always been since his arrival in America as a young, cynical man caught up in a gambling obsession and a desire to possess wholly a wildly romantic sixteen-year-old from Glasgow, Scotland, my mother, whose immigrant gaze, along with his, was fixed on the greatest distance from detestable poverty.

But that's my imagining. Catherine's drunken precision was probably closer to the truth: "Dad looked at me when he left the living room. It was a signal. He communicated with me that way; it was what made me feel special then, but what would later make me sick to my stomach—it was what he required of me if I were to remain special: to attend to his every secret injury that he was powerless to alter, especially when he was stretched out on his bed and I would sit next to him and lay my hand on his forehead while he indulged his drunken moans and groans; and he would reward me with material gifts and with making me feel superior to all of you. That's why I now know it was all a set-up. He knew I would follow him to the basement and cut him down. He hadn't even kicked the stool away; he just dangled next to it, the ball of his foot always ready to take excessive pressure off, and he probably had his pocketknife just in case he couldn't make it back to the stool. When he heard me open the cellar door he knew I was beginning that final descent, those few remaining steps down into his private hell, the home he had always been preparing for me."

Catherine obsessed on reminding me of mom's love for me and rejection of her. I tried again and again to convince her of the circumstances that created that impression, that it had to do with me living close to death the first six years of my life, and that if she had been the one who was dying, she would have been the most loved, that it had nothing to do with either of us as persons. I was sickly—chronic colds and bouts with pneumonia. My mom had to constantly decongest my lungs with a homemade decongestion tent, and there were many nights when she would gently massage my sunken chest while applying Vicks Vapo-Rub and smiling into my eyes. And there were the delicious hot toddies (tea, sugar and Irish whiskey) to help ease me into moments of sleep that seemed to always elude me. She would read to me, sing to me and reassure me every minute of every day that I would be all right, that she would find a way to get me better. She promised.

When you know with certainty that someone wants you to live—no hesitation, not ever, just persistence in keeping you alive—you have certainty that you are loved. And eventually mom would find a doctor who would perform a new procedure, massive wiring and bone grafting, and it worked. I was age 6 when the procedure was finished.


During my initial stay at the hospital they worked mostly on building up my strength for the operation. There were vitamin shots and lots of liver at mealtime. I hated liver, so when they served it I threw it behind the bed. When mom came to visit, she would sniff a bit, look around, and then look at me and ask "What's that smell, love?"

"I don't know, mom."

She looked at me with a big smile, and then went behind the bed to clean up the mess. She would always catch me in my lies, mostly because I hardly ever lied. I would lie only in rare, desperate moments, like being forced to eat liver.

On another day mom came in and I told her in a fearful voice "There's a witch on our ward!"

"A witch?"

"Yeah. It's a real witch, mom."

"How do you know?"

"It's hard to tell at first. She wears a disguise. Everyone thinks she's a nurse. But she lets us kids know. When she comes up to our beds she shows us her witch face and she speaks with her witch voice. Like yesterday. She said 'Well now…what needle is it going to be today, hmmmmm? How about *this* one?' And she pulls out this really big needle!"

"Is she on the ward now? Can you see her?"

I look across the room and see her sitting at a desk doing paper work. "That's her there," I say, pointing to the witch.

"Are you sure?"

I forcefully shake my head yes.

"It's OK," mom reassures me, "I'll take care of it."

And mom gets up and walks straight across the ward to the witch, and with an outstretched arm grabs a big handful of the witch's hair, pulling her up from her chair and walking her quickly in a circle, the witch's arms flailing about as she stumbles around, and then mom moves out of the circle and straight for the wall where she slams the witch's head real hard, again and again, yelling "You bitch!"

That day I was moved to a private room, which saddened me. I wanted to be around the other kids. Mom never hesitated in those kinds of situations. Her impulsive style could so quickly save the day, but would sometimes get her in trouble and eventually drive her into isolation and madness. But her attention, her cutting focus on what was immediate, was something I would inherit from her. And for me, too, it would become a blessing and a curse.

Mom's fault was that she had never grown up. She stayed fourteen. Her father had warned her that if she went to America with my dad he would disown her. She disobeyed him and he never forgave her, not even on his deathbed. By the time I was age 7 mom had moved into a severe, crippling depression, and she dealt with it in endless sleeping and crying. During her crying bouts she would always call out for her dad.

It was then that she began a program of reconstructing reality. No set plan. She would make stuff up as she went along. She learned how to establish new identities (at one point she had 6 different names with a license and social security card for each). Being brilliant and stuck in the world of a 14-year-old, she became proficient at altering every second of wherever she had found herself cornered, and she was cornered most of time.

\*\*\*\*\*\*\*\*\*

Mangled as they were in their respective ways, dad was the more practical and dispassionate of the two—a true utilitarian. His singular warning and advice—"The only crime is getting caught"—stemmed from his core philosophy: "Everything's according to Hoyle." Hoyle, of course, systematized in writing the rules for most card games, but for dad it signified the laws of probability. To win at cards and life itself one must know and abide in those laws. Whatever you want, to get it you must manipulate the odds in your favor. For dad it was never a question of ethics—it was a matter of winning, and if you do something wrong and get caught you had simply failed to master the game. All of human behavior is grounded in some kind of hustle. People are good at dressing it up, even hiding it from themselves, but in the end there is always a scam doing down, every seemingly sincere gesture an accomplished slight-of-hand.

With the information from the doctors after my birth about my deformity, dad knew the odds were against my living any length of time. I'm sure mom's efforts at keeping me alive, attending to my every need, were to dad a series of futile acts. On scientific evidence alone they simply didn't jibe with reality. He wanted nothing to do with it. He kept his distance.

Then one day something changed. Dad and I were home alone. I was 5 and it was only a few months before mom would find a doctor to perform a highly experimental operation on me. He asked if I would like a bath. He wanted to actually hold me and wash me, and he was smiling. I shook my head yes, not daring to utter a sound and risk losing that moment.

He carried me in his arms down to the basement where the two big industrial laundry tubs were. One of the deep tubs had already been filled with warm water. Dad helped me undress, and then with his strong ironworker hands he picked me up and lowered me into the warm liquid. First he washed my hair, and when rinsing it he told me to lean my head back, and with one hand supporting my back he used his other hand to cup water to pour over my head. He was so gentle. To feel him so close, and then his soapy hands rubbing me around the neck and shoulders and dipping down a bit into my sunken chest, and then more gentle rinsing with handfuls of water, and then his thick muscular fingers locking hard into the bones of my emaciated shoulders, and with a swift, violent thrust he pushes my entire body under water, my bony feet crashing hard into the far corner of the tub, massive energy gushing down from my brain to my feet, my legs locking stiff and pushing with great force, my arms crashing wildly about as my heart pounds against a deformed bone, and then a total release, my feet and legs propelling my body upward and over the wall of the tub and thumping down hard on the cement floor, my body shaking and my breathing jagged as I look up into my dad's face. He is smiling, and he calmly says "I was only kidding. Don't be scared."

For a good part of my life I believed I had actually broke loose from dad's death grip with the sheer force of my legs. In a more lucid moment I knew that for some reason he had changed his mind, possibly letting go of my shoulders because my resistance surprised him, forced him for the first time to see me as a person who was living, not dying. Or maybe…maybe I had actually died.

**********

When I was fully restored to good health at age 7, I entered a new realm. I joined my brother in being an object of dad's attacks to help relieve his many frustrations, especially stemming from his escalating losses at the race track. His betting got so out of control he would eventually lose two homes, the one we lived in and a duplex rental. It turned out his philosophy of winning was displaced by an obsession, what we now like to call addiction. In the end what guided dad were not the laws of probability, but the fever of placing a bet.

Anything could ignite his anger, and beating up on Tommy and me was his most immediate form of release. But when I turned 8 years old it occurred to me that what made dad's satisfaction complete was the pitch of our screams when he beat up on us. The higher the pitch the deeper the affirmation of his absolute power over us—what for him displaced the terror of his helplessness in an agonizing spiral ever downward into a hellish poverty pit, proof-positive of his impotency in the actual living of his life day to day. For me it was an epiphany: *if I don't cry, he will be robbed of his power. I could beat him!*

It was a night I had forgotten to do something he had requested of me. He ordered me to go to the kitchen and remove my clothes. This time, though, my fear was displaced by a rabid determination to beat him at his own game. I *wanted* the beating, was anxious for it. *I wanted to win.*

I removed my clothes as ordered and stood there naked. Already he could sense something had changed: I was not cowering on the floor, sitting with my arms wrapped around my legs and shaking, my head buried in my knees. The first lash from his construction belt landed against my upper left arm and back. But instead of falling to the floor and protecting my genitals as I had always done in the past, I just stood there, defiant. His fury and concentration intensified as blow after blow of the belt cracked across my back, arms and legs, and then he punched me hard in the face with his right fist, my body crashing to the floor, the lashings quickening with even greater force, his face turning red, white spittle collecting around the corners of his mouth, his lips curled up tight into the gums of his false teeth, the muscles of his face contorting against his skull—he *knew* what I was doing, and he screamed "You bastard! You'll cry!" But I didn't, the belt tearing at my flesh but losing its sting…and then I moved—out of my body. I was hovering over and looking down at my body and dad's twisted face, his mantric "Cry you fuckin' bastard!" hanging softly in the air. I was calm, silent. And then it occurred to me: *I'm going to die.* And that thought connected as if through a lazy thread to my body below, and with a jolt, like an electric shock, I was back in my body, letting loose a long and piercing scream. It was as if it didn't come from me at all, but from somewhere below my feet, a distant place, now traveling up through my legs, intestines, stomach, heart, throat and out the top of my head. And when the scream stopped, so had dad; but with a crazed deliberateness I screamed again, a futile attempt to capture *that* scream, to *know* it before it left forever, leaving me alone in this final submission—my body now belonging to him.

**********

When I was 10 years old, mom and dad called all us kids into the living room (Tommy, Catherine, Sarah and me) and told us they were breaking up. Mom was leaving. I was happy for her. It turned out she was seeing another man. For me, her getting away from dad was a blessing, regardless what the circumstance. But I didn't like the way they handled it, lining us up in single file, oldest to youngest, and asking each one of us whom we wanted to live with. I knew instantly that I wanted to live with mom, but then it occurred to me that although dad seemed to be in control, this was something he would not be able to handle. His jealousy, loneliness and utter sense of failure would destroy him. Plus, Tommy had defiantly told me he would stay with dad no matter what, having made that total identification with him, connecting at that base level, that philosophical level of brute force, of being in control, and Tommy, dad's number one agent, a serpent birthed from dad's tortured brain, was now giving me a choice, to stay with him or go with mom. Tommy was already the archetypal toughest-kid-in-town of his age group, and that he remained in his way a sensitive and generous soul to all his friends was moving him into mythological status. Once when we were teens walking down the street an older kid bumped into him to impress his girlfriend who was hanging on his arm, and this muscular kid with a pack of cigarettes tucked tight in his rolled-up t-shirt sleeve gave Tommy a nasty look, and with a series of devastating blows Tommy pulverized him, the kid's girlfriend screaming hysterically as Tommy kicked what little life was left in the kid out of him as he lay on the ground in a fetal position. Yet if the kid had simply said "Excuse me" Tommy would have honored that courtesy. He always did. Another time we were all hanging out at the local pizza parlor, and some kids who weren't with us started acting out, and the owner, a bulky middle-aged Italian man, angrily ordered all of us to leave, but Tommy ordered us to stay: "We ain't done nothin' and we ain't goin' nowhere." The owner came over to our table and screamed "I a told a you to a geta outta here. Now you a move!"

"Fuck you!" is all Tommy said, and the owner grabbed him by the arm and pulled him up from his seat, Tommy going with the momentum to gather force and comes with an overhand roundhouse right slamming into the owner's face, stunning him just long enough for Tommy to grab the man's right arm, and with one hand holding the forearm at wrist and the other the elbow corner, Tommy slams the forearm dead center down on the aluminum-edge of the table, the bone cracking, the sound of it making my blood cringe, the owner falling to the floor screaming. For Tommy this was simple justice. For him court was in session every second of every day, and he preferred speedy trials. But he wasn't a bully, not in the technical sense—he never picked a fight or in any way infringed on a person's dignity. And he would give you his last dollar and the coat off his back.

I, on the other hand, was cowardly. I had learned this with finality at age 7 when the Swanger brothers had ganged up on Tommy, challenging him to fight, and I just stood there frozen. I had shut down so thoroughly in my fear and shame that I have never been able to recall the outcome of the fight. I had gained the first, primary revelation of the core of my being, where I reside most deeply—in cowardliness. I would learn to weigh every threatening situation in life from that shameful place. And because I was at the core terrified, whenever I met other kids in any situation, I had developed a technique of quickly discerning their psychological and emotional needs, and always when I talked with them I would take on their voice patterns and agree with everything they uttered. I ingratiated myself in this way to win acceptance at the most basic level: when another kid looked into my eyes he would see a submission to his ideal image of himself, a total affirmation of his personal power, what every fear-based boy desires above all else from his mates and everyone else, and what I would provide. But this also distanced me from the kids. Submission to another sends one's personhood into hiding, a stifling of self to become a lackey. This aloneness in the world is what made my relationship with Tommy so desperate. Only with him did I become visible. He knew me and didn't judge me. He held nothing against me and demanded nothing from me. I needed Tommy and dad needed me. So when my turn came and they asked me whom I wanted to stay with, I chose dad. I was happy that mom didn't get upset. I thought she might be hurt. But she somehow understood. Catherine decided to stay with dad and reap even greater rewards as surrogate wife. And not long after mom left with Sarah, dad was getting polluted drunk most every night, sometimes coming home covered in blood from bar fights. I would always have his coffee ready for him, and I would cook all the meals, do the laundry, keep the house clean and the yard pristine in appearance. But the beatings continued. What I couldn't see then was what I was really after: I stayed with dad

23

because it was the first and last chance to win him over. I knew he would need me, and by attending to his every need he would in time embrace me. But it didn't happen.

Getting over dad, getting away from him, would become an obsession. He was embedded in my psyche by the sheer force of his distancing himself so thoroughly from me. Too often through the years I would imagine I had let go of him, but he was always there like a scab hardened over a deep wound, itching but not hardened quite enough to tear lose and throw away, leaving only a scar, a battle wound common to all of humanity. I was caught up in this fantasy that he would one day turn to me, however fleetingly, and smile, acknowledging in one gesture that I *am* here and that he wishes me well. And until then, every effort to move away would in fact pull me deeper into this longing.

*********

Dad found out where mom was living and the name of the man she was living with— Armando. One night dad waited for Armando outside his home and beat him into the ground so badly he was hospitalized for three days. Dad convinced mom that if she didn't come back to him he would kill her and Armando. She came home, pregnant, and dad arranged an abortion. I was about to turn 11 years old, and it was in that year that everything changed.

Chapter 2

A person once said to me "You got a movie reference for everything." It's true. In films I focus. I pay attention. As a child and teen I hardly ever looked at what was going on around me. I was in a coil position, fearful and alert, prepared to defend or withdraw at the first sign of an impending humiliation or other act of violence. This was not something I was necessarily conscious of. It was a way of life. My early fears and cowardliness over time had altered my chemistry. The terror had become constitutionally who I am and not to be weighed against other possibilities. This is one reason why drugs would play a big part in my life: they altered my chemistry. I could relax.

So at age 14 my objective was clear—to get high and journey into the lives of characters who move in and out of the television tube. I would sometimes do this around the clock. It was a way of having a conversation with myself, a socially sanctioned solipsism. I rarely talked to people, and when I did it was empty—a drug transaction, the parroting of a delusional way out of the drug life or the retelling of a big score. To watch a film was not an escape—it was an alternative, a temporary fix, a way of sticking around, curious, hopeful, and I remain indebted to the masters and those directors who simply entertain with style.

*********

When I was 8 years old I had separated from most childhood clingings and began my move into adulthood. I relished the opportunity to make a difference—sewing, washing and ironing clothes, raising money to buy food (mostly by scouring the neighborhood for empty soda bottles and returning them for cash), cooking meals and comforting mom in what meager ways I could as she moved deeper into her abyss. I found great joy in this. I had no desire for another way of life. It would take an event to push me out, and that event arrived halfway into my 11th year:

My brother at age 12 had made a solid commitment to make the world back off. I clung to him as much as I could, and nothing spoke to my religious commitment more than my passing up an opportunity to walk to school with him so that I could attend the 6:00 o'clock Mass before school started.

We went to an Irish-Catholic school run by nuns who had abandoned the Church's teaching that human beings are made in God's image and likeness and are therefore essentially good. They had bought into an infected religious notion that human beings are essentially corrupt and cannot but act according to whatever desire enslaves them in any given moment, our bad habits wielded like weapons to fight off the good angels assigned to help us, no doubt a Jansenist influence after their priests were kicked out of France by the revolutionaries and they migrated en masse to Ireland. From this view it easily follows that only the fear of consequences can generate morally sound conduct. And this fear was instilled with teachings of an impending after-life of hell-fire for wayward souls, and in present time corporal punishments ranging from ruler-knuckle-beating to head-slamming into walls and blackboards: the nuns saw us poor Irish street kids heading towards inevitable destruction, no help from any realm, including the

Kingdom of God, because we were hell-bent on survival and winning at all costs, with a penchant for brute force. They figured all they could do was be forceful in preparing us for possible alternatives, what wasn't available to us in the now of our lives, and they could do that only by making sure we learned to read, write and know basic math, and by age 9, the age I stopped participating in school, I was accomplished at all three, something poor kids of post-modern times are deprived of inside a matrix of experimenting with competing theories of education, including theories on discipline/guidance, that in fact justify indifference and non-engagement by teachers. This is why today I hold those nuns in high regard: they single-handedly helped prepare me for the real world where I would have a fighting chance.

It was the morning of Tommy's complete commitment, crossing the last authoritarian line carved in stone by the society we knew. A nun had slammed his head into a wall outside the classroom for being late yet again to school, and Tommy turned and slammed his right iron fist into the nun's head, dropping her to the floor like a big black bag of laundry.

Arriving at school the next day a nun walks up to me in the hall, stops and looks sternly down into my face and yells "Your brother is going to burn in hell for what he did! You understand? And if you continue to associate with him, you will burn in hell with him!"

I'm sure the nun had no idea how those words would send me out the other side of my faith. I had never told anyone about my prayer life. I never felt a need to. It was a place where God comforted me and gave me strength to endure and make attempts at bettering the world I lived in, for it was in the joy of those in my family that I found the greatest joy.

I returned home that day and began an exploration of what the nun's words meant. I finally thought to myself, *Tommy is the only person who knows me, who accepts me, who I can be with and be as ridiculous as I want to be, who in his way loves me like no other.* It was he who figured out a way to comfort me when I had migraine attacks: he would fill a closet with pillows, and then tie a belt around my head real tight, and then pick me up and slowly lay me down on the pillows and then shut the door so no light would get in.

I then began to go over in my mind the torments of hell. Although the many vivid descriptions of those torments really played no part in how I lived my life up to that point, I now had to start considering them seriously, because I might go there. You see, when I prayed daily it wasn't from a fear of anything, it wasn't toil—I didn't experience the ground of my prayer life as something I had to do to make other things possible, what is called petitioning prayer. It was a place I resided in at all times, in no way cordoned off from the natural rhythms of life's varied and sometimes unpredictable movements. There was a great deal of joy in going secretly to six o'clock Mass every morning, and after Mass sitting in an isolated, darkened space in front of the tabernacle. God and I had an understanding. The point of it was to just be there with him, no different than spending time with my brother who was always with me in spirit. And our communication was not in words, or in any way a process of coming to know or accomplish anything. It was simply a residing, a being at peace, a *resting with him*.

So to keep those endearing times with (and loyalty to) my brother, I would risk not only the eternal torments of hell, but also forfeit my ground, my participation in the very life of God, where his love and tenderness was a constant. In other words, I would risk residing in a land of spiritual suffocation and judgment. This would be the ultimate act of the will, more than even suicide, for in suicide there is no life in one's experience, only its absence and any hope for it, *despair*, a being blinded to life, and therefore any decision to part from it being no decision at all, for no real choice between life and death is available, only a feeble choice between death and a living death. Whereas my *no* to God would be the deepest break, a fully conscious, deliberate decision to be in opposition to him who had provided and sustained in me a natural joy that naturally sustains hope.

In the moments before my decision I pictured in my mind my brother and I walking through the vast terrain of hell, huge boulders around us splitting with loud cracking sounds from the intensity of an ever-present fire, the ground a solid blistering bed of rock, our flesh burning off our bodies as we walked, and then growing back again only to be melted away once more. But then a strange sense of the rightness of being with him, and I look over at his face and he is smiling. And then the realization that we were already growing accustomed to the environment. It was not unlike life as we had always known it.

The next morning I awoke early as I always did, but instead of heading for the six o'clock Mass, I go to a frozen pond deep in a wooded area about a half mile from home. It was cloudy, dark and quiet, the only sound the humming of electricity gushing through telephone wires overhead. Leaving the road to the pond, even that sound fades. It is a calm quiet, like prayer quiet, eventually arriving at the pond and walking out to its center. Standing still on the ice and looking up into the immensity of God's darkness, without a thought in my mind I start screaming at the top of my lungs: "Shit!...Fuck!...Dammit!...Dammit to hell!" And with every repetition the words intensify in an exultant burst of venom, and I feel in every molecule of my being a heightened sense of power and release, every word a super-charged affirmation of Lucifer's defiant "No!" that still haunts every region of the universe. It was a new freedom...not of love, but of saying *Fuck you!*

29

I didn't go back to school. Not because of the nun's hell-threat or because of what Tommy did. It was new territory. With my *no* to God came clarity, an awareness of the futility of willfully pursuing anything in the world to make a difference, everyone locked as they are into games of cyclical despair, totally dependent on whatever fix of forgetfulness they rabidly pursue in a relationship, a drug or a cult, what they lock into and sometimes bow to, always a trembling and turning away in terror from looking into the dark pit, our rendezvous with Satan or the Void. My focus, my fix, was now on the ecstasy of rebellion, of saying *no* to God's initiative in any degree, and after two weeks of playing hooky from school I was, without knowing it, ready for the big move.

Tommy was out somewhere with older friends and I was at home with my sister Sarah, who had also picked up the habit of not going to school. Sarah yelled at me excitedly: "Sam, there's a car parked outside with two people in it!"

I run to the living room window and peer out from behind the curtain. Sure enough. It was a '58 Chevy and the woman on the driver's side was climbing out of the car. She was a big woman, more wide than tall, her hair rolled up in a bun, wearing a white blouse, grey skirt and big black shoes, and she begins her walk up the sidewalk to our front porch. I turn to Sarah and say "Go to the kitchen and don't make a sound!"

I go to the front door and stand there, adrenaline kicking in. I knew this wasn't good. A loud knock on the door. I wait, trying to think what to say. Then the knock again. I open the door:

"Yes?"

"Hi there," she says with a broad smile. "You must be Sam."

"Yes."

"I'm here to speak to your mother or father."

"My father's at work and my mom's sleeping. She's sick."

"Oh, I'm sorry…I don't want to wake her, but it is important that I speak to her."

"I'm sorry. She's really sick and I'm not supposed to wake her."

"Sam, I have to talk to her…I'm a police officer."

Panic kicks in.

"Can I see your badge?" I demand.

She looks at me for a few seconds. "Of course you can. It's in the car. Hold on." She turns around, but moves slightly backward into the doorway to prevent me from closing the door, and she yells to the person in the car: "Marge, would you bring me my purse?"

Already I have the door pulled way back, and then with my shoulder pressed hard against it, like a football linebacker I run full force and slam the door into her huge backside, her falling out onto the porch as the door slams shut and I lock it. I run to the kitchen and grab Sarah by the hand and then run with her to a bedroom window on the second floor that leads out onto the garage roof, and once out the window onto the sloping roof, just as I had trained her to do in the past in anticipating what was now happening, we hold hands and jump to the high ground of our neighbor's yard and run off to Mystery Land, a large wooded area that was used mostly as a dump, but a place where kids would play. We stayed there until it got dark.

When we got home I tell Sarah to go inside and tell mom and dad what had happened.

"Where are you going?"

"I don't know."

"Can I come?"

"No…just go inside. I'll see ya later, OK?"


I walk for hours, and when it gets real late I go to sleep in a parked car. I get up early the next morning, freezing.

After walking for two more hours I arrive in a town called Rahway where one of the three state prisons is located. I was hungry, so I go into a grocery store and steal a package of boiled ham. I walk a block and then pull out the package, tear it open and begin eating the meat. I keep walking down the street, carefully pulling off one thin slice of meat at a time, savoring every bite.

An older kid, about 14, is walking towards me from the opposite direction, looking straight at me. He is a tall, lanky Italian wearing a perfectly grease-groomed pompadour and a motorcycle jacket.

He stops in front of me, looking right down inside me. Then he looks at the ham, and then back into my eyes. He smiles.

"What's goin' on?" he says.

"Nothin'."

He keeps looking at me, still smiling. Then, with the fingers of his right hand pointing to his chest he says, "Would'ya do me a favor?"

"Sure."

"Good. I like you. Come on." And we begin to walk back in the direction he came from.

"What school you go to?" he asks.

"I don't go to school."

"Good. Neither do I—most of the time. Let's go to my house. What's your name?"

"Sam."

"I'm Frankie."

When we got to Frankie's house and walk inside I see a potbelly stove in the middle of the living room radiating a welcoming heat with a big oval sheet-metal bucket of coal spilling over next to it. I smell a wonderful food-cooking-all-the-time smell. No pretense to middle-class aspirations in sight. Just poor get-along-the-best-you-can living, a blessed resignedness to routine survival. I feel immediately at home and sense I could live there forever. It would be my first introduction to Italian food, and it would remain my favorite. Frankie's mom was in the kitchen, a portly woman with graying black hair pulled back in a big bun, an apron tied around her waist. She was mixing spices into chopped meat on an aluminum edged vinyl kitchen table.

"Frankie. How a come a you a not in a school?"

"I forgot my books, ma."

"Who's a your friend? I don't a remember him."

"His name's Sam, ma. Just moved here. I'm gonna introduce him to some kids his age."

"Why don't a you a take a him to a Gloria's. He a looks a Danny's age." She stops moving and looks right at me. "How a old are you, Sam?"

"11, mam."

"Yes, you a Danny's age. You a come a here after school and a Frankie a take a you to a Danny's."

"Gotta go, ma. See you later."

"Don't a forget to a come a home after a school."

"I won't, ma."

Her name was Mary, the kindest person I would ever know in my childhood.

33

We leave the house and head over to a small horse farm owned by a man in his 80's. His is the last farm in Rahway. Frankie introduces me to him—Sibi Dilts. He tells him I'm looking for work, that I'm a new kid in the neighborhood and I won't be enrolled in school right away and that I can work full-time. Sibi offers me $15 a week to feed the horses, brush them down and clean their stables as well as load up manure wagons when he makes a sale for fertilizer. On the weekends Sibi would give hay-rides to children on a big horse-driven wagon, and I would sit on the back to make sure no one snuck on. I took the job and started right away. Frankie takes off and tells me he will stop by later, that he has to go to school, which was intended for Sibi, I thought.

Sibi pours me a cup of coffee and gives me a powdered-sugar donut to eat. "You can eat here, but I'll have to take out for food." At the end of the first week I get paid $5. But it doesn't bother me. I like the work and I like Sibi. I just have to get used to two things: the smell of urine wafting throughout the farmhouse, and two strange characters that lived there. Sibi had a hard time getting around, and he had a weak bladder. So he would strategically place portable urinals throughout the farmhouse. Eventually he would get around to emptying them, but it wouldn't fight back the stench—it was in the walls.

And the two characters that lived there. One thought he was Santa Claus. He was rotund with long white hair and beard, always wearing big baggy pants with a three-inch-wide belt and suspenders, and always the thick long-sleeved thermal undershirt. In his bedroom—that used to be a dining room on the first floor next to the kitchen, separated by two French, curtained doors—there was a big brass bed with the thickest mattress I'd ever seen, along with two giant pillows. Department stores would compete to hire him at Christmastime, and during the summer

34

he would ride a three-wheeled bicycle ice-cream cart and sell ice-cream to children at the parks. He was obviously harmless, but the other person scared me.

His name was Harry and he would get up in the morning, dress in an old musty pin-striped suit, the same suit every day with the same shirt—a yellowed-near-brown white shirt and tie. And he always had his crunched-up sweat-and-oil drenched fedora hat on. He would sit at the breakfast table all day and just stare out the window. He never uttered a word. He was feared by all the children who, on the way home from school, would sometimes stop and stare at him and then break into a run. But he, too, was harmless—just scary.

Frankie came for me about 3:00 that afternoon: "Come on, we gotta go."

"I got a few more things to do."

"No you don't. Come on."

I turn and look at Sibi who is in the yard. I yell to him, "I gotta go!" He just waves.

As we begin to walk Frankie starts telling me the plan:

"About dat favor you promised me? Dere's dis punk kid. He got me in big trouble. I can't kick his fuckin' ass. Too young. He's your age. So you do dis for me and I'll make it up to ya, ya understand?"

I shake my head yes.

"You don't talk much, do ya?"

"No."

We walk to a park where a bunch of kids in different age groups are hanging out. "Dere he is," Frankie says, pointing his finger to a kid close by. I look at him and get scared. Not of getting my ass kicked. I could handle that. I just wanted badly to impress Frankie. I didn't want to let him down.

"Hey asshole!" Frankie yells at the kid. The kid looks at Frankie and yells "Fuck you!"

"You talk a lotta shit for a little punkass motherfucker! You're just lucky I haven't crippled your fuckin' ass you little piece of shit! Unfortunately I can't beat up on a little punkass sissy motherfuckers like you. It's beneet my dignity. So my man here is gonna do it for me. He's gonna tear you a new fuckin' asshole, bitch!"

The kid sizes me up real fast, and I see in his face a sarcastic confidence. He probably picked up on my terror. I was emaciated, looking like a Holocaust victim, my knees bigger than my thighs. He pulls the cap from his head and throws it to the ground, walks right up to me, and with an over-hand right punches me in the face. I manage to slip a little to the right, avoiding a solid blow. I move quickly without a plan, rushing into him and clasping both my hands behind his head, locking my fingers tight into his hair and then pull his head down with great force while simultaneously bringing my knee up with even greater force, smashing his nose on impact. He puts his hands up to his face, blood oozing through his fingers as he starts to cry. Frankie picks the kid's hat up from the ground, pulls out his dick and starts pissing in it, and then throws the hat at the kid's face.

"Come on, man," Frankie says to me. He puts his arm around my shoulder. "Dat was good, man…real good."

When we get to Frankie's house his mom accepts me like I had always lived there. That night Frankie's girlfriend came over. They went to his bedroom to make out, and I just sat in the living room watching TV. After some time passed, Frankie comes down to the living room and calls me to come up to his room. When I get there, his girlfriend is on the bed. "Peggy," he says to her, "Come over here and give Sam a kiss."

"Give him a kiss?" she asks with a knowing smile (I knew instantly they had planned it). "I don't know. You think he's up to it? I mean, he's a little young to be kissing girls, don't ya think?"

"Naw…not after today. He got his manhood. He deserves a kiss. Come on."

He walks over and grabs Peggy's hand and pulls her up from the bed and walks her over to me, her being only semi-reluctant with a sway that moves her knee-length puffy dress freely about, my eyes fixed on her perfect legs; and once in front of me he lets go of her hand and backs away. She looks down into my eyes with a smile born in fearlessness and all-knowingness, and with outstretched hands her warm body with just a hint of perfume moves slowly forward, her fingers gently pressing into and moving across my temples and behind my ears and down my neck, my eyes closing as the tips of our noses touch and her lips press ever so softly into mine, my entire body and mind melting into pure intoxication, lifted out of this world, no longer trapped in any notion or desire, everything fulfilled in an instant, the perfect kiss—not because it was my first: she just naturally sensed what I was yet unaware of, a crazed longing locked in the marrow of my bones to connect with a woman, a longing that up until then only a hint of which would occasionally seep into my not-fully-actualized propagation-of-the-species hormones, and even in this moment not fully developed, and precisely why that programmed prepubescent distance freed me from lust and allowed entrance to a far deeper place than sexual desire and its fulfillment. She had playfully indulged the sweetness of my sexual innocence, resolving to pull me out of childhood into a flawless euphoria known only in the arms of a woman, the joy of disappearing, of being able to relax inside the realm of a transcendent other, the greatest freedom I could know, and when her warm lips melted into mine that's exactly what happened.

At night Frankie would sneak me up to his bedroom where I would sleep under his bed. The night of my first kiss, lying there on the wood floor, my head pressed into a pillow, I felt for the very first time that I had arrived, and, as I would discover much later in life, these arrivals are far more important than any journey.

I'd been gone two weeks. As usual, Frankie met me at Sibi's after school and we began to walk back to his house. I told him about this strange thing Sibi had told me:

"We were having lunch outside at that old picnic table with the bird-shit baked into it. Sibi just sat there starin' at me, and then he drops his eyes, and then looks up at me again, still not saying anythin'. He just stares. It was odd. He never did it before. He always looks straight at me and tells stories when we eat together. But he wasn't sayin' anythin'. And then he says 'It's strange.'

"What?" I asked him.

"It's hard to explain…I have this gift…Well, everyone has a gift…My gift is I can tell immediately what a person's gift is. But I found out a long time ago the most dangerous thing in the world is a person's gift. When I was a kid, Frankie's age, I told a friend what his gift was. It was exploration. I knew he was destined to travel, that his curiosity about the world and people had no bounds. I could see it clearly, and I told him. He said he had always known that, that his favorite book was by Richard Burton, the English explorer. A few weeks later he starts hanging out near the freight yards, and he told me he was going to run away, that he had been talking with some hobos at a campsite inside an abandoned house, learning the routes and how to get to certain places. He was going to head to Florida first and from there he just didn't know. I didn't want him to go…He was my only friend. I tried to talk him out of it. But he left. About a month later I found out he had died trying to jump a freight, got crushed beneath the wheels.

"I swore I'd never tell anyone their gift again, and I never have. Inside there's Santa Claus. His gift is communicating with children—it's the world he thrives in. A long time ago he had worked at a school as a janitor and bus driver for school trips. It was the day after a snow fall—the streets had been cleared, but some melted snow had turned to ice overnight. Someone on a highway cut him off, and when he slammed on his brakes the bus skid sideways off a small cliff and down an embankment. Three children died and lots of others were injured. He almost got indicted because of protests that he hadn't put chains on the bus, something he was required to do when snow is on the roads. But the prosecutor didn't pursue it…Santa blamed himself. He spent some time in a hospital where he had to undergo a series of shock treatments, and after his release he began to believe he is Santa. And that's the name he goes by. I let him stay here 'cause there's no place else for him to go.

"And Harry. He was a self-made millionaire. He made his fortune in stocks, and he met and married the woman of his dreams. His gift was finance. He had an instinct to make crucial, often high-risk decisions that always panned out. His wife was from established money. Then the stock-market crashed and Harry lost everything. His wife found it intolerable, as did her family who never liked him anyway. They had three children. His wife left him and arranged through lawyers that he would never see his children again. I don't know what's on his mind. I sometimes think he's still waiting for his wife to change her mind.

"It was their gifts that destroyed them, you see, just like my friend…But now I'm sitting here thinking about your gift. It can't possibly harm you, but I don't understand it…not at all."

"What?" I ask him.

"I saw it the day you walked in with Frankie. I know you're playing hooky from school. That's not my business. That's for your family to figure out. But your gift…It's not possible. I don't understand it… But I can't doubt it."

"What?...What is it?"

"Sibi looks deep down inside me really serious and says 'You're never going to die. I know it can't be true, and it certainly couldn't hurt you, but I could see it as clear as I've seen anything in this life.' It gave me the creeps."

Frankie was silent for a second and then says, "Da old coot's a fuckin' lunatic, man! He's always makin' shit up like dat. I used ta listen to dat shit, too…Just fuckin' nix it, man. It don't mean shit."

"What about Santa and Harry?"

"Who fuckin' knows, man? Who gives a shit? Sibi let's crazies stay at his farm, dat's all. It could be anythin'. He likes ta tell stories. Maybe he's tryin' ta fuckin' scare ya, ya know? Dat's Sibi, man. One thing's certain…you're gonna fuckin' die, OK? *Trust* me on dat…OK?"

When we arrive at Frankie's house, his mom is sitting in a chair facing the front door as we walk in. "There's a someone a here to a see you, Sam."

Although his back is to me in a chair I know it's dad. He stands up, turns and looks at me for a half second, then turns back and thanks Mary, and "we'll be leaving now", and Mary tells me I'm always welcome.

Once outside dad orders me to get in the car. I open the car door and get in. He gets in the driver side and closes the door—not loudly as I expected. He doesn't start the car right away, either. He just stares straight ahead, not saying anything. Then, without looking at me, he asks "Do you want to go home?"

I was scared. I knew no matter what I said I was going to get a serious beating. There would be no way to plead my way out of it. So I told him the truth: "No."

He sits still for a moment, not saying anything. Then he starts the car and drives home. When we arrive home he slowly pulls up in the driveway and stops the car and we both get out. I follow him up the porch steps and into the house, and he disappears into another room. I just stand there in the hallway. He doesn't come back. No beating, no reprimand…nothing. Then I understand. I was on my own. This was a new, great freedom that had come unexpectedly with triumphant exhilaration, but in the next second an awareness of a new shackle—a deep sense of an ever-lasting abandonment that dragged my new freedom down into a pit of emptiness destined for despair.

\*\*\*\*\*\*\*\*\*\*

We moved twice over the next year. I was 12 and Tommy 13. He had put together a gang of thieves. There were four of us. We mostly broke into homes. Tommy had opened a bank account in a neighboring city where most of our share of the stolen money went. The light valuable stuff we had accumulated, like jewelry, we buried out in the woods, just like pirates, but Tommy insisted we not write down where it was—we would memorize it. He chose a wooded area near a train trestle. He paced off 10 steps from the 20th plank from the corner of the overpass, using the plank as an arrow to point the way. He reasoned that the land would never be developed because the railroad wasn't going anywhere anytime soon.

We built a small, square shack with 2 by 4's and plywood (painting it brown) in the mountains far from any paths to stash stolen weapons, booze and other items. We made a small clearing, and with an old car seat and a few chairs our gang would gather to drink whiskey, talk nonsense and make plans for our next sting. I never talked, and when I drank with the other two (ages 14 and 16) I would fake it. The taste was just too harsh. That would change in a year.

One of the kids got busted and told the police everything. Tommy and I wouldn't admit to anything. Finally, to avoid the court system, probably arranged among his Irish cohorts who inhabited all areas of the justice system, our dad moved us to Mountainside, a middle/upper-middle class town seemingly removed from everything criminal. That was an illusion. My brother soon discovered the criminal element, the mischievous teen rebels looking to cross lines who can be found in any community. Tommy and I would form another burglary ring, and again when one of the kids got busted and ratted us out, we ended up having a hearing not in court but in someone's house where we were told that we would for the rest of the year go see a counselor at her home with our report cards in hand. Tommy and I never went.

*********

When we first moved to our ultra-suburban home in Mountainside with its expansive living room, larger than normal dining room, three bedrooms, a fireplace, wine cellar, a large sun-deck, huge back yard with adjacent vineyard and a finished-off basement with a living room

42

and a bedroom that Tommy and I would use (we could easily come and go as we pleased through a basement window) I slipped into a euphoric sense of having arrived in a new grand opportunity of altering the way I had lived up until now, having just turned age 13. But in essence this was just another one of dad's periodic, although the most elaborate at this point, ways of creating an illusion that things were hunky-dory in our world, that no matter how bad things got, they were destined to get better with his gambling skills and ingenuity, and these occasional flourishes were mostly a gift to mom because she more than any of us needed that illusion in place, and this time with a windfall in crime or gambling he gave mom money to purchase new furniture for the entire home, but no new clothes for us kids other than Catherine, and still little food in the cupboards.

But for some inexplicable reason I was in, whole hog. I spent that summer in anticipatory joy, working hard at landscaping around the house and preparing to start 8th grade in September, even considering that being apart from Tommy, who was entering high school, might be a benefit: I would be on my own, not drawn to how he moves in the world. I even meditated on an elaborate way of fitting in: I would observe closely what the other children wore and outfit myself in their garb: their khaki pants, checkerboard shirts and penny-loafer shoes. I would adopt their hairstyle and their every gesture—the way they walked, the inflections in their voices, their hand and facial gestures and their postures when motionless, every nuance of how they moved or stood still in the world. But I thought so elaborately on this plan that I began to be discouraged. It occurred to me that no matter how well I mimicked their lives, at some point, however subtle, someone would catch me in a blunder and I would be found out, and it would be revealed to everyone, and their inevitable humiliation of me would be more intense and unrelenting than if I had just accepted and remained in my detestable state. But I kept heart, determined to proceed.

43

At home the familiar signs persisted: no food in the cupboards, dad's drunken sneers and mom's powerlessness, and especially no new clothes for the first day of school, no investment in my plan. It was over before it began. I was 13 and entering the 8th grade, an age where hyper-consciousness about what one wears takes hold, and on the first day of school all mom could come up with was an old thick tight-fitting black wool suit. In the 90-degree high humidity heat I could feel the wool eating into my flesh, sweat dripping down my face, acne swelling up on my neck, but not ever removing my jacket to expose the too-tight dingy (yellow) white shirt.

I moved fairly quickly into failing every subject, including woodshop and gym. I drank a lot, mostly whiskey, and loved the numbing effect, most especially that initial euphoric glow that eased in after a throat-gag and stomach burn, a realm where I always experienced myself in sync with everyone around me, students and teachers, even though I couldn't talk to them, especially the girls. I would always end up laying my head down inside my folded arms on my desk and stare at their legs and budding breasts, swimming around inside an incipient lust with a strange sense of being exactly where I was supposed to be, that all was well in the world, perfectly fine, no worries about getting bogged down and trapped in life's anxious situations as long as I had booze. I was able to maintain, not overindulge and get drunk, just occasional sips to sustain the mood, with a pocket-full of spearmint gum to hide the smell, in every way keeping to myself, and this more than anything gave me a free pass: the teachers knew I was thoroughly distant from the bourgeois norm of teen life for obvious reasons, with no retrieval in sight, and they were simply relieved that I exhibited no tendency to drag other kids down into my private pit. I called it "the invisibility factor" when explaining it to my brother, as if the teachers were saying, "Stay invisible and we'll leave you alone." It was easy to disappear in booze and hopelessness.

And thus my love for the film *The Invisible Man*, the incomparable one with Claude Raines who was able to give it a comedic twist in a sustained seriousness, right up my alley.

But it was the glue-sniffing I was most drawn to. One particular model glue was my favorite. It had a sweet smell and was gentle on the sinus membranes, a cool menthol touch. I would empty two or more tubes in a paper bag and then form-fit the bag to my face. This would take a good minute of blowing out, folding, rolling, bending, crinkling, crumbling and creasing the paper, a ritual not unlike any ritual associated with drug use. The big difference with glue-sniffing is that it can be, after PCB, the most dangerous drug-induced journey—physically, psychologically and spiritually. If you stay in the bag it can lull you through mild hallucinations down into the most hidden of the darkest depths of the subconscious, and once arriving you are no longer aware you are hallucinating while the glue chemicals eat away at the brain: you part company from the apparent world in every respect.

My routine was finding a comfortable spot on the ground with my back propped up against something. With the first deep inhalation I could feel fumes move up into and coat my sinus membranes where the chemicals with haste enter my bloodstream and go directly to my brain. My body completely relaxes inside a mild, long-drawn-out reverberating synthesizer sound that hangs in the air a few seconds with every breath and then drifts away, but with each new breath it returns with more intensity as my cranium begins to dissolve, my mind expanding ever-farther beyond my lungs and the paper bag, the bag itself with a few more breaths disappearing along with my body and brain, leaving only my long-drawn-out breaths alone inside a vast chamber with a distant sound, like paper-thin sheet-metal softly reverberating, lulling me into a free-floating realm deep in the subconscious where I am no longer aware that I

45

had induced this transport. The sound disappearing, I become immersed in a dream world deeper than normal dreams, now with no awareness at all that I had ever sniffed glue.

The Dream World is no doubt with us in every second in some degree, for the Dream World in all its manifestations is after all the praxis of the *will to be whole* in consciousness. The Dream World can help liberate us piecemeal into a deeper presence in the real world if we make the connection, what it reveals, what it wants to help us understand, or in a resistance on our part it can trap us ever deeper into fantasies utilized as salve for our tortured souls—it's a conscious or preconscious choice we make; but unlike the variety of dream-states while awake, preconscious or asleep, the glue-dream has a heightened immediacy: more residual clarity, more vividness and more lingering power upon a return to consciousness, not easily dismissed, no natural re-entry fading. In awakened states even our nightmares can easily find a home in and coalesce with the nightmares that surround us—in our lives, the world, in books and in cinema— and our minds utilize the same powers in contending with them: the filtering, softening, displacing, dampening and blocking out what impinges on our second-to-second cognitive adaptations and goal-oriented actions that cling to surface life. But glue dreams are more intense in insisting that we pay attention, the Id in a rebellion that won't quit, attempting in a disguised fashion to dominate our thoughts with its concerns, refusing to cooperate with ego, and I am certain this is related to symbolic formats of glue dreams pointing to concerns that go deeper and broader than what our normal dreams (including nightmares) are pointing to, confronting us with questions that would test our security in what we think we know and are certain of in our radical fear-based clinging, especially a clinging to false hopes and desires or social constructs that falsely reassure us we are safe from falling into the Void. This is why glue dreams can be more exacting in taunting and terrifying us: they grab us by the scruff or our necks and force us to look

46

at truths we are quick to cower under and deny with every ounce of our psychic strength. The lush symbols are often comically horrifying in heightened fashion, poking fun at our willfully entrenched denials that we rivet in place in lieu of our dying day when our minds in one fell swoop will open onto a feared unpredictable afterlife or the Void. When waking from a normal dream there is a transitional mode that in some fashion parallels daily life, a sense of familiarity between the dream and the awakened state, the dream most often connecting with an actual event no more distant than the day before, a dream that invites inspection of a theme shared in common by accessible interior and exterior concerns longing to connect into a broader conscious awareness or vision, encouraging another hopeful step into the future, but when departing from glue dreams it is always a stark departure, an exiting from a world deeper than the dream world, as if it exists independent of us and our dreams, daring, even demanding, that we risk interpreting it, and, without thinking, we run from it, not having the wherewithal to interpret it even if that is what we desire.

But occasionally a glue dream will speak to an all-encompassing event that we find ourselves trapped in with elements of conscious and preconscious awareness. On one occasion at age 14 I was with a friend, a friendship based in glue obsession. We were both leaning up against a huge oak tree inhaling glue from our bags. Suddenly, unaware that I had been glue-sniffing, I was in a graveyard sitting up against a tombstone. I looked to my immediate left and saw a dark hole in the ground where a coffin might go. I then looked up at a tall thin man in a black suit on the other side of the hole. He began to explain matter-of-factly that I had died and that he was preparing to bury me. I was frozen in fear and was about to explain that this wasn't a good idea, but he cut me off saying in tones that seemed to be bathed in electricity, "Hey…I understand your concern, but there has already been a funeral, your family and friends have left—*it's over,*

OK?...No point being dead in the world—for what? It's irrational." Then I turn around and see my headstone that I had been leaning against.

I leap to my feet and start running in terror, and the tall man with his long legs was on my ass with a furious pace. I leap over tombstones, not wasting a second going around them, but the man soon catches up with me, his long right hand with boney fingers landing on and locking into my right shoulder, and in that second a release, a peacefulness taking hold of my body and mind. I knew he was right—there was no place for me now but the grave, and in calm resignation I turn to face him and go with him, but when my eyes meet his it is my friend, Ritchie. He is frantic and out of breath. "What the fuck's with you?! I chased you for three blocks! You cleared that hedge back there. I had to run through it!"

Once I was a prisoner inside a three-story clock, part of a team responsible for synchronization in the turning of one of the many slow-turning gear-wheels of time—my assignment attending to the maintenance and precision of just one of the wheels. And there was another time I was shackled to eternity but stuck in time, sitting motionless in a lotus position atop a sand dune in the middle of a desert, light blazing all around me, my sole function in every second to relay every communication from every electronic communication system in existence, from telephones to bus lines to police and ambulance calls to inter-continental missile-guidance communiqués, deprived in every second of a reflection or even a passing thought.

My glue-sniffing partner, Ritchie, was even more caught up in the glue worlds. On one occasion I chose not to indulge, but to instead watch him. He was deep in his bag, crunching and crinkling the paper in rhythmic delight, continuing his breathing in and out, and then, pulling the bag from his face, he begins laughing loudly, making wild hand gestures and mostly having conversations with a bunch of little people who lived inside the bag. I listened closely but couldn't make out the language. He begins to accept tiny bottles of liquid from the little people inside the bag with his fingertips, guzzling the liquid down and then giggling. And then he shouts with joy, "Yeah!—we're getting down to the last bone!"

This shocked me but I didn't know why. Later in the day when Ritchie and I are walking down a road I ask him: "When you were sniffing glue this morning you said something strange. I can't figure out what it means."

"What?"

"You yelled 'We're getting down to the last bone!'"

He falls to the ground and starts screaming, the left side of his body convulsing in spasms, his right arm curling up into his stomach. He keeps screaming "Stop it! Stop it!"

I try with all my strength to pull his twisted arm out from his body but it won't move. He rolls to a nearby tree and begins slamming his head into it, trying to knock himself out, still screaming "Stop it!" as I buffet his head by working my body between him and the tree. Then anguished, muffled sounds come from his throat, his body starting to relax, and then a rhythmic rocking back and forth, eyes closed. The rocking goes on for a while, his breathing an almost inaudible wheeze. Then he stops moving and looks up at me, and with an exhausted but still fearful voice says "Don't ever say that again."


As a child the magnitude of death or the possibility of going crazy just didn't faze me like in adulthood. That's why it was exciting and easy to jump rooftops, float down deep rivers in cement-mixing metal tubs without knowing how to swim and other death-defying actions, especially making crazed getaways when the cops chased me—I always got away. And that's why it was easy and exciting to sniff glue. You don't hear about adult glue-sniffers—it's not something an adult revisits, like marijuana or heroin, and even the rare adults who stay stuck in sniffing glue don't journey down to the depths. They go for a surface numbing effect with looping thoughts and mild hallucinations that simply entertain.

Many years would pass before I realized that my glue-dreams possessed important messages of no interest in my youth, for they were epic concerns. Like the one where I was paralyzed on top of a sand-dune in the middle of a desert in a lotus position, trapped eternally in relaying information that had taken priority over every aspect of my life, a living death that I could now see clearly represents the modern condition of being enslaved to electronic forms of communication that kill off any possibility of a depth-oriented connection, where the human person is reduced to nothing more than one of many relays that enhance the flow of information that has taken on a god-like life of its own, our minds co-opted and utilized solely to keep that information in motion without any possibility of us arriving at any real ground, any real knowing, somnambulists who believe we are in control because we are proud, fine-tuned relays, having abandoned even our powers to reason (which would involve long intervals of discernment that move us out of time) in a continual effort to stay plugged into the endless flow of vast and varied forms of empty communication, from the relentless drone of sitcoms and news programs onto the endless glut of the Internet that includes digital professors who will indoctrinate us into becoming more admired as fine-tuned relays for a fee, the mere velocity of information itself generating an appearance of such magnitude and force that we become convinced it is vital. And all of this to make Time a more polished, intricate and complex idol, something worthy of worship, our best means of not looking into the eternal void that one can hear groaning on the periphery of time, and why more than anything we must stuff up our ears, and precisely why music has the potential to be the most liberating art form. No wonder our fascination with zombie films persists, a constant reminder of our slavery to utter emptiness: we are the functioning dead as a means of avoiding the reality of death: our bodies, severed from relationships in a slavish addiction to abstract forms of communication, we now float digitally toward virtual reality to avoid reality, and in a moment of anxious awareness our bodies seek a rejuvenating union with an other in hyper-stylized, cannibalistic sex acts to convince ourselves that the imagined live flesh of an other is coalescing with our own dead flesh, a humanly-derived means of fleshly communion absent spirit; but because this is not union but sadomasochistic titillation, our hunger for flesh and blood is never satisfied, and only deepens in other equally futile searches for sexual gratification, sometimes on to hyper-violent sex, that final commitment in a sadomasochistic universe, best represented by the cinematic image of Deborah Harry in David Cronenberg's *Videodrome*, pointing to her neck and seductively requesting of James Woods to "Cut me here with your penknife."

As a child a glue-world is experienced without serious reflection. But the sophistication of adulthood with a fully-developed frontal lobe awakens us to the many dimensions of our fear of death and no longer permits access to the fluid naïveté of easy childhood escapes from the many anxieties that would lull us into consciously flirting with the once subconscious, even preconscious, proclivities toward death as a means of romancing or defeating it—to somehow rid ourselves of it once and for all (best repented artistically in Jean Cocteau's *Orpheus*, a film that for me comes closest to a glue dream, and what possibly influenced the making of Bergman's *Hour of the Wolf*). Our fears in adulthood are always intruding on consciousness—especially the fear of being declared insignificant because there is no real personality to signify anything (we most often invest our energies into sustaining transient roles), and every fear is rooted in the fear of death; indeed, every fear is utilized to suppress the fear of death. But a child's unconscious

51

can know all this, long before the conscious mind even glimpses it, and why a child at the deepest level is never really deceived by the deceptive, fearful lives of adults. We obviously know in the depths of our child minds all there is to know, signifying that our lives are somehow complete before they even begin, our future awarenesses an unraveling of what we already know.

Not only in reflecting on the glue dreams from childhood does this become clear. In reformatories where glue and other mind-altering substances were scarce (I even sniffed bug spray at one point, and probably would have continued if the high hadn't been accompanied by one of the worst head-pound headaches of my life, worse than the migraines I suffered from), there was a method to move into the deepest region of the unconscious, far deeper than glue regions, and in that place all is good, a realm of pure light. I became certain it is the ground of being, and it is in that place one finds the evidence that in our depths we always move from goodness, but somehow always end up taking a wrong turn. The method of journeying to that ground, to that beginning, was a rapid hyperventilating, and another prisoner from behind would quickly wrap his arms around my chest as I held my breath and he would squeeze hard. First there would be a tingling numbness all over my body, like Novocain wearing off, as I begin sinking into unconsciousness, and right before I lose all consciousness I enter a pure white light.

And then the arrival, totally removed from the slavery of a distorted worldly view manufactured in egocentric denial, bathed in the ground of pure goodness, a place where conversations with others have no barriers, no resistances, no oppositions, no hidings—a total presence, not a word uttered that is separate from or in any way distanced from its precise and immediate meaning. In fact, there is no grammatical language at all, just pure communication. And then consciousness grips me by the neck and pulls me away, and my return to surface consciousness itself wipes out all memory of where I had been, but the residue of the experience

remains for a short time in every molecule of my being. And that's why I kept going back, trying

desperately each time to hold on to the experience, but it remained elusive—it was simply not

purposed to be a part of a consciousness that clings to a delusory existence. I learned how to

knock myself out without help from other prisoners, and I would return to my cell at night and

do the repetitive returns. Eventually it would become clear that consciousness—at least in the

modes that we are accustomed to—is opposed to and refuses access to clarity, to Truth,

preferring instead the delusion that the chaos we jog around in is in fact an organized and fruitful

arrangement, that the new barbarism, most especially our egomaniacal slavery to "technological

progress", is the most beneficial mode of existence while it obliterates every inch of ground

beneath us, mocking every virtuous impulse, but this dynamic in no way numbs the longing for

clarity that clings to all our dominant drives to adapt and forget while moving *ever forward* into

the grand Nothingness, and this longing becomes most apparent in the awareness of the failure of

all our empty, obsessive forms of forgetfulness, including sex, drugs, power and intellectual

titillation: their utter failure itself the revelation that there is no solace, no definitive sense of

having arrived in the essence of who we truly are, no real rest for our weary souls in our rabid

and relentless attempt to escape the Void, and it is precisely in this moment of truth that our

genuine longing becomes unbearably oppressive, for it is this longing itself that points

incessantly at the futility of all our actions that distance us from fulfillment and rest.

The only parallel to this coma-induced white-light clarity that comes to mind is a

particular way of mainlining cocaine, maximizing the dosage, where the rush takes you to the

point of death, what I call the *point of clarity* (where I would sometimes speculate I had actually

died), the mind opening up and *all* is understood—all of one's relationships to others and the world. But again, the problem is that afterwards one cannot recall the essential contours of what was perceived in that clarity. Like with the violent thrust into the deepest region of clarity in the subconscious in knocking oneself out, one is left with only a residual sense of the experience. But the strange thing is that this residual sense washes out the crash, the severe depression experienced in coming down off the drug: no depression and no desire for more cocaine. The entire next day would be energized with a heightened joy that accompanies every exact and unalterable knowing. That's how I knew I had touched the real, but could not hold on to it.

Chapter 3

Alternately playing hooky and getting suspended from school got comfortable. Resuming

minor criminal activity like shoplifting and breaking into soda machines and parking meters, I

had enough money and more time to get high and watch television, the commitment I had moved

back into, especially in those days when movies aired around the clock. On one of those hooky-

from-school days President Kennedy was killed. I was watching the first television airing of *The

Loneliness of a Long Distance Runner*, one of those rare films that is more than an escape, one I

could commune with, like *The Man with the X-Ray Eyes, TheTingler, Invasion of the Body

Snatchers, Between Two Worlds* and *Carnival of Souls*. So when the movie was interrupted with

a newscast that "The President has been shot!" I experienced a temporary dislocation of

consciousness, a suspension, but thankfully the movie came back. And then, after a few minutes,

the announcement returned—on *every* station, and it wouldn't go away. The film was lost. This

upset me. I turned the TV off and started looking for something to get high on. No glue, booze or

pills. I had heard about sniffing gasoline, so I tried it, and it worked—not clean like glue, but it

did for a while get me away, but I started vomiting and for the rest of the day I was plagued with

nausea and a pounding headache.

Drugs can in their limited way substitute for every need or want—that's their pull. But most importantly, they kill pain, and for me the absence of pain provided a prolonged interior time-space where I could softly fantasize deliverance from my private hell.

Of course the problem is drugs cost money. At age 13, my brother, now 14, was arrested for assaulting the principal at his high school. He had this habit of showing up for school at whatever hour it pleased him, and on a particular occasion he not only showed up late, but walked through an entrance reserved for staff only. He was stopped by the assistant principal and taken to his office. The principal, a big German man with a bald head came to escort Tommy to his office, but the principal made the mistake of angrily grabbing Tommy by an ear to drag him through his office door. When the police arrived they found the principal with a battered face and unconscious behind his desk. This got Tommy his first reformatory sentence, and when I would visit him and he sent mom to buy treats from the visiting room store, he would tell me where to hide cigarettes on the grounds to be picked up by trustees who did landscaping. It was these visits that started me having second thoughts about stealing. I was scared not of doing time, but of being raped, and worse yet, my brother finding out and how he might then see me, a disappointment in his eyes that I would be unable to bear. Thus my cowardliness kicked in and I had to find another way to get money for drugs, for I wasn't going to stop. Selling my body to men seeking child flesh was the only alternative.

The psychosexual problems that afflict men who purchase boys' flesh are complex and varied. For me as a youth there were three main types of ephebophiles. Of course they all share in common the power they have over child flesh when purchasing it or otherwise acquiring it for pleasure without emotional complications. But there they part company, or, in many cases, the types overlap. There is the lonely, pathetic man who for any number of reasons in his psychosexual weakness cannot engage women or men in sex, directing his sorrowful and degrading lust to the least threatening object he can find, a person he can control in every respect, not feel threatened by, a boy, and then elicit (*pay for*) a grateful response from the child that solidifies his sense of the child's complicity, but even more he hopes the child will look on him with pity, a delicate response that more than anything cleanses this predator from all his guilt, for in that response the roles are reversed: the predator becomes the child and the child the adult.

And then there is the predator who envisions himself set apart, the decadent artist, the sophisticate, the consummate outsider—the prototype so clearly drawn by Tennessee Williams in his masterpiece, his most poetic play, *Suddenly Last Summer*: Sebastian, the Dionysian artist/saint seeking sensual dissolution unto death, territory reserved solely for the mystically unrestrained gnostic who would abuse, denigrate and destroy corrupt human flesh, one's own or another's, as the only escape available for the soul sensually fettered to and trapped in that flesh. Heaven's sullen, powerless angels bear witness first to his sexual denigration of impoverished youth—who in the film version are Third World children on a beach caged off like wild, beautiful, beasts of tantalizing flesh from those of wealth and status who can choose to purchase that flesh for a price—which instills in the youth who succumb to this financial arrangement a resentment buried deep in their interminable shame of being robbed of their manhood, and who will, as a final resolution to their dilemma, join forces with the Dionysian demand for a violent, ritual slaying of Sebastian's flesh, the necessary slaying of bound flesh to free the spirit for union with the superior god of light who is untainted by creation, a god who knows only contempt for this thoroughly corrupt fleshly world generated by a lowly, corrupt Demiurge.

57

Sebastian, who, after looking on the violent face of this lowly Demiurge who thrives on the torture of all that lives and breathes, chooses in an artistic vision union with the transcendent god as prophet and warrior son, what is tantamount to self-worship in imaging oneself the bearer of the light of truth in great darkness, becoming simultaneously high priest and victim in a grotesque ritualized act of rabid, spontaneous disintegration, an imagined martyrdom as saintly artist who gives first his life and then his body as food, his holy gift, for the ignorant lowly youth, a food that will over time inspire a superior wisdom that liberates, their first step in ritually transcending with Sebastian their accursed state, to eventually escape with finality in some suicidal act the corruption of organic life unto other-worldly, transcendent bliss, or simply onto the guaranteed absence of all corruption in Nothingness—both agreeable ends. Sebastian's transcendence begins and ends in violent, hedonistic sexual undifferentiation, a nihilistic assault on what he views as a degenerate Demiurge's plan to perpetuate his corrupt creation (the propagation of the species) who jealously hates the human creature who has the potential to transcend his corrupt creation unto union with the transcendent god of light. Sebastian's assault includes nothing short of the destruction of all distinctions between man and woman, adult and child, even parent and child, categories that serve to justify a commitment to corrupt creation, an assault that is a Sadean counter-offensive designed to annihilate all slavish and mundane sexual morality utilized to mask a corrupt creation, and with incomparable genius he manipulates and thereby becomes superior to the creatures who mobilize most against him in absolute service to the Demiurge, *women*, those breeders of more corrupt life. Sebastian's artistic commitment is to reveal the nihilistic truth of man's alienation and aloneness and how he is forever under assault by the forces of corrupt nature, and he remains fierce in not feigning concern for anyone committed to this abject slavery, a holy indifference, especially for the impoverished, ignorant child he holds in contempt and sacrifices on his bloodied altar of unlimited sexual gratification together with the women who would maliciously trap him in corrupt flesh, a violent commitment that he perceives as stimuli to beget his masterpiece, his poem of ritualized self-sacrifice, not recognizing that a poem birthed in this commitment is always stillborn and will in fact always remain an unfinished chapter of a degenerate and meaningless life, for in every instance it fails to redeem.

Billie Jim, the youngest of the children I knew who sold their flesh, suffering from a high fever and having difficulty breathing, fearfully told us that a big blob of coagulated blood had dropped from his rectum. He thought he should go to the hospital and wanted our advice, and one of the kids derisively rejoined, "Another blood baby!" One of Sebastian's children.


Then there is the predator who indulges child flesh with an elaborately developed political philosophy, an entrenched world-view that justifies his slithering movements about the earth. He will talk about how boys who hustle are searching for themselves, that these children are fringe dwellers because somewhere inside they prefer boys to girls but cannot admit it to themselves because of a repressive hetero culture that stigmatizes their secret sexual orientation, and thus hustling becomes the only route available to these sexually deprived children in finding their true sexual identity. This predator sees himself as helping the boys in every way he can, an advocate and liberator, saving the child from society's suffocation: he will let the boy stay at his apartment, take care of him, and eventually (during the first night—why waste time!) help him find himself through therapeutic sexual engagement. One of these lunatics had given me some pills (although the pharmacological/alchemical mixtures vary with these predators, there was a group who had a designer drug that included life-threatening belladonna, and we had heard of one child who had committed suicide while under its influence) and told me to sit in a really comfortable armchair. He put an album on, an instrumental, tunes I was unfamiliar with. I began hallucinating—large musical notes from the speakers made visible and undulating in the air, slowly drifting towards me, and then softly crashing in cinematic slow-motion into my chest, lifting me up from the chair and suspending me euphorically in space, paralyzed, held captive to the predator's gaze as he begins a rant about the ancient Greeks and how they understood the superiority of man-boy love, how the "breeders, women who emit foul smells, serve the minor function of birthing children, not making men!", and that it was left up to the courageous, enlightened men to mold boys into powerful creatures of wisdom and strength, referring at one point to his genitalia as "jewels of transmission", and soon after I drift into unconsciousness and no doubt taken to some subterranean temple to be transformed into the predator's image and likeness through commingling semen, blood and various diseases, where I would become interiorly lost in a sexual confusion that to be undone its dynamic of shame must be sought out, understood and resolved, but the shame itself was something I sought to *escape* from, and in the process of this psychic distancing from shame and confusion, accomplished mostly from drug use, I at some level became enslaved to its dynamic, and thus completed the predator's perpetual domination and reign over my existence, especially in the addiction to drugs, what I used to escape his lair but inevitably drove me back to it. But what he didn't know, or perhaps did, is that his reign is only a mirror of a more substantial, complex and thoroughly entrenched reign imposed by my father that subsumes and dilutes all other reigns into what constitutes his absolute reign, turning these predators into his agents whose only real purpose in relation to me is to affirm dad's absolute power over me, and why the predator resorts to an obsessive fantasy that the child is falling in love with him, and to honor this imagined love the predator in return

60

will protect the child in his temple of prostitution in service to *thee* god, the predator himself, who views himself as superior to (in his violation of) all the forces of nature, and through union at the deepest level with this force (sexual engagement) the child will become one with the predator and thus liberated from his father and all other forces in the absolute superiority of the predator, he who has defied every moral impediment to absolute power in absolute willing, for there is no more powerful expression of the will than the absolute domination and imprisonment of another human being, cutting him off from even a glimmer of self-actualization; but even then, if this impossible fantasy were actualized, the predator would eventually discover that he himself, like the child he dominates, has not escaped the grip of the child's father, that he, like Renfield, is in sycophant service to the true master, that his true nature is one that would munch on cockroaches and other vermin to sustain his decrepit soul, and the predator would then begin to detest the child for mirroring his own miserable servitude and begin looking for a more worthy temple prostitute, a child he will seek out with a glass slipper to determine the beatific worthiness of the child, and when found and chosen, the predator will decide this time to invest more lovingly in his captive while sacrificing the former, as it turns out, detestable child, on the altar of his hidden, insatiable desire to poison every semblance of innocence, what he himself had been robbed of—his every sexual expression rooted in this jealousy and hatred of innocence. A cinematic portrayal, and in one sense a sorrowful idealization, of this predator was perfectly captured in Michael Cuesta's film, *L.I.E.*

Even at this young age, ignorant of psychology and being unsure of the meaning of my own experiences, one thing was clear: these men needed to believe what they were telling us. At the level of titillation unto death, they want to freely experience the sexual pleasure of a child's flesh without guilt, an imagining of a legitimate other in the child that constitutes an actual relationship, and a desperate street child, trapped in an immaturity that escapes his awareness, is the safest object in this grotesque assigning of a sexual identity—a sexual imperialism with no serious threat of rebellion. These predators essentially take an errant sexual desire and build an ethos out of it to justify it, sometimes elaborately constructed, but it's always just an obsession with having sex with children. I would pick up on their signals and feign interest in what they were saying, understanding that this was required, part of what they were paying for, occasionally in my drug stupor saying something like "Wow…I never thought of that." And that every child hustler is at some level complicit (intentionally hustling to get money for drugs or a night off the streets) only feeds into and heightens the predator's delusion that sex with men is what the child either wants or needs; or, in cases where the child does not provide affirmation of the predator's delusion, he will perceive the child as decrepit, out to take advantage of his good nature (a failed relationship because of the child's corruption). I can think of four highly acclaimed, close to universally applauded, films that argue in their fashion the predator's point of view: *Our lady of the Assassins, L.I.E., Hedwig and the Angry Inch* and Allen Ginsberg's lament in Jennifer Bachwal's excellent documentary, *Let it Come Down: the Life of Paul Bowles*, where an aggrieved Ginsberg explains how he was *used* by an impoverished child he engaged in purchased sex, how the child gave him crabs and then tried to manipulate him into helping his younger brother who was ill. All these films, other than *Let it Come Down*, in some way justify the violence of the predatory adult by pointing an accusatory finger at the apparent complicity or outright predatory impulse of the child, as if this complicity in any way sets some stage of equal culpability. And film critics mostly applaud the predator's point of view.

The major problem the child hustler has with the philosopher-predator is that the predator works hard at paying little or no money at all. That would threaten his delusional justifications and activate his dormant guilt, a resuscitation of conscience. He will offer consumer items and shelter to the child (to get ever-ready low-cost sex) to sustain the fantasy that he is out to either help the child or engage him in a serious love relationship, not to in any way use him. I would often have to go into an elaborate story of desperation, how I had to go home to whatever state I had left, that I needed money for a bus ticket or whatever. This was just more work for me, and rarely effective (these predators are far too sophisticated, cynical and vicious). Sometimes I would keep it simple and just look for an opportunity to rip off their drugs or things I could sell and hit the streets again. Little did I know that they counted on this (they never keep anything of real value visible). It was a small price to pay to enhance their secondary defensive delusion that it is the child, not them, who is the predator, the real criminal.

\*\*\*\*\*\*\*\*\*\*

Moving into heroin use at 16 changed everything. The first time I used it I mainlined a g-shot (an amount so small you can't see it in the syringe casing). I was told I would feel it immediately after the injection. So right after the liquid was squeezed into my vein and the needle pulled out I said in disappointment "I don't feel anythin'!" And in that second the rush of the drug hit my heart, brain and stomach, everywhere in every molecule, gravity suspended, my jaw and eyelids dropping, total release, even the pain that I had not been aware of, the emotional pain and minor physical discomforts that are locked into the body unawares and remain a constant in one's life—it was all gone.

"I'll n e v e r  s t o p" is all I could slur before nodding into lethargic bliss.

63

There is a partial truth to the junkie line that he keeps using junk to recapture his first high, and he fails because the first high is an ambush, beyond anything he could expect or imagine, an unrepeatable event. No one can know how much pain he's really in, not until it's gone. This *knowledge* comes once, only once, and because it is experienced in the flesh, it is absolute from a materialist point of view, although it parallels what mystics describe as transcendent bliss—a *knowing* that illumines and gives rest to the ravaged soul; but the mystic lives *in* the knowledge of what he experiences in faith through grace, a knowing that is eternal and thus occupies past, present *and* future in an eternal now, and why the illumination is for him a source of life in every second, for it is centered not in the emotions, sensations or intellect, but in the soul from which all that is of lasting value emanates, the ground of being, what some call the very image and likeness of God. For the junkie, everything that follows the illumination— every thought, every movement—involves an obsessive quest to recapture not the pain relief, but the illumination, now buried in the past, and his repeated failure will first fray and then rend the curtain that conceals the Void, for the knowledge *of* or *about* anything is not a knowledge *lived*, what Gertrude Stein no doubt meant with her "a rose is a rose is a rose": the experience of an encounter with a rose, an ambush, is never an abstract sense of what it is. The most the high can now provide the junkie is a physiological reminder of what he now knows only in the abstract. He thus begins in earnest to construct an alternative: a fantasy of a better way of life, an eschatology of his own creation, a phony-future-now-knowing that will dominate all his imaginings like a puppet taking control of its master. This because the fantasy provides a world free from the complications, hazards, hard work and mystery of the virtuous life, the only place where life is actually lived. For a junkie the mere thought of that life exhausts him, what the ancients called *acedia*, and why he finally dismisses it; he instead pines for what is lost forever,

64

the easy absolute, the ambush in first shooting up, and the fantasy as the only accessible alternative becomes his only respite, the beginning and end of nowhere, the safest place on earth, requiring no effort—a region somehow palpable, more real than reality, because as praxis it successfully destroys a junkie's innate dread of every terrible possibility, from spending his life in prison (why he so easily becomes a rat) to a future controlled by terrorists with nuclear weapons, for every future possibility is terrible in some fashion. He controls this threatening future by displacing every concern about it, the fantasy itself transporting him the farthest distance from possibility. The fantasy becomes a pseudo-life of certainty, a gnostic fulfillment: a *knowing* (a secret knowledge available only to the junkie) that has the power to dismiss all of what is associated with life itself, a life the Demiurge created to hold him captive, and why his junkie life is the only freedom he knows. And so it is *there* in the fantasy, not the first high, that the junkie in maniacal determination seeks to return, a place of power over all of life, absent every agonizing demand in conscience for heroic love, precisely what creates in the junkie his cool indifference and manipulative skills in relationship to others, his pride in having found a cure for meaninglessness: a utopian absence of pain and every anxiety-ridden concern for self and others, a concern that always has its origin in a seriously considered future happiness or eschatological end intricately fashioned in the now of the real world. And that the fantasy itself ultimately fails him he simply chalks up to "failing to recover that first high".

Heroin got expensive real fast, especially for me—I tried to stay high 24 hours a day. Hustling predators was no longer possible. Not only because it didn't provide enough money to sustain my habit, but at the old age of 17, with obvious signs of addiction, customers dwindled; and my expanding awareness of shame and wretchedness in feeble maturation of how I had

65

decimated my budding manhood dug ever deeper into consciousness. When I washed my face in pubic bathrooms I couldn't look in the mirror. I moved quickly into crime, mostly boosting and burglaries. I knew jail was inevitable, but the agony of heroin withdrawal takes care of that fear. Once, on our way to cop some dope in New York, I told Tommy about this fear. Having done reformatory time, he gave me some singular advice: "Ya gotta remember one thing: in the joint ya gotta fight at the drop of a pin. It don't matter if ya win or lose. That's not the point. They'll respect ya if ya fight. Ya don't fight, they'll fuck ya in the ass. Ya don't wanna live with that. The worst that could happen is ya get killed, but ya won't be aware of it, so it don't matter...Just fight."

   *That* stuck in my brain.

Chapter 4

Jail was around the corner, and the terror of this thought instilled in me a keen sense of avoiding it. I got real good at boosting and burglaries. I was breaking into at least three stores every night, and during the day I would steal from department stores. My fence, a big burly balding Italian who always had an unlit cigar stub stuck in his mouth, with shirt sleeves rolled up to his armpits, caught on quickly how good I was. I was bringing him mostly televisions and leather coats to his pizza parlor on a regular basis, items he could sell fast. On a day I was really sick from withdrawal I brought him a top-of-the-line console color TV. He could see the sweat popping out on my forehead, and he decided to take advantage of it, cutting his normal price in half. "No way, man!" I yelled at him. "Get the fuck outta my store!" he yelled back after pulling the cigar from his mouth and raising his hand in the air.

I took the TV to my drug dealer and told him what happened. He gave me a hundred dollars' worth of heroin for it, and later gave it to a couple who dealt drugs for him out of their apartment. I blew my only fence, making life a lot more difficult. I didn't like the idea of peddling what I stole. But my brother found a way out. He got a hot wire on a big score, the one that would get us enough cash to get to California, what we fantasized about almost every time we got high. Lots of East Coast addicts got California fixed in their minds. I never figured out why. Maybe it was the heat, the notion that one would never get cold (and heroin withdrawal shakes is as cold as it gets), or that it was as far away from New Jersey as you could get. That's what New Jersey had become for us and a lot of others—a place to get the hell away from.

The owner of the store had over 50,000 dollars in a safe, and Tommy had the combination. He knew this was the one, the one we'd been waiting on for years. He turned to me and said "This is it, bro—after this we're outta here."

Tommy had knockout keys for all General Motors cars. We went to one of the biggest car lots in Newark. "Take your pick, man," he said as we walked down the street and stared at all the cars.

"You know it's a Cadillac for me, man."

"Yeah," he said, smiling that blue-eyed smile of his.

It takes seconds. A big black Cadillac Fleetwood with black leather upholstery and a primo radio. Tommy pulls off the lot and drives a few blocks. He parks the car and pulls out a screwdriver and small wrench from his tool bag, and then removes the license plates from a parked car and puts them on the Cadillac. When he pulls out I ask him where the store is. "Out in the boonies, man."

I turn up the music as we drive out to the suburbs. I am already getting muscle cramps and sweating profusely from the withdrawal, but the adrenalin mixed with the sensation of a Cadillac in motion and a big score up ahead eases the pain. The small town we arrive at is quiet. We pull into the alley and a parking spot waits for us right behind the store.

"Are you sure about the money?" I ask.

"It's all set up, man. It's the dude's wife. She and her stud get half. If I let 'em!" He laughs. "The husband's been stashin' big bucks to avoid payin' taxes. It's illegal money. Like it was meant for us, man. He can't even report it stolen. And it's more than easy. I got a key."

And it was easy. Tommy had a door and an alarm key, turning it off as we enter, and then going right to the safe. And it was true: all the money was there.

"What about the drugs?" I ask.

"We got time. Grab all the morphine, speed and barbs [barbiturates] you can find. Put it in a shopping bag." I hear him laughing to himself.

I move quickly through the isles and Tommy joins me after filling a shopping bag with the money. It takes about five minutes to find all the drugs. We dump the bottles into the money-bag after downing some morphine pills.

Outside we get in the car. The morphine starts coming on as we pull out. I can feel tingles all over my skin and I start to itch. I look over at Tommy and he is laid back, his right wrist resting on the top of the wheel with his hand hanging down as we ease through the empty streets. I turn the radio on and the music fills our minds and hearts. We had gone about three miles. It was only two more blocks to the highway entrance.

A siren from a cop car pierces my brain and sends a shock through my body. The morphine had induced a calm, but the adrenalin kicks in and I'm alert in my pain-free state. I look at my brother and he says "Hold on" as he slams the gas peddle to the floor.

I love Cadillacs. They're heavy, but once they start rolling they move fast and maintain their balance and comfort, and this one moved at high speed right out onto the highway, Tommy burying the needle in no time at 110 miles an hour.

It was then that I understood how much I loved him. I look over at him. The iron-clad focus as he holds fast to the wheel. I smile. I know we are busted, but it doesn't bother me much in my morphine haze. Tommy's criminal focus, as always, had him taking seriously only this second he was living in, determined to stay true to his commitment to make the world back off and let no one pull him down. He wasn't about to cut anyone any slack, no compromise: you're in or you're out, and not even death meant jack-shit to him when he focused. The cops' red

swirling lights were flickering off shiny objects in the car, sirens now all around us and piercing

my ears, and then Tommy eases into an exit without slowing down, but he can't maintain and the

car slams through some small trees and bushes and out onto a road, but unable to get control

back, the car crashes into a telephone pole, my head slamming into the windshield as the car

twists sideways and stops.

There are cops with guns raised yelling at us to get out of the car with our hands in the

air. Their screams seem distant, and they keep it up. A cop finally pulls my creaking door all the

way open: it had already been knocked out of its closed position. I move slowly out of the car,

and once out the cop slams me up against the car, yelling at me to put my hands behind my head.

I can't coordinate that move, but it ends in him handcuffing me. Then the door on the driver's

side being opened and Tommy being dragged out by a cop, and once on his feet his whole body

pivots with that force of anger I know too well, his right fist crashing into the cop's face.

I see lights all around us, like it was a 5-alarm fire.

Handcuffed I am shoved into the back of a cop car. I don't see Tommy until we arrive at

the State Troopers' barracks. I am standing handcuffed as five cops enter with Tommy.

Handcuffed behind his back, they quickly drag him across the floor to a room to one side of the

Sergeant's desk, the cop standing next to me yelling "Sit down!", shoving me down into a chair,

then saying "You want to see what happens to a creep who assaults a police officer?" and he

grabs me by the hair at the back of my head.

The five cops take turns beating on Tommy with fists and sticks, him standing his

ground, not going down to the floor. Then one of the cops yells "That was my partner, you

bastard!" and punches him in the face with an overhand right. When a nightstick lands sideways across Tommy's skull I hear the bone crack, twisting my insides. Tommy goes down on one knee, and then with a force from the depths of hell he jumps up, and with his shackled body crashes full force into the cop who had hit him with the nightstick, driving the cop across the length of the room and slamming him into the wall, and then, the cop stunned, Tommy in staccato fashion is crashing his bleeding skull into the cop's face, breaking the cop's nose and tearing eyebrow flesh open, blood running down his face. All the cops are now on top of Tommy, forcing him to the floor. They are kicking him and beating him with nightsticks all about his head and body, and then drag him across the floor and lift him up on top of a table. The cop whose nose and eye are still bleeding profusely comes over to the table and yells "Take the handcuffs off!" They turn Tommy onto his stomach, cops' forearms pressing into his neck, back and legs, and a cop removes the cuffs. "Hold that arm down!" the bleeding cop orders the cop standing next to him. Then he begins pounding the arm with his club full force, blow after blow, down on Tommy's forearm until broken bone is visible through a deep laceration. The cop then grabs a piece of the broken bone with his left hand, and with his right hand he comes down hard three times with the nightstick and cracks the piece of bone off, and then throws it to the floor, yelling "They won't put this back in your fuckin' arm, you fuckin' piece of shit!" One of the cops in the room looks over at me looking at them from the floor where the cop now has one foot on my neck, and he slams the door shut.

The cop standing next to me pulls me up from the floor by my hair and forcefully walks me to a cell area. There were only three cells. He pushes me into one and slams the door shut.

I curl up on a wooden bench that is supposed to be a bed, my mind fixed on what had been done to Tommy. The morphine stills the horror, but my mind is not able to kick the sound of Tommy's skull cracking—it is stuck and twisting around in my brain. An hour later a cop is at my cell door, opening it and ordering to me to move out. He places handcuffs on me, this time in front. He escorts me out by the sergeant's desk first, where my mom is standing, her face contorted with terror. He won't let me talk to her, but she fearfully speaks to me as I am moved along: "They're going to let you go. Just cooperate!"

I'm taken to the second floor and into a room where a detective is sitting behind a desk. The cop orders me to sit down in a chair in front of the desk. The detective is an Italian man of small stature, bordering on emaciation with his hollow, hair-shadowed face, his receding black oily hair combed straight back, his dark blue silk-mohair suit with its subtle sheen, perfectly tailored, hangs loose from his small frame. He tells the cop to remove my handcuffs and then asks him to leave. With an elbow on the arm of his chair, he holds a cigarette in a relaxed, half curled hand.

He looks at me for a few seconds, and then down at a large crystal ashtray on his desk, slowly moving his cigarette over to it and carefully putting it out.

With not a hint of animosity, he speaks calmly with matter-of-factness:

"Like a cigarette?" holding out a pack of Lucky Strikes and shaking up a few for me to look at. Not a trace of Italian heritage in his voice. He speaks television news English.

"Yeah...Thanks" as I reach across the large oak desk and pull a cigarette from the pack. He picks up a Zippo lighter from the table, gently flips it open and thumb-scratches the flint to produce a flame and looks right into my eyes as he moves it across to me. I bend forward and draw hard on the cigarette after it's lit. The smoke fills my lungs and I feel the morphine again like a wave passing through my body. I thought it had worn off, but I should have known better. I wasn't in excruciating pain, although I should be.

"You alright?" he asks.

"Yeah."

"You're lucky you're not dead. You're not hurting anywhere?"

"No."

"We could send you to County hospital."

"No…I'm fine."

"You have a nasty cut on your head."

I reach up and feel the damp coagulated blood mixed with dry blood. "It's nothin'."

He just stares at me expressionless, and then says "I have a statement. I want you to read it and sign it. If you do, you can go home with your mother. I'm sure she can get you to a doctor who can do better work than what you would get at County. Besides, from County Hospital you go to a cell and wait on trial. You're a juvenile, which means no bail. That's the downside. Of course, being a juvenile means the state can only hold you until you're 21—four years. I guess you could look at that as an up side."

He picks up the statement and reaches across his desk, carefully placing it in front of me. I pick it up and start reading. It's mostly accurate, except for the part that states that I saw my brother trying to escape by jumping out a second story window.

"I know what you're thinking" the detective says. "Do you know why you were pulled over? You both looked too young and too slick to own a top-of-the-line Cadillac. Vanity, like everything, has its place, but not on a heist. And then your brother assaults a police officer. That's the worst thing a criminal can do, and your brother did serious damage. He will go to prison, and he won't be out for a long time. You understand?… And there you sit. It's simple…You have a choice: You sign the statement and your mother takes you home. You sign the statement and there's an excellent chance the judge will not send you away. You sign the statement and you get a drug program and probation. You don't sign the statement, you go to jail right now, and it's certain you will be sent away, and you won't get out until you're 21. That's your choice."

I felt the morphine beginning to wear off. Or maybe it was the clarity of the sobering choice offered by the detective. But he was asking the impossible—I couldn't sell my brother out. But I am analyzing everything quickly. I had heard that a statement wouldn't hold up in court if it was signed under duress, and they could never get me to actually take the stand to testify even if the judge allowed it. Signing the statement was a way out, a temporary fix. I couldn't do Tommy or myself any good in jail. The only hope was on the outside.

I pull the statement closer to me and pick up the pen. This was worse than anything, worse than standing by and watching my brother be beaten by the Swanger brothers years ago. It was worse than turning my back on God. But only if I testified in court, and I knew I wouldn't. Getting out and finding a way to help Tommy—that's what mattered. It wasn't like he had any chance of beating the rap, but I could in some fashion find a way to help him if I was on the outside, even if it was just sending him money to make his time a little easier, or helping him escape. That's what I tell myself as I sign the statement quickly. A thought then occurs to me: I would go to New York. I would never show up for court.

"You're smarter than I thought" the detective says. And then looking to the cop who is standing at the doorway, he says "Take him downstairs and process his release."

\*\*\*\*\*\*\*\*\*

74

Mom is hysterical in the car. She is crying, scared because they told her Tommy is in the hospital under guard and she won't be able to see him for at least a day or two. Then she yells at me: "Why did you do this? You're killing me—you and your brother! Killing me! I can't take it. I can't! Oh God!"

"I'm sorry, mom."

"I don't want you to be sorry. I want you to stop!"

This is what hurt the most every time. Mom having lived nothing but a tortured life, and I was adding to the torture. This hurt far more than any jail cell.

"You can let me off here, mom."

"What the hell are you talking about? You have to go to the hospital."

"I don't need a hospital. I'm OK."

"What are you doing? Listen to yourself! You're trying to drive me into my grave! That's it, isn't it? You want to see me dead!"

When she stops at a light I open the door and jump out.

"Sam—get back here!" Her scream rips through my body. I keep moving, not looking back.

"Don't do this to me!" she screams as I break into a run.

## Chapter 5

It is late, cold, and I am in a strange suburban territory, no bus stops in sight, and I have only two dollars and change. If I get picked up this soon after my release I will be back in jail and won't get out. I find a parked car on a side street, climb in and curl up on the back seat, painfully tossing and turning in the cold until the sun comes up.

The cold settles deep down in my bones and coalesces with a heroin withdrawal, severe cramps lock up and twist the muscles in my back and legs. I can't close my fists, blood pounding at the top of my head, and when I reach up to feel my scalp there is a big mound of encrusted blood, and then a stabbing pain running from my neck down my back with even the slightest movement of my head. It is whiplash, no doubt. When I leave the car and start to walk, the shakes hit and get so bad I can't move. I crouch down on the sidewalk and wrap my arms around my legs real tight to still the shaking. I have to be careful not to move my head at all, just keep it balanced as best I can on top of my shoulders without using my neck muscles. The slightest movement in any direction jams sharp pains throughout my body. Then the heat hits, a stifling heat, sweat jumping out of my pores as nausea wells up in my stomach. At least I can walk now, although with extreme caution, careful not to let my head move in any direction. I finally find a bus that takes me to Newark, and from there I get the Hudson Tubes into New York.

*********

In New York it doesn't take long to get connected. I run into Nick, an old friend, a New York City street hustler who, because of circumstances similar to my own, had moved on from hustling predators to petty crime. Nick shares a sleazy Midtown hotel room with two other addicts. They don't mind me staying as long as I chip in on the rent. I can sleep on the floor. Although Nick and his friends dip into heroin on occasion, they mostly take pills. Nick's lithe body and formerly handsome, angelic face with its smooth white skin that had made him a favorite of the predators, is now deeply scarred all about his eyes and mouth. It is from the severe pill addiction, going into seizures and falling down hard on table edges and other surfaces. He has a huge gnarly scar indented to the bone on his right forearm. He told me he got it from nodding out on heroin and barbiturates while unknowingly leaning against a section of a radiator. Nick turns me on to some decent painkillers, but they mostly just take the edge off my sickness and ease the pain from the whiplash, enough for me to clean up, put on some clothes Nick gave me and go do some shopping. Getting shoes is easy enough. I go into a shoe store with Nick and he tries on different shoes, keeping the clerk busy in the stock room while I put on the ones I want and walk out, and then meet up with Nick afterwards. Boosting was always easy for Nick and me. Getting dress slacks and Italian knit shirts and a leather coat was next, and then the drug money.

We move fast, going into a store, Nick pulling his hat slightly down as I buy a pack of cigarettes in front of him, and when the cashier opens the till to make change for the five dollar bill I give him, Nick with an overhand right punches the cashier in the face, him half-falling half-ducking down to the floor as I grab all the 20s, 10s and 5s.

For about a week we mostly boost and do jostling scams (selling prostitutes that don't exist, something we were both good at). I manage to stave off withdrawal sickness and the pain from the accident, but I wasn't getting high unless I mixed barbiturates or pain killers with the heroin, a sloppy high, one where I lose track of whatever fantasy I'm indulging.

One night I'm doing a jostling scam with a bald-headed middle-aged John hovering over me as I talk into the phone to a non-existent prostitute: "…Yeah. Yeah…I'm sure. I'm tellin' you—the guy's cool. Decent, ya know?...Yeah…I know…No, No…I'm *tellin' you* [I look up at the guy]—he's a regular guy. I wouldn't bullshit you…Yeah…Ok—I'll bring 'im over."

We walk up to this decent hotel and I give him the room number. "You can go right to her room. Her name is Eileen…Oh, my ten dollars."

He reaches into his back pocket (which signals he's not from the city) and pulls out his wallet, takes out the ten and hands it to me.

"Room 904. She's sweet" I say to him as I start to walk away. And then it happens, what had never happened before:

"Wait!" he yells to me. I stop. "I've changed my mind" he says while walking up to me.

"That's your business."

"I want my money back."

"No way, man. I did what you wanted. I put my time in on this. You don't want the pussy—that's your decision."

"Give me my money!"

"Fuck you!" and I start to walk away. He walks up to me and grabs my shoulder, turning me sideways and insists: "Give me my money!" With that turn pain crashes down through my body, I don't think: with both hands I push him hard in the chest and he stumbles backward, and I start running. If I wasn't in so much pain, I would have just given him the money back, chalk it up as a wasted effort, not risk going to jail. But the pain from the accident grinding into my nervous system coupled with cramps and nausea hurl me over the edge of reason. I run fast down Midtown streets. No way in hell can he catch me. I'm fast, real fast. I never get caught on foot. And then a man in a white Corvair up ahead slams on his brakes and a man on the passenger side jumps out in civilian clothes and points a gun at me, screaming "Stop! Put your hands in the air!", and I comply. He shoves me up against the wall of a building and slams his gun down hard across my head and then down across my right kneecap, yelling "You move and I'll fuckin' kill you, you fuckin' prick!"

And here comes Mr. John all out of breath yelling "He's got my money!"

I.m held at bay until a police car shows up. It turns out the two men in the Corvair are undercover cops and were responding to a Midtown robbery and saw me running and thought I was the suspect. They handcuff me and shove me into the back seat of a patrol car. Before pulling out one of the two cops turns and asks me my name. I don't answer.

"Don't fuck with me!" he yells. "What's your fuckin' name?"

"Sam Jones."

"Don't be a fuckin' smart ass…What's your fuckin' name?"

There's graffiti all over the back of the front seat, and amidst all the scribbling I make out a name, "Charles Cappers", and I respond, "Charles."

"Charles what?"

"Cappers."

From the sickness in my stomach up through my heart and into my throat pressed an urge to laugh. But I suppressed it.

After being booked I am taken to the Brooklyn Atlantic Avenue Jail, a holding jail for youth ages 16 to 21. It's brutal. First into the shower room—stripped, searched in every cavity, drenched in liquid bug killer with an industrial spay-gun, showered, given jail clothes and a wool army blanket that is, I would soon find out, infested with crabs, and then taken to a cell. That is the easy part. The next morning begins the pure hell-torture campaign.

Metal everywhere, except in a huge dining/recreation area during day hours, with big picnic tables—every table ruled by a different racial group. I am quickly taken under the wing of an Italian kid, a heroin addict who obviously isn't cut out for hard time. I can see the deep sorrow in his eyes that always appear to have excess liquid, as if he would break out crying any second, a truly sensitive soul with a good heart. He is as scared as I am. He quickly runs down the rules to me:

"Whatever you do, don't ever talk to a Yom [black prisoner]. If anythin' of yours touches a table, even a cigarette, you gotta throw it away—alright? A Yom mighta touched the spot where the cigarette touched the table, and if you smoke the cigarette you end up kissin' a nigger by proxy—ya understand?"

"Yeah."

"And the Spics…They're mostly neutral. No one fucks with 'em 'cause they don't fight. They cut you. It's their style. But you gotta stay with your own. And them over there (pointing to two prisoners standing by themselves in a corner), they're Geeks. It's always open house on them. The Yoms fuck 'em in the ass, take their food and cigarettes, and they get no help from us. Most are stool pigeons, nigger-lovers and faggots, and sometimes just Geeks by nature. Stay away from 'em."

"Yeah."

"Everythin's straight forward here, man. Nothin's complicated. You stick with your own and you'll be OK."

I nod.

"You play pinnacle?"

"No."

"You'll pick it up. We'll play...be partners."

**********

I had a plan: keep low, be cool and just go along with the shit until I got to court, cop a plea, get 30 days and get out, time served. Just keep my mouth shut, nod yes to everything and play pinnacle.

But wicked fate reared its head. Jimmy Jack, a black street hustler, a friend from way back, walks into the dining area after I am there for only a week. (I don't know the origin of it, but a lot of child street hustlers back then created aliases with two first names.) Jimmy, like Nick, is a pretty boy—blue-black silky baby face with a perfectly trimmed small Afro and fly clothes, easing up on old age at 16. He still didn't have to shave, and he would pluck and thin out his eyebrows not to appear fem, but to create what today some call a metro look—he could go either or any way. That was his style—dress to the max, silk and gold, always smiling. The only one of us who had a pad with a phone. He had it all figured out, not living day to day in drug-induced fantasies like the rest of us. He had a plan. He had a Rolodex file system with names and phone numbers, and when he got a call, he would quickly check his file, and if the person's name wasn't in it he would nix him. He would build a clientele based only on word-of-mouth. He was already servicing mostly elite clientele from around the country and the world, and he would one day have his own callboy service. (I ran into him walking down the street two years later, and already his operation included two penthouse apartment outlets, and he was sporting on either side of him two Titan black shaved-headed bodyguards in black fishnet shirts).

The thing about Jimmy is that everyone liked him. He didn't habitually do drugs. He was an encouragement. He had class, attitude and genius, and he was quick throwing bucks your way if you were in a squeeze. He was bold, witty, outspoken and fun to be around. To him mostly everything was a joke, and I suppose it's always best to laugh your way to the bank.

So here I am looking at him walk into the dining room in his red, body-tight black-striped silk t-shirt and perfectly tailored tight black silk-mohair pants with thin-belt serving mostly as an accessory item for the pants that meet the top of his pointy-toed corrugated leather half-boots with three small buckles at the heels, wearing that perennial smile common to those confident and clearly focused. I couldn't hide forever. The guards don't give you an option to stay in your cell during rec time. Everyone has to go into the dining area during day hours. I tried not to make eye contact, but I couldn't resist—I stared up and he was looking dead at me with a broad smile. "Sam!" he yells across the room. "What's goin' on?"

I looked across the table at Lennie. He had just turned around from looking at Jimmy with shock all over his face. He had gone pale. He doesn't say it, but his face screams it—*Don't do it!*

But I do do it. I get up from the table, walk over to Jimmy, and we embrace. "What's up, man?" Jimmy asks. "Whatcha down for?"

"Jostling."

"Jostling? You gotta be fuckin' kiddin' me! Damn...Now you know what I told you about that, right? It's dead end shit, man. It'll always be about goin' to jail. What?...you hanging out with Nick again?"

"Yeah...and I know. What'd they get you on?"

"They ain't got shit on me, man. I'll be outta here in a minute."


It wasn't exactly a minute. It was more like an hour and a half. Jimmy made bail and I was a Geek.

Don't get the wrong impression. There was nothing heroic in what I did. Anything I ever did that might be construed heroic was actually either a part of a cowardly long-range plan to save my ass, or something spontaneous, no deliberation, coming from a place inside I didn't identify with or was inaccessible in the moment—it always surprised me more than anyone else. For example, a sense of honor was my core virtue, my last stand—the last thing I would give up in a moment of cowardliness. But it wasn't something I in any way reflected on. Holding on to it was an interior determination to safeguard the only refuge I had for the little dignity I still possessed. I would no longer be a "self" if I let it go. Counselors of the first drug programs in New York figured this out about recalcitrant addicts, and the first thing they would take from them is their sense of honor by first making them dress in infant clothes and suck on their thumbs or baby bottles and then make it a condition for release that they rat on their friends while in treatment. These counselors figured if they tore an addict down to a sniveling non-entity, they could build him back up into a respectable person, but what in fact happened is that they created a squadron of stool pigeons that would work with narcotics agents to stay out of prison when they went back on drugs, and the addicts began to take pride in this behavior, experiencing it as yet another liberation from moral constraints that impinged on their chosen life of drug use, the first established class of moral relativists in America, Nietzschean supermen in their own right. And so it was that my embracing Jimmy Jack was in fact a desperate attempt to save what little dignity I possessed on my own terms deep in my conscience as a human being, not in any way altruistic. This is how I would later come to understand that one's real identity has its origin, its ground, in conscience, a conscience that hasn't been reshaped by a moral relativity often grounded in radical conformity, including a conformity to rebellion, and I would think of the film that most terrified me as a child, *Pinocchio*, and how my terror became complete when Pinocchio starts turning into a donkey; in other words, not only not becoming a real boy, but regressing to slavery in a dumb animal existence. And years later I would read the original story, and there it was in the beginning, even more frightening than the film: Pinocchio's first rebellion is complete when he stomps on and kills the cricket, destroying his only chance of ever becoming a real boy (person), but later in the story the cricket returns as a spirit to guide him home.

The blacks wasted no time. On the food line that night, a tall light-skinned black with a big Afro serving food said "Hey Geek—gonna give up some pussy?"

"Fuck you!"

"Yeah…right" he says nonchalantly, head held high. "See you in the dining room."

And everyone gathered around for the fight. I remembered what my brother told me: "Fight at the drop of a pin. It don't matter if you win or lose. They'll respect you for fighting."

But I developed the strategy a little further, a strategy that would get me through three reformatory bits. I knew I was too frail to win against this guy, but there's always a chance I could win if I fought hard. You know—get lucky inside crazed determination. But I decided no matter what, I had to lose. It was the only way. I had to fight hard enough to convince everyone I had that crazed determination to defeat my opponent, but to not let a vengeance mode to work its way into the soul of my opponent or his friends by actually winning, which could result in my getting jumped by a bunch of blacks right there in the dining room or possibly gang-raped later, for there is no way to predict the outcome of a vengeance that resides in a bitter pool of resentment. No, I had to let the black have his glory, but also instill in him the possibility that he might lose if he fought me again. And if I staged it right, I could instill this fear in others, the spectators. I reasoned that the thought of losing a fight with a Geek would induce enough fear to make anyone keep their distance. Who could risk it?

My long Scottish nose from my mother's side always bleeds easy and copiously, often spontaneously, without being hit by anything, so whenever I get punched in the nose, the blood flows. This was good. It didn't take long—early in the fight I get smashed in the nose and blood starts to spill all over the front of my shirt, but I keep punching, connecting blows to his head, and then his retaliatory blows, splitting an eyebrow open, and more blood streaming down my face, and when he knocks me to the ground, I jump right back up with my eyes swollen and move in on him with a flurry of punches to his body and head. Thanks to my dad, an ass whipping is nothing to me.

Finally the siren sounds and the goon-squad comes rushing into the dining room and they drag us off to the hole. Three days later we get out and the black tells me we will pick up where we left off. "I'll be there," is all I say.

85

That night he walks up to me and says "You got heart. I respect that." And he sticks out his hand. I grab on to it and hold it firmly for a few seconds, and then we go our separate ways. I then begin to enjoy peace and the company of my fellow Geeks the remainder of my time.

I copped a plea for the 30-day time-served sentence I was offered and go back to jail to collect my belongings, and then walked out of the jail into the bright sunlight. No matter how illusory the feeling, it's always grand walking out of a jailhouse, and I stood there in Brooklyn penniless and feeling like the world was mine. And then a gun at the side of my head. Two men in suits, one of them slamming me up against their car and handcuffing me.

"What the fuck you doin'?" I demand

"Shut the fuck up! You're under arrest."

"For what?"

"Assaulting a police officer."

"You're crazy. I ain't assaulted no cop."

"Shut the fuck up!"

*********

It turns out they are two detectives from New Jersey. Juveniles couldn't be extradited across state lines in those days for juvenile offenses other than homicide, and although I was involved in my brother's assault charge, being equally culpable by law, it was still a juvenile offense. The detectives turn me over to the authorities at Union County Jail in Elizabeth, New

86

Jersey, reporting they had picked me up on Main Street in Elizabeth, and I am read the charges against me: 25 assorted burglaries and an assault on a police officer.

After being booked, two guards escort me to a wing where only black prisoners are jailed. Even though it was 1968 in the North, segregation was still practiced in some jails in New Jersey. It wasn't official segregation—it was just an informal practice with a practical purpose. Racial tension and violence was common enough, and if a white prisoner got out of line, the guards would put him on a wing with the most hardened black prisoners (the more pliant blacks were jailed with pliant whites on desegregated wings). I knew why they were putting me on a wing with all blacks: the guards had their own way of handing down a sentence involving an assault on a guard or police officer. But what was worrying me most was my brother. He was in the jail somewhere and he had to know I signed a statement against him.

And sure enough, after the clanging of the key in a metal door and the door swings open, I walk onto the tier, and the door slams shut behind me and a black prisoner is in my face asking me angrily, "You prejudice?"

Adrenaline pumps into my body and brain, totally alert and scrambling at warp-speed for an answer, an answer that won't offend, but knowing if I say "No" he will know I am lying (all blacks know—even if any particular white doesn't—that every white growing up in America is infected with racism), but that a defensive, worming-my-way-out answer, regardless how true (in this case that I had indeed been infected with the race virus, but that I had never acted on it) will only sound like a dressed-up (a lying) "no". I knew in that second I had to keep it simple, up front and direct, and so I told the truth:

"Yeah."

"Well I'm prejudiced, too!" he yells into my face. "I hate all you white motherfuckers!"

I didn't respond.

"Whach ya gonna do motherfucker? You got a tier full of niggers here. I know you ain't gonna live with that!"

"I don't hate anyone, man."

"Except niggers, right?"

"I never said that."

"You prejudiced, ain't you?"

"Not like that."

"Like what? Like behind my back, motherfucker?"

"I got no beef with you, man."

"Yeah you do, you racist motherfucker! So make your move, motherfucker!" as he pushes me and backs off a half foot with hands up. "Come on, motherfucker!" he yells, holding his open fists in the air.

"I don't wanna fight you, man."

Then he slams me with an overhand right into my face and we're in it, and I'm in mode, the strategy I had devised in the Brooklyn House of Detention, hitting hard enough, but not in any way trying to win the fight. *I have to stay conscious* was my main thought, defend myself as best I can, do damage but in the end take an ass-whipping and hope it turns out for the best. And with my reliable bleeding nose, in the end I was covered with blood. He was breathing hard, minimal damage.

"We'll take it up again in the mornin', motherfucker" is all he says before walking away to go play cards. I go into my cell and begin soaking the blood out of my shirt in cold water. It is déjà vu, getting a crash course in prisoner race-relations.

In the morning, after my cell door opens, ten seconds later the prisoner was in front of my cell and says "You ready?"

"Yeah."

"You know I'll fuck you up."

"Yeah."

He walks into my cell and sits down next to me on the cot, staring me in the eyes.

"Whach you got against niggers?"

"Nothin'"

"That ain't what you said yesterday."

"I said I had prejudice. Everyone I know is prejudiced. Except my mom. I really got nothin' against anyone. You asked me if I was prejudiced. It's there in me. I didn't ask for it, but it's there. I don't act on it. I figured lyin' would only make it worse."

"Why'd the pigs put you on this tier?"

"I'm charged with fuckin' a cop up really bad. They're gettin' paybacks."

The sound of food trays in the hall interrupts our talk. He looks outside the cell and then back at me. "We'll pick up after breakfast."

When we got our trays of food he motioned for me to sit next to him on a long bench out on the tier.

"What's your name?"

"Sam."

"I'm Frank."

A black person with the name Frank, a name I associated with being Italian. It struck me as strange. And this was the third person I had met in my life named Frank—each time marking a major shift in consciousness.

We continued our talk, covering a lot of ground. He liked the story of how I had first met a black person:

"Dad told me to never to cross the tracks into Roselle to play, that that's where the blacks lived. So one day I had to do it—you know, that curiosity and rebellion thing. And sure enough, in the train station dividing the towns there were three black kids, and one of 'em picked a fight with me, and we got into this knock-down dragged-out fight, at one point both of us rollin' down the cement stairs of the train station, breaking off a piece of my front tooth, and I panicked, grabbin' a handful of his hair to slam his head into the cement stair, and when my fingers tightly gripped his hair the hair felt soft, not like steel-wool as I'd been told. It was the first lie about blacks that was undone for me. I was stunned."

Frank and I became friends. He knew the guards were using him and the others to get me. That pissed him off. We became pinnacle partners, and I got really good at the game.

After about three weeks the guards couldn't take the harmony anymore. So they came down and ordered me to step off the tier, that I was being moved to another tier. I went to grab my stuff. "Leave it there! Just step out" the guard ordered.

They were hoping the blacks would rip me off. But later that day a black prisoner from the laundry room came up to the new tier I was on and asked for me. He handed me my stuff through the bars and said "Frank told me to make sure you got this, and if you need anythin', let 'im know."

"Thanks, man."

*********

My brother was in the hospital section of the jail, still recovering from his injuries. But he was able to arrange through his court-appointed lawyer to get us together. Even though I would be tried in juvenile court, we were still co-defendants, and the lawyer had argued successfully in court to allow a consultation.

When a guard rolls my brother into the room where his lawyer and I are sitting, he is dressed in white hospital clothes, head wrapped in bandages, his face barely visible. They had obviously broken bones in his face, his swollen blood-red eyes barely open, his left arm in a cast. Tears well up in my eyes. He is calm and looking right through me. I am seized by terrible guilt.

The guard tells us we have 30 minutes and then leaves, locking the metal door behind him.

"Tommy can't see you" the lawyer says. "The doctors say it's temporary, that he will gradually get partial vision back."

"How you, bro?" Tommy asks with garbled words.

"I'm OK, man" and I break into tears. I try to stifle them, but they turn into gut moans as tears pour down my face. "I'm sorry, bro…" and the tears don't stop.

"Everythin's cool. We don't have much time. Listen. Do what ya gotta do to get outta here. I don't care about the statement. If it gets you out, I'm glad. I just want you out."

"I went to New York. I thought they couldn't use the statement. But I'm not testifyin'. I'll say they made me sign it to get out of jail."

"No...I don't want you involved. What I want you to do is get out. That's all I want. I'm not gettin' out. I don't want us both goin' down, ya understand?"

He winces for a few seconds. I don't know where he's experiencing the pain.

"Just get out. Hear me? Do it for me." There's a silence. Then he says "I gotta go."

The lawyer goes to the window of the door and motions to the guard. The guard walks over and opens the door, the lawyer saying "Tommy's going back. I want to speak with Sam for a moment."

The guard rolls Tommy out and locks the door again. And in that moment I don't care what happens to me. I know I will not testify.

After he sits down the lawyer says, "Look, the Court can use your statement whether you testify or not. I've spoken with Tommy a number of times. He wants you out. That's all he cares about. That's all that worries him. He figures you got a shot at turning things around if you get out. He's convinced it's your only chance. He's going away regardless."

"But I can help him!" I say in desperation. "He didn't try to escape. He never jumped out a window. They just kept beatin' on him after his arrest."

"I know that. I represent your brother. Believe me—I spent a lot of time trying to convince him to press charges against the police who did this to him. I even contacted the American Civil Liberties Union, and they wanted to include your brother in a class action suit on police brutality. But your brother was adamant in not wanting to be a part of that, saying 'It goes with the territory.' He won't press charges. But I still represent him, and I have to do everything I can in his best interest, and that's why I have to be honest with you: I believe if you retract your statement and give a new statement telling exactly what happened, there's a good chance I might be able to work out a deal. It would give me a lot of leverage. I'm certain I can at the very least get him a lighter sentence. That's something you'll have to think about."

"I'll do it."

"I want you to think about it. Tommy mustn't know that I talked to you about this. You understand? It has to be your decision, not mine. I'll come back to see you tomorrow. You sleep on it."

"I can tell you now—I'll do it."

"Think about it first. I'll see you tomorrow."

He gets up and goes to the door window, signaling to the guard. He then turns back and looks at me. "Your brother really is a remarkable person."

The tears return, and I bow my head

Chapter 6

A probation officer interviewed me for a pre-sentencing report. The court-appointed lawyer kept insisting that if I continued with my plan to implicate police officers in a police brutality suit, I definitely wouldn't stand a chance of getting out. As things stood, if I continued to cooperate as I had originally agreed to do, I still had a chance to get a suspended sentence, probation and a drug program. But I insisted on retracting my former statement and making a new one, telling the truth this time, which I did. But my brother wouldn't allow me to be called to testify for him. He knew it would go bad for me if he did. I would be sent to reformatory, but as a first offender and a juvenile, according to every prisoner I talked to I had a good chance of getting out in 6 months.

\*\*\*\*\*\*\*\*\*\*

Pulling up to Farmdale Reformatory I was impressed with the outside. It looked like a renowned European university campus. The administrative offices, large mess hall and all the cottages used for imprisonment were built out of huge hand-chiseled stones by adult prisoners a hundred years earlier. The idyllic grounds were impeccable and meticulously cared for—not a blade of grass, hedge or tree branch out of sync in an elaborate landscape.

Once inside the reception cottage everything changed. In the main reception area, also designated the "recreation room"—originally designed for no more than 50 prisoners, now

94

housed over a hundred. Prisoners had to sit against the walls or in the two rows of back to back chairs at the center of the room, not allowed to leave those chairs except to use the bathroom or to go to the mess hall at mealtimes. Where the long line of prisoners sit along the walls in the main gathering area, there is a wide long black oil stain circling the room from the thousands of heads that had rested against the walls through the years. This was true of all the cottages except Cottage A. This was the cottage touring bureaucrats, social workers and other career-folk in the criminal justice system visited, a cottage that housed compliant first offenders destined for early release. This cottage also had the benefit of freshly painted walls and more spacious living quarters.

Every new prisoner has to spend 10 days in quarantine, locked in a room with no human contact other than receiving meals on a tray. Officials say this is for health reasons, but it is more of an introduction to what is in store for any prisoner who steps out of line: solitary confinement.

On the eleventh day us "fish" were released and given khaki clothes, a mattress and a towel, and then a shower. There were about 40 prisoners in the shower room that had five showerheads. I was looking at a black prisoner who had effeminate features, thinking that he was going to have a rough road ahead.

"What the fuck you lookin' at motherfucker?" he yells at me. I don't say anything. "You want some of this?" he says, shaking his dick at me.

It is fearful self-defense when I reply "I thought you wanted some of this" as I shake my dick at him. And that was it. We were fighting in the shower, the one place prisoners usually manage to keep their cool.

I was out of quarantine less than an hour and found myself in the hole for another 5 days.

Reception period lasts 30 days, at the end of which you are assigned a cottage and a job. When I go before the Assignment Board (which also functions as the Parole Board) the chairman, who is also the warden, asks what cottage and job I prefer.

"I was hoping I might go to Night Farm [easy time for first offenders only]."

"You're not serious, are you?" the chairman asks with a sarcastic tone.

"I'm a first offender. I thought I was eligible."

"Who told you that?"

"It's just what I heard."

"You heard wrong. Night Farm is for inmates that demonstrate a desire to reform their lives, and you have given every indication that that is not a part of your plan; in fact, the opposite. In any case, you better get used to the idea that you are in a reformatory, which is not a place to believe everything you hear. Inmates for the most part are not adept at truth-telling strategies. Their gifts lie elsewhere." And then he looks down at some papers and begins leafing through them. "Let's see. You get in a fight the same day you get out of quarantine. And your attitude towards drug abuse is….[he looks at the other members of the Board and back at me]…you like the feeling?"

"That's not true!"

"Are you calling a staff member a liar?"

"No…I mean…yeah, I said I liked the feeling, but there was a misunderstanding. There's more to it than that."

"I'm sure there is, but I'm certain I have heard it a hundred times before. In any case, it has been decided. You will do your time here. You will be assigned to Cottage 8 and you will work in the kitchen."

"That's the worst cottage and job here."

"You will have an opportunity to prove yourself. If your attitude improves, so will your situation. It's all on you, you see. We don't decide—you do. That's all," he says abruptly as he closes the folder. "Tell the inmate waiting to come in on your way out, please."

It turned out way worse than I had expected. Prisoners in reception told me because I was a first offender I would go to one of the camps outside the reformatory (less violence, better conditions, more food) or at worse go to Cottage A or Cottage 1, both easier than the other cottages.

About a week later in Cottage 8 I was talking with another prisoner about what had happened. He said the assault on the cop didn't help, and neither did the fight I had in reception, but worst of all was the intake interview with the counselor I had told him about:

"When he asked me why I use heroin, I was agonizin' over what the correct response should be. I decide in my panic that he had probably heard it all, that my best shot was to tell 'im the truth, so I told 'im I liked the feelin'."

"You like the feeling?" the counselor says with a shocked look on his face.

" You know—it feels good. That's the truth."

"You like the feeling?" he asks again, this time with anger. "Do you know my best friend was found dead in the trunk of a car from a drug overdose? What the hell do you think liking heroin will get you?"

"I didn't mean it like that."

"Oh? How did you mean it?"

"Well…I…I don't know…It's just that—"

"It's just that you like using drugs! Isn't that it? And I suppose you like to assault police, other inmates and anyone else who gets in your way? Isn't that it?"

When I told the other prisoner this, he just shakes his head. "Man, you got a lot to learn. You never tell those assholes the truth. That's the last thing they want to hear. Tell 'em about your wicked childhood, about how some older dude turned you on to drugs, got you hooked and then fucked you in the ass, and how gettin' off drugs and confronting your shame is all you ever really wanted…Damn…you'll figure it out, man. If you wanna get out."

When I had first arrived at Cottage 8 and walked through the front door with my mattress on my back, a prisoner came up to me and asked for a cigarette. I put my mattress down and pulled out one of the five cigarettes I had in my shirt pocket to give to him. "Make it three" he ordered.

I knew this was it. My brother's words again flashed in my mind: "Fight at the drop of a pin. It don't matter if you win or lose. They'll respect you."

"Fuck you!"

"What motherfucker?!"

"Fuck you!"

"Step into the bathroom, fool."

That's where the guards let you fight, which insures that any anger a prisoner might get caught up in will be directed toward the prison who offended him and not later be the cause of instigating a riot or result in a guard getting assaulted. I walk to the bathroom and employ my standard. I fight long and hard in a confined space, bouncing off tiled walls, holding back just enough to let him eventually win. He walks away slightly injured, exhausted and justified. Here I was this scrawny white boy in a cottage packed with 120 prisoners—6 Puerto Ricans, 20 whites and 94 blacks—and I knew the assailant would think twice before ever attacking me again, because he knew I possessed the potential to whip his ass, which would irrevocably demote him in his homies' eyes.

Between the cottage and my job, a job consisting of 95% blacks, I had 6 fights in two weeks, the second to last one in the basement. I was talking with this other white boy, Roger. A black comes up and asks me for a cigarette (most fights in jail are over cigarettes or sex). I give him one and then he asks for the pack. "Fuck you!" And we are fighting. But this time I slip into one of those passive-aggressive moments, that deep, dark, spaced-out intestinal region, again surprising me more than anyone, and in the middle of our exchanging blows to the head I grab him with both hands by his hair and with wide sweeps I start slamming his head with full force into a cement pillar—his skull cracking and blood oozing out as he goes to his knees, and out of the corner of my eye I see Roger running up the stairs to get away from a gang of blacks rushing at me. I fight hard as blow after blow pounds into my body and skull, finally going down, them kicking me from every angle as I lie in a fetal position. A guard shows up and blows a whistle.

Only one more prisoner tried me after that, many months later. (Prisoners in reformatories, unlike in prisons where stabbing others with shanks is the norm, usually stick to fisticuff rules, and when a prisoner steps out of those confines, like I did in cracking the prisoner's skull, that prisoner becomes at some basic level feared because of his unpredictability—the reason, for example, that no black or white prisoner messed with Puerto Ricans: they preferred not to fight, but instead cut your face up with razor blades melted into a toothbrush). When I went to work in the dairy, another job reserved mostly for blacks, wild man Toby, a black from another cottage, started it up with me in a cow barn, but this time I decided to

99

fight hard and win, not a passive-aggressive interiorly unannounced decision, but a calculated and practical one: It was too easy to get knocked out and raped in the dairy—way too many blind spots with no guards around. After exchanging a number of blows we crash down to the ground, and he grabs me by the hair and moves to shove my face in a pile of cow shit in a gutter, and the thought of that humiliation, always more terrifying to me than being pummeled, went off like an alarm in my brain, maximum adrenalin kicking in. I snatch onto his ear with my teeth, trying hard with locked jaw to tear it off. I fail, but his ear is torn and the fight ends when he screams for me to stop. I would meet up with Toby years later in prison. He was down for a string of armed robberies and three homicides. He loved to tell other prisoners the story of our fight in the barn. For some reason he thought the whole thing was hilarious. He was quite mad, a wide smile always etched on his face, the happiest-go-lucky person I've ever known. And we had bundles of respect for each other.

That fight with Toby ended it. I would do three sentences in Annandale without another one. It wasn't just the respect. Through daily workouts and sparring matches (body boxing, where blows with full force could be landed, approved by guards, as long as there were no punches to the face, and with my masochistic streak I always went the distance). I had considerable skill now, coupled with endurance and, like my brother, able to endure relentless punishment, something all the prisoners would witness as I boxed with prisoner after prisoner, not stopping until the bell rang for us to return to the cottage. A potential enemy had to consider not only the sure knowledge that I would fight to the bitter end with a physical force that might make me victorious, but also that unforgotten scene where I broke the fisticuff courtesy, a trait now permanently etched in how prisoners analyzed my character. Fear mixed with respect gives

100

you close to full license to move about in the most relaxed state possible in reformatories. For me that meant having a license to be left alone.

Farmdale was severe. No books, magazines, comics or radios—and television 2 hours a night for 120 loud prisoners in a cramped recreation room. I was never able to hear anything other than musical tunes I was familiar with and the satirical, campy Batman series, the prisoners' favorite show, the only show they quieted down for, except during the impact-captioned fight scenes ("pow!" "bang!" "smash!" "zonk!" etc.) which always produced howls of laughter. That's why the marching flag was a big deal for most prisoners. All the cottages, eleven in all, were required to march to the mess hall at mealtimes in military style. Points on form and precision were tallied by the guards, and whatever cottage scored the most points at the end of the month got to stay up late and watch an extra 2 hours of television on the night of their choice.

Cottage 8 had a tradition of not ever marching. We were the fuck-ups, and we took great pride in not competing with our fellow prisoners for the one bone offered each month. We purposely marched out of step and talked shit on our way to every meal.

There was this prisoner we all loved. He was a black dude from Newark named Auggie. He was hard core, for that time one of the rare youngsters who was doing time for armed robberies, but one of the very few prisoners who came from an educated background, his mom a single parent and teacher who had devoted her life to him. He also had the handsomest face, the biggest smile, a pure heart and not a racist bone in his body—he was the great exception on every level. I asked someone who knew him one time why, if he had every advantage he was still into crime, and all he said was, "Adrenaline junkie. And he likes to get high." He also had that great gift of being able to see humor in everything, and you would always catch him laughing at

101

something. He had nothing but kind gestures for everyone, even stool pigeons. You just couldn't cross him, and no one ever did, not even the stool pigeons.

The most important event in Farmdale was the Motown Review Special that aired once a year on television, and it was scheduled to air on a Thursday night at 9:00 pm in the new month coming up. The only way to see it was to win the flag. The show featured top stars from the Motown label—the Supremes, Temptations, Smokey Robinson and the Miracles, Stevie Wonder, Martha and The Vandellas, Dionne Warwick, Mary Wells, on and on—a non-stop lineup. Auggie had a set parole date and would be leaving in two months. He wanted more than anything to catch the Motown Review before leaving, and he asked all of us if we would this one time march for the flag. *Motherfuckin' right, man*—our pleasure!

And we, all of us, tried real hard, knowing in our hearts that there was no way we could get down like those other prisoners who had been doing it for years. But we gave it our best shot. And it turned out the guards were so shocked at our effort—Cottage 8 for the first time in memory trying to march—they decided to award us the flag, to encourage us in our miraculous redemption. And the day after seeing The Motown Review we were back in form, out of step and talking shit.

A week after Auggie's release he was gunned down and killed in Newark.

**********

The first time I was released from Farmdale I had to sign a check for $25. I was told I would get the cash when I reported to my parole officer in Elizabeth, supposedly a way of insuring that I showed up at the parole office.

On my arrival, the first thing I ask the parole officer for is my money. "Not so fast" he says. "First you find a job and an apartment—then I'll give you the money."

I understood. I wasn't getting any money. No way to find a job and an apartment without a phone and a place to live. It was pocket-change for the parole officer.

When I was arrested for a parole violation and sent back to Farmdale and released again, this time they had me sign a check for $15.

"I thought I was supposed to get 25?"

"The last time you didn't make good use of the money. So this time you get 15."


When I arrived back at Farmdale for the third time on a parole violation, I was twenty years old. I had status—I was an old-timer. I didn't have to worry about fighting to prove anything. I knew all the games, all the strategies of survival, and just being relaxed creates an aura of self-confidence that makes the touch-offs (prisoners looking to establish they are men with violence) back off.

My brother was still in prison, and although we weren't allowed to communicate, I had gotten word that he was being heavily medicated, that he was in a severe depression and the prison doctors were looking to give him electro-shock therapy, something really dangerous for Tommy because of the brain damage from the police beating. This news plagued my mind every day. (I would find out later that the rumor was a bad wire: Tommy had been a major suspect in some kind of violence related to a drug war that resulted in the death of three prisoners, but the administration couldn't prove anything, and for whatever reason he had been shipped from lock-up status to the Vroom Room, the state psychiatric ward for criminals, supposedly to give him an elaborate psych evaluation, but it had nothing to do with him being depressed—it was strictly a ruse in removing him from the population for an extended period to prevent escalating violence.)

There was nothing to adapt to at Farmdale. I had mastered the game. It had become boring. I got that itch, the one that even in childhood would make me move on without any truly definable reason, sometimes across country on boxcars just to get away from wherever I was standing. It was just another inner turmoil, not feeling comfortable in my skin. I was sick of the drug lifestyle. I was sick of doing time. And I thought my brother was on the edge, ready to go under. I made my decision: I would try to get to prison. I put in a formal request. I was denied.

There was only one way. I had to become an extreme escape risk.

Early one morning on line walking to the mess hall for breakfast, I break away in a sprint, running around the back of a cottage and out into the darkness towards the 12-foot fence 200 feet away. When I get to the fence there was no one behind me. *What the hell's going on?*, I thought. Finally two guards come running up to me out of breath (I had slowly moved halfway up the fence), hands out in front of them, one yelling "Get down! Right now! You hear? Get down!"

I wasn't going anywhere, except prison.

It was strange. I was interrogated about how I knew they were two guards short that morning. They wanted to know who told me.

I found all of this amusing. It was simply coincidence. But they were reading everything they could think of into it. They wanted names.

I was in the hole waiting for my transfer to prison. The warden himself comes to my cell, a tall, big-boned hairy Greek with greased-down hair combed straight back in a pinstriped suit.

"You think I don't know what you're up to, Jones? You think I'm stupid?"

I didn't answer. I just keep looking at him from my position on the floor, on my back, clasped hands pulling my head up from the floor.

"Look, asshole," he went on. "You put in for a transfer to State Prison. You were denied. You're still denied. Understand? You make a ridiculous escape attempt and it turns out we're short two guards. So what do you do? You could have made it over the fence and into the woods, but you wait! Who do you think you're conning? You're not going anywhere. Got it? You will max out on your sentence right here, in Farmdale. So get used to it!"

I slowly get up from the floor and look him dead in the face:

"Now get *this*, you fuckin' asshole. You send me to State Prison. That's your only option. If you don't, I swear on my mother's life I'll escape for real. That's a fuckin' promise. And when I do I'll steal cars, rob old ladies, kill motherfuckers, whatever it takes, ya understand?—I'll do everythin' I gotta do to stay out. And when the investigation goes down, it'll be your stupid fuckin' ass that'll be on trial. It'll be you who decided not to send me to prison knowin' I'm an extreme escape risk. A violation of a strict code for the first time in Farmdale history. Put that on your fuckin' resume, you stupid fuck!"

I lie back down on the floor and get comfortable, him just staring at me. He has nothing to say. For me it is the pure fear of not getting sent to prison after being thoroughly finished with reformatories. I had already crossed that line with both feet, and at that point there is no turning back. To turn back would trap me in a realm of pure boredom. Three days later I am transferred not to prison, but to Gillette Reformatory, a reformatory for young adults, one step away from prison. And although I wouldn't get to see my brother, I was that much closer to him.

Chapter 7

Gillette Reformatory, like most reformatories, sits out in failing farmlands. Unemployed farmers in economically depressed areas is what gives bureaucrats a fast ticket to build prisons and reformatories in those regions, creating jobs that save families and communities.

There was a wooded area that blocked a view of Gillette from the New Jersey Turnpike, and that Turnpike was a singular torture for us prisoners. Late at night, alone in our cells in sheer country quietude, structurally isolated even from the sound of crickets, we could hear only the trucks rolling down a long stretch of road to unlimited points of freedom.

I was processed in and assigned to wing B-2. This was the wing for all the shot-out crazy loons, prisoners with no conscience and escape on their minds. Of course, as the system was designed back then, the higher up you go in the prison system, the better life gets—we were allowed radios, newspapers, magazines, books and a television and phonograph for every wing that could be played any time, day or night, before lock-up. But I had no real interest in any of it. I was dwelling most of the time on what I would do once I got out.

Most of the prisoners on B-2 didn't give a shit about anyone. For them it was all game, no principles. I didn't know this when I arrived. So when a well-respected prisoner on the wing came to me and said, "Look man. You're gettin' outta here soon [I was maxing out on my juvenile sentence, which was about 3 months]. I'm not. They won't be lookin' at you as hard as they're lookin' at me. You're cool. I know I can trust you. I need someone to saw a bar out for me in an empty cell. I'll play chicky. No way they'll suspect you. And I'll make it worth your while. Name your price."

"Yeah…I can do it, and it won't cost anythin'."

I smuggled a stainless steel bowl from the mess hall. In no time I was able with multiple bendings to tear it in half, and then begin cutting the bar with the bowl's torn edge every chance I got, metal on metal, the bowl's steel stronger than the old iron bar. Within a few days I was halfway through the bar.

I was lying on my cot absorbing angelic sounds from Miles Davis, John Coltrane, Red Garland, Paul Chambers and Philly Joe Jones—Red Garland's piano notes easing into space and hanging there in the air—when the tier guard shows up with another guard. "Get up!" he orders, jarring me out of my dream mood.

"What?"

"Get the fuck up!"

They lock me down in shackles and pressure belt and take me to an interrogation room. A lieutenant and another guard question me about cutting the bar. I told them I had no idea what they were talking about.

"Doesn't make any sense to me, Jones" the lieutenant says. "You're getting out in three months. You had to be doing it for someone else. Give us the name and we won't press attempted escape charges against you. That'll get you another three years."

"I told you—I don't know what you're talkin' about. You wanna charge me—go for it. Just stop wastin' my time."

They took me to the hole where I would spend the next two weeks. The next month the prisoner I had cut the bar for got a parole date and a transfer to a protective custody wing consisting mostly of stool pigeons and fem gays. Then I got it: he had set me up, got me to cut the bar and then ratted me out for an early release. This was a whole new scene consisting mostly of drug addicts who had been to drug programs and conditioned to rat on one another, part of a rehab philosophy to break down their criminal self-image by violating the basic principle of honorable thieves: you don't rat. It turns out I had a lot to learn, but no desire to learn it. It was all too depressing to think about. Even my obsessive need to meet up with my brother was vanquished. It became clear: prison life was over for me. Ennui set in big time. Gravity ruled.

\*\*\*\*\*\*\*\*\*\*

There was this young kid on B-2. I took a liking to him. I liked his smile and his enthusiastic appreciation of my every failed attempt at humor, and especially his groundless faith in the possibility of some good in the world. I felt sorry for him. He was 17-years-old, originally arrested at age 10 for stealing a pocket book. He was trying to get movie money for him and his friend. He was sent to Denselburg Reformatory, a place where imprisonment begins at age 8. He had a small frame, super-fine hair and milky-smooth skin, which made him an enticing on-going sexual object for other prisoners. His strategy since age 10 to make other prisoners back off was to just keep getting in trouble, playing crazy, spending record-breaking time in the hole. He wore glasses that had been smashed so many times he had only one lens left, all of the broken frame's pieces tied together with loops of polyester thread, and all of it held to his face with a shoelace tied at the back of his head.

He admired me and he knew I liked him. He came up to me one day and said, "There's this big dude who works in the kitchen. He says he's gonna fuck me, and if I don't like it we can fight."

I look at him. I know this had to have happened to him at many points in the past and he had a way of dealing with it, even if it meant succumbing to the threats, submitting to the violent humiliations. He'd been down for 7 years. But something in him had changed. What was certain is that he was relying on me to help him, something he might never have asked for before, not in the way he was asking me now. It had nothing to do with being in prison. He just wanted to know if I would help him, pure and simple, no ulterior motives. It was like he was putting his trust in humanity on the line with me. I couldn't say no, not to someone that innocent and still trusting after a brutal child and teen life in reformatories.

I don't know where it came from. That's how I moved in the world in these rare, genuine moments, moments that had the nature of an arrival of some sort, a summing up, more important than all the moments leading up to it, an event, clearly a destined moment with all that that demands outside every machination, all my fears suspended along with an accompanying rationality that would engage only what is in my self interest: "You got ta kill 'im."

"What?"

"You got ta kill 'im…It's the only way to make him and the rest of 'em back the fuck off. It's the only way you'll ever get to relax. At the rate you're goin', you'll never get out. You got to fuckin' show 'em, man. There's no other way. You gotta kill 'im. You know that. And I'll help you."

"What do I gotta do?"

"He works in the kitchen, right?"

"Yeah."

"Ok. You go to lunch. You get in line like you always do. When you get to 'im you tell 'im: meet me in the dugout [a blind spot leading up to every wing from the hallways]. Tell 'im 'You wanna fight? Fuck it...I'll meet you in the dugout at B-Wing!' I'll be there, man. I'll get you a shiv. Keep it on you. When he walks into the dugout, I'll grab 'im from behind and hold 'im. That's when you move fast and stick 'im as many times as you can—in the stomach first: that's the most painful; even if he survives he won't soon forget it. Just keep stickin' 'im, ya understand? And when it's done, we'll shove 'im under the stairs...You got it?"

"Yeah" Donnie says with a big grin on his face.

"OK...tomorrow at lunch."

I got a shiv. A solid, heavy one, long enough to pierce the lungs and heart, and I give it to him. "See you in the dugout" is all I say after handing it to him. He smiles and says "See you in the dugout."

And that's where I was when the prisoners began returning from lunch, standing at the entrance looking down the hall until I see Donnie coming towards the dugout, and I move back in to the right side of the entrance, pushing my back, arms and head tightly up against the wall. For me it was simple: Donnie was a good kid who was being systematically destroyed by the State, ending in some asshole fucking him in the ass to rob him of what little dignity he had left.

Donnie shows up, moving into the dugout to the back wall and turning around, the shiv under his shirt. He looks at me and grins, then quickly removes the grin from his face and stares at the entrance, waiting on the dude with arms at his side. And then, although I couldn't see him, the dude is standing outside the dugout, Donnie now motioning to him with his hands to step inside: "Come on, motherfucker! You wanna kick my ass? Come on! Kick my ass!"

Adrenalin is pumping as I prepare to grab him and put him in a hammerlock as he walks through the door. But he doesn't. He must have smelled death because it was hovering thick. "I *should* kick your ass you little punk ass motherfucker," the dude says to Donnie, and Donnie retorts, "You're the one mouthin' shit and not movin'. I'm here, waitin' on your big punk ass. So make your move, bitch!" "Man—fuck you!" the dude says and walks away.

Donnie wouldn't get out of Gillett for another three years. After his release he hooked up with two young criminals and went in to rob a store. The proprietor started gathering up the money, but Donnie, holding a machete, for no reason begins hacking on the man with wild swings. The proprietor was pleading with Donnie to stop, the two thieves Donnie was with chiming in with screams for him to stop, but he wouldn't—he just kept hacking on the man until he turned into a bloody corpse, the two other thieves running out of the store and down the street, Donnie just standing there blood-soaked waiting for the police to arrive.

**********

Maxing out on a juvenile sentence made a difference somehow. I was anticipating for the first time being on the outside without any of the games involved in the parole system. In the past I had always violated my parole within the first week, never calling in and never reporting after the first show; it made no sense to, knowing what my commitment was, to drugs and crime. This new way was its opposite: a commitment *not* to do drugs or commit crimes. I would work any job I could find and live in any rat-hole I could afford, as simple as that. And the more I focused on that possibility the more aloof I became to everything around me in Gillette, to the point of relaxing inside the sheer boredom, not oppressed by it. I had made fast friends with this

111

prisoner named Ray, another happy-go-lucky type with long hair and goatee who, like my brother, devoured books and liked to gamble. In fact, he was the only criminal I had ever met other than my brother whose first and primary addiction was books. On one occasion he was trying to convince me to partner up with him in a pinnacle game to make some money as I had done in the past. I didn't gamble, but he did and he always made money when we were partners, but I was sitting on the floor in the hallway with no incentive to move:

"No, Ray…Ain't got the energy for it."

"What? You depressed? I got somethin' for that."

"No. Just ain't got the energy to move from this spot, that's all. It's exhaustin' even answerin' your question."

"I know what it is, man…Acedia."

"A what?"

"Acedia, man. It goes deeper than boredom and depression. It grips you right down there in the marrow of your bones, a big-time disconnect, a lack-a-interest. It's just that everythin's over for you here, man," and he looks around. "I get it. I know where you're comin' from. It's just a question of gettin' out."

"Exactly."

"But my concern is that you might give 'em a reason to keep you locked up. You get too far out there they could send you to the Vroom Room…ya know what I'm sayin'? They can do it, man, even if your time's up. Get you on some psych shit, ya know? Convince a judge you're too nuts to be released."

"I'll keep that in mind, Ray. But I ain't playin' pinnacle."

Ray laughs: "That's cool, man! But you shouldn't be sittin' out here on the damn floor. Just go in your cell, man. You know…outta sight, outta mind, though I live day to day, I'm here today and gone tomorrow kind of thing."

"What the fuck you talkin' about?"

"Never mind, man. Just don't let the pigs fuck you around, ok? It's only a waitin' game. And there's a proper way to wait…out of sight. You got it?"

"Yeah, I got it."

Waiting game. Yeah. That was it. That's all it was. Don't make it anything else. I begin to rise up off the floor with Gravity pushing back at every little push I make until standing and moving into my cell, lying down on the cot and staring at the ceiling. This is where I discover a new life-strategy, *ceiling staring*, a check-out point from any repetitive movement that grinds down into a rut. Lying still, non-resistance, is the only way out, a waiting until some benevolent force lifts you out, for anything willed only burns the rut that much deeper. I would name this strategy so as not to forget it: Ceiling Staring, something I would employ often down the road, and its duration had a built-in time clock: three days to the second.


There was this prisoner, Dave, short with a medium build and conservatively-cut dark brown hair against pale smooth skin with a skimpy goatee, the best he could manage with minimal facial hair growth. He was also the most accomplished gambler I had ever met, and he had no conscience. His family moved to America from France when he was 13 years old, and he once confided that he had been influenced by American crime cinema more than anything in his life. He was the one who first instilled in me an interest in foreign cinema other than the plethora of Kung Fu films that had hit 42nd Street in new York for a time, and the first opportunity I got I saw the films he recommended in New York's revival theaters, films like Duvivier's *Pepe Le Moko*, Melville's *Le Samurai* and Godard's *Breathless*. It wasn't long before I became accomplished at reading subtitles while watching these and other foreign films, a whole new roadmap in understanding the wily ways of the world and the machinations of man in his misguided attempts at establishing some recognizable good for the world or, in a more humble aspiration, a better balance in doing the right thing for one's loved ones and self outside a social matrix comprised of infinite deceits. One film in particular summed all of this up for me, Renoir's *The Ruling Class*. Nothing like it: a bubbly, good-time film, loads of fun, but every gesture concealing one of many machinations of a world sewed together in sadomasochistic delight for the initiated, the Ruling Class, the master game-players, reveling in their awareness that there is no redeeming feature to being human, that life's a game of expropriation, and one need only master that game, which the ruling Class with its manners and fine education, especially in the Age of Psychology, were best prepared for. I could see all of this so clearly because all of them were obviously my dad dressed up in wealth, manners and an education. I would eventually discover only one American writer who knew this as deeply as Renoir from a uniquely American perspective, F. Scott Fitzgerald, and why I would come to believe that his novel *Tender is the Night* is in fact that great American novel that most of us are still waiting on. Fitzgerald figured it out: the ever-blossoming plant we call America, although continually watered, pruned and otherwise cared for by the miracle we call the Constitution, actually grew from the corrupt seed of slavery, genocide and self-assertiveness at the expense of others. And I could see Europe patiently waiting for our inevitable comeuppance that they, too, had to live through and humbly endure in a past not so easily forgotten.

Dave was ecstatic when his parents decided to move to America after his dad got a job offer, and for reasons I never discovered he had a cynical view of everything and no sense of humor—his singular, dominating focus was to become a successful criminal. He gambled, pimped prostitutes, sold drugs, did stick-ups and whatever else he had to do to immerse himself in a criminal lifestyle, and on the inside he gambled, and he was the master. We had casual, short-lived conversations, and without really getting close he considered me as close as he'd ever gotten to a prisoner or anyone else.

He was the consummate loner—there was a wall between him and everyone, including me. He never really saw me, never engaged me at any level other than as a person he felt he could trust. And that's the only thing that made me different than others in his eyes. One night, to help him loosen up, I told him about my experience in an 8th grade French class, the then mandatory foreign language requirement:

"The French teacher was hot. I mean HOT! And she knew it. She would sit on the front of her desk, slowly crossing her legs in her tight skirt, occasionally flingin' her long blond hair around, revealin' and then hidin' her perfectly chiseled facial features and her blue sensual eyes. She would play a French conversational record, and I would fixate on her legs, and in my hypnotic gaze I would unconsciously memorize every line on the record—not knowin' the translation, but I can accurately repeat every line of the conversation to this day."

Dave looks at me with a non-committal stare, his thin lips not budging, a blank stare from his brown beady eyes, and then:

"You know why the French hate Americans?"

115

"No" I said in a confused tone, because it had nothing to do with what I was trying to accomplish, and I knew nothing about history. He was silent for a few seconds, never altering his cold stare into my eyes.

"I'll tell you: we were all in it together in the beginning, during the war—a religious war, Pagans against a Jewish/Christian civilization. But when American soldiers freed us from the grip of the Nazis, they took the youngest of our French stock as payment, the 12, 13, 14 and 15-year-olds. Nothing kills principles quicker than lust. But unlike hordes of Pagans who tie young girls to trees or throw them to the ground and rape them, your soldiers gave our girls Hershey bars and silk stockings, and it was our little girls who provided the hidden dark places for the act, making them complicit. Our little girls were raped with consumer items…Now, the war won, we don't talk about it, but the French are still pissed off, only at this late date probably not knowing why—it's just buried in the genes. Anyway, no court would even want to hear the case—it was a one-time humiliation begging to be forgotten. Out of all the Americans, only the criminals get it right—the best of them anyway, and why we French are fascinated with them: they're honest about what they want and how to get it; they don't dress it up as anything but criminal, and I've never met one who fucked a child, and those rapos on E-wing in protective custody ain't no criminals. They're something else. That's why they keep them separate from us."

\*\*\*\*\*\*\*\*\*

It was a Friday night. Most of the prisoners were out at the movies. Dave stayed back to gamble. He was involved in a poker game with four blacks. He won all their cigarettes. The blacks who had lost were mulling around in the hall talking deep shit about this white boy who thinks he's hot shit. One of them said, "I'm gettin' my shit back, man."

When they moved on Dave he was ready. The blacks figured they'd beat him unconscious and take all his cigarettes—simple enough. But Dave had something else in mind: with a toothbrush that had six razor blades melted into it (he was a white who had obviously learned from the Puerto Ricans) he sliced the first prisoner's face to shreds who was at the door and entering his cell, and Dave was ready for the next one, staying up front at the door to limit movement into his cell. It was probably the scream and all the blood and shredded flesh that made the blacks back off, returning to the injured prisoner's cell to make butterfly stitches for his wounds and work on another plan.

When the movie crowd returned, the wounded prisoner started talking shit to the blacks. He was trying to instigate a race riot to divert attention from his humiliation. But it involved more than exacting revenge. There was still the hope that he and his friends' gambling losses could be recovered. Then there would be a total lock-down, but he would have his dignity and plenty of cigarettes to smoke through the duration.

It all brewed quickly. The racist whites played right into it.

There was this prisoner, a heavyweight-boxing champion—a big black dude, 6'3" and a solid 230 pounds. We called him Blue because his skin was blue-black. He came up to me and said "Can I talk to you, man?"

"Yeah."

"Come to my cell."

We went to his cell and he laid it out with precision:

"Look, man. I got a shipment of drugs comin' in. I can't afford this shit. The pigs'll lock us up for a month if this shit goes down, ya understand? We gotta stop it."

"Yeah, well…what's your plan?"

"It's simple, man. The brothers want blood. Their man got cut up."

"Yeah, but I wasn't involved."

"The brothers say you warned Frenchie."

"That ain't true. I wasn't involved in that shit, and I ain't cut nobody."

"Exactly. You ain't involved. The brothers know Frenchie got into this because he had legitimately won at cards. They're tyin' it to you precisely 'cause you ain't involved—get it? I mean, they know you're the only one that got a rapport with Frenchie, and they also know that Frenchie's next response if he's attacked might kick off a race riot, and most of the brothers, even though they're talkin' shit, don't want lock down. They don't want to blow their visits and drugs. And that's where you come in: you can offer yourself up, a kind of scapegoat, ya know? But you and I can plan it and control it, make it effective. I'll go back and tell the brothers that you and I will settle this shit, and we'll put on a show for 'em, give 'em a good fight. We can prolong it, a really good show. You're a loner and so am I—and you're friends with Frenchie. We're talkin' 'bout stoppin' a race riot where all of us would lose. Whatdya say? A little show. It's perfect."

I feel my exhaustion more than ever. All I wanted was my cot, and I could care less if they locked the joint down the rest of my stay, but I say "Sure. Whata we do?"

"I'll talk all the shit, man. I know you're not into that. Gotta get 'em riled up first, make 'em focus on you and me, a white motherfucker and a black motherfucker. That's all it'll be: you and me; we got to focus on the entertainment value, and I'm sorry, bro, but in the end you got to lose. It's not only what's obvious, but mathematics: it's 80% black out there, and they're the ones that feel slighted 'cause one of theirs got cut up, but you'll get your shit off on me, too, to satisfy the whites. We got to draw blood on both sides and prolong it for as long as it takes to satisfy their bloodlust. That's the only way they're gonna back off...You with me, man?"

This pissed me off. I was tired. I wanted out—out of everything. I wanted out of Gillette and out of a life of drugs. I was finished. This request was the culmination of all the demands ever made on me, the absurdity of it all, and I wanted to say "Fuck you!" But I didn't.

"Ok, man."

We moved out into the rec room.

Lee was a great showman. He walked around the tier broadcasting the event, how he was going to fuck this white motherfucker up, making sure everyone showed up. And the guard was seasoned: he knew what was going down, preferring a fight over a riot, sitting at his desk behind locked doors, turning his head as was custom when an organized fight was about to go down.

Lee swung the first punch, an overhand right into my face, me slipping to one side and coming back with a solid roundhouse to his ribs, the smack of flesh against flesh audible to all, the whites yelling "Yeah!" and I could hear a black yell "Kill that white motherfucker!" And we fight on and on, the cheering and epithets bouncing off walls but now distant from my ears as I focus on the game. It was mostly Lee who had to do all the calculating because he could have put me down fast: he was the best and most powerful fighter in the jail. All I had to do was fight as hard as I could without restraint, focusing solely on a solid, willful act to destroy Lee. It was Lee that made this all look legit, taking a punch in the face here and there, me splitting his lip at one point and one of his eyes slightly swollen. But my nose was already bleeding profusely, my chin and chest covered in blood, and at one point, not knowing if Lee was trying to knock me out, he came down hard with an overhand right on my left eye, and that single punch split the corner of

my eyebrow wide open in three gashes, a Y design, which sent me flying across the room, a big

roar going up in the air from the blacks, and I jump right back up and charge into Lee with a

flurry, hitting mostly Lee's forearms but landing a solid punch to his jaw that elicited roars from

the whites. But with no round breaks, our breathing began to get heavy and our arms started to

weaken, mine more than Lee's who was in excellent shape, but he took on the rhythm of

exhaustion as a good actor, winding down the spectator hysteria as our left jabs, overhand rights,

upper-cuts and right crosses slowed, and finally Lee connecting hard and sending me to the floor,

and as I slowly try to lift myself up off the floor with lacerations around both eyes, top and

bottom, Lee puts his hand in the air with a black power salute, and cheers go up, and Ray comes

out to the floor and puts his arm around me, saying "It's over, man." Both my eyes were swollen

near shut, blood pouring from the gashes, my chest and arms covered in blood. Lee got it right:

the blacks and whites were appeased with only minor, hardly audible racist murmurs of elation

or protest, everyone returning to whatever they do to make the evenings pass without having to

think about serving another day in jail, and not having to feel their dignity in any way had been

effaced.

After showering and going to my cell to butterfly my lacerations, I was pissed. I had an

urge to get a pipe or anything and crush Lee's skull. He hadn't done anything wrong—he didn't

deserve to have his skull crushed. But he represented that thing, that demand on me to sacrifice

myself to a dead end where nothing is ever made right, just another beginning of an endless cycle

of people getting their shit off on one another.

\*\*\*\*\*\*\*\*\*

I was healing and easing back into listlessness. I was going to be released in 45 days and had lost every residual incentive to get involved in anything of what was going on around me. Doing time was now like having viewed for the last time a favorite film that no longer holds an abiding interest, the director's visual alchemy, insights, concerns and encouragements from the angle of the crevice I resided in and all of my projected realignments of the story to possess and incorporate it into my psyche exhausted at every level. Boredom (the absence of meaning) creeps in, finding myself again in zombie fashion walking through musty corridors of futility, the former enthusiastic response to a liberating truth now a "so what?", and with it the terrible probability that every arrival will end this way, just another impasse, so what's the point? In that moment all the illuminations of my life are displaced by a revelation that all my experiences in life and art will never amount to anything more than a series of diversions, a refusal to turn with eyes fully open, not squinted, and looking headlong into the endless pit of meaninglessness, the book of life slammed shut and placed in a museum for its cover to collect dust.

In Farmdale I had been more fortunate. There I had been stripped of everything I had clung to or envisioned clinging to to create meaning outside—films, money, clothes, cars, music, comic books, television, drugs, sex and the rest—and thus I had no choice but to move closer to those I associated with to defeat the emptiness of a thingless world through paying closer attention to the person sitting next to or across from me. I had no choice but to rely on others for entertainment, the only escape from dreaded emptiness, and I would discover that persons are far more fascinating than things, possessing far more power to sustain one's interest, for there is always another hidden nuance from endless nuances, however slight, of a story continually emerging from a unique and inexhaustible life when trust and an abiding interest goes deep.

121

Every day, sitting in chairs against the wall, was another opportunity to catch a finer point of a story told, a glimpse of a deeper motivation birthed in a vulnerability hidden from the barbarians camped out at every station in life; and for me, I mostly listened—which only deepened my appreciation of the stories. I had unconsciously come to prefer this to all of what went down on the outside, and why on the outside there was always a nudging nostalgia for prison life, and why I had always at some deep level enjoyed my return. The outside was mostly a journey down an empty corridor of desire (and in my world it was the pursuit of drugs, a game that gets old real fast), a labyrinthine corridor Proust discovered and wrote about more elegantly than any writer in history. For me there is nothing more depressing than to see an old heroin addict nodding out with a burning cigarette he is not able to lift to his mouth in front of a McDonald's, advertising with his attire and nod his permanently adopted identity, his dead-end commitment to a tired fantasy and pain relief, and how he rightly feels superior to everyone who walks by, for he perceives that they, unlike him, have not figured out the great secret to life, that there is in fact no secret at all, that it "eeees what it eeees" in all its gloom and doom, and all any reasonable person can do is ease the pain. One old junkie said to me, "Think about it: Why da ya think the only industry that keeps expandin' with out-of-control profits is pharmaceuticals? Everyone wants out, man…anyway they can, and drugs are the easiest route. It's just that street drugs are better than everythin' the pharmaceutical companies are offerin'."

In Farmdale it was the stories told that kept me centered in the world. But now I could see that even those stories in their endless looping were just more fragments of the endless drivel of diversions, a means of avoiding a glance into the endless pit.

Something in my consciousness had radically shifted. Doing time at every level had become just one more disappointment. I wanted to move on, to go somewhere else, to not ever return. *I had to find something outside.*

I was sitting on the floor, my back up against the wall in the recreation room. Like never before I felt the full weight of Gravity, and could in no way deny that it had always been the greatest force in my life, even in my most exalted moments of denial. I was now being pressed into a numbness much like Kafka's Prometheus who turns into the rock he is chained to. It took a terrible effort to push myself up from the floor and walk down the stairs, out into the corridor and straight to Control Center. It was the center of all traffic through all the halls, three guards behind a bulletproof octagon glass and brick enclosure, a fat sergeant sitting closest to the hole in the glass (the edge lined with thick brass) that prisoners talk into. I walk up to the hole, standing there, blank-staring at the sergeant.

""Whatdoyouwant?" the sergeant demands.

I lean close to the hole. "I refuse your program."

"What program?"

"The Gillette Reformatory program."

No rebellion in my voice, just a tired monotone. He looks at me for a few seconds, then says "Stand over there against the wall."

I turn and look at the wall on the other side of the corridor. I walk there, turn around and stand with my back against the wall in a relief that always accompanies an action that turns an abstract, highly unlikely decision into reality, especially a decision so radically foreign to one's options only an hour before, and one that is opening a door to a great unknown, for I had no idea where this decision was taking me.

About a half hour goes by and a prisoner I know comes walking by and asks "What's goin' on, man?"

"Nothin'"

A guard yells to the prisoner to keep moving. I was glad he did this—I had nothing to say. Where would I begin?


Eventually two guards walk up to me with a pressure belt (a thick 3-inch leather belt with handcuffs attached to a big metal ring bolted into the leather at its center, with a connecting chain that runs through the ring and hangs to the floor with leg-irons attached, the buckle at the center of my back). They lock my hands and legs into the pressure belt, and when they once again tighten the buckle another notch, I feel a great relief, a deep sense of containment, as if I were in no way any longer exposed to the vagaries of fate, that I had thrown in the towel and submitted to all its decisions without resistance, for the first time experiencing what the freedom of letting go really means. Every sense of being in control or determining the outcome of anything was gone, a terrible weight lifted, Gravity suspended. This was good—I didn't have an ounce of energy to invest in anything. I just wanted to lie secure on the floor and watch my thoughts move about, a return to that newly discovered activity, *ceiling staring*. The guards took me to the hole where I would spend the remaining 45 days of my time.

Chapter 8

I had a lot to think about in the hole, but everything kept bringing me back to a moment in a park in Summit, New Jersey. I was 18. I was waiting on my crime partner to show up. I was in no hurry. I was twisted on heroin. I sat on a bench chain-smoking cigarettes, looking out on the people and cars passing by. Then I saw this young couple walking down the street towards a laundromat, each carrying a bag of laundry.

What caught my attention was the guy—I had done time with him in Farmdale, and although I didn't hang out with him on the outside, I would see him around on occasion. But I hadn't seen him in a long time, figuring he had moved to another town or was doing time somewhere. Then I got it: he had let it go. He had found a girlfriend and was making that trek into what I could only fantasize about, falling in love and working through all the bullshit, caring for each other, carving out a space, a personalized fortress, regardless how small, that would secure and protect them from every onslaught for the rest of their lives, abiding in a love that repels every evil, even the degenerative and depressing thoughts of the mind. It was pure clarity. No mistaking it. No heroin illusions like living without problems on some beach in California. It was clear that even with their problems it was going to be better than anything they had ever known, including heroin. That's what I had to find when I got out. That meant no drugs. Just getting a job, any job, and waiting for everything to open up. Without any warrants and off parole, I would be able to visit Tommy and maybe find a way to help get him out. I was certain the mere fact that I was happy in the world would give him relief. The possibilities were endless. All I had to do is take that first step: get a job.

125

**\*\*\*\*\*\*\*\*\***

Donnie was waiting on me the morning two guards escort me to the tailor shop to get my release clothes. He followed close behind. The two guards stopped at the Control Center. I was still dressed in white hole-pajamas. They told me to stand against the wall, that they were going to arrange for me to go to the barbershop to get a haircut.

"I ain't gettin' no haircut."

"Oh yeah?" one of the guards shot back in anger. "You're getting a fucking haircut, asshole. You don't like it, you'll get one at the Vroom Room!"

Donnie walks up to me: "Get the fuckin' haircut, man. They'll fuckin' do it!.. They'll shock you up and turn you into a basket case. You're free, man. Don't let 'em fuck that up!"

"Move it out!" the guard yells at Donnie.

"Get the fuckin' haircut, man!" he yells as he moves away.

"Keep moving!"

"Get the haircut!"

Donnie was right. My time wouldn't officially be up for another 24 hours. They always release you one day before an actual max-out date (most prisoners leave with parole time hanging over them and have to submit), just to keep you in line that last day where you feel free from the system, especially the jibes from that one sadistic guard that always seems to show up on your release date and hangs around to taunt you. And in those days shock treatment was used as a tool for control and punishment. The standard psychiatric line was that acts of aggression were externalized forms of acute depression, so any act of aggression got a doctor's approval for shock treatment if requested by the guards. I was once sent to see a psychiatrist at Farmdale, a mad German with a thick accent. He screamed at me: "I send you to tha Vrooooom Rooooom!" There was this kid in Farmdale who had beat up a guard who had smacked him. He was sent to the Vroom Room, and when he returned after a series of shock treatments they put him on bed time, reserved for prisoners with high fever or other sickness where they weren't able to work and were allowed to stay in the dormitory all day sleeping or just relaxing. And this prisoner just slowly shuffled up and down the dormitory all day and night until told to go to bed. This was a tactic, parading him in front of us as a warning. Then one day I noticed the prisoner was starting to shadow box—only light action at first, some uppercuts, slow flurry moves, his head dipping a tat or moving to one side at moments, and he was now walking instead of shuffling. But as the days progressed he got more active and actually started doing footwork with more elaborate and faster fist movements. When the guard he had assaulted saw this, he walked up to him and said "This ain't a goddamn gym! Knock that shit off!" The prisoner just looked at him for a few seconds and then with a furious flurry beat the guard into the ground again, and as the guard lay unconscious on the floor, the prisoner continued to do his shadow boxing, as if he were waiting for the guard to get up to start the next round. When they took him away this time he never returned.

They buzzed my head and fitted me in ridiculous looking clothes the guards had picked out, the pants hitting far above the ankles with white socks that had no elastic, the socks continually falling down over the heels of my shoes. I was handed an envelope with $13 and change and a cheap watch I had when I arrived. Then I was escorted to the outside, always a good feeling, and I was directed to step into the back seat of a car. The guard who drove me to

127

the train station, after pulling up with a look of superior disgust, hands me a one-way ticket to Newark, New Jersey. When I step out of the car he says disgustedly "You'll be back."

"Yeah, for killing some stupid punkass motherfucker like you" as I slam the door shut.

Obviously even in my cowardliness I had become what they call hardened. No doubt the process began when I cursed God at age 11—I just didn't know the implications and what interior places it would connect to, attitudes and behaviors now randomly unfolding in my life, surprising me as much as anybody, but definitely forming more of who I was becoming, but what I just as easily dismissed, determined to get on with my plan.

These were the times before community support systems were put in place with work-release and other transitioning means for ex-cons to find their way back into the fold. I went to Summit and called Kris, my main man, a tall muscular but slender Polish/Italian kid who always wore a pompadour and always dressed to kill, most of the time sporting a sarcastic grin, like he was in on some kind of cosmic joke. He never was a criminal at heart. He was a kid who loved his good looks and the company of women. To this day I feel the guilt of having dragged him into the heroin world. The best I could do was make sure he never did time. This was the ethical compromise I reached in dealing with my aloneness in a drug-world of total self-absorption, a needing someone, a good friend, and I loved Kris as deeply as a man can love another man. When I called him "brother" I meant it. I didn't want to lose his companionship, meaning I didn't want to be alone in the world. I knew in my heart it was wrong to lead him into the drug world, but I conned myself into believing it was all his free choice. Every time I got into a new drug Kris would try to talk me out of it, and I would say "Hey, man, you ain't got to do it. As a matter of fact, you shouldn't do it. But I'm goin' with it." And he would relent. But he never took to crime, not in the sense of making a commitment to that life. He hovered at the periphery, dipping in every once and a while, but never anything serious.

When I got hold of him we agreed to meet at the train station park, an old hang-out. He told me I couldn't stay at his house, his parents not wanting me around.

"That's cool with me, man. They're bein' lovin' parents. Hell, I wouldn't want me around either, but I ain't figured out a way to get the hell away from myself. But I got to get a job—I don't care what it is. I got thirteen bucks. That ain't gonna last. Can I use your phone number?"

"Yeah, man. That's no problem. My mom mostly answers the phone, and I'll explain it to her. My dad rules the roost, ya know, and he got this attitude 'bout you, but mom will understand. I know she'd like to help."

I went on interviews, picking the lowliest of jobs, mostly factory work, to insure employment as quickly as possible. But every time I asked Kris if anyone called he told me no. I began to suspect that his parents might have gotten a call but wouldn't tell Kris, figuring that could only help in distancing him from me. It was April, the nights still chilled when sleeping, and when I woke up after sleeping in the park, I would go to the train station to wash up. There was no hot water. After the third morning, the cold water mixed with the hard grainy soap from a dispenser felt like it was tearing into my unshaven skin. I looked long into the dull, scuffed-up metal mirror at my stupid tie and stupid hair. It was all a fuckin' joke.

I was 20 years old, not old enough to buy alcohol. It was early morning, but I found a wino and gave him the last of my money to buy me a bottle of rot-gut wine. I drank it down, and just sat there in the park, falling easily back into my old voyeuristic routine inside what Leonard

Cohen called "a visionary flood of alcohol", totally calm in that warm glow and believing that things would somehow work out, that there would be this big turnaround, that this was only a temporary set-back, that I, too, would find a way to move freely as the persons I was watching, especially walking hand in hand with one of those pretty women that walked by who, more than anything, reminded me of my plan. How hard could it be?

A kid we called Greek, whom I had in the past made every effort to avoid because he was a known stool-pigeon (he could fight, a golden gloves champion, and in his mind this, together with a drug-program-indoctrination belief that ratting was a sign of maturity, gave him license to stool to keep himself out of jail) came up to me: "Hey, man! I heard you were out. What's goin' on with you?"

"Nothin', man."

He sits down next to me on the bench.

"Look, man…I got this set up. I know this bitch who works at Corby's laundry. She told me where they stash the money after closin', and it's never under $2000. It's sittin' there waitin' for us."

I look at him. "Why haven't you grabbed it?"

"It's getting in, man. They got alarms. You're good at this shit. You're like the Houdini of B & Es, man. I know you can pull it off. I trust you, man."

"I don't know, man. I'm tryin' to get a job. I'm finished with all this shit."

"I under*stand*, man. But you need some cash. Look at you. No offense, man, but if you want a job you got to get your act together—get some decent clothes and clean up. Get yourself a room and a phone. I don't like seein' you like this—it ain't you, man."

I take what he says to heart. It was true. It wasn't me. Nothing about where I was was me, good or bad.

"Alright…I'll check it out."

"We can check it out now."

"Yeah, ok."


And we walk a few blocks, and then walk around the building. I notice there are ventilation windows up high on the building in the industrial laundering part of the building, and that we can access those windows from the roof of the building next door. I was certain I wouldn't have to worry about dismantling alarms on those windows. I tell Greek we will need some rope, masking tape, a giant screwdriver and a small ladder.

"I'll get it, man. I'll meet you at the park at 10:00."

"No. Make it a little before 12:00. The best time is when the police are changing shifts."


The wine had worn off by the time he showed up. I had a slight hangover, enough to hook me into a deep despair and confusion about where I had arrived. Here I was doing a burglary with the Greek, something I'd never have done in the past. I was operating out of desperation and nothing more.

Greek pulls up on a side street. I walk to his car and get in.

"Don't pull into the alley. Just park near it."

He pulls up and parks and we get out of the car. The entire square block is made up of stores, no apartments. The city is quiet. I look around and see nothing moving.

131

"Ok, let's move quickly." Greek pops the trunk. I grab the ladder and rope and Greek grabs the masking tape and screwdriver. I didn't expect the amount of money Greek said would be there, but I was sure there would be enough to get me some clothes, rent a room and get a phone.

We walk into the alley, Greek complaining that he is scared of heights, asking why can't I go in first and then open a door for him.

"Look, man—I don't want to mess with the alarm system. This is the only way I'm doin' it. Those are ventilation windows up top, and the laundry section is at least two stories high without ceilin' separation. I'm certain no alarms were installed up there, and I'm sure lots of pipes will be runnin' close to the ceiling. We will be able to make our way down and to the front office. I'm not openin' any doors. You're either in or out on this. There's no other way I'm doin' it."

"Ok, Ok, man."

I tie the rope to the first rung of the ladder and then climb up the adjacent building onto the roof, and the ventilation windows are easily accessed with the ladder. I look closely and see no alarm tape or devices attached to the window. I tape up one of the six panes in the window and break the glass, pulling out the glass and opening the window from the inside. Just as I suspected—no alarms. Then we begin our descent down pipes and industrial washers.

When we get to the front of the store there is a clear opening into the front office. Once inside Greek points to where the money is supposed to be, and using the big screwdriver I break open the locked drawer with one shot. Just papers inside—no money. I turn to Greek: "What the fuck, man? There ain't shit here."

"That's crazy, man. The bitch told me that's where they keep the money."

"Yeah, well the bitch lied...Fuck!"

And then I hear a voice talking loudly through a megaphone: "We know you're in there, Jones. Come out with your hands in the air."

I look at Greek. "What the fuck, man?"

"I don't know! They can't know it's you. They're assumin'."

"Yeah. Like that fuckin' matters!"

Then again: "We're telling you one more time, Jones. Come out with your hands in the air."

"I'm goin' out, man" is all Greek says and heads for the door yelling "I'm comin' out! I'm comin' out!" He looks back at me: "I won't tell 'em you're in here, man. You can hide. I'll tell 'em it's just me, OK?"

I run to the back of the laundry and there are red lights spinning outside the back door. There's a small maintenance room at the other end and I head for it. I hear the back door entrance being forced open and an alarm going off. They were already entering the building. I go into what I thought was a maintenance room but it was a small bathroom, but it had a diffused glass window, a possible way out, the only way out. Going inside I lock the door, assuming they might think it's a locked storage area. I lay on the floor, my back pressed hard up against the toilet, my knees locked and feet pressing against the door, my mind jammed with rapid-fire thoughts about a possible escape, but I could see the red lights flashing about the diffused glass. *I got to try the window. Maybe they'll all come inside and I can make it.* They were still pounding on the door: "Open the door, Jones! We know you're in there!" *How?*, I thought. *Did Greek set me up?* No way. That made no sense. He wouldn't have come in with me if that were the case. Maybe someone had spotted us on the roof. The cops knew I was out and probably saw me walking around unshaven in my clown clothes and were just waiting on me to do something desperate. But how did they know? I would never find out. I had never got caught on the premise of any of the hundreds of burglaries I had done, and I wasn't about to let that happen now. I had to figure a way out, to at least give it a shot at getting away. The cops were now banging their fists on the bathroom door, yelling again: "Open the door, Jones!" My feet lock harder against the door.

They start body-slamming the door, and the door flies open with me on the floor, a cop sticking a 38 Smith & Wesson in my face, his hand shaking in fear: "Don't move! Don't fuckin' move!"

## Chapter 9

The thing is it's over. I'm sitting in a city jail where the cops aren't even going to bother to interrogate me with an offer for a deal. They all know me. I'm a loser pure and simple. They got the goods—they caught me on the premises. But this rap is not going to get me into prison where I could get some comfort in knowing I will see my brother, because I'm still 20-years-old for another four months. The crime isn't serious enough for prison time. So I'll be back in Gillette with that guard sarcastically reminding me that I'd be back. I'm lying on a wooden bench, but the discomfort has no relevance. That I will have to go back to Gillette is the only torture consuming me. Regardless what I think about it, I know I don't belong there. If I did go, I would have to escape. It would be my sole meditation.

It's early morning of the next day. I'm being processed to be sent to the County Jail. A cop comes in and says "You made bail. Get your things together."

This was a shock. I had never made bail. It was a totally unsuspected reprieve. And I hadn't a clue as to who it could be. I knew Kris had no money and he wasn't working. And it wasn't like anyone would loan him money.

I walk out to the desk sergeant, and standing off to one side is Kris, and he's with a young woman named Angela whom I had known briefly four years earlier when she was age 14. Kris says "Just sign the papers, bro."

I sign the release papers and they give me my belongings—a wallet with no money, a cheap watch and a comb. We walk outside. Angela has a 65 Mustang convertible parked out front. Kris says "I went to the park lookin' for you, and then I find out you're arrested. What the fuck you hangin' out with Greek for? You know he's nothin' but trouble, and a fuckin' stool pigeon to boot."

"He had something that looked good—some fast money."

"You mean a fast ticket back to the joint. Come on, bro—why you wanna be stupid?"

"I know, man."

"I gotta go—give me a call."

"Whataya talkin' about?"

"Angela got you out. Talk to her. I gotta go." And he walks away. Angela looks at me and smiles.

"Can we get out of here?" she says.

"Yeah."

She walks to her car and unlocks the passenger side and then moves to the driver's side. When we're both in the car, she starts it up and pulls out of the parking lot without saying anything.

She moves quickly through the center of town, and once on a main arterial outside downtown she asks "You need a place to stay?"

"Yeah."

"You can stay with me until you get your own place."

"I appreciate it—but why?"

"Why?"

"Yeah—why'd you bail me out?"

"I owe you—that's why." And then we both remain silent.

**********

I met Angela when I was staying at a run-down mansion. I was 16 and strung out on heroin, and there was this old, frail alcoholic woman who had many years before suffered a nervous breakdown after the premature death of her husband, a brilliant physician who had founded a psychiatric hospital. She was wealthy, but her finances were controlled by a lawyer who was also a judge, a man who gave her a monthly stipend and arranged minor repairs on her mansion when it was needed. She would sometimes walk around town late at night, and that's how I met her. More than a few times she approached me when I was nodding out on heroin in the park by myself. She felt sorry for me, a kid living alone on the streets, and told me I was welcome to stay at her house until I made other arrangements—she had plenty of room. I finally took her up on the offer. Sometimes she would sit with me and tell me stories about her husband, how she had met him on a cruise liner and how he was the most remarkable man she'd ever known, and when he died her world crumbled. But mostly she stayed to herself inside her drunkenness, and I inside my heroin nod.

My ritual was simple enough. I would sit in front of a television and shoot up. On a particular night there was a severe rainstorm and I heard a knock at the door. I went and opened it, and there stood a 14-year-old girl soaking wet and shivering—it was Angela. "Someone said I might be able to stay here. I can't go home. They said you're a runaway, too, and old Mrs. Duffy lets you stay here."

"I ain't a runaway. I'm a stayaway. But you're welcome. Come on in."

I showed her a room she could use. Mrs. Duffy was already asleep, and she never questioned who I had over because first, it was rare that I had anyone over other than Walt, and I was always quiet, withdrawn, not the partying type. I told Angela I only had men's clothes for her to wear until hers dried (I had stacks of new clothes, mostly Italian knits, silk-mohair pants and leather coats, laid out over banisters throughout the house that I had shoplifted and sold when I could). She was fine with that. She was a short, close to plump Italian girl with dark brown hair and dark eyes.

I rarely talked. I had nothing to say. But over the next few days Angela would come around me, trying to engage me in conversation. Then one day we were alone in the house. She came on to me sexually, closing her arms around my neck and kissing me. We went to the floor and I was on top of her, pulling her dress up to her waist and running my right hand along her legs, our mouths sucking on each other's tongues. And then I smelled one of her deep breaths. It was the smell of deep emptiness—a dark, dank loneliness and desperation, and when I looked at her legs I could see into the pores, and they too were breathing from an abyss of sorrow. I got up off her and walked away. She stayed a few more days and we didn't talk to each other. I just sat in my chair high on heroin. I never knew what had happened with her. I never saw her again after she left the house, although I would sometimes hear from someone who had talked to her and that she was asking about me. I figured it had to do with my status as a convict with a reputation among fringe dwellers. But here she was four years later bailing me out of jail.

\*\*\*\*\*\*\*\*\*

138

When we got to Angela's one-bedroom apartment I was impressed. It was a modern apartment on the second floor of a duplex with big windows, a balcony and lots of natural light. The apartment was moderately furnished—a kitchen table with four chairs in a dining area that was a section connected to but set off from a huge living room, a cream-colored sofa, a tall lamp, a stereo and television. She didn't show me her bedroom, and this was a relief. She told me she had extra blankets—I could sleep on the couch or the floor. She told me she worked for a man whom she believed would give me a job reference.

"That'd be great" I said.

"I'll get you a set of keys, and you'll need some clothes."

"That's OK."

"Look. You helped me out years ago when I was in trouble. I want to return the favor. Walt came to me and asked me to help you. What could I say? It's not a big deal. I'll get you some clothes so you can go on interviews. When you get a job you can pay me back. It's really not a big deal. And the apartment [she looks around]—it's not much, but you're welcome to stay until you get your own place. I'm hardly ever here, anyway. I spend a lot of time at my boyfriend's house. Things will happen for you pretty quickly, I'm sure. Just relax and accept a helping hand, OK?"

She left to get a copy of the keys for me. And when I went to the kitchen cabinets to look for something to eat, I found nothing but a jar of instant coffee. No sugar, and no cream in the refrigerator. Just a container of orange juice. That emptiness. It was still there. Nothing had changed with her. That's what I thought, and it was creepy.

When she returned she gave me a set of keys and fifty dollars.

139

"I'm sorry there's no food in the house," she said. "I eat out. It's just easy. Buy what you need, and if you need more money, let me know."

"I'll be fine. Thanks."

"Well…I guess I'll see you tonight—if you're awake when I come in."

"Yeah. Thanks. I appreciate it."

"OK. I'll see you." And she leaves.

I call Kris:

"What's goin' on with you, man?" he says, "I've been waiting on your call. You gettin' laid or somethin'?" and he starts laughing.

"I can't stay here, man. No way."

"Are you crazy? Angela digs you, man. You're in like Flint."

"Yeah, and I want out like Jimmie Hoffa."

"I'm tellin' you, man. I scoured my brain tryin' to think where I could get bail money, and then I remembered Angela. Whenever I ran into her when you were in the joint she would always first thing ask about you. She's got a thing for you, man—always has. I tracked her down and when I told her about your arrest and that I was tryin' to raise bail money she leaped at the chance. Serious! You might as well dig in; otherwise you might be lookin' for a way to dig out!" and he starts laughing. He always saw himself as some kind of comedian. And I don't know if he was or wasn't—he just made me laugh all the time. But not this time.

"I gotta get outta here, Kris."

"You're fuckin' nuts, man. I hook you up with a good thing and you want to blow it? That's not cool, man. Where you gonna go? No way can you stay at my house. You know my dad would never go for that. So whataya gonna do? It's not like you got all these options, ya know. Don't blow a good thing. It fell in your lap, so just go with it. You'll have plenty of time to figure somethin' out. Plus you can pick up where you left off on that big romance."

"Fuck you!"

"Hey…I'm just tellin' you not to be stupid, OK? You should be grateful. You're out on bail, get it? I mean, that's a first, and I just don't see an alternative."

"Yeah—whatever…Look—meet me at the park about 6:00. Bring some works."

"You're not serious?"

"I wanna get high."

"What about money?"

"Angela gave me some, enough for a half load."

"Man, you're deranged. You got a good thing and you're lookin' to blow it."

"There ain't nothin' good about being here, man. Just be at the park at 6:00 and have the works."

"I'll be there."

(About a year later Angela and her boyfriend were busted. They had hired an ex-con to kill her boyfriend's wife, and there was a big insurance policy. But the convict turned them in after taking some money up front. He wore a wire and got the boyfriend on tape. Angela cried the blues about how she was a mistress who was used by a cold-hearted killer. She turned state's evidence and got a 5-year sentence in a women's reformatory.)


I take a shower and catch a bus into Newark. I get some cheap food and then do some shopping: a cheap pair of dress shoes, pants and a shirt, and I got enough left for a half load of dope (15 bags), enough to get Kris and I high for a week.

141

Kris was there at the park when I arrive. We shoot up in a gas station bathroom and get twisted. We walk back to the park and do some catching up, and then he had to go: "Sheila's waiting on me, man. I was supposed to be at her house an hour ago. I'll meet you back here at 11:00. Be here! Don't do anythin' stupid!"

It was always like this with Kris. He was like a brother. He really wasn't destined to be a drug addict. It just wasn't his thing—he never crossed over into a commitment. He was essentially a ladies' man. He had to have a woman in his life at all times. And the heroin would give him sexual prowess. He would say "Man, I can fuck all night on this shit." And I always suspected that that was the main reason he stayed with it for so long without ever getting totally strung out—once he got a chipper he would stay away from the drug until he was able to go back to his regular dosage. It's rare to find a maintenance heroin addict, but they're out there, and Kris more than anyone I'd ever known had mastered it. His family doctor would even prescribe a drug to help him kick his chipper habit without too much discomfort when he needed it. Probably the only drug he could totally get strung out on is Viagra, but that wasn't around in those days.

And there I sat in the park—just like it had always been with me. But this time my thoughts weren't fantasies. I was considering the arrest on the burglary charge. Even if I got a job it wouldn't matter. I had been down too many times. The longest I had been on parole was two months. No, they would put me away. I couldn't kid myself. Then I thought of a way out: I could go to California for real, get fake ID, finally give substance to the drug fantasy. I liked that, especially the new name. I could name myself, and in naming myself I could easily set a new

142

course. The name "Alex" came to mind. I always liked that name. Yeah, I would name myself Alex.

Kris showed up and I was ready to shoot up again, put myself away for the night. It was midnight and the gas station was closed, so we risked using the train station bathroom. Little chance of anyone coming in at that hour. We moved fast, one at a time in a stall. We went back to the park, nodding out on a bench.

"So whataya gonna do?" Kris asks.

"I don't know. Get a bus into New York. There's still one runnin'."

"New York? For what?"

"I don't know. Walk around. I wanna see the city anyway. I like walkin' 'round the city at night."

"What goes on in that skull? You got a place to stay—Angela's. What the fuck's with you, man?"

"I'm not goin' back there."

"I got an idea. Wait here. I'm gonna call Ritchie. He got his own pad. He might let you stay. I gotta call Sheila, too. Told her I'd call when I got to the park. I'll be back in a bit. Don't go anywhere!"

Kris goes back up to the train station to a phone booth. I move into a heavy nod.


"What the fuck you doing out here, Jones?"

I look up. It's a cop.

"Waitin' on a bus."

"Bullshit! You're nodding out on that crap you shoot up."

I could smell the whiskey hovering over me in the air and I looked at my watch. It was close to 12:30. He had probably gotten off work at midnight and downed some whiskey at a bar, or maybe started before he got off work.

"You Joneses are scum of the earth. You know that, right? I mean, it's not hard to figure out. I don't think you're *that* stupid…And I'm sick of looking at you—all of you!"

This pissed me off. Yeah, I was scum of the earth, but he had no business bringing my family into it. But I kept focused. I had some dope on me, another felony on top of the burglary if he searched me. I stood up slowly and began walking away.

"Where the fuck you think you're going, asshole?"

"I'm leavin', man. Goin' home."

"What home? Like someone is going to let a piece of shit like you stay at their house? Who the fuck you kidding?"

"I'm leavin'." And I start to walk away again. He quickly walks up to me and grabs my right arm and attempts to put me in a hammerlock, but I break away.

"Ohhhhhh! A fuckin' tough guy!"

I start to walk away.

"Don't move!" he screams, and I turn and he's got his gun pointed at me. "Don't fuckin' move!"

"What?"

"You got a choice, scumbag. You go over there [nodding his head towards the darkness of the park between the big oak trees] and take the ass-whipping you deserve or you're going in for loitering."

I just stood there, not saying anything.

144

"What's it going to be, scumbag?"

"You gonna shoot me?"

"Shoot you? Hell, no. That ain't no fun. I'm gonna kick your fuckin' ass." And then he holsters his gun and says "Come on, tough guy" as he walks into the darkness of the trees, unbuckling his gun belt and throwing it to the ground.

"Come on, scumbag. What the fuck you waiting for? You and your brother are the big cop killers, right? Well, come on then!" he orders with both hands in the air with fingers outstretched motioning me to come close.

I move in slowly, head held down, arms at my side, a posture of submission, and when I get within three feet I dash into him with an overhand right, putting every ounce of my moving 160 pounds into the punch. If he weren't drunk it wouldn't have been so easy. My right fist smashes into his face, and it stuns him good. I never could hit very hard, not those bone-crushing blows that my brother could deliver, but that stun gave me an edge, enough time to inflict a flurry of punches to his face, then backing off before he could get a punch off, totally in control—and seeing the blood gushing from his nose, I move back in again, overhand rights and lefts, left and right hooks, bobbing and weaving, him not being able to connect once, just blindly punching into the air, and at one point in utter frustration he tries to grab me and drag me to the ground, but me slipping away and delivering more staccato blows to his head, and he starts to stumble in a daze. He never got a punch off. If he had he might have done serious damage—he was tall and stocky. I come down hard on his left temple with a roundhouse and he falls backward to the ground. I immediately drop down on top of him, sitting on his sternum and continue the staccato pounding of his face; it was hypnotic, methodical, like a machine—blam!, blam!, blam!...It went on and on without a thought in my mind. He was unconscious but my fists

145

kept crashing into his face, flesh tearing loose from around his eyes, his lips teeth-torn, bloody and swollen. Then arms under my armpits and being quickly pulled up off the cop and suspended in air. It was Kris.

"We gotta get the fuck outta here!" he yells, and we move fast out of the park and over to Ritchie's apartment.

This thing with me. The psychs in reformatories called it passive aggressive. I'm cowardly at every level. All the heroics I had planned over time or in an instant, like the bold burglaries and outrageous escapes when cops showed up, were simply actions to avoid a greater evil—heroin withdrawal or a prison cell. Raw survival. My historical non-responsiveness to varied forms of violence against me, especially the more subtle acts of ridicule, the snickering children at a distance when focusing on my rag-torn clothes, or in the same distance poking fun at my physical emaciation and emotional deficiencies, clearly categorized me forever as the dirty, scrawny poverty-stricken kid who couldn't talk; and then what for me was the worst: the kids' indifference, their intentional ignoring of any utterance I dared on a rare occasion to allow passage through my hesitant lips, and me taking it, always in service and submission to their detestable and degrading violence to gain any form of acceptance. I, of course, because of this, had to deep down in my gut loathe every living thing. Down there I would kill everything that breathed. But I didn't know this back then. Instead I was mostly moved by a great and genuine gift of liking everyone I met. I didn't know the why of it. But it was always there. No matter how despicable, degenerate and mean a person would be, I could always at some point see through to his goodness, the place where he smiles on himself and others while lamenting his own private hell, for no one gets away, and this would happen early on. Even when I hurt an enemy, someone out to destroy or humiliate me, I would immediately feel their humiliation and pain and move into guilt and sorrow. When I arrived at Ritchie's I was already feeling sorry for the cop. I realized that when I had locked into a hypnotic daze and just kept pounding his face after he went unconscious, it was the furious release of a vengeance for every injury that had ever been inflicted on me, especially by dad, but somehow with a magnitude that went beyond even that, and it simply wasn't fair—it wasn't justified. He was a cop with problems, and no one, including himself, would probably ever get to look at the heart of it, and he was drunk. Just another victim held captive to a sadomasochistic world.

The guilt that follows these lashing outs always grip my mind like an inflammation and won't let go, sometimes for days, and still recur in flashbacks throughout time, one more dimension of my existential hell.


Animals exclusively employ their instincts for survival, their "intelligence" simply a logical mechanism in that survival, especially in determining acts of violence; but we, unlike them, possess in our puffed-up intelligence nebulous motives for every act of violence, why we can't escape afflicting ourselves with *ideas* about it, a vortex of habitual considerations when attempting to discern its nature, vain attempts to make it appear reasonable, pinpointing precise justifications when there really are none, not ultimately, never arriving at a notion in substance that portends a lasting solution. Every hundred years we arrive at yet another "Aha!" that lasts until the next ravaging. We sometimes chalk it up to catharsis, a perennial favorite, what we call a dispensing of an inner-turmoil rooted in a dilemma that somehow escaped our control or got out of hand for a moment, a turmoil that always leads to unjust acts of violence, a silly escapade considering that cathartic acts always serve to conceal as much as they reveal about our violence. Instinct and intelligence are always in conflict and there is always that gnawing desire of wanting

147

out, a desire when put on hold only gnaws deeper with the teeth of species survival, which can only result in demanding an escalation of catharsis—wars, genocide and violent indifference. Nietzsche wrestled with this dilemma, believing he had his finger on it, but it escaped him, too. His running after it tore him apart because he was unwittingly but understandably running from it. We can see important elements of it dramatically portrayed with deliberation and grace in bullfighting where it is raised to an art form, where we are still permitted that primal excitement (apotheosis of titillation) of intentionally maiming and killing while taunting the karmic horror of retaliation poised in nature itself, our showman prepared to sacrifice himself for our temporary sense of containment and protection. The blood sport of boxing, even if raised to an art form as grand as what Muhammad Ali gave us, cannot reach this apex of surface cleansing for it is corrupted by the idea of *winning*, which fulfills not a gnostic stand against nature, but a stand against each other, oppositional self-imaging which reveals nothing but self-hatred, something we know like the back of our hands that we want to slap people with. It is precisely in this unbearable and persistent frustration at not being able to finally discern, distinguish and control the conflict between instinct and intelligence that a unique characteristic is born, what we will always in the end succumb to in some fashion: bloodlust. To surrender to bloodlust is the only real cure we know for the only real malady of mind—our getting whipped about in moral demands that are always in conflict with our instincts that generate insatiable desires, for there is never a complete satisfaction, never a lasting fulfillment—there is never enough. Bloodlust is the only apex of relief available to us, our only hope, a hope that kills every vestige of hope.

The mystics, of course, view it otherwise. They tell us that in the final analysis the real battleground is a duel between love and bloodlust—or rather love and its opposite, power, a power that can only fully actualize itself in a heightened act of violence birthed in the purity of

148

bloodlust, the Cain-factor, rooted deep in the mysterious darker realms of desire that seeks absolute ascendency. And although I am certain love can defeat bloodlust, in a perennial thirst for some ever-revived need to willfully escape the impending horror of where we stand alone and threatened in a hostile universe on our own autonomous terms, bloodlust maintains its edge, most often disguising itself as an act of survival or a just response in a difficult-to-discern-situation, as in a violent act of indifference against someone's cry for help whom we suspect hasn't earned or doesn't deserve our assistance, and to choose *not* to act, to not even listen, is an act of power itself, an identification with, an alliance with, the bloodlust of the ascendant ones, choosing a side, the side of power, and feeling in that alliance a protection from "the horror the horror", however fleeting. Power keeps daemonic vigilance, whereas love in its purity just *is*, ever-present, and easily ignored, stifled or shoved to one side in its powerlessness; for unlike bloodlust, it demands nothing, imposes nothing—its only movement a letting go, an opening up and receiving, willingly exposing itself to every assault in its passionate concern for ever other, even while moving in an act of gracious, legitimate self-defense, without judgment, its willingness to be destroyed in avoiding an accompanying bloodlust its resounding virtue; in fact, we know in our DNA that the only infallible exit from the matrix of bloodlust is what we witness in the life of martyrs, themselves the living witnesses to love.

They tell us that in every second we reside either in love or power. And what love does exist when moving about in the realm of bloodlust is always love-in-diminishment, love-in-defeat, a negation-of-love-in-motion, never an assertion of love, never a connecting with and loving the other.

A Jean-Luc Godard character says "I think we aspire to live in hell because we can't bear to be loved and forgiven." This speaks to an arrogant, although mostly hidden, addiction to bloodlust at love's expense, for it is love alone that distances us from the violent perpetuation of self via the slaughter of the innocent, those sacrificed in our name or an ideal that services self-aggrandizement; and it is precisely our own innate, cowering innocence that will inevitably lead us in disgust to cutting our own throats on that same altar, and why bloodlust, if it doesn't kill us, bleeds us into exhaustion, the only rest available outside the healing power of love; and of course there always remains that unfathomable guilt that screams from our bloodlust and will not relent in its demand for everlasting punishment, a demand that goes far deeper than our ability to comprehend it.

*********

Kris insists that I move to New York. Every cop in the state would be looking for me. Ritchie says I can stay at his place for a few days until the heat died down. The story was in the papers the next day. The cop had been hospitalized. He was hemorrhaging and he would need facial and dental surgery. A week passes without getting motivated. I lounge in a deep depression, lying on the floor around the clock, long past my 3-day ceiling-staring routine, now staring more deeply inside my life that had become a swamp. Ritchie finally tells me I have to leave. I tell him I will, in the morning.

That night I walk to a car dealership and steal a black '68 Cadillac Eldorado convertible with red rolled and pleated leather interior. I had broken into the dealership and got the keys and stole plates off a nearby car. But I couldn't find any money. Once on the road my spirits are lifted. Behind the wheel of a car is always the best place for me to generate false hope. I turn the music up. Then an idea. I return to Ritchie's, go inside and grab a ball-pin hammer and a pillow-

150

case and go to the train-station parking lot where there are all-day parking meters that take quarters. It's easy. It takes only one swing for the small round ball of the hammer to crush the weak cast iron metal plate, and with a jerking motion tear the plate off and the quarters pour out. I move quickly and in no time have over $300 in quarters.

I go back to Ritchie's and call Kris in the morning. I ask him to get some quarter-roll packs from a bank as soon as one opens. Ritchie is still gently but persistently reminding me I had to leave.

Kris shows up with the quarter packs.

"Where you goin', man?"

"California. Wanna come?"

"California…Right. How you gettin' there?"

"Got a car down the street—convertible."

"Great. Goin' ta California in a stolen car. Real smart, man" he says with angry concern.

"Why not?"

"You're better off on a Greyhound. You got a better chance. A ticket's like thirty bucks, and you'll have money left over. Come on, man—make sense!"

"I don't think so. I'm not gettin' arrested at a Greyhound station. Maybe I'll get one once I'm outta the state…I gotta go, man." I grab the bag of quarters. "Mind if I borrow this pillow case, Ritchie?"

"Hell, I don't care…." Obviously glad just to see me go.

"You comin' or what?" I say to Kris sarcastically.

"Real fuckin' funny, asshole."

"I'll call you from L.A."

"Or the County jail...You know, I don't get it, man. It's not like you're stupid. You just act that way sometimes, and it don't figure. What the fuck's goin' on in your head, man?"

"Later, man." And I walk out the door.


It's the car. Behind the wheel. Route 66. Flat lands, high lands, mountains. All that shit. I knew Kris was right. It was lunacy. But there is no other place for me to be. I get in and pull out, and *that* feels totally right. I roll through the center of town with the roof down like I'm in a parade, not thinking about a cop seeing me. The only thought I have is getting to the highway, and this was the quickest route. Three minutes later I am on Route 22 heading west.


When I get to Pennsylvania I stop at a liquor store and get two fifths of Jameson whiskey and a carton of cigarettes. Then I go to a bank and get $200 in bills for quarters. I'm back on the road, and the farther I move west the better I feel, especially with the whisky running through my veins and the music blasting on the radio.

Chapter 10

The whiskey more than the driving wore me down, so I check into a motel. The clerk is suspicious the moment I walk into his office. He smells the booze and looks at the new Cadillac sitting outside. His obvious suspicion is a sign I ignore. Instead I go to my room and pass out only to be awakened a short time later by the police.

I don't take it hard. After getting through the hangover I'm scared about the whole prospect of going to jail to kick the incarceration wheel in motion, but even more about a return to Gillette—how do you adjust to a dead end? So I start concentrating on seeing my brother. I could now allow myself to experience the weight of how much I missed him. I begin working right away on a strategy that would guarantee prison over reformatory: I would play crazy, criminal crazy, and another assault on a cop would be a good start. This would insure a hardened image of a sociopathic personality and high escape risk and quiet any speculations about sending me back to Gillette where I could easily escape from. Yeah, I was heading for the Big Dusty, The Last Stop—Denville State Prison, and this thought actually puts me at peace.

I waive extradition and within a week I am back in New Jersey, and my first opportunity comes the second day when a guard with a trustee brings in breakfast. It's oatmeal, and a prisoner three persons ahead of me on line complains to the guard that it's cold.

"You don't like it, find another hotel."

When I walk up and he hands me my oatmeal through the bars at a 12 x 8 inch opening, I take the bowl and smash it in his face.

The guard blows his whistle and seconds later a lock-down alarm goes off where every prisoner on every wing gets locked in his cell, and a minute later the goon squad shows up.

The tier has 12 cells. Outside the cells is a long walkway for prisoners to mull around on about three feet wide, a long metal bench a foot wide bolted in to the exterior bars of the catwalk that separates the guards from the wing. I get inspiration. I walk to the end of the tier and stand against the wall.

"That's the one" the guard with the oatmeal all over his shirt says. "It's Jones."

"Everyone in your cells!" a sergeant yells, and the other prisoners comply. He yells at me: "That means you, too, Jones!"

"Fuck you!" I yell back, standing naked except for a pair of boxer shorts.

"Get in your cell, Jones! I'm not going to tell you again!"

"I guess you didn't hear me the first time: Fuck you!"

The sergeant pulls the long metal arm and all the cell doors slam shut. Then the clanging of the key and the entrance door opens. There are six of them, and they move fast toward me. I keep my position, standing against the back wall until they are almost in reach, and I jump up on the long metal bench and start running past them on the bench toward the entrance door. They stop in their tracks disoriented, thinking I'm heading out the door in an attempted escape, and in that second of their hesitation I stop and turn as the guards in confusion run fast towards me, and being elevated above them on the bench it is easy to swing hard with an overhand right and connect to the first guard's face, and then jump down off the bench and grabbing the stunned guard by the hair, ram his head into the bars of the cell door of a prisoner to the side of us, and then a burly arm around my neck and hard blows into my ribs and head, and then pulled to the ground, and once on the ground fists and feet slamming into me, but they can hardly hit me because all of them are trying to get to me at the same time, getting in each other's way. They finally get it, some of them backing away to let two do some serious damage—they have to *show* the other prisoners what happens when you assault a guard. I wrap myself in a fetal position with my hands up against my ears, and they just keep kicking and punching my head and body, and when they are finished, three of them pick my body up and hold it like a battering ram and run, the rest following, and they run me all the way to the Green Room, a specialized isolation cell, and once inside the cell they don't stop, slamming my head with full force into the far wall and dropping me to the floor. They pull my boxer shorts off and one of the guards kicks me in the balls real hard, and that was the best acting job I ever did not letting out a scream, and after kicking me around on the floor came the high-pressure hose—blasting me into the wall and holding me there, and then a quick hose-down of the entire cell to increase the damp cold (there is no heating in the cell). Then they walk out, slamming first the barred-cell door shut, and then a solid exterior metal door.

The Green Room is 10 x 10 x 10 feet. The walls are green tile. The ceiling has a caged-in lamp that's never turned on except when the guards open the door. The floor is crude, porous cement that slightly slopes down to a small drain hole in the center. Lots of blood, shit and dirt are caked up in the deep crevices of the cement that is intentionally never scrubbed clean. When they hose down the cell, it activates a slime substance in those crevices. But that's not the worse part. The solid metal door outside the cell door is perfectly fit with rubber molding on the edges so that when it's closed not a speck of light comes in. The *darkness* is the curse. I can't see my hand in front of my face. I stand up. My nose and right eye are still bleeding and there is for a while an incessant ringing in my left ear, but it doesn't faze me: I am taken over by the darkness itself. I walk slowly around and the shivers start kicking in from the cold. But the darkness. Being trapped in one's thoughts in total darkness is different. The mind naturally seeks diversionary sights and sounds of some kind, regardless how minimal, and when the ringing in my ear stops all I have is a dead dark silence. My thoughts spiral in on how I had reached this dead end with no way out, how I had failed miserably to have even a semblance of a life, with no way to turn any of it around. These thoughts turn into a hellish affliction, a heightened and all-encompassing vision of my Great Impasse. No delusory fantasies, only the ever-so-clear evidence of my meaningless life in rapid-fire thoughts buzzing around in my mind like a crazed hornet's nest. I can see my dead end in that darkness with absolute clarity. It is amazing how quickly it becomes unbearable—about ten minutes.

I knew what they wanted. They wanted me to pound on the door and beg to let me out. No prisoner I had encountered knew of any prisoner who had went the distance, the 72 hours legally permitted, and it was rare for a prisoner to last more than a half hour. In fact, I, too, had arrived at that same place in a half hour, of wanting to bang on the door, and if not plea, at least apologize and promise to be behave from now on, but I didn't, not only as a defiance, as an affirmation of being tough inside a refusal to be humbled, but the more important goal of building on a reputation that would get me to prison. With that one thought, that singular goal, came certainty I could go the distance.

I knew I couldn't just stand for 72 hours shivering. The shivering was already making the muscles spasms around fractured ribs intensify in pain (fracturing prisoners' ribs was a common practice because they didn't need medical treatment to heal; for example, there was this technique of strapping a prisoner to a table on his back, his ankles and wrists tied to the legs of the table at each corner, and then placing a telephone book across the chest and pounding it with a baseball bat, and even if the ribs didn't break, disrupting the cartilage around the ribs was as painful as broken ribs with no physical signs of the assault).

I had to figure a way to get rest and a modicum of heat. I lay down on the floor in a fetal position, my arms crossed and locked at the top of my chest. This maximizes the containment of heat to my upper-body. The slimy ground is cold at first, but the slime turns out to aid me. My body generates heat and the slime soaks it in and becomes a source of heat against my skin and some protection from the cold cement. After 5 minutes I slowly turn over to my other side, fitting my body as best I can into the slime that is heated, enough to lull me back into deep rest; back and forth I go, and it isn't long before I start getting snippets of sleep. The plotting to get these snippets of sleep becomes my dominant focus, actually distancing the dark thoughts of my wasted life. The guards are required by law to feed me, and even though it is cold slop I figure it is fuel to keep generating heat (I did for a second consider refusing to eat for the posture-pose effect in establishing a reputation with the prisoners, for I did need to build a reputation in their eyes too for the confinement years up ahead in prison, but I then realize the other prisoners won't know of this, and for the guards I only have to go the distance, the assaults having already made the major point).

I did the entire 72 hours in the Green Room, and when I left they put me in a regular isolation cell for 30 days. Probably to give time for the evidence of my wounds to heal. And this was fair because they didn't press charges for the assault on the guard.

When I was released back to a tier, an opportunity presented itself within a few days to build on my rep. It was late in the evening when a few guards brought in a screaming lunatic. They put him in the cell next to mine with a young prisoner who was in for the first time. This

157

was the guards' idea of rehabilitation for first offenders—scare the shit out of them! The lunatic went off on a tangent immediately, screaming "I kill pigs!, niggers!, spics!, God!! I kill all you motherfuckerrrrrrrs!"

I picture the kid cowering in the cell terrified out of his mind. I bang on the metal wall and yell "Shut the fuck up, asshole!"

There was a dead quiet. He didn't say another word.

I am awake the next morning before all the cell doors open. I lay there in fear. I am not looking forward to a confrontation with the lunatic, but it has to happen—another item that will bolster my resume; and besides, some greater good would come of it: the kid will get a reprieve from the guards' vigilante rehab.

The cell doors on metal rollers all at once slide and then bang open. Survival strategy has it that I should move directly out onto the tier to maximize freedom of movement, but I hesitate, and the lunatic within seconds was in my cell with his long black greasy hair and wild eyes, lit cigarette in hand , trying to shove it in my eye. I side-step him and smash him in the face with an over-hand right. He falls sideways and loses his balance for a second against the metal cot bolted into the wall, giving me that precious second to throw a series of right and left punches downward into his face, and he slides to the floor on his knees, head bowed low as if in prayer, and then with full force he slams his open right hand up into my balls, then clenches my balls into a tight fist, squeezing and twisting real hard as he gives off a loud scream. All I can do in my excruciating pain is grab two handfuls of his greasy hair and begin slamming his head into a small porcelain-on-metal sink, slamming it over and over as hard as I can, but his grip will not loosen as he screams between smashings: "I ripped Jesus Christ's balls off!" And then the guards rushing into the cell, and immediately the lunatic lets go of my balls and wraps both his arms

158

around my legs, pressing his head gently up against my thigh, pleading passively in a grieving lament, as if he might produce a tear: "He's my friend...don't hurt him." My stomach turns upside down and nausea creeps in—not from the pain but from being so directly implicated in a madness I could not begin to fathom.

*********

No Green Room this time, but I went back to the hole for 30 days. When I get out they put me back on the same wing, but with the lunatic gone. One of the prisoners, James, a black man with a tall muscular body and hard chiseled facial features with a scraggly beard in his early 30s, caught up in a quiet melancholy and in for armed robbery, walks up to me with a deep sternness: "Why'd you hesitate, man? Why did ya leave yourself open like that?"

I cringe inside, and say flatly "I don't know." And that was the end of it.

He knew. He was on to my game. He was in convict mode, ready for the long haul and paying close attention to every detail, preparing a survival mindset for prison life. He had made his commitment a long time ago. That much I knew, and I knew he would never miss a trick at any level in that commitment. The question he put to me was the most important survival lesson I would ever get. He never made an issue of it, never brought it up again, and we became fast but aloof friends at prison, mostly hanging out at the weight pile. I correctly speculated he understood that playing the role of a tough guy was just as deadly as being one, for every situation would play out the same as long as the coward is committed to his role, and I was... and James knew it. One's interior life is irrelevant, for in prison the barbarian's only real concern outside of successfully planning his raping and plundering is if an intended victim might successfully retaliate with deadly force during or after an assault. And the only relational mode for those on the defense (those who maintain a moral center) that has ultimate value in the end is how real a person is in friendship—*would a person put his life on the line if it came to that*. I would. This is what James picked up on, and I knew it was true of him, too, and this is where we connected. This is probably why he so thoroughly dismissed his detection of my error, my hesitation, revealing my fear, my cowardliness. He saw the flaw in my plan, no question. I had slipped. I couldn't let that happen when I got to prison where all the antes are upped and the antennas are fine-tuned. Perhaps if I were on my own I could resign myself to a life of ongoing humiliation, but I doubt it—I always feared humiliation more than death. But what I was absolutely certain of is that I couldn't live this cowardly life with my brother as a witness. His judgment mattered, for he had totally embraced me as a person in his confidence. No, I had to ensure that I never let myself become vulnerable at any level or in any second ever again, insuring that no one would ever detect that I reside in fear of the barbarians.

Years later James would escape from prison and get gunned down in an armored car robbery. He was in the back of a getaway commercial van as the police chased it down a highway. James opened the two back doors and with an assault rifle in hand, fired on the police cars in pursuit. He became a folk hero for a lot of prisoners. And he became that for me, too, but for a different reason. The man had heart on more than one account.

That's the basic difference between the inside and outside of prison: inside everyone consciously fine-tunes their antennas, those intricate feelers, the barbarians always ready to detect the slightest opportunity to strip someone of their possessions, especially their dignity, the ascendancy program always in full swing, no break in the action, or, for those on the boarder of being frozen in terror, an elaborate plotting for survival, every second a time for positioning, establishing oneself as a person who in no way should ever be fucked with; this or a submission to some group's ideology or criminal activity for protection, to not be a target from every angle in every step one takes through the chaos of bloodlust. But it is only in standing alone that one can maintain dignity, the only genuine break in the action. To in any way become who you really are in any significant degree, you have to agree to face death.

Karl Menninger in *The Crime of Punishment* quoted Dostoevsky: "The degree of civilization can be judged by the insides of its prisons," and then explains Dostoevsky's concern, that how a society treats its prisoners will reveal the degree of its compassion and other noble characteristics, but I'm convinced that a man like Dostoevsky, who spent five years in one of the worst prisons imaginable and then offered a reprieve in being assigned to kill people for the state in military service, saw something more entrenched: the infinite masks and mazes of any given culture utilized to conceal a widespread sadomasochistic arrangement, and that all these masks and mazes are ripped away on the inside: the guile, the manipulations, the one-upmanship, the seeking to dominate, all servicing self-ascendancy, a becoming *thee* God in any given second at anyone else's expense, the crazed itch to grind one's foot into any face, or at the very least to satisfy a rabid impulse to grab whatever there is to grab, especially what my neighbor has and I don't, all orchestrated in the hustle and bustle of an ever-spiraling downward in eternal dissatisfaction. He knew that a prisoner stabbing a man in the neck with a knife was not that far removed from cutting someone's throat with an emotion, a cynical aside or a dangerous piece of gossip. It was in prison where he got the first fundamental insight that mostly everyone is looking for an equal opportunity to oppress. And all of this to rid the mind of a poisonous resentment toward God and neighbor or to avoid an inevitable assault on one's being by a person, group or futile universe, a desperate and delusional search for health and safety in personal power.

Chapter 11

At sentencing the judge gave me exactly what I wanted: "Mr. Jones, after reading the probation report it is clear that you not only at no point have expressed any regrets for your criminal acts, but that you persist in what Doctor Herder identifies as a careless disrespect of authority that often finds expression in acts of violence. Dr. Herder also notes that while in Farmdale and Gillette reformatories you refused participation in rehabilitation programs offered there. In fact, in your present situation you have rejected every offer for rehabilitation services; in particular, treatment for drug addiction. It is apparent that you are not interested. What most concerns the Court in light of this adamancy in refusing treatment is your history of violence and propensity to escape…I really have no choice here, Mr. Jones. I see you have just celebrated your 21st birthday. You have fully arrived at adulthood. And although it is normally not my desire to send a young man to prison, in your case I see no alternative. This Court therefore orders that you be handed over to the proper authorities and taken to Denville State Prison for a term not less than five years and not to exceed seven. There will be no bail set pending possible appeal." And down comes the gavel.

Five to seven years in prison was perfect. If I managed to avoid trouble I would be eligible for parole in two years. My mind was now set on seeing my brother.

\*\*\*\*\*\*\*\*\*

Denville State Prison got its "Last Stop" designation because it is the end of the line in New Jersey's prison system, and "Big Dusty" because of the dust from the solid dirt ground in the prison yard. The rest of the prison is all stone and steel, but there is that occasional blade of grass or other piece of life that will rear its head from some dark crevice on the ground or in one of the dust-filled and moistened stones of the massive walls, and there is a work detail, headed by a guard who bears a striking resemblance to Elmer Fudd, that is entrusted with the sole task of scouring the prison grounds and removing these budding signs of life. When the dust blowing around gets so excessive it interferes with the tower guards' vision, they bring in this huge contraption with a big barrel of oil attached to it that spreads layers of oil over the ground to solidify the dust into a sticky clay-like substance that eventually hardens into solid dirt ground again.

When the prison transport bus pulls up to the old prison, I can't block out the terror, nerves jangling all along the wall of my stomach. The huge almost black stones were obviously chiseled from human hands. No visible signs of human life except for a guard in a tower atop a 30 feet wall. The bus waits for two huge metal doors to swing slowly open to allow our passage into a holding area. When the metal doors close, two more metal doors open and we move into another area where we are ordered off the bus and then to move inside a metal door that opens from a building. It is an empty room we enter, and once that door is secured, they move us through another metal door into a receiving area where we are fingerprinted, strip-searched, de-liced, showered and given two sets of prison clothes, two sheets, a pillow-case and pillow, a wool army blanket, a bag of rolling tobacco (something that was never given out in reformatories) and a roll of toilet paper that we are told has to last a month. Then they move us through another door into the guts of the prison. I hear a loud kissing sound and a voice: "She's mine." I don't look, but the terror goes deep. It is clear in that moment that I would be raped and possibly murdered if I wasn't totally prepared to kill. And I decide instantly that's what I'd do without hesitation. I knew in that second that anything short of that decision and the absolute internalizing of it would be a major flaw that would be quickly detected, and once detected it would be wired to most everyone throughout the prison.

We are then taken to a barber shop and given buzz cuts and then taken to a reception wing where we are to be housed for the next 30 days, undergoing medical and psychological testing to produce evaluations for prison assignments, but unlike reformatories our quarantine did not mean isolation. We still get to go into the mess hall for our meals and we can go to the yard after a week of medical and security screening. This and the bag of tobacco is the first sign that I will like prison better than reformatories. In prison there is obviously a fundamental respect. Perhaps this is generated from fear or us just being adults with frontal lobes loosely intact or a combination of both. It is a relief understanding that touch-offs, prisoners like apes who play the game of talking each other down, an in-your-face grandstanding to establish authority and stature, doesn't play out here. It is explained in orientation the place a prisoner has a license to kill: "You don't at any time belong in another prisoner's cell. If you get killed in another prisoner's cell he won't do another day in prison for it, understand? You belong in one of four places—your cell, the mess hall, your job or the yard."

My cell is a 5' x 7' metal box, thick sheet metal flats riveted together with a small sink and a toilet set in a small enclave in the back wall also made from riveted metal flats. There is a small table but no room for a chair—I have to sit on the edge of the bed when writing. I am given a one-ear heavy, hard-plastic mono headphone that can be plugged into one of three holes in the wall. There is a choice of three stations: country, rock or blues/jazz/big-band (displacing the former classical station), and they play from 8:00 to 11:00 p.m. seven days a week. I like this arrangement because no radios are allowed: being forced to use the headphone no one can impose their blaring music on you as I was told was the case in the other two state prisons, considered a privilege, but for me would be a "humanitarian" assault on my nervous system. We are allowed one visit a month for 30 minutes on a phone behind a foot-square high-density bulletproof glass window riveted into thick sheet-metal walls. But that doesn't concern me—I won't be getting visits. We can order books and magazines from the outside, and there is a library, and prisoners upon request can get a list and select from that list and have the books delivered to our cells, another major improvement over reformatories. I will be paid for working, enough to buy basic cosmetics and rolling tobacco, another big plus. But the best improvement of all was having my own space. Granted, it was only 5' x 7', but that is far better than sleeping in a dormitory. A friend in reformatory told me I slept with my eyes open, and I speculated that this was a defense mode I had developed—even while asleep my mind would be taking in moving images, giving me at least a half-second's edge if I were attacked, an ongoing subconscious vigil. But now when the doors slammed shut at night it would be a12-hour reprieve: I can relax into real sleep.

On the second day my cell door is opened and a guard tells me to go to the hospital for my physical, which consists mostly of answering a questionnaire and getting a blood test for syphilis. The hospital is adjacent to the reception wing I'm in, which also serves as a regular wing. There is a guard seated inside a barred door leading into the hospital, and when he sees me he gets up from his chair and asks to see my hospital pass, and after showing it to him he unlocks the door and lets me in, ordering me to sit in a waiting room. And when I walk into the waiting room, there he is sitting on a bench—my brother Tommy. "Hey, bro" is all he says as he stands and walks towards me. Our arms wrap around each other and tears come to my eyes. "I missed you, man." "Yeah, I missed you, too."

"Com'eer" he says to me as he grabs my arm and we walk to the bench. "We haven't got much time."

He reaches inside his shirt and pulls out a device that is taped to his side, and tells me to tape it to my side. I don't look at it too closely until I get back to my cell. (It is a shank he had someone make in machine shop, a six-inch ice pick with a metal base for a handle consisting of three parts that can be dismantled and placed in separate places in the cell so they can't be identified as anything dangerous, only contraband. The ice pick itself I can hide in one of the sockets that I plug my headphone into). "You're gonna need this at some point. Anyone fucks with you, stick 'im. Don't think about it. Just stick 'im. And make sure it's a vital organ. The stomach's always an easy shot, and it's the most painful if they don't die. You can work your way to other organs from there if you're fast enough. And make sure you keep the shank pointed upwards, not down—this way you get more leverage, more mobility." Then he pulls two packs of cigarettes from his pocket and hands them to me. "I'll have some more sent to you tomorrow. I'll see you on the yard in a week."

Then he gets up and walks over to the prison guard and tells him he's ready to return to his cell. Another advantage in prison: you get just about anything you want except a woman if you got the money, even a private meeting with a prisoner in quarantine.


After a 30-day processing I am brought before a three-person assignment committee. Captain Shields is the head and does all the talking. He is a barrel-chested man with thick arms and neck with strands of side-hair combed across his bald head, dressed in full uniform except

167

the jacket, Captain bars on the collar of a starched white short-sleeve shirt. He speaks matter-of-factly:

"There's a lot of chatter about a new day. The bleeding hearts want to take over the prison system, give the fools among you more excuses for doing what they want to do at everyone else's expense. The poor childhood crap. They haven't arrived here yet. They want to coddle the little babies first. So for now I run things, and for me it's simple: All of you are prisoners of war. You're the bad guys, we're the good guys. You waged war on us and you lost. We want at least two years of your life for what you did to us. The coddlers want more than that—they want your dignity, turn you into whining idiots. But I'm not after your manhood. This is internment, not hospitalization. You want to be an *inmate*, play crazy and we'll send you to the nut house. They'll fire you up with enough electricity and Thorazine you won't be able to do anything *but* pay attention. I guarantee you'll beg to get back here. Look at something for what it is and you can change it. That's how I see it. And it's on you. We're not here to make you into anything. We just want to be as certain as we can that you won't wage war on us again. And because we're the good guys, we treat you fairly. The rules were read to you during orientation and you were given a manual, which I encourage you to memorize. All you have to do is follow the rules and everything else will fall in place. I don't care what you did to get here—everyone gets a fair chance to get out and change his life, because that's where your life really changes if it changes at all, on the outside. You're eligible for parole in two years. You're a first offender. You follow the rules and you will make parole first time before the Board.

"We're assigning you to work in the bakery. You work there for two years and you leave prison with a trade. When you get out you decide whose side you want to be on. You choose the wrong side, we'll catch you and bring you back. The third time you'll be here the rest of your life. Nothing complex to figure out. Just decide whose side you're on.

"You'll lock on 6-wing. We normally don't keep prisoners here your age, but the Court required it. You brought that on yourself. I'm sure you know by now 6-wing is for prisoners who stand the best chance of making parole. Like I said, we're not out to make life difficult for you. We're giving you every chance to turn your life around. And I won't tell you to stay away from your brother. No one would keep me away from mine, and I don't expect it of you. Just keep in mind your brother crossed over and he's not coming back. We know his every move. From this moment everything is in your hands. It's on you."

*********

I had been too long without sunlight. Walking out to the yard the first time is blinding. One corner extending to the center of the yard is a baseball field, and an entire wall six handball courts. In another corner is a weight-lifting area, and in another a marked off boxing area and a bocce ball court, a reminder that at one time Italians were the majority in prison, and before them it was the Irish, and now it is the blacks. I was looking around for my brother, and he came out of nowhere. It was sudden. He was just at my side. "Let's walk" he says.

As we begin walking he asks without looking at me: "Had any trouble?"

"Not really. A few prisoners stopped by my cell and offered me some cigarettes, candy— you know. One of 'em said he heard I was someone's kid in reformatory."

"Yeah. They're testin' you. Just want to see your reaction. They're all punks. They start spreadin' rumors that you took it in the ass in reformatory so some other prisoner will make his

169

move on you. They'll lay in the cut to get sloppy seconds. That's how it goes down. Just keep the shank close by when your cell is unlocked. It'll happen soon. It's your age. The rapos can't resist young meat. At most you'll get 30 days in the hole. The pigs ain't got no sympathy for rapos, or for those who don't stand up for themselves. Most of the rapos that run in packs here are tree-jumpers out of Camden. Punks. Bunch of slime-buckets...I don't know what it is with this new breed of rapos showin' up here. They used to hide in lock-down tiers, but now they take pride in it, and most other prisoners relate to it. That's new. It don't figure: they could've raped your wife, mother, sister or daughter. How the fuck can you respect that shit? I don't know what the fuck it is. Maybe they're just stupid, or have no idea what respect is...for you, me, their mothers or anyone else—except death. I used to figure a little respect goes a long way, but now it just goes right down the toilet with everythin' else. It's like respect is seen as a weakness. But like I said, they respect death. That's why you can't hesitate when it goes down, ya understand? Don't fuckin' think about it, man. They're like fuckin' demons—you gotta send 'em back to hell."

*********

And it wasn't long. About a week later. And I got lucky. He had the reputation of being the baddest black dude in prison. He went by the name Hannibal. He stood in front of my cell, at least 6'3 in shorts and tank top with thick wool socks folded once beneath his knees. He had to be at least 250 pounds of solid muscle He had come in from the yard, still glistening with sweat.

"After dinner you be ready to fuck."

I don't say anything.

"Just be ready" he says again and walks away.

It was immediate—my stomach tied in knots and I was shaking everywhere under my skin. I had about two hours. This was it. I am comforted only by the thought that if I manage to kill him I will be for the most part set. Taking down Hannibal would make everyone back off. He didn't belong to any gang. He stood his own ground. It was perfect.

I can't stop shaking inside, but I have no idea if it is visible. It is the longest two hours of my life. I have to plan it in a way that he will come into my cell. I have to kill him there if I am to avoid getting more time.

I undress, naked except for a pair of boxer shorts. I sit up on my cot in a half lotus position, my hands flat on the bed at my side, but the tip of my middle right finger just touching the base of the ice pick concealed under my pillow.

Then he arrives. All the cell doors remain unlocked during meals so prisoners can return to their cells after eating or take care of business out on the flats or on a tier. Hannibal just stands there for two seconds in front of my cell staring at me, and then grabs onto a bar and violently pulls my cell door open. "You ready?"

I bend my head down in a fearful, submissive welcome.

He just stands there, quiet. A few seconds later he says "I'm givin' you a break this time…But I'll be back." He shuts my cell door and walks away.

*Dammit! I blew it. This could have been my ticket out of madness. I should have done something differently. Not sit up in the bed but lay down with my head towards the wall, a cowering and enticing posture. I didn't play it right.* I realize I acted more out of fear than calculation. I didn't yet possess a wanton desire to kill, to kill him for even thinking about raping me, and enjoying every angry second of plunging an ice pick into his stomach, lungs, heart and

171

throat—that's what was missing. I sought only to avoid being raped, not execute a death, even though I had certitude of killing him. That wasn't enough. I half-stepped, missing a perfect opportunity for long-term survival.

After languishing in this regret for a while another thing dawned on me: *Hannibal is no tough guy*. He just has excellent radar and a desire to indulge any pleasure he imagines, and to prolong his own life for as long as possible to keep the kicks rolling. He isn't a tough guy—he's a hedonist! With his acute radar he knew in a split second I was going to kill him, and he backed off. He's just as much a punk as the next guy—all of us punks, all scared of the gaping abyss, but he is caught up in heightened diversion, a wanton lust for power, sex, drugs and whatever other titillation is available to lust after, and he had devised his own methodology of maximizing fulfillment of those lusts over the longest stretch of time. Hannibal had long ago mastered a plan of action, knowing he had a genetic advantage in building a powerful body and a mental strategy, and with that he developed an elaborate game in getting whatever he wanted, far better than the strategy I had devised to survive. And then it hit me: with a piece of metal and a willingness to kill or die, cowardly punks have pure equality with tough guys. This epiphany is in itself a liberating thought, but I am still not able to take it to the next level where real superiority in a sadomasochistic world resides, a saying the ultimate "fuck you!" by committing to kill anything that gets in my way for any reason; actually not even needing a reason, becoming one with death, or at least partners in crime. I now knew this was the ultimate freedom for man on his own terms in a futile, absurd world. And it can be had without any prior conditioning, biological or social, but with a simple decision. And I wondered exactly when Tommy had made that decision, what the circumstances were. Before I had imagined that it was his sense of who dad is and wanting to be like him, that total identification, and in that identification gradually growing into his commitment. But now I knew he had at some point *decided*, and I wanted to know when it was.

Chapter 12

Two days later a prisoner shows up in front of my cell, a transsexual hustler, looking more like a woman than anyone I had seen since arriving at prison. His skin is smooth, moist-black-silk, long curled eyelashes, subtle red lipstick applied to full thin lips and a short meticulously-cut Afro, wearing a white dress-shirt (the only personal clothes item permitted at that time) custom cut with the tails tied together at the bottom of his ribcage to reveal moist hairless stomach flesh, his custom-cut prison pants revealing ankle flesh, no socks, low-cut white sneakers, the fabric of his khaki pants sewn tight around his calves, thighs and jutting ass. It happens on the inside where there are no women and the deprivation sets in—the pull of the appearance, tugging at the heart and groin. On the outside I would see a person like this as a curiosity, an example of how far we humans can go imaginatively when moving into realms of psychosexual desire and obsession. This did speak to something grand about us, a grandness explored in Jennie Livingston's film *Paris Is Burning*. I am reminded of a club in the Village where I would meet up with a drug dealer, his favorite hang-out. While waiting on him to show up one night I catch the stage show—three singing female impersonators doing Diana Ross, Patti Labelle and Ruby of Ruby and the Romantics. I know they are men, of course, and I enjoy their performance, but at the finale when they pull their wigs off, I experience a dislocation in my mind. It jars my ordered perceptual field even though what they did is no surprise, no revelation. I am stunned. It is a testament not to the power of appearance, but to how when a surface appearance has no real depth, our ongoing interior alignment of appearances to conform to

174

predetermined notions of what constitutes reality to feel safe in the world automatically kick in without conscious participation. It is a subconscious survival mechanism that staves off any potentially threatening information, any disruption in the flow of appearances, imbuing a makeshift, artificial depth with deeper meaning unannounced, realigning any particular world of shallow appearance to accommodate an overall sense of security about living in a world of appearances prearranged for maximum comfort and relaxation, diverting our attention from an abyss of undifferentiated data that points to an incipient chaos that might start banging on the door. I realize we do this all the time, and why at an early age as criminal I had become successful in shoplifting with a preconscious understanding of this phenomenon: a minor manipulation of appearance to give the impression, for example, that a boxed-up television I am carrying on my shoulder and saying "excuse me" to people in line at cash registers as I walk out of a store, everyone certain the television was delivered to me from the storeroom after purchasing it. Cashiers and shoppers do most of the work for me after making my casual hint at what is real, ordering their perceptions to accommodate their sense of safety. And no doubt this plays a significant role in destructive political movements, as when ideologues with absolute power start to move masses of innocent lives into graves unnoticed, even though it is apparent to everyone. In fact, this abstract power of perception is more threatening than any standing army.

His name is Kenny. He gives me a carton of cigarettes. Then he speaks in an effeminate voice:

"This is from your brother. He doesn't like to go to the yard. The other day was the first time he's been out in over a year. He wants you to visit."

"Visit?"

175

"It's taken care of. On your way to the yard, going through the Center [a circular area connected to all wings like spokes connected to the hub of a wheel, and where prisoners must pass through going in any direction outside their wing, a sergeant and two guards behind a brick and bullet-proof glass octagon enclosed area electronically controlling the doors], instead of turning to the yard corridor, turn right and walk to 4-Wing. We're in cell number 7 on the flats. The 4-Wing guard knows you'll be coming. It's all arranged. I have to go…You're cute." He smiles and walks away.

4-Wing has large cells, high ceilings with walls made of stone instead of steel like the other wings, and the door is made of solid steel instead of bars, with a small latch window. This gives prisoners more privacy from guards and roaming prisoners. Usually you had to have connections to get to this wing, someone on the wing or other source. Rumor had it that 100 years earlier they were horse stables, but after the automobile won the day they were converted into additional cells. Each cell could house as many as four prisoners. My brother had arranged for just him and Kenny to occupy cell 7.

When I entered their cell Tommy is sitting on one of the two cots.

"Come on, sit down" he says.

I sit down next to him and notice the thick scar running from his forehead to the back of his skull, the shape of a big Y imprinted on his close-to-bald head. I hadn't seen it when I first met him because he had his khaki prison hat on. Then I scan the cell. Kenny had obviously done the decorating. It was an incredible layout for a prison cell. A large pine bookcase filled with books covered most of one wall. "Everythin' you might wanna know that's in a book is on that bookshelf, but it don't amount to anythin'" Tommy says. "You could say I carved away all the bullshit and kept the crap. Pick out what you want."

176

I walk over and start looking at the books. One title jumps out at me right away. I pull it from the shelf and ask "What's this about?", holding it up in the air.

"What's the title?"

"*The Denial of Death.*"

"Yeah. That's a good one. Torture, murder, annihilation—what we humans can't kick. Kinda sums it all up. Nothin' wrong with gettin' yourself an education while you're down. Plenty a spare time, ya know? Besides, it's the only way to find out it don't change anythin'. Don't want to mull around in false hope. Don't want naggin' regrets. I'm talkin' 'bout who you are and whatcha gotta do."

(When Tommy was in reformatory they had given him a test. It was supposed to indicate what he was best qualified to pursue as a career. Two results came up: librarian and judge. We all got a kick out of that. The first one was understandable because he always had a book in his pocket, and he had mentioned how in reformatory he had paid cigarettes to get books smuggled in, books on psychology, philosophy and literature. When two or three of us would be nodding out on heroin and talking shit, he would be in a corner consuming books. I asked him once why he read so much. "Habit I picked up in the joint. Plus, I don't want any pompous idiot thinkin' he got anythin' on me, especially when he don't know jack shit about anythin', no matter how much he's read." And it was true what he had said—none of it changed him.)

I walk back and sit on the cot with the book in my hand and look around some more. My eyes fall on an 8 X 10 photograph of Fred Astaire and Ginger Rogers glued to the wall. I obsessed on Astaire films when I was a kid, and as I stare at the picture I can hear him singing "Dancing in the Dark" as he dances with Cyd Charisse in Central Park.

"You like Astaire?" Kenny says. "Isn't he wonderful?"

"Yeah. I was just noticin' how Ginger Rogers is starin' directly into the camera, but Astaire is starin' directly at her."

"Of course! She's a goddess!"

"Cyd Charisse was my favorite…That dancin' in the dark scene—you see it?"

"Of course. *The Band Wagon.* Central Park. "That's Entertainment"—my theme song! Get your laughs before the light goes out. Don't turn your back on love! Celebration—what else is there?…But my all-time favorite scene was the opening pink number in *Funny Face.* How they got away with that, making us believe an entire fashion line could be pink. It's crazy, right? But they pulled it off…Amazing…Well, I got to tell you, honey—you got taste. But you don't know a goddess when you see one…Oh well. But it's nice to know we have something in common."

There was a little kitchen area built next to the sink with a double hotplate. There was hot coffee on one plate and something extraordinary cooking in a pan on the other (Italian sausage, peppers, onions, potatoes with a variety of spices added, and Kenny would stuff it all into pita-pocket bread).

"You ready for some food?" says Kenny

"Yeah."

"Ya wanna get high first?" says Tommy. "Got a little of everythin'. Outta scag, but plenty of weed, some Quaaludes and hooch."

"Shit. I'll have a 'lude and some weed."

"Might as well wash down the 'lude with some good hooch. It's my special—pineapple crush. You'll love it. Kenny—"

"Yeah, yeah—I'll take care of it."

Kenny asks me to get up, and he pulls the cot away from the wall and with a handle end of a spoon works a stone out from the bottom of it. He pulls out a bag of weed, and 'ludes from another bag, then turns to Tommy: "You having any?" and Tommy waves his hand no.

Kenny hands me a pill and then goes to the small fridge to get the chilled pineapple hooch, pours me a glass and puts some crushed ice in it from a bowl in the small freezer. After handing me the glass of hooch he grabs the bag of weed and throws it on a small table in front of Tommy.

"Looks like Kenny's losin' his manners."

"Fuck me!" Kenny says with attitude.

"You mean *fuck you!*"

Kenny walks over to Tommy and gently rubs his hand across his face and says softly, "No, sweetheart—*fuck meeee*."

"Fuck you!" Tommy blurts out, and they both laugh.

Tommy looks at me and says "Everyone thinks Kenny's my kid. Some shit went down when I first got here and I had to take out two fools, one of them Kenny's man."

"Ain't nobody my man, honey. So you can cut that shit out right now...In fact, I ain't met a man in this joint yet that's more man than me."

"And here I was all this time thinkin' I rescued you."

"Rescued? Pa-lese! That beating you took must have given you serious brain damage."

Tommy got that smile on his face, the one I remember most. He reaches under his cot and pulls out a bucket and places it in front of him. He then pulls out from under the cot a quart of his special stash in a plastic container, Jameson whiskey, smuggled in by a guard who supplies heroin for him to deal. He unscrews the lid, and with both hands, one underneath and the other at the side of the container, steadying it in front of his face, he just stares at it for a full fifteen seconds, perfectly still. Then he tilts it, putting the opening to his lips and then thrusting the container upside down above his face, glug glugging the whiskey down at breakneck speed. Finally he quits, putting the container on the floor, taking a deep breath, head bowed down, his hands clenched tightly to his thighs. About a minute goes by, his face blue, huge veins jutting out the top of his mostly bald head down into his forehead, blood starting to drip from his right ear. And then explosive, projectile vomiting into the bucket, blood mixed with whiskey vomit. Then deep breathing as vomit spittle hangs from his lower lip. He gets calm, wipes his mouth and then grabs the container and fills a glass half-way on a small table beside him. He wipes his face again and begins rolling a joint.

"Somethin' 'bout alcohol" he says as he lights up the joint. "You can't get it from any drug...It's like your senses are intact, no distortion of reality—just relaxed, at peace with perfect clarity in whatever you're doin'. The other shit removes you in some fashion, but not alcohol, unless you drown yourself in it. It's hard to keep down anymore. Once I get some in my system, my body calms down and I can sip it. But I can't give it up. I like it better than scag."

After eating and talking nonsense for an hour, it is getting time to leave. I have to ask him:

"Tommy. Do you know when it happened? I mean, when you moved into your territory. You know what I mean?"

"No, I don't."

"You know...Like when I was kid. That time you punched the nun out at school and they told me I would burn in hell if I kept hangin' out with you. I chose hell, and everythin' changed."

"Oh no" Kenny says. "Not the heavy shit. Right after I smoke a joint!"

180

"I don't get your drift, bro."

"I don't know…It's just that…I mean, I know how you are. And I can't remember you bein' any different. But all of us were different—way back, sometimes real young. I mean, even at 8 you were pretty much like you are now. You know what I'm sayin'? But there had to be a time when that wasn't so. Do you remember that? I mean, for me…I made a decision and everythin' changed. Did somethin' like that happen to you?"

He just sits there, his eyes glassy and red, like he is in a fog or looking through the wall at something. This went on for about a half minute. Then carefully he says "I don't know…There was this time, when you were in the hospital…I had just started 1st grade. I'd only been in school 'bout a month. You know those shitty clothes we had to wear, hand-me-downs that were always too big for us. I hated it. It was the only thing that really bugged me. I knew kids were talkin' shit behind my back, makin' fun a me. But then this one mornin' a kid sittin' next to me starts in. I didn't have a belt on and my pants were too big. So I used mom's curlers. You know, that grey cloth on wire. I looped 'em through two belt loops on both sides of my pants and twisted them to secure the pants evenly. And this kid starts laughin', tellin' the other kids around him to check it out, how stupid I looked. The teacher told him to stop it or he'd be sent to principal's office. But he didn't stop. He kept gigglin', and so did the other kids. I'd never been that angry or humiliated, not ever. I didn't plan it. I just grabbed the sharpened pencil from my desk, stood up and stabbed him as hard as I could in his face. He was screamin', the girls were screamin', and I saw a look of horror on the teacher's face as she yelled 'Oh my God! Oh my God!' She ran to the cryin', tremblin' kid, grabbed 'im and rushed 'im outta the class. I got up and left school, and I wasn't allowed to return. That's when dad put me in Catholic school.

181

"But...ya know—it wasn't the act that changed me. It was afterwards. I mean, I didn't feel anythin' but joy. I was proud of what I did. Real proud. When the boy screamed it pierced my heart in a good way, an exciting way, every fiber of my bein' experiencin' it as an act of purity, of honesty. Yeah—the first act I ever thought about bein' honest, really honest...ya know? I didn't care what happened, an ass-whippin' or anythin'. Nothin' could take that joy from me. And when I pictured the horrified faces of the other kids and the teacher, I knew I stood apart from them, above them, and everyone else, kids *and* adults. It was crystal clear: I knew they had nothin' on me, and that's where I wanted to be all the time. And when I got in fights after that I was focused, man, my only goal to hurt the other person as much as I could so they'd never forget who they fucked with. How many times someone hit me meant jack shit. The only real damage they could do is win, and that ain't happened yet. That's the satisfaction I carry with me all the time, knowin' they can't win.

"Yeah...I guess that's where I changed. Where I made a decision as you call it. And I've never had a regret. Gettin' mine like everyone else is secondary. Knowin' I can destroy anyone is first, and I'm still ahead of the game. The drugs are cool and I get mine. The sophistos and robber barons get their shit anyway they can, and if it came down to it, they'd do more damage than I could ever imagine to keep what they got, and all of what they got in the end don't amount to shit, 'cause it's all secondary, never havin' a real thought about where they stand separate from their shit, some goal that reigns deep inside that they'll never look at 'cause they wouldn't be able to handle it, the truth of who they really are, and why they're lost, and that's another reason I'm ahead of 'em. They're livin' a secondary life, and that means they're livin' a fuckin' lie. Shit...in every hamlet in Germany people lined up to steal stores from the Jews and then sent 'em to the ovens, makin' sure they didn't come back to claim what's theirs. Educated idiots stole university chairs. Everyone was in on the big grab. And if Americans had grown up there, they woulda been in on it, too. That's what history is, the story of how people can't get past a secondary life, a life of things, building up their stash as insulation, includin' ideas they never earned and don't belong to 'em, none of it havin' anythin' to do with who the fuck they really are, just collectin' and peddlin' shit to get some recognition and a comfortable cage, not figurin' out that a cage is a cage after all and you might as well concentrate on gettin' high in it. The honest ones are always in trouble—kept at a distance in some fashion, and even when they're not forced out, they travel there themselves, like Fitzgerald, Kafka, Proust, Dostoevsky, Arendt, Eliot and O'Connor. They're all there on the shelf. They're the ones you wanna read. They're the ones who go where they gotta go and don't give a shit about the consequences, whether they get shit or don't, and ain't no one travelin' with 'em; and goin' where they gotta go is what makes 'em honest, not what they write. And that's why the rest are liars, 'cause they don't go anywhere, just parrot and parade and build on popular shit to furnish their cage and imagine they're better than everyone else. You wanna see the horror of a dead-end secondary life? Read Fitzgerald—he mapped it all out, includin' the pompous delusion that any person can save anyone from anythin', like there's such a thing as a heroic act, like there's anythin' real outside of a love that burns the shit outta ya in the end; but the idiots conned themselves into thinkin' it was all about a profligate Jazz Age. Well…he gave 'em an out, an escape hatch: he was kind that way—didn't want to lay the absolute horror of it all on 'em in one shot, ya know? They'll read *Tender is the Night*, his masterpiece, but ain't no way in hell they gonna look at the night he's talkin' 'bout. *He* got it: when man killed his useless God, buried 'im and drove 'im from memory, he could invent his own god, any idol of his fancy from whatever canister caught his eye, which is man's first prerogative; for me it's alcohol or whatever other pain relief's available, especially when a delusion gets nudged to one side or blown up. They called Fitzgerald a romantic—yeah, he was, the real ticket—he lived in that bunker to the end, crawling up in a corner as every illusion around im' got shot down, leavin' 'im with nothin' but a desire to disappear, humanity's new destiny, a disappearn' act, meant for every one of us; that or the ICU room called television. Yeah, he fought the good fight for all of us. And where did it lead 'im? I'll show you…Kenny—get me that book." Kenny goes to the shelf and pulls a worn copy of *Tender is the Night* from it and opens it to a page selected with a marker (162). "Read it Kenny." Kenny reads: "…he was thankful to have an existence at all, if only as a reflection in her wet eyes…[S]uddenly there was a booming from the wine slopes across the lake; cannons were shooting at hail-bearing clouds in order to break them. The lights of the promenade went off, went on again. Then the storm came swiftly…with it came a dark, frightening sky and savage filaments of lightening and world-splitting thunder, while ragged, destroying clouds fled along past the hotel. Mountains and lakes disappeared—the hotel crouched amid tumult, chaos and darkness." Kenny puts the book back on the shelf and Tommy continues: "How tender is that night? Sounds more like a fuckin' apocalypse to me. Like I said, he gave it his best shot as the carnival of progress mocked his every step into isolation and death. All he could give us was the first and only great American novel, but we don't want it, ringing as it does the death toll on any semblance of a lastin' love or that we can in any way work our way out of the pit in this age of the big grab, love itself just another tool in negotiating for more shit to pile on the shit we already got, while Madison Avenue works tirelessly at advertisin' an endless list of shit to purchase and lose intrest in, includin' endless boxes of ideologies sold at ever higher prices at university stalls, all of it to stop us from thinkin', 'cause only a fool would want to think when he's stretched out in a casket. How long can you stare at the walls of a coffin, no matter how pretty the inlay? It's *all* about the big hustle now, figurin' out what scam's goin' down and gettin' in on the action early—and I'm sayin' there ain't no point to it unless you're out to get enough cash for pain relief, unless you're a masochist. But the liars won't even take responsibility for bein' in on God's murder, pride-filled co-conspirators, especially the pompous Christians—masters that they are at self-deception, preoccupied with takin' pride in their coffins, their tomb-worlds, each with its own veil that can be embroidered with any initiative after purchasin' a pattern. Step right up! Enjoy the big fuckin' show! It's their amusement park, man, their final fuckin' achievement, and if you don't applaud 'em they'll stick a fuckin' screw-driver in your eye…You'll figure it out, bro. You got some time on your hands. I don't see you optin' to be a fuckin' liar or goin' stupid on me."

I had forgotten about Rose, the love of Tommy's life when he was 16, the most gorgeous girl in Summit, an Italian beauty with long dark hair and a perennially tanned, buxom body filled out perfectly in low-cut, revealing silk mini-dresses she loved to wear like an advertisement. When Tommy was with Rose he hardly ever came around. He wouldn't even introduce us to her. That was the only time he talked about getting off drugs. Anything Rose asked for Tommy got her, even bought her a car when she didn't have a license. When he went to reformatory he got news about Rose seeing other guys, and he ended up on Thorazine. During that period of mom and me visiting him he didn't have anything to say: he would just sit there with eyes glazed over. I thought he was high on drugs, but mom would eventually explain that Tommy was having some difficulty, that he was depressed about not being able to see Rose. Nothing in his life had ever hit him that hard. She was Tommy's only link with a world outside drug use and violence, and it all went under. When he got out he said nothing; wouldn't talk about it with anyone. Rose tried to get in touch with him, but he wouldn't see her. The last tie with the delusion of romantic love had been cut, and he wasn't seeking a return.

This is what we would do at least once a week—get together, get stoned and talk shit, usually about some book Tommy insisted I should read because I wasn't getting a point of his in a big way. But something happened to me. I began losing interest in the drugs. I didn't have the hyper brain activity that had cursed Tommy, where even drugs couldn't slow his mind down, and why, I believe, he could so easily slip into madness, which made him absolutely dependent on drugs, street or prescribed. And I was able to go deeper when I didn't use them. Drugs sapped my energy, unable with any rational force to connect associative thoughts, and thereby losing interest in what I was reading, my thoughts falling apart and finally spiraling out into anesthetized chaos on the periphery of consciousness, of absolutely no use to me, something that would frustrate and depress me, and why I longed most for my cell, a place to relax and where my imagination could wander in clarity without impediment, for it was in sensations fixed to my imagination that the things I read would come to life. When I used drugs I could feel them pulling me away from what great artists would reveal and then activate my imagination, the artists who had dug deep, risking everything, life itself, to utter something with clarity, pointing in directions the truly curious longed to travel. Drugs like marijuana trapped me in paltry particulars of what I was experiencing, annihilating the fullness of what authors mined in their inner-depths, and those particulars became hyperbolic abstractions, losing their in-flux relational form in the grand gestalt, existing on their own in empty space, separate from my life. Barbiturates and alcohol always ended in crushing the gestalt *and* the particulars, another dead end. Heroin would numb too much pain and suffering, especially the pain and suffering required for fruitful reflection, glorious melancholy, the artist's closest friend, his best guide in exploring the deeper depths, and for the reader of great art, heroin can push the artist's works into an abstract imagining outside the grounded, concrete gestalt of the artist's intent. And speed would heighten every particular to the point of losing all subtlety, the finer nuances that give the final shape to an exact knowing, especially what is discerned in a bed of sorrow that one must not abandon in seeking clarity. Above all, I wanted my mind to be clear, open, in order to receive the gift of what my imagination had the power to provide, to reproduce as much as possible the original illumination the artist attempts to convey. The books Tommy gave me opened up these amazing realms, like cinema did on the outside, places to go and have a conversation outside the repetitious bullshit that kept me propped up in any given lie. Reading for me now wasn't an immersion into high abstraction to find a justification for anything, or an escape or denial or entertainment for entertainment's sake (even trash novels have points of illumination)—it was a sure guide to deeper interior places that gave me a more accurate view of what was actually going on around and inside me, and the best of times were those rare moments where "I" would disappear inside an unassailable truth, the haze of the past's competing spoon-fed explanations delivered on familiar conveyor belts falling away into a linguistic abyss, the clarity in a newly discovered, honest image so rich there is no interior or exterior movement at all, just the light of illumination itself, not seeing myself or anything else, but more like I am being seen, and that *being seen* is always the best glimpse of myself, a view absent every desire destined for exhaustion. When I read Plato's *Phaedrus* and *Symposium*, I was there in the thick of it. I could smell the grass, hear the soothing, cleansing sounds of the river moving against rocks, the clamor of cups and plates, people mumbling in the background, and I could feel the breeze caressing the hair on my face and arms. I could see the looks on the faces of those caught up in an intellectual

187

drama that they in their rabid egoism had no clue was a matter of life and death, of dying to a dead notion to be resurrected in a point of infinite clarity, a being alive in letting go of a construct that freezes us in fear where we are forced to take on false identities, to don masks in a deluded sense of all-knowingness—unable to be lifted into realms where the dignity of every human person has more value than any ritualized idea that would hammer us into conformity with whatever matrix is provided to contain and stifle our daily death throes, distant from the breathing of those very real persons standing right next to us, lost in roles played out to sustain the lies of zombieland. Socrates didn't represent the intellectual or the intellectual process, but every breathing human being singularly concerned with being open to and receiving every person in all their dignity, knowing that in the instant they embrace a lie to simply get along or to gain a position of prestige, they will disappear and never know love, for how can a lie find love when love is the absolute truth at the hub of a life actually lived?

*********

Tommy laid it all out for me. He had cancer. The arm the doctors had fixed developed a cancerous growth along one of the metal plates that held his forearm together, and they told him they would have to amputate, and if he refused the cancer would spread quickly once it got in the bone marrow. Tommy refused and sure enough, the cancer spread throughout his body. It got to his stomach and that's why it was hard for him to hold down food and booze. He also was slowly going blind, presently seeing in hazy over-lapping triplicates. Kenny was his eyes, even read for him at night. He was the only person he trusted. The other prisoners thought Kenny was his kid who also ran drug-errands for him. Tommy had the most successful drug operation because he

188

was feared and, more importantly, the crooked guards trusted him more than anyone else. The drug programs started in the early 60s turned most somewhat self-respecting criminals into whimpering stool pigeons behind closed doors, mostly with a crazed vision of getting the next heroin fix, their sole meditation, and Tommy was one of the remaining few who didn't have the wherewithal to sell an inch of his darkened soul, and the corrupt guards knew and respected this in him, and what made possible an arrangement. He had to every once in a while make an appearance, and he knew the routes to the kitchen and yard by heart. He was convinced he would die before he went totally blind, but then his life had gone on for two years past his six-months-to-live prognosis.

\*\*\*\*\*\*\*\*\*\*

What I was missing most in prison was films. As much as I was getting into literature, my obsession was cinema. I had been down for three months and not a single good film had been shown. I thought maybe Tommy had a connection:

"Just wish I could see a good film."

"Forget it—the selection committee, a bunch of stool-pigeons, are into porn and shoot-'em-ups. Just go with the books. They're a dead end but they won't bore you."

"I always get more from films."

"Well…I did like Polanski's *The Tenant*. Kind of summed it all up for me. Didn't have any desire to see another one. Shit—you can smoke a joint and watch 30 films in your head!"

"Yeah, well you can smoke a joint and read a newspaper and think you read the complete works of Shakespeare."

189

"Exactly! So shut the fuck up and roll a joint!"

"I don't know if I told you. The doctor said I could get my tattoo surgically removed."

"The 8-ball?"

"Yeah."

"What the fuck for?"

"I don't know. Maybe I'm tired of bein' behind the 8-ball."

I meant it as a joke, but Tommy got annoyed.

"I gave you that tattoo!"

"Yeah…I know. But I was thinkin' about gettin' out of the drug game, doin' somethin' different."

"Different? What the fuck you talkin' about? What's better than scag, booze and weed?"

"I don't know, but I wanna look."

"Exactly! You don't know. And the reason you don't know is 'cause there ain't nothin'!"

"I don't know."

"Come on, man. It's one thing to say you're sick a doin' time or you're sick a the game. I could buy that, as long as you know the why of it. There ain't nothin' wrong with throwin' in the towel and just goin' along with whatever shit to avoid endin' up here. But in the end you ain't gonna find anythin' better than drugs, bro. Every road's a dead end. And if your dead end's a castle, you're still gonna need whiskey ta get comfortable, unless you don't care 'bout bein' severed, willin' ta adjust like some fuckin' zombie, which is somethin' else altogether."

"I don't know."

"Hey…ya know—do what the fuck you want, man."

Kenny interjects, "There's always God. Maybe you should give him a shot. You're always in the Bible. Seems like there's something in there you're looking for."

"What I was lookin' for in there I found."

"You believe in God?" I ask with disbelief.

"Of course…What?…I look stupid?"

"No…it's just that it's somethin' I never think about, and I didn't think you did, either."

"Anyone that's looked at it, *really* looked at it, knows there's a God. But so what? Once you get what he's up to, you know your choices: do his will or yours. That's the way it's been from the beginnin', and that's all there is to it. Religionists go in endless circles tryin' to make it complex, mostly 'cause they don't wanna admit they've settled on doin' their own will, just as adamant as me in saying *fuck you* to God—rebellin' 'gainst God without lookin' at it, hypocrites, and why they never really get all of what they really want, never go all the way—ya know, stradlin' that barbed-wire fence, livin' the shredded life, just sos they can do their own will and pretend they're on God's side for a possible reprieve in the end, really believin' they've conned God, and then act all surprised when they one day wake up in hell, pissed off that they didn't go all the way when they were on earth—and that'll be their eternal torment, feelin' cheated. Anyway, it all comes down to that. And if you choose his will, then you're stuck as his sufferin' fuckin' servant, man. There ain't no other way. If someone says he believes in God and ain't his sufferin' servant, then he's a fuckin' liar and a fuckin' hypocrite, and there ain't nothin' so foul from where I stand. That happy happy joy joy shit is best left to Ren and Stimpy. You choose your own will you're choosin' *not* to be that sufferin' servant. And that's all there is. No way 'round it, bro. And from my perspective, not sufferin' is the best choice, the one I made a long time ago, why I'd kill any motherfucker attemptin' to inflict even a modicum of pain on me, and as for the incidentals—in my experience drugs and alcohol are the best treatment for pain and sufferin'. Everythin' else is a wash. Hell, maybe gettin' high's a wash, too, but there's no question you're puttin' a big fuckin' dent in pain relief."

"What about the heaven and hell thing?"

"Shit! That's somethin' you don't have to swallow. The thing is God knows everythin' that's goin' down, even before you do it, and I suspect he wrote the whole fuckin' script from the jump and just lets us play 'round in it. That's our flimsy freedom, and we'll never be free enough to change his script! Yeah, we write our own scripts and employ idiots who won't write their own, or maybe theirs intersects with ours, and none of it goes anywhere but the shithouse, and precisely why our lives are shit. Why wouldn't we get high? Makes sense, right? I mean, if he just kept lettin' us thrash around endlessly in our meaningless shit, we'd just keep bein' the fuckin' idiots we are and would never get to his desired end, where all of us can be lovey dovey in union with *him*. His providence like river currents move us to his end as we thrash around in the water, if we're even up to the effort, and with his infinite fuckin' patience he sustains our stupid thrashing, our little freedom games—that's what his tenderness is all about: he's amused and takes pity on us in our futile seriousness just like parents with their toddlers. We should cringe in shame when tempted to imagine our freedom's the same as his; and he just keeps tryin' to con us with exhaustion, world-weariness shit, *showing* us how futile our every gesture towards the good life is so we'll come 'round to his plan. Outside of that movement we'd be spendin' eternity not in heaven or hell but in a relentless chaos that would never exhaust our ridiculous ambitions. Talk about hell on earth, and precisely why scientists seeking immortality are the biggest idiots on the planet, like those monkeys trained to be addicted to shocking themselves with electricity to sustain an intrest in stayin' alive! He in fact places all our hopes and dreams on

192

a conveyor belt and lets us take pleasure in shootin' 'em down, what our willfulness is really all about, actin' in the only way possible on the hatred of the futility he's placed us in, 'cause we know deep inside our hopes and dreams are worthless and make us look like the fuckin' blind idiots we are in our utopian deceptions. That's the only history lesson worth payin' attention to, the eternal changin' of the guard, everyone gettin' his turn at destroying the illusions of real freedom if he chooses to step up. You have to at least appreciate God's sense of humor. Yeah, he's a lovin' God and desires somethin' really good for us, makin' us higher than the angels, but it pisses me off that he persists in movin' us there with all his manipulations, *with his script*!...*That's* what I'm rebellin' 'gainst every fuckin' second of every fuckin' day, the only thing *worth* rebellin' 'gainst, 'cause it's the only honest fuckin' rebellion. That's the book I want to write: *Every Fuckin' Second of Every Fuckin' Day!*, and I won't have to fill the pages. The title tells the whole story! I'm only demandin' a right to *my* heritage, *my* origin—*Nothin'*! You get it? He's a lovin' God. No way in hell's he gonna send anyone down into some fiery pit for eternity. No fuckin' way, man! He made us out a nothin' and that's where I wanna go—back to my real home, what I really am, *my essence*—Nothin'! You get it? We're creatures, man, and always will be...Only God is infinite freedom. He ain't trapped in havin' to decide between good and evil, but our creaturely free-will imposes that on us, and does nothin' but whip us around in our petty god-games, everyone inventin' their own notions of what's good and evil, when in fact no one really gives a shit, not deep down inside—they're just lookin' to get somethin' on you so's they can stick their finger in your face and set you straight, make you get on board with their petty power play, an imposition of their great plan for you that serves only to force you into submission to their godhood. You get it? God's pure freedom, and we'll always be less than that, petty power-mongers, and why we, unlike him, can choose evil, even turn it into a good to our

193

great satisfaction, and force you to embrace, even more satisfaction, and why we endlessly rip each other to pieces with ever-shifting acts of so-called freedom in opposition to the moral demands of every other, most especially those we love, for they know our pettiness better than anyone, and to defeat them in their knowledge of us enhances the will that much more—yet our freedom remains forever limited and determined by our inadequacy as creatures in seeking total ascendency, our pathetic lowliness fixed in an ever-shifting moral quagmire of power-plays; in fact, even absent morality, in say Sadean delight, our freedom is still in opposition to real freedom, the freedom that is God, which means it ain't real freedom at all, meaning it's just slavery dressed up in more colorful rags of freedom, which means we're always losers, and why there ain't no such thing as winnin', not ever. Our only option's to choose union with *Him*, which is only a participation in his freedom—it ain't ours! We become the best but lowly approximation to what he is, an image, a likeness, a *reflection* of him, which means we ain't him and therefore ain't freedom! Yeah, we'll get eternal bliss, the wiping away of every tear, but it'll always be *his* freedom, not ours! Jesus showed us this in his creature-self, reminding us that he never did his creaturely will, but the will of his Father, and that's what he's askin' of us, to do *his* will, not ours. Well, fuck 'im! 'cause that's what pisses us all off—the only thing that really pisses anybody off, and it's nothin' but cowardliness not to look at it, 'cause when you look at it the choice is clear, and we *do* have the freedom to decide ultimately—*to do his will or our own*, and the only choice we possess for unlimited freedom on our own terms is to decide against *his* will with finality, returnin' to our origin, *our* absolute essence separate from him—*Nothingness*! Every other decision is slavery, and why Paul, an honest man, told us the only road to everlastin' life is to become slaves in Christ. There's just no way we can ever be the freedom that is God; all we can claim as ours is *submission*. Ya get it? The truth of bein' created is that we are slaves, eternally, *unless* we return to Nothingness."

"So what are you here and now?" Kenny says. "You ain't no hypocrite as far as I can tell, but what *are* you?"

"I'm a fuckin' drug addict!—nothin' more and nothin' less. We really are what we do, ya know? Don't let those lukewarm fuckin' idiots talk their cringin' shit to you; even God chooses to vomit them out!—there ain't no fuckin' fundamental option, man, some transcendent self separate from the shit you do, like those cons claimin' they're innocent for so long they start believin' it: what you do is always a big clue to a big fuckin' choice you made deep down inside; so why snivel and hide from it, why be a fuckin' hypocrite, the worst kind of coward walkin' the face of the earth? My decision's made, and all I'm lookin' for is pain relief, man…It's like Freud said: everyone's lookin' for happiness, and what's happiness? Pleasure! And what's pleasure? The absence of pain, man. Everythin' else is bullshit. My life ain't mine! It belongs to God…but I can steal it from 'im—I *can* will that! and why suicide's an honest option. The only reason I'm on this fuckin' planet is to get high. And if I gotta stay at motel hell, I'd be a fuckin' idiot *not* to get high. It's what I want, what *I will*. I ain't no fuckin' masochist, and if I ain't one of those fuckin' idiots, what fuckin' choice do I got?"

"Nothin' else in life?" I ask.

"Like what? Love? Romance? Money and all the shit you can buy with it? Shit, I've had all that, and none of it's as good as a fix. Why play those games…for what? Ta make anxiety a life force?, to camp out on a ledge you're gonna have to jump from or get throwin' off of? Ya gotta be fuckin' kiddin'. I told ya—I ain't no fuckin' masochist!"

Now I was pissed. But why? It wasn't the drug thing or the God thing he was rambling on about. Then it occurred to me: Tommy had not only given me the tattoo—he had chosen it. It was like he had branded me as an initiation into his world, and for him that meant that we were bros to the end; not just biological brothers, but a total commitment to *his* world, which meant an absolute rejection of any world I might imagine for myself, which I had not a single objection to at the time because it was what I wanted more than anything back then—to be with him. And now I was thinking seriously about moving on, exploring territory on my own, and he was interpreting it as a betrayal, revealed in being pissed off about me removing the tattoo he gave me. This is what was making me crazy.

Much later I would see another dimension: Tommy had found his freedom in power in his total identification with dad, internally registering quite logically that he couldn't transcend dad's grip, so he coalesced with him. Tommy branding me was not only his taking possession of my body and mind, incorporating me into his world, his commitment—he was also unknowingly dad's agent, extending dad's grip on my soul way into the future; and then I remembered the time in the kitchen when I was age 15. I hadn't been home in weeks, and one night around midnight it was snowing big chunks of snowflakes, and with it came that great snow-quiet where the lingering sounds of late evening were absorbed into the billions of soft icy pillows angelically floating to the ground, and I was transported back to that prayer-quiet I knew as a child transfixed before the tabernacle at church. I had been sleeping in cars or on rooftops, but now, in this prayer quiet I was moved to a house where a friend lived and I knocked on the door. His mother, whom we suspected was his grandmother because of her age, an Italian woman from the old country, came to the door, and when I asked if I could stay the night, she said "No, no, a Sam. You a gotta go home. Your a mama she a worry about you. You a go home now, OK?"

196

"OK," I said. And when she closed the door I walk over to the big oak tree in their front yard and sit down under it, my back against the massive trunk, and I immediately relax in the great silence as the snowflakes begin to cover me like a soft blanket. I awake about 5:30 in the morning, brush all the snow off me and walk up to the door and knock. The old woman opens the door and panics: "Sam! What a you a doin' a here? Didn't you a go home?" "No," I said, "I slept under the tree." "O my God—getta in here!" She woke her son up and gave him some money and told him to take me to the bus stop and put me on a bus home. And he did, but I don't remember being on the bus. All I remember is that in the next moment I was in the kitchen at home. It was Sunday morning and everyone was in the living room watching television. I was leaning against the counter in a totally relaxed state. Light was blazing outward in all directions all around me, from the walls, ceiling, counters, floor and appliances, not a dark crevice anywhere, and my mind was fixed in pure clarity. Without intention, I found myself pontificating on what I saw in all its simplicity, and I started with the youngest, Sarah: "Sarah—you always had the most sense. You have always seen everything for what it really is. I can't remember you ever not seeing it. That's how you became an adult at age 3; Catherine—you saw your opportunity early on, when you realized dad wanted you as his wife in waiting, and you took him for everything you could get—it was pure survival; Tommy—you went to war with the world trying to get in dad's good favor, the only way to get his admiration; mom, you just submit to dad's violence like a child as wives often do and you try to keep your sorrow to yourself, escaping as best you can in magazines and lies about your life; and dad…you're responsible for all of it—you had the power to change everything, but you decided to whip us all in shape and serve you, Lord of O'Brien Land, making sure none of us would ever have a life." And on those words I could see my dad moving fast toward me from the dining room with that fearless fuming face of his, a stocky bull

197

of a man, and as he drew close, again without intention, I could see my right hand out of the corner of my right eye rising in slow motion, separate from me, having a life of its own, an overhand right, just as my dad reached me, the fist slamming full-force into his face, and because he was in motion and my body braced at the counter, my punch had a triple impact, stunning him, and then with tight closed fists I grip both his ears, feeling my fingernails tearing into their flesh, and in staccato fashion start pounding his head with full swaying force into the counter in rhythmic delight like a metronome, and after repeated blows his knees start buckling—he was going down and I no doubt would have pounded him to death, slamming his head into counter doors and then floor, but all of a sudden Tommy is behind me with his arms reaching under my arm pits and hands clasped in finger-locks at the back of my head, pushing my head forward and pulling my body up in the air, a perfect position for dad after composing himself, pummeling me with upper-cuts to the head and fierce blows to the stomach, Tommy holding me firmly in place, and I'm barely conscious as dad moves to open the cellar door and orders Tommy: "Give him here" and Tommy hands me over to him. He grabs me with both fists by the front of my shirt and then throws me down the cellar stairs. I wake up three days later in the basement, my mom hovering over me, fearful with tears welling in her eyes: "You have to leave. You understand? You have to leave and you can never come back." And that's what I did.

This is what I had forgotten, and what my recurring thought about Tommy being upset with me for my wanting to remove the tattoo he gave me would eventually jar from memory. And in this recollection I understood that Tommy had no life of his own at all, that for him it was dad's world through and through, that Tommy was just another victim, and I realized in that moment that every person who has ever walked this planet is equally in some fashion a victim—we're all victims, and that we mistakenly believe in the subconscious that the only way out is

198

victimizing someone else; or rather, we believe the only way out is through power, and that dead-end deception is simply a justification for the fulfillment of an even deeper desire, the desire located in Adam's rebellion to in some way be *thee* god by inventing our own knowledge of what is good and evil, and then acting on it, the only dynamic of a life that resides in power. I realized that had our roles been reversed in that crucial moment and it was Tommy beating dad to death, I would have helped him do it, but only because I had identified more with our mom in her dark sorrow and would be acting under her influence, her world, not from whoever I was hidden away some place deep in my heart.

**********

Tommy, Kenny and I were wasted on heroin this time. Tommy had gotten a shipment in, China White, as good as any I've ever used. He was excited because he could step on it twice and prisoners would still be happy with the quality. It was an early Sunday afternoon. We were talking nonsense when the cell door opened and three prisoners move in quickly—two with knives, the other with a pipe. "Where's the dope?" the leader with the pipe demands.

"Fuck you!" Tommy yells as he moves to grab the assailant, the pipe coming down hard across Tommy's forehead, a clean crack opening up his skull, him falling to the floor, eyes rolling up in his head as the second assailant plunges a knife full force into Tommy's chest. I'm frozen in that second with no weapon as Kenny, seemingly from nowhere, at the same time the pipe came down across Tommy's head, was already stabbing the two other assailants, one getting it in the stomach and the other, the one who had stabbed Tommy in the chest, getting it in the juggler vein. And the leader with the pipe starts to run for the door, but Kenny grabs him by his long hair at the back of his head, pulling him full force back into the cell and throwing him to the floor, and when the assailant jumps to his feet, Kenny in an upward motion slams the knife up through the assailant's gullet, the knife sliding easily up into his brain, his body crumbling in lifeless motion to the floor.

I move right away to Tommy and start applying CPR in a frenzy. "Help me, Kenny!" I yell after I breathe air into his lungs, and there's gurgling of blood in his throat as he breathes out, little blood bubbles forming around his mouth.

"Leave him" Kenny says.

"He's breathing, man. Help me!" as I continue pushing on his chest.

"That's not him, man. It's your air…what you're breathing into him—that's what's coming out. Now leave him. It's over."

I knew it was true the second he said it. Tommy's eyes are still wide open, but distant. I slowly move away from his body and stand up. I can taste his blood in my mouth—literally the taste of death, a taste that would stay in my mouth for a month.

There's moaning coming from the assailant who hadn't done any damage, the one Kenny had stabbed first in the stomach:

"Help me" he says in a voice wracked with pain. "Please…help…I got kids."

Kenny grabs a towel and is wiping his prints from the shank, and then holds it out to me.

"Take it" he said.

I just look at him, the sounds still coming from the prisoner on the floor: "Help…please…"

"Take it, and do him" Kenny orders.

"He didn't do anythin'."

"He would have if he got there first. You think they'd let any of us live after the first kill? Come on, man—be realistic. And if he lives he'll make sure you never see the light of day. Trust me on that. Now do it. We ain't got much time."

I turn and look at Tommy, and then at the assailant, still groveling in pain.

"We ain't got time, Sam. Listen—this is what we got to do. It's the law. They killed Tommy in his cell and you're his brother. That means no charges. You got it? We ain't got time to waste. Tommy's a known drug dealer, and they're going to be searching the cell. I have to get rid of the drugs. You don't know anything, OK? You were just sitting talking to Tommy when they rolled in on him, and you did your best to defend him and yourself. Simple as that. You'll walk, and no one'll fuck with you ever again in this joint. It's up to you, but you got to decide right now. If it's yes, take the knife," as he holds the knife out to me.

I had three thoughts in a second: I owed it to Kenny—he saved my life; this would also finalize the reputation I needed to do easy time; and I realized in that second that I never really had a life on the outside other than numbing my brain. The last two months I had begun to feel more real, more of who I really am just by reading, something I would never do on the outside.

"Ok," I said, taking the knife from Kenny.

Then he looks at the body now convulsing on the floor, and then back at me, and then in a voice that had no trace of effeminacy: "You got to do him, man."

"He'll be dead any moment."

"You can't chance it. And quite frankly, it's the only assurance I'll have that you won't burn me. Don't take it personal. I have more respect and trust for your brother than anyone I've ever known, and I would be asking him the same thing if he were standing in your place. It's survival, nothing more."

I walk over to the dying prisoner who is on his side in a fetal position. There's jerking motions now, seconds apart. I grip the shank and come down hard into the side of his neck, and then pulling the shank out I thrust again sideways into his chest, again and again, faster and faster I don't know how many times, but with each thrust I pound harder and harder with the image of Tommy's dead eyes fixed in my mind, my anger and anguish intensifying with each blow, not only because they killed Tommy, but with *everything* that gone before and what no doubt awaits me up the road. Then I stop.

"I got to go" Kenny says. He walks over and pulls the brick out of the wall and grabs the stash, wrapping it in a clean shirt and stuffing it under his armpit, and then grabbing a windbreaker jacket that he puts on. "I'll catch up with you later." He opens the cell door and casually looks both ways before moving out. He looks back for a second with an encouraging tight smile.

I stand still with the shank in my hand. I look at it for a few seconds and then let it fall to the floor and then walk through the doorway and down to the guard's desk where he is seated doing paper work. There are about 20 prisoners out on the flats standing around in little cliques. I feel invisible amidst all the chatter as I make my way to the guard. He doesn't look up when I approach him.

"Officer" I say.

"What is it?" he asks, eyes fixed on some paper work.

"I just stabbed some people in my brother's cell."

He looks up at me and lingers on my face for two seconds, and then picks up the phone: "Officer Jenkins on 4-Wing. We got a code 9." Then he hangs up the phone.

"You OK?" he asks as I hear the alarm sounding.

202

"Yeah…I'm OK."

"Good. Help will be here. How's your brother?"

"He's dead."

Chapter 13

I was taken to the hole. All I could think about was Tommy. Everything would be different. I just keep going over all that had gone down in our lives. I remember a lot of times I had forgotten, like when he was in a hurry one time when we were boosting. "We ain't got time—just grab everythin' you can carry." And I did, all the leather coats from a rack. The owner ran up and grabbed me, and Tommy knocks him out with one punch. We then quickly walk out of the store.

With Tommy it was always different, moving on a plane separate in every way from what was going on around us. And because I loved him so, it wasn't like his actions were separate from mine, not when we were committing crimes. We really were in it together. Unlike most criminals, we had no hesitations, no doubts, because we totally trusted each other. Any act, even a criminal act, that resides in sacrificial love resides in eternity, and thereby dispels, if only for a moment, all fears—even the fear of death. Every act outside of love is futility's breath trying to revive a corpse. I knew now that Tommy is what made the criminal life real for me, not the drugs and adrenaline. It was a way of staying with him. It was always about being with Tommy, because like everyone else, I wanted to reside in love, and with Tommy, however mangled, the love was real and not to be questioned, because at the drop of a pin we would die for each other.

*********

204

I only spend one night in the hole. Early the next morning I am transported to the county jail where I am processed in on a charge of triple-homicide. Two days later I am arraigned in court and formally charged. My public defender, a small young waspish man in a grey suit with conservatively cut sandy hair and wing-tipped dress shoes, didn't have much to say. He didn't even know if he would be representing me. The only thing I said was "It's self-defense, right?"

"Yes" he says in his quick, perfectly enunciated and emotionless style of talking. "But New Jersey doesn't recognize self-defense in homicide cases. There can be mitigating circumstances that preclude jail time, but it's questionable if that applies here. And this new prosecutor—he's on a bandwagon. He's got political ambitions. I think he wants to make a big deal of this, not handle it like other homicide charges that come out of the prison system."

"What's that mean? I mean, it's clear-cut, right? Was I supposed to let 'em kill me?"

"I'm on your side. I'm just saying this new prosecutor…he's hard to talk to. But I'll be getting back to you soon. We have a pretrial hearing coming up in two weeks. I'll have more information then. Take care of yourself. You have my number. Call me if you have any concerns. I'm hardly ever in my office, but my secretary will give me your messages. Just hang in there. This is a capital offense, which means the state can't limit the money we spend in defending you. I'll be in touch soon."

He shakes my hand and leaves. I feel like I'd just talked to an accountant who was adding up numbers to give me an estimate. But I wouldn't have to wait for his estimate—it was a lead story on the front page of the local newspaper the next morning: **PROSECUTOR WILL SEEK DEATH PENALTY**.

I read through the entire story carefully. At a press conference, the prosecutor handling my case, a 2nd generation Italian named Paul Regerrio, a stern, no-nonsense man of tall stature

205

and big-bone-structure, dressed meticulously in a dark blue pin-striped suit and red tie, laid out the facts of the case, and then proceeded to explain the tradition, how murders were permitted in prisons, but that that was going to stop. "Why aren't inmates held accountable for their actions? Should we take the attitude that it's OK for them to kill one another? Allow them to become more and more conditioned to kill and then release them to the streets? That's what we've been doing. But that stops *here*, today. And I promise you—if I don't put Sam Jones in the electric chair, I will resign from office as prosecutor!"

When I next see my lawyer he explains it to me: "Regerrio is going to make the case that you hooked up with your bother in an organized drug-dealing ring within the prison. He's already got two inmates—"

"Whoa! Would you stop calling us inmates?"

He looks at me for a few seconds. "What am I supposed to call persons in prison?"

"*Prisoners*. You know—you're in prison so you're a prisoner, not an inmate. Prison's not a mental institution."

"Well, it's been my impression that 'inmate' is a term that connotes more dignity, more respect...a more humanizing term. That's why I use it."

"Just the opposite! So don't use it 'round me, OK? Either we have an understandin' or we don't."

"Hey...it's fine with me" he says, holding the palms of his hands up in the air, "but I want to get back to the point. Regerrio has two prisoners who will testify that you and your brother were major drug-dealers within the prison. It's fairly certain they are going to get early parole dates in exchange for their testimony, and we can use that to discredit them, but there's more. He's also going to enter the issue of race, because his two witnesses are saying that most of your customers were black."

"First of all, I never sold any drugs in prison. Second, if my brother was sellin' drugs, the majority of the population is black, so it just makes sense they'd be the majority of his customers."

"A point I will introduce at trial. But I've read their statements, and they clearly state that your brother was a racist…'a hard core racist' was the words one of them used."

"A racist? He was sharing a cell with a black man!"

"A homosexual black man. His *kid*. Get it? One of the inma…*prisoners* testifying said that your brother got—…his name escapes me."

"Kenny."

"Yes—Kenny. This prisoner said that your brother got Kenny strung out on heroin and then used his addiction to coerce sexual favors from him for drugs, to dehumanize him."

"That's the craziest shit I've ever heard! My brother and Kenny were friends, close friends."

"Well, I've contacted Kenny, and he won't testify at your trial. He refuses to even talk with me, Reggerio or anyone else. That doesn't look good. Can you get him to testify for you?"

"No…Kenny and I really don't know each other. I'd just see him in passing. I was visitin' my brother that day, not Kenny."

"Well, he won't testify at trial. And, like I said, that won't look good."

"Shit…this is crazy."

"Race is a hot issue—it's going to make and break careers for a while. Regerrio wants to put you in the electric chair, and he's pulling every rabbit he can find out of that judicial hat to do just that, you understand? No jury, even an all-white one, would want to identify with what they perceive as a lunatic racist drug dealer, and that's how Regerrio is going to paint you. He knows he has to paint as vile a picture as he can if he's going to get the death penalty, and obviously that's what he wants. He's staking his career on it…or rather advancing it—the political everyman, covering all bases, and this case is his best shot at catapulting himself into serious contention as a political candidate. What's important for you to understand is that you are going to have to work with me on this, and you are going to have to tell me everything, from day one—how this all came about, what the extent of your involvement was, what you knew and didn't know about your brother's activities. It's the only chance we have of winning in court."

So here I was. The lawyer was right: my best shot was telling everything exactly as it happened, but no way in hell was I going to set Kenny up. A wave of uncertainty washed over me in that moment, but it brought calm, a deep calm, and without knowing the origin of the words I said "You know, I don't wanna participate in any of this."

"What?"

I look dead into his eyes in my calm: "I didn't do it, and I've lost all energy to fight it. I got nothin' to say to you or anyone. Let Regerrio do what he wants."

"That's crazy!"

"Crazy? No…It's exhaustion."

"Call it what you want, but the fact is I have to prepare a defense, and we can't waste time."

"You know, I've always seen public defenders as assistant prosecutors. Not 'cause they're out to help prosecutors win their cases, but because they're all in a buddy system, helping each other advance their careers. You know how many prisoners have copped guilty pleas to crimes they haven't committed because their public defenders told them it was in their best interest? And maybe it was in terms of getting off with a lighter sentence, but what kind of justice is that? The point is they have no passion or concern for the truth, unless the innocent one has no criminal background, as if innocence only applied to those who don't have a record."

"I won't argue with you about that. But whatever you think, I'm telling you—we have what is tantamount to unlimited funds for your case. Our office is going to pursue every angle to get you acquitted. Our top investigators are going to be involved. Whatever you believe about the past, it doesn't apply here. And that is the truth."

"Because it's a capital offense."

"If that's how you want to look at it. But the point is we are here to fight for you, and you would be crazy to turn it down."

"Well, call me crazy, 'cause that's what I'm doin'."

When I return to my cell I think it through. What defense do I have? I already admitted to the slayings. I was too hard on my lawyer, unfairly so, but I was just looking for a way out, to get away from him, to not say anything until I got it all clear in my own mind, decide how I was going to move.

No matter how I sliced and diced it and ran it through a blender, it kept coming out nasty. Regerrio was going to win. He was seizing his destiny because it was calling him with a loudspeaker. Couldn't fault him for that. He was looking at it as honestly as he could with all the information he had gathered. The more I thought about it the more I realized there just wasn't any way out. The only hope I had was on an appeal down the road where, with new evidence and the absence of witnesses, or even a miraculous chain of events, the situation would change, and all I could do now is not say anything, not to in any way give them anything in testimony that might interfere with a future defense, the only way of optimizing my options for painting a now unforeseen scenario for a future trial, and this would give me the time I needed to think it all through in greater detail and start developing a plan.

And there was something else. The prisoner I stabbed. In prison he went by the name Cyclops. He had a bulging eye and a drooping one related to some illness he had. He was a follower, going along for the ride because he was strung out and used to the protection of a group, not a sadistic bone in his body. He loved making fun of himself to make other prisoners laugh, them viewing him as a joker. And the image of him pleading for his life—it wouldn't leave my head. Throughout the day, every day, it kept intruding unannounced—his face with its agonizing plea for life looming large in my mind's eye in all its clarity. I kept trying to convince myself that he would have died regardless, but in my heart I knew I had killed him. Not only because I stabbed him. A decision not to help him was evidence enough. He had a wife and three children who would visit him regularly. There was hope, however distant. Now there was none, not for him, his wife and children. I deserved the death penalty because it was a cold-blooded murder. Even the horrible image of my brother's death would not assuage the guilt. Cyclops' face with its pitiful plea and convulsing body always carried the day. It would become my singular meditation, my no exit.

*********

My quietude becomes addictive. I have no energy to respond to anyone. Any urge to open my mouth and say something to anyone dissipates before a word can be formed by the muscles in my mouth. A few times I agree to see my lawyer when he visits, but it always ends the same way: I have nothing to say. Then one day he caps it for me:

"I've arranged to have you evaluated by a psychiatrist."

"No way!"

"Sorry—it has already been ordered by the court. If you refuse, the court will have no choice but to send you to the State Hospital for the evaluation. It's your choice."

"Fine! I'll see the idiot. But I don't want to see you or anyone else from your office again. Leave me the fuck alone! Got it?"

He says nothing, just stands up, takes his briefcase and calls to the guard outside, and when the guard opens the door he leaves without saying anything.

The interview with the psychiatrist lasts all of twenty minutes. When I enter the room he is seated at a desk and doesn't rise to greet me. He just motions with a fat stubby-fingered hand to the chair opposite him at the desk, and then mutters almost inaudibly: "Have a seat, please."

His obesity is unsettling *not* because of the massive flesh that appears to be suffocating him. It was the color and texture of his facial skin, hair-stubbled chalky clay with no pores, drool dripping from one corner of his mouth, occasionally wiping it away in slow motion with a handkerchief, his long greasy graying coarse but thinning black hair combed back away from the huge horn-rimmed glasses weighing heavily on his face. My first thought is that he must be taking the medication he would prescribe to violent prisoners.

"Tell me about your childhood" he mumbles with eyes half-closed, as if the words were struggling through all the fat around his neck and wearily rolling off his tongue. I had to make sure of one thing—avoid state hospital. That was my singular focus.

"Not much to tell. We were poor and I liked street life."

"What about reformatories?"

"You do the crime, you do the time."

"And what about the crime you are charged with now?"

"Self defense."

"You believe it was justified?" he asks, his eyelids raising and looking directly at me for the first time.

"Well…it was them or me. No other choice. If self preservation is a justification…then yeah, it was justified."

"You had heroin in your system after the murders."

"Do they test marines for drugs after they kill the enemy?"

"Do you see marines as criminals?"

"No. When they defend themselves and us they end up killin' the enemy. I tried to defend my brother and myself. I obviously failed on one count. It doesn't make me a murderer. I was visitin' my brother in his cell when three prisoners come in with knives and a pipe. My brother moved first to grab the pipe, and I knew in that instant we would die if I didn't stop them. It was knee-jerk—I didn't think about it. If I hesitated I would be dead, too. I just arrived at prison. I didn't know what my bother was involved with. He turned me onto some heroin. That's all. Does that make me a murderer?"

It went on like this. He never asked any of the questions I thought he would ask, the psychobabble, the Freudian shit. Just mundane questions anyone would ask.

A week later I agreed to see my lawyer to find out about the psych report to see if there is any advantage in it. My lawyer's upset. He has the psychiatrist's report with him.

"This guy's nuts," he says. "I don't believe what he's written here. Listen to this: 'Although Mr. Jones is perfectly capable of standing trial, having no mental incapacitation, it is clear that he is not capable of emotionally distinguishing between the inside and outside of institutional environments. This makes him particularly dangerous because there is little, if anything, that could deter him from committing crimes.' Do you believe this nut case?"

The clarity and precision of what the psych wrote surprised and impressed me.

"Actually," I said, "he has a point. It never occurred to me, but it rings true."

"What?"

"I don't suffer any more in prison than I do on the outside. Actually, I suffer more on the outside. Once I start doin' time and get used to it, the boredom more than anythin' gets to me, not the sufferin'."

"That sounds like a disturbed mind to me."

"Forget it—there's no way I'm coppin' an incapacitation plea. Don't even think about it. I'm not goin' to any nut house. And this psych report clinches it. I'm *not* incapacitated! Got it? And you can't do nothin' 'bout it."

"We still got to talk about going to trial."

"No we don't," and I look to the guard standing outside the metal room. "Guard!...I'm ready!"

"Before you go. I heard from your mother. She called my office from California. She wants to come out."

"Forget it! I don't want her here…You make sure she understands that. Tell her I won't take visits, not from anyone. I'm doing this on my own."

(Here I was facing the death penalty. Mom—spiraling in her agony over Tommy's death and my being charged with triple homicide—couldn't bring herself to write or visit, but now she was considering it, grasping at straws, but I couldn't allow it. She would just look at me through the glass, unable to speak, her face and neck muscles twisting in an effort to stifle her moans, tears pouring from her eyes. This always happened on those rare occasions she dragged herself down to visit me in jail, and how I had been adamant in telling her I would refuse all visits in the future; it was always a torture program for both of us and made absolutely no sense. After those visits I would think only of returning to my cell to cut my throat. Sarah, who had originally talked mom into moving to California to get away from her environment and the bad memories associated with it, only ended in mom isolating herself in her grief, continually ripping her mind apart, evaluating every step of where she might have gone wrong. I knew she was seeing it as herself having failed. It wasn't possible that *The One*, the child whose life she saved for great things, the one she had put all her faith in because my daily dying had forced her to attend to my every need those first six years of my life, had failed her with such finality, destroying her only remaining refuge from the real world, the notion that she had been a good mother to at least one of her children.)

"Is that fair to your mother?"

"Fair? What the fuck you talkin' about? I'm facin' the death penalty. Got it? Ain't nobody goin' to that chair but me. This is my time—no one else's, not even my mother's. I decide from now on—*no one else*. And I'm tellin' ya—don't let my mother come out here. Don't be a piece of shit. It's on you!"

"She's just worried about you."

"She's better off worryin' in California—she'll do less of it. What's she gonna do here, hunh? Get a job and come down to cry every day? I don't want it. I'm tellin' you! She'll listen to you. She would've been here by now if she really believed it would help. She knows there's nothin' she can do, but she can't accept that, and it'll really piss me off if you encourage her, ya understand? You wanna torture her by makin' her close to everythin' goin' on? Every fuckin' second of every fuckin' day?"

The guard is inside the cell: "You called to leave."

"Yeah...I gotta go, man."

"Look...if you want another attorney I can start the process today."

"It's not like that. You're all the same to me. I just don't have the energy to help you guys. I need rest. It's like I got all this time and no time to rest. I just wanna be left alone."

Walking out with the guard I turn and look at the lawyer: "It's not personal."

When I return to my cell I write a letter to my mom, pleading with her not to come out, that I just couldn't handle it if she did, that this was something I had to do on my own. I explained I had put in a request for no visitors and I would stick to it. Her traveling out here would be a waste of time. I told her I would write as soon as I got it all resolved, that I got it all figured out and that if she came out it would mess up my plan.

Chapter 14


I lost all interest in my case. The light at the end of the tunnel looked more and more like Freddy Kruger with a flashlight. The only real hope would be to tell the truth, but I couldn't involve Kenny. I wrote a letter to my lawyer and told him I felt like I was being railroaded and couldn't trust anyone, not even the public defenders, any of them. I wasn't going to talk to him or anyone else from now on

I passed time mostly playing pinnacle. My partner Buddy was a former musician with a band that had one hit song, doing 6 months for marijuana possession. He resided in an inner-calm, constantly twirling in easy motions the corners of his thick handlebar mustache as we played on hour after hour, day after day.

One evening during lock-up Buddy hands me a book by Jess Stern on yoga, *Yoga, Youth and Reincarnation*, explaining that he did some of the exercises at night in his cell and it helped him a lot: "You might want to try it out. It works for me. Anyway, it's a fast read."

That night in my cell I read most of the book and like the idea that there are about 40 positions that Stern claims can produce great benefits. I decide to give it a try, but not at night like Buddy. I start doing them during the day in my cell. And then I take Stern's recommendation on Kundalini yoga, and I begin doing radical meditation exercises, sometimes for hours in a clip after finishing the physical postures. It was easy for me. I slipped right into it because it was not unlike the contemplation that came natural to me in church before starting school every morning. Then as now I could stay motionless, thoughts passing me by, off on their own journey separate from consciousness, not connecting in any way with my concern centers. It became an addiction early on, having no desire to leave a state of cool indifference to everything around me. One day I had the thought that it made perfect sense that audiences in the Village listening to jazz in cafes in the '50s would applaud by snapping their fingers lightly—to clap would be way too much involvement for an Age of Cool.

Buddy ended up getting another pinnacle partner. He was right: it was changing me in many ways. I severed from the workings of my trial. It was something happening way over there, too distant to take any interest in. I was more and more living a relaxation response, letting go of all my attachments. I didn't have a single care—I was absorbed in the calming effect. But it in no way was a radical separation from my immediate physical environment, what was concrete for me in any given second, for in every second I was experiencing the perfect rhythm of every sound and motion. I recall thinking *Of course, wherever I am in any given second is exactly where I'm supposed to be, so there is no reason to be anxious.* Where I was traveling interiorly was in perfect sync with the flux of the exterior world, like we were all subconsciously participating in this great jazz ensemble, joyfully improvising in perfect harmony in every second, and this was way better than any drug experience I had ever had, and the problem of the "why" of drug use no longer needed an answer: it was just another silly choice from a smorgasbord of distractions that beat back the music playing for us all the time.

Stern's book made it simple: basic yoga breathing techniques while sitting in a full lotus, something that was easy for me because of my years of practicing contortionism. Then I would concentrate on gradually directing Kundalini energy up through and stimulating the 7 Chakras. In the beginning, no matter how long I meditated, I couldn't get past the third eye (6th Chakra) where I would concentrate all my energy on maintaining an image of a cloud, and this in a short

217

time began to detach me from the ravages of my rowdy, uncontainable thoughts about anything. Eventually I do tap into the 7th Chakra, the illuminative realm just above my head where the *willed* (effort-driven) concentration on the cloud, my meditation image, was dispensed with, leaving me alone with my cloud, void of all willfulness other than a near-effortless focus on the cloud, a place where time and space lost its hold on me.

It went on like this for about a month, and then one day while meditating the cloud disappeared. I was left in a state of having in my mind no thought or image, no dark, no light, no gray, no anything, and it shocked the shit out of me! It was the shock of experiencing awareness independent of any thought or image, something impossible to explain or experience in the imagination.

(About a year later I was devouring as much philosophy as I could get my hands on, and I was struck by the words of Rene Descartes: "I concluded that I was a thing or substance whose whole essence or nature was only to think, and which, to exist has no need of space nor any material thing or body." This "father of modern philosophy" had single-handedly ripped human existence from its physical and metaphysical moorings, its true home; now what one *thinks* becomes the grand Idol of a new philosophical age, a fully actualized idolatry of self, and it demands an ongoing sacrifice of everything in the physical/metaphysical realm that had in stages served for millennia to illumine our unfathomable essence that exists prior to and independent of any thought or image, and what every molecule of life with or without thought groans toward, easily witnessed in how life *grows*, its destiny configured in the most deeply rooted desire, beyond any thought, to be wholly what it is. Thoughts remain abstract, limited and ephemeral, and as idol, reductionist; they can exist as a positive force solely to serve man, to help guide him to his essence, and in poetic power alchemically conjure what cannot be put in words or grasped

218

with any thought, but only experienced in one's heart. To make thoughts our god makes all the meanings they manufacture equally ephemeral and thereby farcical, and why we no longer laugh at ourselves in recognition of the foibles of our falleness, but in self-contempt, for we can never measure up to our notion of being gods unto ourselves in our thoughts, and why we sense it is best to do away with ourselves. Words at best can guide us to meaning or tear down a false edifice of meaning, but they can never be meaning itself, and why wisdom is always a knowing beyond what we can know with words alone. What Descartes ecstatically creates is a Babel revisited, using new and improved mortar and brick to construct an idol-edifice that can like never before dazzle, amaze and amuse, and we name this god: Reason—Reason liberated from essence in *man's* image and likeness, his thoughts. But like everything man absent essence constructs, it at some point either crumbles to dust or in frenzy dances the red death of chaos into Nothingness. And because of my Kundalini experience, I knew all this before I ever thought about it.)

Many other things occurred during my Kundalini days in the county jail:

Buddy loved to gamble. This more than anything was what motivated him to do yoga. The more relaxed one is, the more one is able to concentrate on the dynamics of winning, including avoiding tells (physical clues to how good or bad an opponent's hand is). And we *were* the reigning champs of pinnacle on our tier. We were also able to communicate beyond skill and imagination, perfectly aligned in the gestalt of how each of us played the game: it was a connection we made as fast friends, and it was just another, perhaps the most important, dimension in winning at double-deck pinnacle against accomplished opponents. And on a particular day Buddy is telling me about a football game he is betting on, and an hour later in my cell meditating a scoreboard appears in my mind's eye that has the underdog winning the game by 12 points. I tell Buddy, and the first thing he says is "You wanna bet? I'll give you ten to one odds."

"Buddy, you know I don't gamble. I'm just tellin' you it's what I saw. I don't wantcha to lose a bunch of cigarettes."

"I ain't gonna lose. So put up or shut up."

And when his team loses by 12 points he starts to interrogate me, wanting to know about another game coming up.

"It don't work like that, man. There's this letting go. You don't even think about it. In fact, you can't even let go because that would be a part of not letting go. I don't know how to explain it. When you're not in the fray, you see it, but when you're in it you'll never see it. You can't control or manipulate it 'cause that kills it."

"You're talkin' crazy. Just do the thing you do and see what comes up."

"That's just it—I can't do it 'cause it's not about doin' anythin'."

"Fine—you don't wanna help, that's your thing."

"I'll tell you what…if I get any visions about football scores, I'll let you know right away. That's all I can do."

"That's all I'm askin', man. Shit!"

Of course, nothing happened.

Another time a young prisoner is assigned to our wing right at lock-up. He introduces himself and I shake his hand. And when I go into my cell, lie down and close my eyes, I see him clear as day running along a fence and into the woods.

The next morning at breakfast I tell him what I saw, and he looks at me startled. "I got busted for shoplifting. I ran out of the store and the manager chased me forever, and I ran along a

220

fence next to a football field and out into the woods. I tried to hide after I got exhausted, but the police found me."

But the most amazing occurrence happened after I was into the Kundalini for about 3 months. One day Buddy says "You're way too caught up in the yoga thing. It's not healthy, man. You're gettin' way too self-absorbed."

"That ain't it, Buddy. I'm more in touch with everythin' around me than ever before."

"Naw—you just don't see it. There's nothin' healthy 'bout isolation, man, and that's what you're doin'—isolatin'. I can't remember the last time you played pinnacle. You don't even read books. At least books have somethin' to do with other people."

"It doesn't intrest me."

"What—you think you can't get anythin' from books?"

"I'm not sayin' that…if you got one you think would intrest me—"

"Sure. I'll be right back."

Buddy goes to his cell. He has a stack of books. When he's not playing pinnacle he's almost always reading. He comes back with a book:

"This might intrest you" he says, handing me a copy of Shakespeare's *Macbeth*.

"Yeah—I'll check it out. Thanks."

That night I sit on my cot and open the book. I begin reading the first lines of the opening scene, a conversation between three witches:

First Witch:


"When shall we three meet again?

In thunder, lightning or in rain?"


Second Witch:


"When the hurlyburly's done,

When the battle's lost and won."


Third Witch:


"That will be ere the set of sun."


And while reading these words little bits of white light begin creeping out from behind the letters and start dancing around the words till all the words of the entire play are on fire with this light. There is no effort in reading it. I go straight through to the end, the thought of time never entering my mind, like I had read the play in less than a second.

The next day I return the book to Buddy saying "That's the best book I've ever read. Everythin' I need to know was in there. I won't have to ever read another book."

"You ain't serious?"

"Yeah."

I can't remember what made me decide to stop doing the Kundalini. Maybe it wasn't a decision at all. I one day found myself playing pinnacle again. I kind of floated back into where I was before, but I still had a calm connection to everything around me in an abiding detachment, meaning I was connected without being pulled into anything—I just floated freely; and I still did the yoga, but not to get anywhere, not to seek enlightenment or anything else. Maybe it was just letting go of letting go.

Another important event occurs after another prisoner casually mentions during a pinnacle game while he is arranging his cards, "Ya know, if you die in a dream, you'll die in real life." This thought drifted into my consciousness and hung around, but it didn't send me off in any deliberate reflection—I just sensed a subtle shift in consciousness with no meaning attached to it. Thoughts for me now floated in and floated out, but this one hung around. This was in tune with what occurs next: some prisoners start to argue about the statement being true or false. Although I am taking it all in, or rather the discussion is passing through me with some interest, I have no desire to comment. When I return to my cell at lock-up and lay back on my cot, the thought of dying in my sleep if I dream my death still clings to consciousness as I drift into sleep.

While sleeping I dream I fall off a cliff and begin a furious descent, about a 3-mile drop, and when I hit bottom I crash hard into the ground, every bone in my body breaking and my skull crushed, and my spirit is ejected from my body at great speed, at least a thousand times faster than the speed of light, straight out into space. I pass many galaxies before entering a zone void of anything. Then it hits me: "I don't want to die", and in that second my spirit instantly without resistance (no slowing down or speeding up) reverses course and begins its equally fast trajectory back to my body, and when I crash into my body, it is more painful than when I had

223

first crashed into the ground. I wake up and my body aches all over, as if all my bones are broken.

I can authoritatively state to the prisoners the next day that a person doesn't die in his sleep if he dies in a dream. But there was another surprise waiting for me:

About a week later I have a dream I am being executed by a firing squad. And when the six guns are fired and the bullets pound into my heart, I die in a flash of light. And when I open my eyes it is obvious that the tier guard had just turned on the main overhead lights.

But it didn't stop there. I am executed in dream after dream, week after week, with all the historical methods of execution I had known. And the last one is the most elaborate:

I am in an antechamber waiting on electrocution. Everything is vivid down to the minutest detail. Two guards walk up to my cell and open it:

"It's time, Jones."

I get up and walk outside the cell. They escort me down a long hall where we arrive at a solid metal door with a hole and metal sliding cover-latch. One of the guards slides the latch open and looks in, and then bangs on the door with a big key. He shakes his head yes to the other guard. The door opens and we walk in. I look to my right, and at the far end of the room up against the wall are three prisoners in three electric chairs, all strapped in and ready to go. One of the guards looks at me and says, "It's the busiest night we've ever had for executions. You're going to have to stand on that plate over there with four others," and he looks over against the other far wall where there is a long metal plate about three inches thick, two feet wide and ten feet long hovering an inch from the floor.

The four other prisoners had been led barefooted up on to the metal plate, and then a guard tells me to take my shoes and socks off and roll up my pants and get up on the plate. I do as he asks, and standing there my legs begin to shake. I worry that someone might see it—I don't want anyone to think I went out on a cowardly note, but I can't stop my legs from shaking. And then a sense that I might pass out—that would be the ultimate humiliation. I wanted them to hurry and pull the switch to prevent that. And that's what they do, and when the electricity gushes up from my feet to my brain, I go unconscious, and then wake up.

Buddy says "Your mind is preparing for what it perceives as the inevitable. It's a biochemical thing. Your mind's adaptin', that's all. The mind doesn't like to be surprised if possible; but the thing is it's not inevitable."

"No?"

"Come on, man. Even if they convict you, you can go on forever with appeals. I don't see them making this stick, not ultimately. It's self-defense. I just don't see a jury wantin' to fry you for that. No way, man."

That must have been the way the head prosecutor felt, because a week later I am offered a deal: life in prison on each count to run concurrent, which meant it would be the same as one life sentence and I would be eligible for parole in 14 years. If I got my act together, I would be no more than forty when I got out, a young forty because I would be exercising regularly and not boozing and drugging. Anyway, I needed that much time to figure out what the hell was going on with me, and perhaps eventually make a real life for myself. I experience joy with the thought of pursuing my ongoing investigations and my conversations with my author-friends. It was like they could help me devise a plan that would actually work when I was eventually released, and this would take time. They were persons I could trust, whereas authorities involved in the prison system had no vested interest in helping me stay out of prison. That for them would be counter-intuitive at the deepest, subconscious level, for it would undermine their job security

225

Chapter 15

The judge on the day of sentencing asks me if I have anything to say before he sentences me. I look at my lawyer who is standing at my side, and he nods to go ahead and say something. I had told him before going into the courtroom that I had nothing to say. He insisted: "It's important that you say something. Talk about your childhood, how you were a street kid and got caught up in drug addiction, that your life spiraled out of control, and then this terrible thing happened."

But now standing in front of the judge, him sitting tall in his saddle with broad shoulders in his black gown, looking down inside my soul over his reading glasses, I figure, what's the point? I'm getting a life sentence. If I don't say anything I won't say anything stupid. That's how I look at it.

"No, your honor."

"How about you, Mr. Waters? Would you like to address the court?"

My lawyer looks at me and then back at the judge: "Yes, your honor."

And then he goes on with a litany of sad situations I had grown up in and how I had never really had a life. He tells the judge that I wouldn't allow any family members to visit because I didn't want to put them through an ordeal, that I was just a kid who got lost in the shuffle, and he concluded with the words "My client is just as much a victim as the persons he killed, your honor. It could be them standing here facing sentencing today with my client dead. His reaction was solely self-defense. What else could he have done?"

It was the weirdest thing: while my lawyer is talking about my childhood, especially him telling the judge I wouldn't accept visits, I am afflicted with rumblings in my intestines and tears pound at the back of my eyes. I'm feeling sorry for myself! I had to fight real hard to hold back the tears. That would have been too humiliating. My lawyer is just participating in protocol. Everything is already carved in stone. He's just being true to a matrix he's invested in, keeping things moving as they are meant to move. And all I want is to get my sentence and get the hell out of there.

The judge is silent for a moment after my lawyer finishes speaking, then:

"Anyone else here today who would like to speak?"

And the prosecutor (not Regerrio—he had refused to accept my plea) says, "Yes, your honor. There are six family members of the deceased who would like to address the court."

"That will be fine. Please bring them forward one at a time. Mr. Jones—you and your attorney have a seat."

And the litany of pain and sorrow goes on for more than an hour. I *do* deserve to die. I know that when I listen to the tearful animosity from Cyclops' wife when she discovers I am not going to die for her husband's death: "My husband didn't deserve to die. I don't care what Sam Jones says—my husband was incapable of hurting anyone. He's never hurt anyone in his life! And his two daughters keep asking me why we aren't visiting daddy. How can I tell them—how can they understand it? It wouldn't be real to them. All they know now is that they don't get to see their daddy. I just can't bring myself to tell them they never will see him again." Tears start steaming down her face. "He loved them so much, your honor. Sure, he had a drug problem. But even that never got in the way of him playing with his children. He had the most beautiful laugh, and when he laughed his daughters laughed. They imitated his laugh because they loved the

227

sound of it, and when they imitated it they laughed even louder. That's how close they were. That's how he was—he made people laugh, even during bad times. And now he's gone. And he's not coming back, your honor. What am I supposed to do?" And she begins sobbing uncontrollably.

The judge orders a recess, and when we are all back in the courtroom he orders me to stand, and he begins to read the sentence:

"Mr. Jones, I doubt you are even capable of taking seriously what you have pleaded guilty to simply because you have nothing to say to the court. I happen to agree with Mr. Regerrio's original assessment that the time has come to end the cyclical violence that results in so many needless deaths in prisons. As you witnessed here today, the persons you killed are persons with families, families that will know no end to their suffering. But according to all the reports I received, you are not fazed by any of this. And I don't buy your explanation that you were simply defending yourself. You don't have to stab a person 17 times to defend yourself, especially after the first two blows to the stomach and neck. It was more like you going the distance in making sure Mr. Williams would die. And I'm particularly concerned with Dr. Kesselhurst's report, that you are not capable of being deterred from committing crimes. A message needs to be sent that society will no longer permit this brutal behavior. Either life is sacred or it is not. The death penalty would have been appropriate in this situation. Four persons died as a result of ongoing violent drug transactions. And you were at the heart of that activity. Your own brother's death could have been avoided if you had decided to remain within the boundaries of lawful conduct. You chose to enter that world and now you stand before this court with a nonchalant attitude, not once expressing any remorse for what you have done. Your actions not only resulted in the death of three inmates—you have engendered ongoing suffering in the lives of their family members. The testimony you heard from close relatives in court today is but a fraction of the ongoing rippling effects of your bloody actions.

"I don't have any choice in this matter: For the death of Michael Williams, the court hereby sentences you to life in prison. For the death of Howard Blake, the court sentences you to life in prison, to run consecutive. And for the death of Ronald Gibbs, you are sentenced to life in prison, to run consecutive. That will make you eligible for parole in 45 years. And if I were you, I would consider that a reprieve from a deserved death sentence."

"That is the sentence of this court," and down comes his hammer. He turns to the bailiff and says, "Remove the prisoner from the courtroom."

I can hear women sobbing as two guards come up to me and place handcuffs on my wrists. I am not stunned by the sentence. I even at one level agree with it. But I am angry about the betrayal, them going back on the sentence agreed to.

\*\*\*\*\*\*\*\*\*

Back at prison I am brought before Court Line, Captain Shields once again sitting between two other guards. I'm actually glad to see him: an honest man is always a breath of fresh air:

"This is the last you'll see of me, Jones. I'm taking an early retirement. Looks like the Nanny State now wants to camp out here. I don't like crooked guards, but pretentious fools in suits I like even less. I'm sorry you didn't take my advice. And I'm sorry about your brother. I don't agree with the sentence, but it's just the beginning of a new day.

"I'm going to have to cool your heels for a while, put you in indefinite lock-up."

229

"But Captain—"

"I know. It was self-defense. I don't disagree. But I can't risk more violence. And it's actually in your best interest that you go to lock up, even if you don't see it. My men will find out if anyone is out to get you, and they will make sure they're transferred to another prison. It's just going to take time. You got close to forever in here. It's best you learn how to take it easy. 'Walk slow and drink lots of water.' That's what the old-timers say. You didn't take my advice when you first got here. Maybe you're more open to it now. With your sentence, you can't afford to get involved in any more violence. If you do, you'll be looking at a lot of years in lock up. You're a lifer now. Figure out a way to settle in.

"Indefinite lock-up."


My lock-up time turns into 26 months. It actually does turn out to be in my best interest. The lock-up section of the prison isn't as severe as the hole. I can have books and I get paid a stipend making braille bingo cards, enough to buy cigarettes and extra food from the commissary. I easily get back into yoga: I can lift the bed on hinges in my 5' x 7' cell up against the wall, and that gives me the space I need to do my posturings on the floor, this time doing little meditation; instead concentrating on building up my strength and flexibility—hand-stand push-ups my favorite. They allow us one hour of exercise each day in a small cement court yard. Two prisoners at a time. I spend most of that time playing handball off one of the cement walls. Can't waste time talking when you only get an hour to move around.

I devote my cell time mostly to improving my writing skills while exploring philosophy and psychology. When I come across a word I don't know, I look it up in a dictionary, and then write out the definition along with the sentence I found it in and then construct a sentence of my own within a one-paragraph essay or story. When a page is filled, I stick it to the wall with jelly I save from my breakfasts, and then go over it for as long as it takes to firmly plant the word in my mind. The dictionary itself becomes an adventure because many words in an author's text require seeking out other words to help grasp the writer's sometimes subtly nuanced sense of the word. It is these artists who convince me that words are alive only in an engagement with the world they have come to know in an activity of mind disciplined to stay as close as it can to a deeply personal approach, from where one resides uniquely in the world, the only realm where one can access truth, what make events breathe, a vertical as distinguished from horizontal writing, exemplified in the writings of Flannery O'Connor, a radical non-conformist who refused to parrot the ideas of any other for self-aggrandizement or acceptance on any level, but instead to write from where she resided uniquely, in the deep South; in fact, this is the greatest power of the imagination, making events, however close or distant, real by having it rhythmically coalesce with one's deeply interior experiences, not what has been dictated by any consensus at dinner parties or in academic certainties, what made Fitzgerald the greatest American novelist, traveling inside our culture the greatest distance via the excruciating depth of his own honestly perceived experiences, knowing too well that he was a product of an American ideal that was crumbling fast in his generation. Unlike the horizontal artists of his generation who were devastated by the reality of WWI, an epic awareness, Fitzgerald chose the only place he knew with the authority of a true artist, inside the American Dream.

My reflections began to return to what I had once known but had learned to forget in survival adaptations. A friend in prison, a self-made historian, once said that the best way to get to know another culture is to go to war with its people. In that confrontation and its aftermath what is real appears out of the dust of bombs exploding and bodies bleeding, convulsing and

231

writing in pain, or simply ripped asunder, lifeless limbs scattered amidst the rubble of gutted buildings and devastated landscapes, all our prior abstract considerations of what constitute the lives of these alien others to justify their extinction equally destroyed, for in their bloody cries and whispers or in their lifeless bodies one can hear the wailing of parents, wives, husbands, grandparents and children whose only interest is a return to the daily routines that had brought them together in love. "In boot camp," my friend said, "a soldier learns to diminish the other to a reprehensible thing with a dignity never to surpass that of a cockroach, but in battle that other returns to his true nature, even if only as a ghost."

Freud helped me most in the beginning, what Tommy at one point in our discussions about books insisted I had to learn: "It's best to wrestle with what Freud revealed till the end of time, especially how we assign roles to those we meet as tools to work out our dilemmas in a cyclical pit we only burrow that much deeper into, and when we eventually dig our way out to the light of day, we're back where we started. Look at Woody Allen. All that time and money in therapy just to find out he never had any incentive to get the hell away from where he was actually standin'. And Allen Ginsberg readin' a poem to college students about his only real fear in life is his asshole being stretched so far he could no longer experience the pleasure of someone's dick plunging into his ass, and William Burroughs steppin' up and readin' 'bout one of his sexually learned alien characters strippin' and sexually molestin' a child inside out until the child learns to love it, liberatin' the child into full sexual expression. And the students stay suspended in awe...And there it is: all one can do in the end is pack up and go home with Freud's pleasure/reality dichotomy, what puts all of us under suspicion in a world of the big grab, constantly slapped back into the awareness that pleasure = the absence of pain, and who the

232

hell wants to be in pain? And no pleasure's ever enough! The laughable irony is that so much of what he got right is being kicked to the gutter while his flawed imaginings on infantile sexuality, children sexually lustin' after their parents and other adults, are being revived to justify turning kids into sex objects. And they call me a criminal? The slithering perverts, like the ones they lock up on E-Wing, are now college professors and respected philosophers—look at Foucault who can't stop droolin' when lookin' at children! You gotta laugh, man. It's a circus out there, and every one of them vanguards is a clown. A scary clown!"

It was here that I first thought about *the hell of reciprocity*. I mean, if we are seeking pleasure to knock out pain (from every origin), and if this is our prime motivation, why would we allow anyone to get in the way? I mean, doesn't this formula imply that we are all libertines at heart, what, through an imposed faulty, controlling moral fabric we become irrationally convinced we must suffocate? Sure, we can through negotiation strive for the "reasonable" libertine ideal Bob Seeger sings about ("I used her, and she used me/but neither one cared/we were getting our share/working on the night moves"), but there simply is no escaping the feeling we are being slighted at some level, which inevitably moves us into the resentment that Kierkegaard, Nietzsche and Dostoevsky said would poison the 20th century and beyond. It makes sense that Freud was strung out on cocaine while exploring the pleasure principle. On cocaine even conscience, the center of all our psychic pain, gets annihilated by pleasure. Of course we would crush the life out of Jiminy Cricket to liberate ourselves from this suffering!

I knew a woman who took Freud's flawed Oedipus Complex seriously to justify her own ends (we now know from Rene Girard that this complex involves mimetics, not sexual desire). Her name was Cindy, but she liked to be called Cat. She went through three abusive relationships with drug dealers, and then set out on her own dealing heroin and cocaine (how I got to know her). A potent model of sexual liberation and how anyone can become a vanguard, she had 3 children. For her there would be no negotiations inside a phony reciprocal arrangement—what would for her be tantamount to compromise, what she declared anathema in the adventure of true liberation. Everything would now be on her terms. Her 13-year-old son, Jeremy, was her main carrier, and she would pay him well, mostly in cocaine, which no doubt helped to keep him in bed with her at night to satisfy her sexual longings, but his sexual penchant was for his 8-year-old brother.

I am at her apartment one morning, nodding out on some excellent heroin on her living room couch. She had just taken a shower and is walking around with a short silk robe tied together with nothing on underneath. She has the music on loud, and she begins to dance in front of me. I look up, barely able to keep my eyes open. Her hands are pressed tight into her swirling hips as she moves to the music, quickly jutting her head back and forth to keep her long strands of silky brown hair moving in space. She rolls her tongue across her upper lip slowly and then smiles at me. I am transfixed in my heroin high, but I can't take my shocked eyes off her. And then it happens: she moves forward and plops herself down on my thighs, her legs spread far apart, then undoing the sash of her robe. She is grinding away on my lap making deep breathing sounds as she looks up at the ceiling, and she then moves forward, grabbing the hair at the back of my head and rubbing her breasts in my face, then moving backward and looking at me intently, and then stops moving. She quickly gets up and angrily ties her robe back together.

She looks at me sternly and says "You could've told me you're gay."

"I'm not gay."

"Oh, you're gay! You think I give a shit? To each his own. You suck pussy or dick—who gives a shit?" And she walks away.

I don't argue with her—never do, about anything. It makes life easier. She is my main connection, and she lets me hang out at her apartment.


After a year in lock up, I was contacted by a young Indian psychologist, Kaushal Naidu. He was 4'10" high, brown skin with a frizzled, close to foot-high Afro hair style combed slightly backwards, as if he were moving at lightning speed to get the hell away from where he was standing. He had told me that he was interning and that he had practiced psychotherapy in India and England, and that since arriving in America he had developed an interest in criminology, especially the young criminal mind. The reason he chose me along with nine other prisoners was that I was one of the youngest prisoners and I had never received any counseling in my life. If I liked he would see me an hour each week. I agreed—not to get out of my cell as many other prisoners do, but because I was really interested in him helping me explore my mind.

At one of our sessions I ask if I might be sexually repressed.

"What do you mean?"

"I've never had sex. I had opportunities, but I passed on all of them."

"Explain."

"Well…for example, I had a friend when I was 14—he hooked me up with this girl. It was a double date. Their parents would be out late. It was clear that we were going there to have sex, and my friend and his girl ended up in the bedroom pretty quickly. I stayed in the living room talking with my girl. She was real pretty, and she was nervous like me, and we just talked. I was not one for conversation in those days, and she did most of the talking. And the more we

235

talked the more aware I became that we were not going to have sex, even though her smile, low-cut blouse and perfume were intoxicating. And on another occasion, I lived in this house with an old alcoholic woman, and this girl came by asking for a place to stay. She was a runaway. I told her 'sure', and the next day she came onto me sexually and I didn't respond."

"Why not?"

"When I looked in her eyes I saw fear, and it was like the fear was coming from every opening in her body, some dark abyss. I could actually see into that abyss in the pores of her skin."

"I see. But that doesn't sound like sexual repression. It sounds like an existential dilemma. You had this hyper-sensitivity towards girls who had overwhelming problems in their lives, problems most likely having their origin in some type of trauma, and you didn't want to make it any worse—you didn't want to use someone who had been used up. Whatever balance that girl had in life was fragile, and you didn't want to be the one to give her that last push off a cliff. Where I come from that is considered noble. And besides, before meeting with you I went through your file, and in the many psychological examinations you have taken through the years there is no sign of sexual repression. I suspect there is none with any of your siblings, either. There just weren't any causative factors in your environment for sexual repression. Just the opposite I would surmise".

This was a major revelation for me. I had to find out if it was true. I reasoned that if I had no sexual repression, then I could not only pursue any sexual interest, but even sex that I had no interest in. I had to find out.

It was easy to get hold of porn books. Even in lock up. And in every sexual encounter within a given book, especially the ones I didn't identify with, and most especially the ones I found repulsive, I would, via my imagination, put myself in the situation and tear down every resistance to the point where I could masturbate and in orgasm claim the perversion as mine, which, in essence, was an affirmation of free will over conscience, biology and every external force that would in any fashion trap me in a pre-determined mode of sexual activity in the world. I viewed this dynamic as an enhancement of free will by a broadening exercise of same, providing more space for it to operate consciously. This activity would not be determined by anything other than will. In Sade's *120 Days of Sodom*, for example, there is a scene where a young man, a sophisticate, walks into a room that is empty except for a small dining table, and there is a toothless old woman who dines with him at that table. At the end of their meal, he gives the old woman a vile to drink from, and after she takes a sip and swallows it, he, too, takes a sip and swallows. They stand up and embrace. He puts his mouth on hers, and there is rumbling in their stomachs, and then the woman starts projectile vomiting, the man swallowing in big gulps her hot vomit into his stomach, and then him vomiting back into her mouth, her taking his vomit down, and it goes on like this, back and forth, until the man reaches orgasm.

There was a young, handsome and buff prisoner who was being visited by a woman in her 70s, a renowned psychiatrist, and as a doctor she was allowed to visit the prisoner in a closed consultation room. It was rumored that they were having sex, and that she was going to get him released in exchange for his amorous affections. I had always looked at her in amazement. Her wrinkled face with thin jutting jaw and sunken thin lips gave the impression that she had no teeth. No way, I thought, could I have sex with her, even to get a parole! So she obviously became the object of my quest in the Sadean scene with the elderly woman. And I found that place inside. And when I found that place and entered it, I knew any sexual place could be accessed. This is when I coined the word "omnisexual", displacing the obviously reductive sexual-identity signifiers "heterosexual", "homosexual", "bisexual", "transgender", "onanist",

"fetishist", "sadomasochist" and the others used to obstruct a person from moving freely in a

world of uninhibited sex, slamming the door shut on any possibility of exploring and discovering

in physiological and psychological truth the sexual mores of others that reveal how an aspect of

self rebels against and conquers its gestalt and brings it under its reign as an act of the will, a

solipsistic imperialism of the body, similar to cancer cells, taking on a life of their own, a

determined opposition to the gestalt, its defiance having no concern with how the gestalt of self

is deprived of its harmonious interconnectedness; indeed, interiorly, in the heart of rebellion, it

exults in disrupting the self with sadomasochistic delight (why, for example, in pure Gnosticism

a willed sexual rebellion against the entirety of the body becomes a heightened religious practice,

represented by the image of a snake consuming itself starting at its tail), for the rebellion of an

aspect as agent of the will conquering the gestalt of the body is always in essence a consolidation

of the body as pure will in rebellion against the tyranny of nature, a rebellion that resides in the

futility of nature itself! (will defying the natural mechanism of reason that wills harmony), a

futility that entered the universe at the Fall, the body thereby becoming a total rebellion against

life itself, *the highest expression of the will to power*, and taking on a sexual identity becomes a

means of "normalizing" (masking) this rebellion against how we are biologically constructed

and purposed in nature, and this masking secretly fosters guilt which moves the person more

deeply into denial, denying the power of the will that sets him apart and elevates him in his

rebellion, and precisely why this raw, immediate and direct rebellion is filtered into a superficial,

surface rebellion, in politics or in the courts, which only sidesteps the praxis, the guts of rebellion

as an assault on conscience, for a rebellion against the biological determinism of nature that

exists in nature itself is always a rebellion against conscience, the spiritual domain of the body,

refusing to be subjected like slaves to the guilt that is the wrath of that spirit. In Rainer Werner
Fassbinder's masterpiece, *In a Year With Thirteen Moons*, an existentially ravaged savant, Soul
Frieda, states, "What in expressive terms I regard as my body…is in fact my will. Or, my body is
the objectivization of my will. Or, apart from it being a concept of my imagination, my body is
merely my will." A sexual identity, after all, is no identity at all, but simply a role one takes on to
gratify sexual urges, mostly an advertisement, a way of saying "Here I am!", regardless how
elaborate the role is constructed and reinforced for ever-easier access to gratification of sexual
desire, a process Proust came to understand better than anyone, finally knowing it as a way of
life in slavery to desire in all its manifestations, not just sexual. If a person in sexual rebellion
against nature transmutes a sexual role into an identity, the rebellion is diminished in coagulating
with the praxis of denying guilt and he will lose sight of his will's commitment that resides in
rebellion, for there can no longer be the free-flow of the blood of his rebellion, most especially a
rebellion unto death, its purest form, for in rebellion, even if battered and barely alive in a trench
of warfare, he would still be alive in an exaltation of his solipsistic self. But in a sexual-role-as-
identity he loses sight of this rebellion, his metaphysical stand against nature, a lukewarmness
setting in that is a submission to mere titillation, serving yet again another Grand Inquisitor who
doles out petty pleasures. He loses sight of how his personhood-as-will is established and can
only be fulfilled through dominating unto death, and there remains only one alternative to
willing-in-the-world or a pathetic submission to gratifying sexual urges as a way of life, a letting
go in spiritual freedom, what the non-gnostic mystics East and West insist is the only real
freedom for body and soul. No matter how much the rebel's now lukewarm role/identity might
glitter like gold in his and the eyes of others, an idol is always a thing, never a person who wills
without justification (even Christians seek to be free from law, from the slavery of continually

239

seeking justification in moral and ethical constructs). The lukewarm rebel is like a child who in

exultation steals a candy bar but when caught blushes in embarrassment and makes a silly

excuse, like "I was hungry." The ancients knew destiny as a journey to a destination where one's

true identity is revealed, not in any role at the surface, but in an interior place beyond

appearance, language and history itself, the point of the first three Chapters of the *Bhagavad Gita*

where the holy warrior prince Arjuna arrives at his destination but there is no way to explain the

arrival, no context to reveal its meaning, for it goes too metaphysically deep. We moderns

interpret identity as a social and/or behavioral construct of predetermination, which classifies and

diminishes us inside assigned roles, defining freedom as an embrace of those roles to get petty

rewards and handouts on whatever scale from some Grand Inquisitor, often one who pontificates

from some pulpit, political or religious, or sits on the Supreme Court, which robs us of our

dignity as *persons* (what can unfold only in our destinies, and destinies always exist in defiance

of assigned roles, for a role inside a destiny can be thrown off like a set of clothes that no longer

fit or belong to a cultural understanding that no longer guides us to the Omega Point of our

Homeric journey in life). For me the evidence of this is in Kafka's *The Trial*. His perennial

character K stands alone in his persistence against every impediment to self-justification

(determined not to be guilty), including those who have mastered the game of submission in

lukewarmness along with the arrogant transgressors who have paradoxically found a niche for

their rabid willfulness equally locked inside an institution that denies freedom! (One cannot

grasp the essence of Orwell's *1984* until one acknowledges that the interrogator Obrien is just as

imprisoned as his captive, Winston; indeed, Winston is but a recapitulation of K.) K fights the

good fight against those who would define him out of existence, but he does it from the roles

assigned to him in the matrix of desire, unaware that it is the roles themselves as identity that

240

doom him, that make death itself the only escape. In other words, there is only one malevolent force, a force that would rob us of our destinies where our true identities reside, who we are as persons beyond every assigned role in the matrix of desire. And what makes Kafka majestic as an artist is that he never submitted to any role, not even the role of writer. If he had, he could never have penned his masterpieces. To those all around him, including his loved ones who would encourage him to embrace assigned roles to help free him from his existential affliction, he had a singular protest: "No more psychology!"

I now understood that we humans, unlike all other creatures on the planet, can choose to enter any sexual realm for any number of reasons, consciously or unconsciously, and stay as long as we like if we will it (this was Foucault's fundamental insight), an act of power in directing our lives into whatever realms we please for *any* reason or as a *defiance of reason*, a satisfaction deeper than sexual, revealed especially in a willed enjoyment of what one initially experiences as an abhorrent and destructive sexual act, directing the libido towards what it abhors and thereby becoming will itself independent of all classifications constructed by authorities from the past and present, which means we *are* will. It is not unlike teens in Third World countries who are in no way sociopaths, far removed from any apparent desire for bloodlust, but are nonetheless enticed by the power held by rebels and proceed to make a series of choices to access that power, eventually resulting in not only becoming torturers and murderers, but craving the slaughter inside an addiction to the power that is its inspiration, much the same as your average serial killer. Of course it is different when captured as children by those same rebels and indoctrinated into becoming vicious killers (as children are now in many public schools being herded into sex education classes and indoctrinated into taking on sexual identities), although the indoctrination

241

itself could not be successful if the potential to rebel against conscience did not exist in the realm of the subconscious just waiting to be called on by the will to power (why in every situation there is a degree of complicity); and the realm of sexual desire is the most enticing, for, residing as it does in a drive for the survival of the species, at the heart of creation itself, it has the potential for the greatest heightening of one's sense of power in controlling and directing the sexual act in opposition to conscience (nature), and why sexual plundering of the innocent during wartime, young and old alike, makes perfect sense: why in those circumstances where we dance at death's door would we restrict expressing our will to power, possibly our last opportunity before death to take an absolute stand against conscience?

Much of what is now presented in sex education classes as "normal", "healthy" and "intimate" sexual acts—for example, various forms of anal sex—was at one time considered abnormal and abhorrent precisely because it is unhealthy and defies the constitution of the body, an assault on the gestalt that is self, but now with the daily indoctrination of its "normalcy", the will to power is easily awakened into a desire to overcome an innate, natural abhorrent sense of life-threatening sexual acts, an indoctrination that will over time lead children into engaging in those acts as an affirmation of their power, a singular attraction for their teen angst (the will to power banging at the door of consciousness) and rebellion (its release). This, for example, is why boys anally penetrating their girlfriends (whether the girls in a masochistic embrace accept the pain and humiliation or not) has skyrocketed since universal sex education was introduced and why an epidemic of boys strangling their girlfriends during orgasm (it heightens orgasm) broke out for a time in New York until dead bodies started showing up and boys rediscovered their consciences, looking down in blushed embarrassment and saying, "We were just trying to be intimate." Make no mistake—the real pleasure in these instances is in the exercise of the will to

242

power, a negation of love, for love always involves forms of surrender, a letting go in an abiding tenderness, never the inflicting of pain and humiliation. These children are being introduced to a sexual methodology of self-empowerment, the modern battle cry, defying conscience by defying the sexual mores it inspires, and over time whipping conscience into shape, forcing it to serve one's will to power, no doubt the greatest enhancement of the will, and to "purify" the act, one need only dismiss etiological understandings of it in religion or psychiatry, allowing it to be what it is, an act of rebellion against nature, and why truths involving psychosexual mangledness are so easily dismissed in our time. Indeed, religionists, psychiatrists and sociologists are being called upon by the power-oriented to dismiss the hard-earned truths of their professions, threatened with discreditization and subsequent loss of their careers, and this works because they, too, have mistakenly established their identities inside the roles of their professions—they are now as lost as the victims they were at first determined to help. The opposite would be adults guiding children through a process of submission to the harmonious laws of nature (not its inherent futility, the afflictions in nature) in defiance of our willing-unto-death (personal power's highest expression, and why the question of suicide/homicide still hasn't been answered). The initial attraction, therefore, of sexual liberation in essence is a defiance of nature, the ultimate affirmation of the will to power always heading towards a Dionysian frenzy unto death, a defiance of life itself as life's greatest expression!—a gnostic dream come true, and why even the role I invented, "omnisexual", is itself just another trap, a role that incorporates many aspects, a fusion of roles, into a false identity that still serves as a denial of destiny and a masking of will.

Now I had to think more clearly on the unavoidable consequences of pursuing my freedom via sexual transgression: When the will to power displaces the will to discernment (the

243

will to understand in truth) we necessarily dismiss an understanding of the complexity of our psychopathologies (our derailments from nature's intended path of the affirmation of life in its flourishing, its propagation), pathologies that have their origin in dead-end desires aligned with the will to power, basking solely in this willing-in-the-world-unto-misery-and-death, a pathetically weak construction of meaning coupled with high anxiety, an intensified fear and trembling rooted in a loss of meaning, a relentless slide into Chaos, a slavery to non-distinction as we pick up speed on that steep slope, holding on as we are subjected to the whims and fancies of unlimited others we are incapable of understanding *or* controlling, for if it is truth that sets us free as Socrates claimed and demonstrated, and why Aristotle placed the intellect at the top in a hierarchy of human faculties, and not unlimited power over anything (Meister Eckhart, the founder of the Rhineland mystics, placed understanding above even love, arguing that genuine love is not possible without understanding) then our willing-in-the-world in power becomes a radical form of slavery, the gestalt of our faculties for discerning being enslaved to the angst of a willing unobstructed by understanding. Conscience, the ontological ground of the will-to-understand (what makes love possible), nature's innate guide into the harmony of her ways, becomes the primal enemy of the will to power. Why, our power-oriented minds ask, should we be controlled by conscience into not indulging sexual engagements with persons who are the objects of our sexual liberation because they are trapped in degrading sexual compulsions via trauma or what whittled away at their freedom to move unimpeded in psychosexual maturation (viewing them as victims instead of paths of liberation)? They *want to cooperate* with our willing! To engage with them is not harming them, but indulging them, what they are adamant in insisting is *their* act of freedom in pathetic submission to external and usually unknown powers wildly at play in the realm of Chaos (why Johns have no compunction in purchasing child flesh

244

for sexual fulfillment). They more than anyone would oppose the revelation that their sexual identity (including the identity "prostitute") is a degradation imposed by ghostly figures from a haunted past, having now established their enslavement as their meaning in life, believing their lives mirror the lives of those willing-in-the-world in power (why, for example, many gays who disagreed would eventually agree with Foucault's assessment that willing as an act of power, not genetic sexual orientation, is what makes sex meaningful and intrinsic to identity), when in fact they are slaves who fixate on whatever sexual benefits, what crumbs, they are left to enjoy as slaves, as victims, what their masters had long ago shackled them to. The sex liberationist would explain that the "noble child" in me who was resigned to sorrow when confronted by victims in the past did not understand that those victims had long ago resigned themselves to enslavement. They willingly forfeit any claim on my conscience in my quest for sexual liberation in relationship to them. And then there is the added dilemma that my fullest expression of power can only take place in an absolute defiance of conscience, so how does one proceed? Does one venture from the path of Sade to that of Jack the Ripper?

It finally occurred to me in my reflection that to be free one must at some point be free to dismiss even the desire for freedom itself, a transcendent freedom not available to consciousness through the cognitive constructs of a language trapped in understanding freedom in the matrix of desire and the liberation from constraints. Proust *proves* this, what made him one of the most powerful novelists of the 20th century. His aesthetic in essence is a poetic elaboration on the dead-ends of desire, and that once arriving at the last dead end, Nothingness is made visible, what Ingmar Bergman arrived at in *Persona*, his final dead end (artistic vision made whole), where he also explores the fact that the pursuit of desire is always narcissistic and thus solipsistic, killing off every possibility of relationship, even to one's child. But Proust and

245

Bergman could not find freedom, only a salve, a detachment, a beautifully cool indifference, a transcendental condolence of sorts, a kind of freedom I suppose in an aesthetic absent any lasting, unwavering good other than the artistic process itself.

But I reasoned that I had to begin somewhere in this process towards freedom, this deconstructing of desire-identities (roles) that kill off one's true identity, or rather continually and exhaustingly suppress its emergence, and it was clear the most powerful and all-consuming desire-identities are sexual, and therefore the best place to start, otherwise I might simply be conning myself via high abstraction—I wanted to *experience* the truth of what was being revealed; but that process could not begin in prison, for the elaborate, concentrated and life-threatening games of crazed sexual passions in the power-games of prison life would endanger me beyond my ability to maintain any process in my self-interest, my own self-aggrandizement. I no doubt early on would become overwhelmed by the interests and life-threatening machinations of others trapped in power-identity-role enslavements. After all, forms of rebellion inside a powerful institution like prison that is designed specifically to curtail free expression are limited, and that concentration of institutional power as a constant is precisely what makes the passions concentrate and escalate in conjuring a deluded sense of being free, and that rebellion feels most active and alive in sexual conquests that totally degrade and destroy the other in conquest (physically and/or psychologically-emotionally), an expression of absolute power over a human person as a completely functioning representative of all of humanity, and this degradation, this comprehensive assault on humanity via any person, cannot be accomplished if the person being degraded is a willing participant, as is the case in mutually agreed upon sadomasochistic engagements in sexual-identity subcultures on the outside (lives of lukewarmness). This is what makes games of deconstructing sexual identities impossible in prison. For a prisoner it really

246

isn't about playfully establishing with others a cooperative and mutually beneficial juggling of sexual identities to experience a freedom of control over the sexual drive, of directing it to one's own fancy, but either a submission to a mangled and pre-programmed sexual identity servicing a sexual inclination, or establishing a sense of power with a desire-identity-role of power over another human existent to deflect a conscious or subconscious awareness of total enslavement to the omnipotent and omnipresent forces of the institution one is held captive to, an institution that is only one minor manifestation of a larger, all-encompassing institution called American Culture with its built-in and mostly subconscious controlling mechanisms (mirroring all institutions of power in human history), easily perceived in how we go to war endlessly with no favorable results other than an accomplished sadistic imposition for extended periods of time of a collective will to power, which is why the word "imperialism" is misleading: expropriation of resources, land and people is always secondary to a culture's imposition of its collective will to power.

I reasoned the only way to have concrete proof that I had honestly dismissed the traps of sexual identities would be by first entering and then freely exiting them; otherwise the dismissal would be abstract, not real, and therefore possibly imagined. But this couldn't be accomplished in prison where sexual deprivation as corporate expression restricts sexual engagement to realms of sexual expression that are provided alternatives to what has been thwarted as part of the punitive process (why many prisoners who engage in homosexual acts in prison drop the desire immediately upon release from prison, unless, of course, they had entered prison with a preset homosexual or other sexual inclination of dominant force) or to power plays of domination, a kind of battle ground or, more precisely, a gladiator ring for the enjoyment of the rulers who dominate our lives, who gawk and make fun of us in battle, especially in a battle to the death,

247

*their* affirmation of the will to power, controlling a large concentrated group of power-obsessed transgressors, as well as deflecting the violent energy of that group away from themselves. To engage in these desire-identity-role games of power would be putting my life on the line in every second and not in any way achieving what I was determined to do, but instead affirm the power of others, most especially the power of my rulers who pull all the strings of desire, rulers who image themselves as lion-tamers, masters of the violence inherent in nature, a principle of aggression that knows its birthplace in futility.

But then again, maybe all of this could be chalked up to nothing more than curiosity, that interminable enticement that can easily distance us the farthest from truth; in fact, all these ruminations as well as acting on them might be simply another ploy, a way of delaying what is really required, an absolute exit from the matrix of desire, that relentless and pointless pursuit of dangling carrots, including most especially the carrot called power.

\*\*\*\*\*\*\*\*\*

Big Bill was the librarian, and he would come by twice a week to lock-up wheeling a rolling cart with the books we had ordered. He was about 6'2" and always wore a crew cut. He had thick legs, but he carried most of his weight in an expansive gut. He had slim shoulders that bent forward, the flab of his chest hanging down like women's breasts under his white T-shirt, a perpetual smile on his pale smooth face. Prisoners would jokingly refer to him as Baby Huey.

Big Bill was addicted to books, and he became my best ally. He would tell me what ones to avoid, the "non-essentials": "You could spend three life sentences reading books that don't matter." I once asked him if he was a teacher on the outside.

248

"Naw. And I don't like talking about any of that."

That was fine by me. In filling my requests he would even dig into his personal stash, sometimes managing to persuade me to read some of his personal favorites: J.G. Ballard, Philip K. Dick and Par Lagerkvist (he laughed like a child sharing a sinister secret when he handed me Lagerkvist's *The Dwarf*, saying "You'll like this one.") No question Bill in his philosophic explorations had a penchant for sci fi and a touch of the grotesque.

Early on it would dawn on me that I had a poor memory, and this more than anything frustrated me. I could read a work as difficult as Lonergan's *Insight* and grasp much of what he was saying, but within moments lose it. Sometimes in returning to the text I was unable to grasp what I had grasped previously! When I told Bill about this, he said "There's an advantage to that. A person with a good memory will remember all the important themes and their elaborate details, but often miss exactly what he needs to know in a particular, important moment of his life, not catching the connection in how he moves organically in the world, becoming lost to himself in his knowing—what he is remembering actually masks what he fearfully wills to forget, his grandiose image of his intellectual accomplishments becoming his best disguise, his mask. Memory, your best ally, can become your worst enemy in warehousing raw material in the construction of systems that dazzle and then lull you away from your center, your experiences, trapping you in an obsessive desire to gain status inside some popular mindset, to hang out at some Proustian Salon, always struggling for recognition in competing with members of your Salon or the Salons of others, never having time to hang out with your own sense of yourself, why in the end Proust preferred his bed of isolation that an affliction drove him to, and why his affliction was a secret pass to his inner-vision. But you're not seeking any crowd, so what's the point? You're not going for a degree in anything or looking for a pat on the head at some empty academic gathering. Might as well go with what you relate to right now, especially what you intuit. When I'm reading, something always jumps out at me that is more important than what I'm reading because it affirms where I reside, and oftentimes instructs me on what my next step must be. Last week it was Kierkegaard. I laughed at something he had written and a piece of clarity flashed in front of me, and I wrote it down, something like, 'Kierkegaard looked out over Christendom and saw no Christianity; Nietzsche looked out over Christendom and saw a dead god, killed by Christians themselves; Proust saw Salons populated by persons competing for a dead god's throne; Dostoevsky looked out at a dead god who in the twilight of his death vomited a pool of resentment, from which evolved the underground man.' Just listen to your own take on what you read and write it down. Anything worth remembering can be summed up in a Haiku, or, in perfect clarity, in one word. You're fighting your own demons, not mine or anyone else's. We all live in terror. Great writers are no different. I read somewhere that Sandy Dennis lives by herself in an apartment with 200 cats. She doesn't trust human companionship, which makes sense, so she creates her own world, inhabiting it with 200 complex characters that had formerly camped out in her head; she prefers this place, seemingly removed from a chaotic and deadly world. Hegel was no different, except that he projected his many conversations with himself into concepts he logged in books like a room full of cats, with the added advantage of universal applause. You're not marked for any of that. At least I don't see it. You're destined to live in the real world. So your bad memory is a blessing. It will only assist, not hinder, in getting you to where you have to go. Your only real problem is that you are trapped in the worst possible place, inside a decision you haven't made yet."

This turned out to be the best advice Bill ever gave me. I stopped wasting time trying to remember what anyone said or wrote. I could now speed through the classics, Dostoevsky clarifying best how we maneuver inside power games, Kafka dragging me into the depths of unfathomable longings locked away and out of reach that weigh heaviest on the heart, far deeper than the dead ends of desire revealed so brilliantly by Proust. Like an Irish monk who gets his brothers to wall him up in a stone hut with only a hole to pass food through, Kafka's every word a brick sealing me up in a vision of a pointless world where everyone, from the lowest to the highest, has a list of legitimate points, but none of it leading anywhere other than a cyclical maze—no psychological breakthroughs, no calming encouragements, no satisfactory conclusions, every seeming certainty (the ground of real rest) apparently gifted only to those who embrace and bask in the evil of the mundane, willing participants in the absurdity of the Institution that continuously demeans and finally slaughters, what Arendt called the "banality of evil", persons who remain resourceful and enthusiastic inside an all-encompassing power that feeds on examination, organization, humiliation, persuasion, postponements, sexual lasciviousness and indifference—an end in itself, especially the escape into random or committed sexual encounters to deflect deflect deflect. Reading his stories was like living in glue dreams—frightful, funny and familiar, no distractions, like watching a holographic film from inside a coffin buried at the center of the earth, a weary comfort found only in a futile reminder that what I'm reading is not real, yet…how could one *not* pursue to the bitter end its logic that abides in mystery, its great unknown that has coalesced so thoroughly with worldly flesh, with what seems obvious?

Bill was doing the rest of his life in prison for burning down an inoperative warehouse where six homeless persons were camping out, one of them a young woman who had been missing for three years, all of them dying in the fire. He would eventually confide to me that he

251

had been staying with his brother and his wife and their two children. He never had any incentive to seek employment and get an apartment of his own, trapped in what he once called "the castle of acedia" and "the joy of melancholy". His brother's wife kept insisting that he leave, but his brother kept making excuses for him. They were under a terrible hardship, his brother's business going under and finding it difficult to make mortgage payments on his home, which placed Bill squarely in the role of an emotional scapegoat with the "facts" clearly establishing his guilt. His brother had received a warehouse in his father's will, but it needed a lot of expensive repairs to get it up to code before he could rent it out. Bill never told me if his brother had asked him to do it, or if he did it on his own, but when he burned the warehouse down there was an insurance policy that his brother cashed in on that saved his business and home. After the bodies were discovered, his brother's wife insisted that they have nothing to do with Bill, concerned that it might implicate them in the eyes of the prosecutor, something they must avoid at all costs, which made perfect sense even to Bill, something he would himself insist on. After he was sentenced to prison for the rest of his life he was able to get hold of a small hook knife used for cutting leather. He waited for the tier guard to pass by on a head count, giving him optimum time to die without being discovered in the process. He then cut a deep laceration across his left wrist with the hook knife, revealing everything under the skin, and then hooking the knife under all the ligaments and pulling upward, he severed them, leaving a big gaping hole, insuring there would be no obstruction in getting to the arteries beneath them. Then he carefully hooked the beating arteries into the crescent of the knife and pulled hard. He then lowered his bleeding wrist into a bucket in front of him, not wanting a prisoner to have to clean up all the blood.

It was Big Bill's bad luck or good luck that the guard's count was off, a simple miscount, and the guard had to return for another count and saved Bill's life. Bill slipped into an incapacitating depression at the state mental hospital. They tried 15 series of shock treatment to force him out of his depression, and having failed, they opted for a lobotomy to get to the source. He eventually came around. You would never know from talking to him that they had cut away a piece of his brain. He had a perfect handle on all the intellectual stuff. I was curious, though, whether he had that permanent grin on his face before the operation, if he had always been overweight and not interested in any form of exercise, if in fact he had changed at all. I never asked him. He had little to say about his life, only about the books he delivered with joy, and maybe not being able to stay for long when he delivered books had something to do with it. I just sensed he didn't like long conversations. He had a way of summing things up when he did speak. He had been down for ten years. I told him I would do what I could to repay him once I got out of lock-up, but he insisted that wasn't necessary: "I always get a kick out of helping someone get into serious reading. It's a kind of mission. You don't owe me anything."

But when I got out of lock-up and was assigned to work in the bakery, I wasted no time contacting him and telling him I would have a big slab of cake for him every morning for the rest of the time I was in the bakery. He lit up, his perpetual smile broadening out and up into his cherub cheeks.

Chapter 16

When I was released from lock-up I was assigned a cell at the end of the 4<sup>th</sup> tier on 6-Wing, the highest, most isolated spot on the wing, which made me the most vulnerable to attack (the 4<sup>th</sup> tier is the least visible to the guard on the flat, and the last cell provided only two exits from an attack: through the attacker or over the rail to one's death). This wasn't Captain Shields' doing, for he was long gone into retirement. Someone either had it in for me, or it was just a coincidence, possibly the only cell available at the moment of my release.

I was released from lock-up in the morning, but I didn't go to the mess-hall until dinner at 5:00. I had to decide whether I was going to take a shank with me or not, and decided not to. Tommy's words came to mind: "If you get killed, you won't be aware of it."

When I arrive in the mess-hall, I wait in a long line and get my food on a stainless steel tray. I walk to one of the big picnic tables. Two of the three prisoners at the table get up and go to another table. The one that stays finally gets it after a few seconds, and then he gets up and leaves. If someone was going to kill me he wouldn't waste time. It would be today or within a few days, not longer.

Then Kenny sits down across from me:

"What's up?"

"Nothin'…so far."

"We ain't got much time. I'll make it quick: Things are pretty much ready to go. You got big points. The suppliers want to talk to you. We can be in business within a month. It'll take

254

some maneuvering to get you over to 4-wing. They'll have to move someone out of my cell to get you in there. It's already arranged…just can't rush it."

"I'm not gettin' into the drug thing, Kenny."

"What are you talking about? You're going to have to get a lawyer. Where's the money going to come from? We're not talking small change here. You can get a bank account and put money in escrow for an attorney. I know you don't want to die here."

"I don't know what I want. I do know I don't wanna get involved in the drug thing."

"You think someone's going to fuck with you? Forget it. You got a reputation now that won't quit. You didn't plan it that way, but it's here—it's in your lap, and the opportunity will never get better, not for you or anyone else. You'd be crazy to pass on it. And you won't have to do any of the running. I'll take care of all that, like it was with me and Tommy. All you'll be doing is getting the dope, and it's not from another prisoner, you understand? No way to get busted."

"I hear what you're sayin'. I'm just not interested, Kenny. I'm sorry, man."

"Sorry? What the fuck you talking about? Staying in this joint is as sorry as it gets. This is your ticket out. There ain't no other way. That's what we're talking about here, OK? [he holds the palms of his hands up] Don't answer, OK? Don't say anything. We'll meet here tomorrow night. Just think about it, OK?"

"Kenny…Somethin' happened in lock-up—"

"Yeah—I see that. But there's a cure."

"I'm serious. I got this book. It's titled *In the Penal Colony*, by this writer, Franz Kafka. I thought it was a book about someone in prison, but it's a collection of short stories, and there's this one, *Before the Law*—"

I see it in Kenny's eyes, giving me that fraction-of-a-second edge—his eyes simply averting from mine, looking over my shoulder, and I know there is someone behind me. I quickly move to the left in a slight dip, as the person behind me is coming down like a guillotine with a stainless-steel tray, dead center on my skull, which would split my skull wide open if it hit right, but that movement of mine to the side results in the edge of the tray hitting the side of center as I am in motion, which is enough to tear flesh and TKO me, but I remain conscious. Unfortunately, in the TKO state I can't move a muscle to defend myself, continuing my descent to the floor. And while in motion, the assailant comes down again with a fierce blow to the side of my head with the tray, but again he hits while my head is moving, not making a solid connection, but the blow is hard enough to knock my senses back—I can move! And energy from my brain gushes down to my legs and feet, and once in my feet I jump up, slamming my right shoulder into the assailant's gut, and like a football player begin running with him across my shoulder, and I run fast up to the huge counter where the counter pots had been removed from the scalding water, and I dump him onto the counter, shoving his head down in the boiling water. He tries to break loose, screaming, but I keep pushing his head back into the scalding water, and at that moment guards are on us, pulling me off him, and my assailant leaps and falls to the ground, and then jumps up, possibly blinded, his right foot coming up from the floor with full force, slamming it into one of the guard's groin, the guard falling to his knees and buckling over, the guard who was holding me joining with the other three guards to subdue my attacker. I just walk away, up the stairs leading out of the mess-hall, across the Center and to the prison hospital.

When I arrive the guard at the entrance can see the blood running down my neck and tells me to sit in the waiting room. He had already received a message that guards were on the way with one of their men. No one says anything to me as they rush the injured guard past me into the hospital. A half hour must have passed before someone calls me in after taking the injured guard to an outside hospital. While sitting there the only thing I feel is blood oozing down my neck, or rather, not feeling it so much as being aware that it is there, flowing. There is a humming in my head but it doesn't interfere with my hearing; in fact, my hearing is more acute. I can hear the guards, nurse and a doctor talking in the distance with perfect clarity, but their conversation doesn't interest me.

They shave and then sew my head up and I am sent to the hole for ten days, but I don't go to lock-up. I did make a mild protest at Courtline that all I had done was once again defend myself. But I didn't have my heart in it—I said it more for the record in case I did decide at some point to appeal an unfair sentence. The new civilian director who had replaced Captain Shields, after sending me out and then calling me back in, explains "We're concerned that an officer was injured in this brawl. Obviously boundaries are being crossed that must be addressed. Violence is simply unacceptable, and violence directed at personnel in any capacity simply will not be tolerated. We understand you didn't assault the officer, but the nature of your actions alone, we believe, only escalated the violence to the point that an officer was injured. We therefore have decided that ten days in isolation will be the sentence, and considering the nature of what occurred we consider this sentence lenient. The next time you are involved in an incident of this magnitude will result in a return to lock-up status. Do you understand?"

"Yeah."


**********


257

When I am released from the hole and return to my cell, something is radically new. The calm and total absence of fear I had experienced in the hospital after the attempt on my life, what was no doubt a state of shock, still remained, but it is not a state of shock. And I feel with certainty that it will remain the rest of my days, and in this moment I move into a euphoric state, an exaltation, as if crowned with the greatest gift of my life—a freedom from the fear of any person or group, and this liberation would remain forever, an abiding calm similar to what I had experienced in my Kundalini days, but now with an added dimension: an abiding curiosity about life and its endless possibilities for the future, especially the possibility of finding an exit from drugs and crime. This was not the cool indifference of my Kundalini days, but a real hope for a future lived *in the world*, not suspended outside it. I feel a *purpose* in my calm. I think about something I had read in lock-up, that how we move in the world is like a helix: in deep, honest reflection we can accurately perceive the horror of being trapped in a circle, a maddening repetition, regardless what pleasures we encounter in that loop, a being doomed to a cyclical and eventually a weary meaninglessness, and this horror was not only in our nature, but in all that transcends it, as in Nietzsche's eternal recurrence that he experienced as freedom, but for me is the greatest horror show imaginable; but if we tilt the outer edge of what appears to be a single circle to one side in angular focus, we see the rotating loops of a helix formerly hidden behind the first rotating loop, a helix that moves us ever forward (right now I recall a film, *Before the Rain*; in the opening scene kids are playing marbles in a circle, and an elderly Greek Orthodox Patriarch who is close by says to them "The circle is not round.") My cell is glowing now, a glow that emanates from the center of this calm awareness that now extends far beyond the walls of the prison. *I had arrived*!, an arrival more real and more important than any journey that moves inside a thrash-city circle that always ends in yet another rut. This arrival is not a finale,

258

but in it I can grasp the clarity of what it points to, an Omega Point of a great unknown after exiting the last loop of the helix and sent to the other side of every universe, an exit from the matrix of cyclical futility, and in this clarity, this absence of fear, I sense my personality altering, or rather bringing me closer to it, for I no doubt am closer to who I really am outside all manipulations controlled by fear and melancholy, knowing in this instant that "resting" inside a blind addiction to a cyclical rut is no rest at all, that real rest exists beyond it, and this arrival is a knowing with certainty that there is a way out.

Kenny never came around again. I am assigned a long-timers job, cleaning the shitter in the big yard. This was a prized job because it only took about ten minutes to do, but I would get paid for a full day's work. It is a job the guards reserve for those whom they believe will never see the light of day. Most guards, like most everyone else in the world, have a good heart and basic respect for others, including prisoners. Assigning me that work detail is an expression of that. All the other jobs in some degree have an air of rehabilitation about them, the 8-hour day that conditions a prisoner to embrace a life of habitual work, along with a basic skill that can be applied to a work search on the outside (tailor shop, license plate shop [working with industrial machinery], bakery, shoe shop, industrial laundry, etc.). I spend four hours a day (two in the morning, two in the afternoon) in the yard working out on the pull-up bar and weights, and then run 5 miles around the yard. At night I read until the lights go out. I am a loner. No one talks to me except Big Bill, who is still my book supplier and advisor. If I mention a book I saw referenced anywhere and want to check it out, Bill finds it for me, sometimes ordering it from a university book store outside prison. When he stops by to deliver books, the guards let him spend extra time at my cell because they know it is the only conversation that interests me and that I am not planning any criminal activity. They know I'm also in a non-threatening state, no thought or desire to go anywhere other than my cell, including out of my mind. I'm settled in for the end days. With the money I get from work I buy Bill cigarettes, him trying to refuse and me insisting: "Bill, you got your addiction and I got mine. Let's support one another in this, OK? Whataya want from me, to stop requestin' books I need?" I simply have no use for the money, and Bill knows it. I quit smoking and lost all desire for drugs and alcohol, and the prison food is more than adequate to meet my needs.

A year passes. I receive a letter from my sister Sarah, the one I was closest to growing up, the one who would applaud my childhood circus act. She and her husband had been taking care of mom who had been diagnosed as paranoid schizophrenic and was refusing to take her medication. The reason Sarah wrote to me was because she and her husband were trying to have mom committed to the state mental hospital in California, the state where they now resided, and the lawyer she hired said it would be easier to get a court-ordered commitment if she got letters from everyone in the family requesting it for her safety. Mom had always been fearful of commitment, and she instilled in me that same fear. For me it was a fear far greater than the fear of death because psychs have ultimate power over any patient: they could with pills lock me inside a suffocating inertia, a being dead and still conscious, like being buried alive with a brain that never shuts down. Only the will can guide self-reflection and a passage out of a rut, and the will is illusory if it is deprived of bold action birthed in a lucid decision or, better yet, an impulse, its purest expression. I'd seen pharmaceutical suffocation too often in reformatories and knew its aim.

I read my sister's short letter over again, her ending with "Please answer as soon as possible. Love, Sarah."

I grab a pencil and paper and write:

*Dear Sarah,*

*I'm really in no position to make a decision or even participate in making one. The truth is, I can't offer any alternative. But the way I feel is that I would rather see our mom dead in the streets than see her in a state mental institution.*

*Love,*

*Sam*

When the tier guard comes around for the count I give him the letter to mail. It's done. I love my sister, and she has a good heart, but I feel like the universe is spinning out of control and that she, like everyone else, is trying to imagine stability when bodies all around are being ripped from the ground and hurled through space, including our mother's. I'm angry. But who am I to judge? There is fraudulency in my anger—it is unmerited, perhaps invented, a self-righteous emotional mask concealing the depths of my own vile nature and the damage it has done to others, especially mom. I more than anyone had led her to her no exit, her everlasting hell on earth, perhaps unconsciously exacting revenge on her for having decided long ago that I would be the one to redeem the unredeemable, placing that impossible burden on me, utterly trapping me in a hell of an impossible reciprocity. If love is truly a gift, there can be no expected return, reciprocity amounting to no more than a surface social game, a deluded attempt at establishing a

261

*fair exchange act* in the commerce of goods and emotions at every level of existence, even at the heart of intimacy: "What can you give me? I need! I need!—Oh! And what do *you* need?" And that becomes the ground of our relationships, always returning there, to the resentment of being slighted in some degree. We street kids had a saying: "When you give someone somethin', take your fuckin' hands off it!" It's the absolute law of a real gift, especially the gift of love. What it came down to: the gift of mom's love, expressed in her daily efforts to save my life as a child, although certainly true in some great degree, was now in question, because I was trapped in feeling I had to contribute something, anything, to undo all the damage done to her, to reciprocate what couldn't be effectively reciprocated because there was no way to even discern where her torturous internal disintegration began. As a child, beginning at age 8, I would cook, clean, sew and raise money for food—all of this to give mom relief from her abiding depression. But it had no effect—her sadness went too deep. Now I was under a double judgment: from dad I was judged as having deprived him, via my deformity, of his wife's affections, and he sentenced me to never in any way make it appear that I had become better than him as a person, as I did when I cared for mom and my siblings, for that would justify her neglect of him, having to turn to a child because of his failure as a man, and if I betrayed him in this manner, he would, with constant beatings and humiliations, destroy all my hopeful imaginings of receiving his love in the future, my only hope for true liberation in love; and mom's judgment, that I had failed to right the wrongs of her tortured life, to reciprocate her enduring and successful efforts at saving my life, I was sentenced to despair until I could find a path for her deliverance. So perhaps I had decided at the deepest level, in a revenge-oriented resentment towards her for having assigned me as her redeemer (which was a more insufferable burden than dad's demand), to create an everlasting hell for her, the anger I had towards anything at the surface of life in any given

262

moment serving to mask the original resentment towards myself for having failed in mom's mission so decisively, and how that resentment had shifted towards her for having assigned me the mission in the first place! What other motive could there be? As my sister Catherine had observed in one of her drunken, snarling rants: "Mom always saw you as special. She loved to talk into empty space with that stupid smile on her face, always repeating 'He's the one', like she and the Void had this big secret. I *hated* it when she did that. And it was about more than all that time she spent keeping you alive. She really believed that crap that you would somehow turn everything around or give it some fucking meaning, that in the end you would justify what couldn't be justified."

Sarah on the other hand had made a simple choice at age 5—to become rich. Her argument went like this: If there are two kids identical in every respect, except one is rich and the other poor, tallying the score of enjoyable moments in life, the rich one always wins, and that's why she wanted to be rich, and although I didn't agree with her, I didn't state as much—I just got a kick out of her staunch determination and singular focus, like it was impossible that she wouldn't one day be rich.

I began to see it when I found out she had been stealing money from dad's wallet when he was drunk. At age five she had offered to give me a dollar when I told her how badly I wanted to see a movie that was in town.

"Where'd you get money?" I asked

"From dad's wallet. I always do when he gets drunk and passes out."

I panicked because it hit me immediately that if dad found out money was missing from his wallet he would blame me and Tommy: "Are you crazy? You know what dad'll do if he finds out?"

"He won't. He never remembers how much money he lost gambling when he gets drunk. I always take at least ten dollars, sometimes twenty. He never misses it."

How much did you take this time?"

"Ten."

"You got to put it back."

"For what? Don't you want to go to the movies?"

"Yeah...but I don't want to get killed when I get home!"

"I'm telling you—he won't know. He never does."

"I'm telling you: You have to put it back—right now! And I'll make sure you do."

"Jeeeez...Ok...But I only have five left."

And I watched her from outside dad's bedroom door. She was so nonchalant, not a drop of fear. She went up to the bed, slowly pulling dad's wallet from his back pocket, putting the five dollars in and then sliding the wallet back into his pocket. She never offered me movie money again, but I'm sure she kept stealing it, probably on that occasion returning to get another ten dollars after I was out of sight.

And now she wanted me to help put mom in a state hospital. When I got past the anger I felt after mailing the letter, I reasoned that Sarah had probably dissociated from affections for mom and dad at a very early age, that she had somehow figured out that she was on her own and had to remove herself from the dynamics of family life and fend for herself, but this distancing cost her, and it was obvious now, because Sarah had always been a good person. It was not in her to decide to exploit women to make money, and it was not in her to have mom put in a state mental institution. She was robotically caught up in a severed indifference, like those people who chant for money more to distance themselves from the horror of life than to get a new Mercedes, most often a distance from the hell of childhood.

Two weeks after sending my letter out, two days before Mother's Day, I am confined to my cell on the tier for a week (chain wrapped around the cell door and bars next to it to prevent me from leaving when the doors opened for any movement) as punishment for stealing a bowl of milk from the food line. The wing guard comes up and removes the chain and tells me to report to Center Control. I walk out to the Center and a sergeant from behind a bulletproof window says "Your mother died. Here's a phone number you can call when you get off lock-up status," and he hands me a small piece of paper through the porthole. It's from Sarah.

I walk back to the wing, and the guard—the best kind of guard, friendly but no nonsense, just doing his job, career-oriented with no chip on his shoulder—looks at me and says:

"Ordered you to return to lock-up status?"

"Yeah."

"I'm not buying it. Go to the phone section in the education department and make your call. That's between you and me. I'll notify them you're on your way."

I walk to the phone area where a guard is sitting.

"Officer Jackson called; said you're priority—go make your call."

I walk to one of the three phones at a long desk. I dial the number from the piece of paper and Sarah answers. I have no emotions. I am in shock—like I got hit by a truck.

"Hello?"

"I just got the message."

"Sam?"

"Yeah...I just got the message."

"It was an accident. I'm so sorry, Sam. I know how close you and mom were. It was an accident. She got hit by a car."

"A car?"

"Witnesses said she wasn't looking when she crossed a main arterial. The car was going about 50 miles an hour. She experienced no pain. She died instantly, they said."

Then the words of my letter came to mind: *I would rather see our mom dead in the streets than see her in a state mental institution.*

"I've got to go."

"I'm going to try to arrange for you to come to the funeral. My lawyer said he might be able to arrange it, although being out of state it will be difficult."

"They won't let me go. I'm what they call a red-dot prisoner. Exceptions are never made."

"Let me try."

"No...don't...I don't wanna go."

"Call me."

"I gotta go."

I hang up the phone and walk back to my wing. Officer Jackson returns me to my cell and puts the chain back on my door.

"I'm sorry about your mom" he says. "Anything I can do, let me know."

"Yeah...and thanks. Thanks, man."

"It's OK."

My disintegration begins that night. I don't feel any sorrow, just deadness. I lose all initiative to leave my cell. When the chain comes off my door I don't return to work, and the guard doesn't make a thing out of it. I also lose my appetite, but I manage at first to crawl down to the mess hall and force-feed myself basic food, but I soon lose interest in that. I think thoughts like *Sarah knew how close mom and I were. Maybe she left my letter on a table or on a shelf, and mom found it. Maybe that was the first time mom knew they were trying to have her committed, and she decided to kill herself to escape that horror, but in a way that no one would know it was suicide. And maybe I knew inside that that is exactly what would happen. Maybe I killed mom, drove her to suicide.*

Bill would come around a lot more and ask me how things were, and he would bring me a pint of milk.

"No thanks...Really."

"Forget that. Drink this. I'll bring it twice a day. I know you don't have an appetite, but if you drink this twice a day it will sustain you. So just drink it."

I look at him. It is real concern. Baby Huey with big breasts bringing me milk to keep me alive. It's like a hallucination—he decides to be my mom, to take care of me just like mom did when I was a kid. He is really in it. It is for *that* reason alone, him ordering me to drink the milk, that I am able to drink it, and he sometimes bring bits of solid food, something special he had probably bought from a prisoner who got a food package, like cold heavily seasoned veal and Southern-fried chicken. I just keep following orders.

On one visit Bill tells me there is a movie playing in the auditorium that night that I would like.

"I can't, Bill...I can't leave my cell."

"You like movies. You like them better than books. And I worked it out. I got them to order a B-film, a thriller. Most of it takes place on the ocean, this guy with a yacht pulling into ports, scenic, lots of island hopping. You know, something light, take your mind off things for a minute. It can't hurt. So make sure you go tonight when they call it out. I'll save a seat where you like to sit."

"I don't know, Bill."

"Just do it, Ok?"

"Ok."

"Ok…I'll see you tonight."


I don't like the weight of my body walking to the theater, or the weight of others walking around me, or the possibility of the weight of conversation. I am just praying no one says anything to me, guard or prisoner. Bill is different. He doesn't talk much, but when he does it is something I need to hear. I wouldn't always get it at first, but later it would register.

When I enter the theater Bill is there at my favorite spot—5th row, two seats in from the right side. The sound system a big mono speaker above the screen, the sound being the same no matter where you sit, so I would sit at the side of the screen to catch the resolution of the image that always hits best at an angle; and there is also the advantage of having more space to maneuver if someone tries to assault me. Bill is still in smile mode when he looks up at me approaching:

"Glad you made it. You're going to like this one."

"Yeah, right…What's the name of it?"

"*The Last of Sheila*. It's got James Coburn in it. You like him."

268

"Yeah…Coburn can do no wrong. He'd save a sinking ship."

"Hey…that's good."

I almost smile: "Let's hope it's a joke."

"Man, you have to get out of that mood. Give the film a chance."

"What's the name again?"

"*The Last of Sheila.*"

"Never heard of it."

The lights go down and up comes the opening scene. A woman who looks a lot like my mom leaving a party late at night. She is crossing a dimly lit street to get to her car, and from around the corner comes a speeding car, crashing into her. With a thud she dies right there, in the street. Terror strikes me like a knife in the spine.

Next scene cuts to a yacht. It's a year later. James Coburn plays the best friend of the woman killed, and although her death was ruled an accident turned hit-and-run, he is convinced someone intentionally killed her. His guests, the persons he suspects, think it's a yacht party, and the elaborate fun party game he devises becomes more elaborate as the yacht moves along island to island in an attempt to discover who the killer is. And when he refers to his dead friend's name, Sheila, I hear instead my mother's nickname, Fay, and I continue to hear her name throughout the film. My body is gripped with tremors. I slink down a notch in my chair with arms folded tight across my chest to still the shaking. The film goes on in my mind to explore all the details of events leading up to my mother's death. And I haven't a clue as to how things turn out in the actual film—who killed Sheila, that is. The floor is ripped out from under me, floating in tortured space, spiraling into a crazed hallucination, the film revealing what I already knew deep inside, what every clue pointed towards— it was *I* who killed mom!

I can't control the shaking when the lights come up. Bill gets up from his seat. I try to stand, but my trembling knees stop me. Bill looks at me, putting a hand on my shoulder. "You OK?"

*He's in on it*, I think. It's instantly clear: agents from every corner of my mind and the cosmos conspiring to force me to look at the fact that I killed my mother. The film was an intentional interrogation. I look at Bill. The smile tells me everything: *He wants me to confess, to own up to the deed. He's not in on it with the others, those that want to kill me. He thinks it will help me. He's not against me, not in his mind. But what does he know? Or maybe he is helping them. But maybe he doesn't know that he is...or does he? Maybe he's been at this from the beginning—intentionally giving me psychology books and literature that would work on my defenses, forcing me into the truth. Yeah, the first Dostoevsky book he gave me,* Crime and Punishment, *and the Lagerkvist book,* The Dwarf *("You'll like this one")—all the time trying to show me how I am consumed by egocentric hatred and have been calculating the deaths of not only my family, but everyone, anyone, one person at a time, for as long as it takes, that somehow Sibi was right—he, too, saw it, but he didn't tell me everything; he was too scared, too cowardly, but he had to warn me, and it was true—I'll never die...but he didn't tell me why...but now I know—I have to keep killing...the killing itself possessing the magical properties that keep me alive, and that is precisely what has been keeping me alive, and the closer a person is to me, the more powerful the potion—*

"Come on, Sam. We got to leave."

(*Leave? Where to? Who's waiting for us?*)

"No…you go ahead. I'll catch you tomorrow."

"You sure?"

"Yeah, yeah… Just go."

"OK, man…I'll see you in the morning."

After Bill leaves I brace myself. I lean forward, and with trembling knees I push myself up, not able to stop the trembling. I lock my legs shut in a standing position and begin to walk, stiff-legged, real slow, out of the theater and back to my cell, the trembling shifting to and intensifying all through my chest, muscles jumping off my ribs.

I lie in bed waiting for the sound of my cell door to double-lock for the night. There will be no sleep. I begin my descent into the deeper regions, deeper than glue dreams, where it is all revealed to me, every sinister detail, how I had conspired from the beginning to kill my whole family, my first victim Tommy, now mom, and eventually the rest, and how I might have to destroy Bill because he is the only witness to my crimes and my plans for the future. He is definitely on to me. He knows everything. Even what I was just now beginning to understand: dad has been behind my every move, that to get his love and acceptance he required that I kill mom and my siblings, but now I could also see, as Bill sees, that in the end I will kill myself, too, that I couldn't live with what I must do, and of course dad knows this—it is part of his plan: I would be the last to die, or even worse, my cowardliness would prevent my suicide and I would remain in his control, continuing to kill persons into eternity, and with every death a new installation in his edification, his ascent to the high heavens. Killing others outside the family would be an ongoing, endless reprieve—it was the only crumb he had to offer, yet that gift didn't originate in any of his intentions, but from the very nature of how he moves in the world, the slaughter of the innocent the purest expression of his will, his insatiable bloodlust. And he is

271

moving on to another life to begin the orchestration of the death of another family, and he needs to thoroughly clean house before leaving. He has already collected the insurance money for mom's death. Does he have insurance on all of us? Of course. Maybe I should kill myself now? It's the only way to stop my participation. But I'm too cowardly. The best I can hope for is to make someone kill me. Yeah—it's in the line of that pop song I keep hearing in my head: "I'm looking for someone to take my life/I'm looking for a miracle in my life." Yeah—the miracle: make someone kill me, someone who *needs to kill* to break through his wall, and there will be no guilt for him to bear because I deserve to die. What is good in me has already set out to accomplish this. It's the surreptitious reason I came to prison in the first place, where there is a wealth of candidates who will easily accommodate my need to defeat dad's designs on me. It's the only battle being fought. Either I die or dad wins, and flawless winning is everything with him. It is a real possibility to defeat him. I can see it now, and for the next two months my rabid, turbulent mind would in every second force me to explore in detail how I have been involved in his program since childhood, how I have always been complicit, willing—that it was all I was ever really involved in with any abiding interest, an ongoing silent deliberation beneath my surface life, aiding him in his blood-sopped tyranny. And something else is revealed to me: every person crawling across the planet is in on this preoccupation with masking what our lives are really about, the abstract surface life simply elaborate constructions utilized to hide us from the truth, almost all our energies invested in concealing what we really conspire towards: torture, murder, annihilation; and whatever person is with me in any given moment necessarily becomes an object of control (if not *everyone*, then *this* one standing in front of me—my wife, my child, my friend, my co-worker.) I can see it everywhere, with rare exceptions—the Cosmic Joke, the tabloids sticking their fingers in our faces and laughing the truth at us every day, from the front

272

pages to the letters-to-the editor, persisting in showing us who we really are, our crazed desire for the destruction of the other, forever in grinding fear pointing our fingers at *them*. How maddeningly ironic! Dad, it turns out, is the honest one, the one who knowingly in a lucid awareness grabs hold of his destiny with unmitigated zeal, embracing it with verve. Like he always said: you're in or you're out. We are in love or we are in power, and because everyone is opting for power, it would be foolish not to respond in kind, with brutal and fixed determination. The real winners play the game like three-card-molly, creating the illusion that the other has a chance at winning while in every second arranging for them to lose. I hadn't been paying attention. The game of life *is* according to Hoyle. To win is to destroy, to lose is to die. And who wants to die?

I can't remember if Bill had brought me food and milk for the next two months. I don't recall that he had, but he must have. Bill *was* on my side. He was a good friend. And I miraculously came around. On the night of my liberation I hear a tapping in my cell. At first I think it's a rat. I tear my 5' x 7' cell apart and find nothing. When I lay back down, I hear the tapping again. I tear my cell apart three times. Then I get it: it's mom—she wants to talk to me. I lay back down on my cot and we talk all night. I explain to her in detail how I had been conspiring with dad since I was a child to kill her, and that finally I was successful. She explains that I wasn't the only one, that Tommy, Catherine and Sarah were all in on it, that they, too, were agents of dad, but ignorant of how he had manipulated them since birth, how he had planned all our deaths before he had ever met us, actually birthing children to use and then destroy them, child sacrifice being the ultimate expression of his ascendancy, his becoming *thee* god, the only guaranteed act of true ascendency. She explains how dad had truly loved her, a real romantic,

273

and how over time he grew to hate her, because the love, real as it was, was never his decisive ground, but only feelings utilized as fuel to feed his real obsession with power, the same as his love for entertainment as he moved along inside his real mission, like his gambling habit—all of it adding dimension to his real obsession—his will to power, doing whatever the hell he wants whenever he wants, especially when it is at someone else's expense, his losing having more meaning than winning because it tortures his captives into a deeper submission in his power over them, trapping them in a pit of depression. And after willfully annihilating her chances at any semblance of a real life by polluting the realm of her heart, it was time to crush her skull, the final and only absolute expression of power. He had completed the process of leaving her trembling in hopelessness, now permanently on her knees with head bent low in exhaustion, waiting for the final blow. She was tired of her major and only reliable diversion, continually changing her name to escape every sense of who she had become in any given time frame of her delusional adult history, running from frame to frame inside the stories she would tell persons she didn't know in a newly created identity, seeking only to hide from dad's death sentence. Dad wanted out because his work was essentially done—he now had other plans. To complete that work, to absolutize his power, mom had to die. There was a time when the possibility of her ending up in another man's arms would generate in her a hope for redemption, a restoration, a rebirth—and then all his work would be undone, robbed of its final victory. But he had played his cards better than anyone, and there was no other way: she had to die. And to manipulate others into doing it for him would satisfy even more his ravenous will, ruling with absolute authority as far as he could reach. That's when he began to recruit his children for the deed. I then told her about the time she had found someone else, someone who was gentle and kind, and how I had smacked him across the face in anger, him humbly accepting it, and how that had brought anguished tears to her eyes and ripped my own heart to pieces. And she told me how she had put far too much on me, had made me into her little man who would take care of her, and how that had destroyed my chances at ever having a life. We covered everything, our whole history, and when it was over we forgave each other everything; she left, and I was at peace. I had been up all night, and when I laid back on my cot, my hands clasped behind my head in genuine rest, the rays of the rising sun came crashing through the 3-storey high windows of the cell block, flooding my cell with glorious light.

*********

I now knew something with certainty. I knew that getting comfortable with spending the rest of my life in prison, like a monk in some kind of intellectual monastery, was a sham. As rewarding as it was, the fact remained that I had been cowering inside books, glorifying the experience of them as a means of avoiding my real dilemma, that dad still had me in his grip, and it was my throat he gripped in keeping me pinned to the wall. I knew what I had to do, especially if I were to confront and defeat him. There was no way around it: I had to escape.

Chapter 17

I had escaped before, but never from a maximum security prison. This didn't in any way discourage me. The basic principle of a successful escape doesn't change: we humans are creatures of habit, and guards, like prisoners, have their habitual and thus predictable movements. It was simply a matter of mapping the guards' movements and finding spaces in-between those movements to slide past them. And I was fortunate to be in an old prison. In my 5' x 7' thick sheet-metal cell the toilet was a rectangular metal box inset in the back wall with a metal seat plate with a hole in it welded into the base of the metal box. And the years of that plate rusting away on the underside would make the metal that much easier to cut through.

Bill was able to get me everything I needed. "Don't tell anyone," he warned. "That's how they get you. I've seen it more than a few times. I don't even feel comfortable with you telling me, and I know I won't tell."

"I appreciate what you're doing, man."

"Look, Sam…This is it—I know you're leaving, and it's good for me, too. And it's not vicarious joy. In a way, I'm glad I'm in prison because here real friendship goes real deep real fast, if you're lucky enough to have one, and you are the best friend I've ever had. For me the joy has nothing to do with anything more than knowing you have to do this and that I get to help you do it. It's clear as a bell to me: it's in your cards. My way of getting out of here is staying. I have certainty that this is where I'm supposed to be. Every day I commit to staying is another day of freedom…And Sam…I know I won't be seeing you again. I know they won't bring you back. I'm certain of it. And I've been thinking: what is the one thing that I would want to tell you if I had only one thing I could say…and it's this: Your dad, when he was drowning you…He stopped at that crucial moment. That's your ultimate meditation…the only mediation that will matter in the end. Find a way to honor that place, a way of honoring him, because that's the only place you will free yourself from him. You are like everyone else crawling across this planet, trying to snatch some happiness. But destiny is more important. It's the only place you'll find yourself. You can't let anything get in the way, not these walls, and especially not your dad. Like in the first 3 chapters of *Bhagavad-Gita*. Remember? You can't question it."

*********

Over a three-week period I cut away the toilet seat, and wait on the first rainstorm, and when it arrives it was like Bill said, destiny, because the rain was so thick I can't see my hand in front of my face. It is too easy: up the plumbing at the back of the cells to a skylight, out the skylight and down to the ground, over to the wall not too far from a gun tower, and then up and over the wall with the rope and hook I had constructed.

277

Chapter 18

I grab a car and drive for two minutes and then make a call to Kris at a phone booth.

"Kris…It's Sam."

"Who?"

"It's me…Sam."

"What the fuck?"

"Listen…I just escaped. I gotta talk fast and ya got to listen real good. I can't call back. Your phone'll be tapped as soon as they find out I'm gone, so ya gotta listen and get it right."

"Yeah, yeah…I got it…hold on a sec…Christ, it's two o'clock in the mornin'."

"Yeah, well I figured I'd pass on a bold daylight escape…You listenin'?"

"Yeah, yeah…Fuck!...hold on…I'm lookin' for a pencil…Fuck!...OK…Go!"

"Is that Restaurant still there on E. 87th Street, the 24-hour joint we used to go to?"

"Yeah…I still go there."

"Good…I'll be there in two hours. Bring me some clothes. And don't forget a hat. Park as close as you can to the East River. It's dark down there."

"Got it."

"Get what you can together fast and leave your house. Don't stick around. Like I said, they'll be taggin' you as soon as they find out I'm gone. Find a place in New York to hang out until I get there."

**********

When I walk into the restaurant Kris is sitting in the last booth looking straight at me with his hair-sprayed pompadour and Italian Knit shirt (no way would he succumb to the popular Hippie-long-hair look: his commitment wasn't exclusively to fashion, but to being cool, street cool, like in "Yeah I'm a white boy who can walk the streets of Harlem.")

Real friends grow inside you, no matter how much of a hassle they might be, and I've always considered myself fortunate to have had one on the outside and one in prison. The thing with Kris is the same with Bill: I can't explain it. It's just a fundamental trust that this person for whatever reason is more important than my life. Bill would call it destiny, and maybe he was right. But looking at Kris sitting there in that booth all nonchalant except for that perennial sarcastic grin on his face, as if this moment were no different than any other time we met up at the restaurant, said it all: he was cool to the bone, and who can resist cool that goes that deep? Like the time we had just copped an 1/8th of heroin. It was simple: the cops knew there was no way in hell two white boys would be easing down Howard Street in Newark, New Jersey in an old Cadillac refurbished to the max if they didn't have dope on them, but they had on every other occasion left us alone. Not this time. The siren came on and the red lights flashed. I said "Oh shit…we're busted." And Kris says matter-of-factly in his determination not to go to jail or lose the 1/8 of dope, "Not necessarily." And he punches the gas pedal, speeding through the black

279

part of town that we knew so well. "There's a parkin' lot comin' up" he says coolly, "and when I make the turn I'll hit the brakes: you jump out with the drugs and roll into the parkin' lot." And that's what I did, him slamming down the gas pedal before I hit the ground, and Kris gets arrested for speeding and a failure to respond and was out in his parents' custody the same afternoon.

I slide into the booth and Kris says "I knew you were out of your fuckin' mind. I guess you had to prove it."

"There ain't nothin' crazy 'bout gettin' outta Denville."

"Good point."

"You got the clothes?"

"Yeah." He hands a bag across to me. I look through it: green silk mohair pants, a two-tone green Italian knit and green alligator shoes.

"You gotta be kiddin', right?"

"Hey…it was either blue or green, and I wasn't givin' up the blue."

"I don't wanna be a fuckin' lamppost, man."

"What?...Hang out in Little Italy. You'll disappear!"

"At least the leather coat's not green."

"Watch your mouth! I got one at home."

"Any money?"

He reaches into his pocket and pulls out some folded bills and hands it to me: "That's all I got: I can get you more tomorrow."

"It's enough to get me another pair of shoes. I ain't wearin' green alligator."

He laughs: "Gettin' picky your first day out, ain't ya?...Ya know, Sarah lives in New York, on Staten Island."

"What?"

"Yeah. And she changed her name back to her real name. She's Julie now."

"You've been in touch with her?"

"Yeah. She calls me sometimes when she needs some hard stuff. She don't want a connection in that realm, ya know?"

"She's strung out?"

"Sarah? Hell no! She only deals that Hippie shit. You know...pot and acid. But every now and again one of her people needs the hard stuff. Comin' down off diet pills or somethin', or maybe lookin' for a temporary break from some nightmare...Who the fuck knows? I know she doesn't use the shit and she ain't got no regular customers. She rarely calls me."

"You got her number?"

"Yeah...I'll write it down for you."

"When you get home, don't call her...Not ever, OK?"

"I got it, man...What about money?"

"Don't worry 'bout it. Sarah'll let me stay at her place until I figure out what I'm gonna do. I'll call you from a pay phone. We'll always meet up here, and always one day to the minute after I hang up. And don't say anythin' about meetin' up. You ask to meet, and I'll always insist we can't. And whenever I say 'Gotta go', that's the signal to meet. Always imagine the cops are followin' you. Make like you're in that film *French Connection* and Doyle's on your ass. Keep it serious and ditch 'em any way ya can. You know, on the Hudson Tubes and the subways. Just don't drive into the city."

"Yeah…I got it…Hey, you wanna get high?" He shows me some bags of heroin.

"Maybe this one time. I'll be walkin' through the city for a few hours. But I'm off that shit. I ain't goin' back to the joint. I gotta figure somethin' out. Get new ID, another life. The big thing was gettin' out, but the tough thing is figurin' out what I'm gonna do."

It was strange: when I went to the bathroom and shot up the dope, I got high, but there was no gratitude for the instant absence of pain, as if pain no longer constituted a force to contend with. I obviously had other fish to fry, other priorities. I was stunned by this realization. I knew in an instant I would never use it again. I had lost all desire for it. I called Sarah, and, as always, she was thrilled to hear my voice.

Chapter 19


When Sarah opens the door to her 3-bedroom home on Staten Island she has a big smile

on her face, and I freeze on the doorstep, only able to say her name: "Sarah"

"No, Sam" she says shaking her head, smile still intact. "Not Sarah…Julie. Julie O'Brien.

Reclaimed my real name. But call me Sarah, OK? We'll get to 'Julie' later."

"Yeah…well, I'm still Sam."

"We'll talk about that, too…but come in!" she says, pulling at my arm to drag me

through the door, and when I step across the threshold we embrace, and I hold her tight, recalling

immediately the time I taught her how to jump off a one-story storage height, formerly a chicken

coup, in our back yard and land on her back on an old mattress, and how at age 13 when I would

steal dad's car late at night (I would push it out of the driveway and into the street before starting

it) I would wake her to take with me. Although she was 4 years younger than me, she was my

true comrade. We connected that way. She was an adventurer, and so was I. My brother sought

glory, but not adventure. Sarah was the only one I shared my antics with. Tommy was too busy

growing up, getting tough and staying high.

She still had that sparkle of amazement in her hazel eyes. Not because I showed up at her

door, but because she was always amazed with life and the risks we take to live it fully, and my

escape for her was simply another reminder. I look over into the living room through an opening

from the a hallway entrance where three young people sit, hippie-types, a girl and two guys with

long hair, beards and farmer clothes. Even Sarah's wavy light brown hair is the longest it had

ever been, flowing front and back over her tied-died blouse. Sarah is short, so she has to grab the top of my shirt to pull my head down to whisper in my ear: "We'll just tell them your name is Alex. I always thought that name fit you, anyway. They won't be here long. And remember— they know me as Julie—O'Brien!"

Turns out they are buying some pot and psilocybin mushroom. Sarah semi-hurries them along, telling them I am an old friend from California and that we have some catching-up to do.

After they leave I ask Sarah: "You sell drugs? Never would have guessed it."

"Actually, I don't see it that way. Except maybe the pot sometimes…and the LSD. Pot *can* be a drug, and mostly is…for those who are plagued by their emotions and need to dissociate from them, float above them, ya know? There are emotions that are sometimes best left alone to swim around deep down below as the mind wanders off into la-la land…or the low-lands for that matter. That's mostly true of LSD, too, making perception of some abstract thought or image seem more real than reality. But not mushroom. It's different: I don't see it as a drug, although in small doses it can be used that way, with an intentional and willful staying-stuckness, but that's not what nature designed it for: with the correct dosage and no resistance you can dimension-travel, dimensions not separate from but deeper in the ground of where we actually reside, nor are they heightened perceptions of some particular we have abstracted from where we reside and magnify to appear larger than the gestalt of life. That's what attracts me to it and what I try to inspire others to journey to. They're most often too bogged down in a one-dimensional commitment. Just stuck—floating, not going anywhere, you know? Kind of convincing themselves that their stationary denial-of-where-they-actually-reside routine actually has meaning, and if they stay there too long and even grow old there, they'll be trapped in a corner they decorate to make it appear more expansive, with the emotions they long ago dissociated from always silently banging on a door they refuse to open. But it is possible for LSD and even pot to assist in small ways. I mean, look at Louis Armstrong. Now that cat knew how to travel on weed! But most people use it to separate their minds from a confused emotional life, and no doubt Louis indulged in this, too—we all do: in running from ourselves we think we're getting closer to who we are. But with a proper dose of psilocybin…Forget it! Let go and you are there in the thick of it! Deeper than you have ever gone!"

"I don't know what the hell you're talkin' about."

Sarah chuckles. "Well…I'm glad you're out. I know about Tommy, and I know he liked that death-dance, and that doesn't mean I'm insensitive to what happened. I am, but I know it's not over for him, not yet…But we'll talk about all that later. Turns out this is perfect timing, as it always is with you. I have to make a trip to California and I have no one I can trust to watch the house. I'm going to fly out in the morning, and then take the train back. You can look out for the house while I'm gone, if that's OK with you?"

"You kiddin'? It's perfect. I got to figure some things out anyhow. Ain't got nothin' planned yet."

"Another perfect day. Can't get the mushroom here in New York, and my connection won't mail it. Been wanting to visit LA anyhow. It's got a great music scene, and there are some old friends I want to look up. I'll be gone for at least a week. I'll stock the frig with food and beer. And if you want to try the mushroom, help yourself. There's a bag left, and they're powerful. You'll only need three to travel, if you're up to it. Two will allow you to stay at the surface, if that's what you want." She chuckles again.

"What's so funny?"

"You'll find out if you do the mushroom. You're a traveler…You'll love it. Actually, we're all travelers, when fear doesn't decide for us, not only fears of being harmed or even killed

285

but especially of being found out, our masks being revealed for what they are and what they hide, the only fear worse than the fear of death!" She laughs again. "It's just that… well…I know you won't resist it…you're too curious, which means it will be all good. But I have to get ready and book a flight. Relax. Get some food. Roll a joint! There's some there on the coffee table."

When Sarah was age 5 we were all sitting around watching television. Sitting on the floor she wraps her legs in a full lotus and then presses her hands and forearms through her twisted legs, raising herself up on her fingertips and then walks around on them. Catherine, the older sister, commented dryly "She's possessed." And if she was, Catherine would have known, being the second most avid reader of books in the home after Tommy, but her comment was more a humorous dismissive, not wanting anyone other than herself to be credited with anything spectacular. Sarah had also said at this young age "There's only one way out of all this…money…lots of it." And a straight-A student at 14, she quit school and went to work as a receptionist/secretary during the day and a go-go dancer in a bird-cage in a famous Manhattan night-club at night, also selling drugs to fellow dancers who had a hard time with the grueling hours of being constantly in motion in the cage. Eventually she saved enough money and moved to California, bringing mom out after Tommy went to prison and I disappeared. She would meet Philip, a young man who had just finished film school. Two months later they were married and together they built a porn empire, Sarah handling the business side of it, eventually purchasing and building theaters throughout Southern California and Texas, and then taking control over distribution. A multi-millionaire at age 22 and living in a mansion off Mulholland Drive, she and her husband decided to have a baby, and when Sarah couldn't get pregnant, she went to a gynecologist and her husband to a urologist, and it turns out Philip's sperm count is so low he can't impregnate Sarah. And then three months later Sarah is pregnant, and Philip insists she get an abortion, that the baby isn't his, that she had cheated on him. Sarah insists this isn't so, and Philip begins to get violent, at one point beating her into semi-consciousness and then repeatedly kicking her in the stomach, resulting in a miscarriage. After getting out of the hospital, Sarah becomes despondent, losing all incentive to do anything, just sitting around the house stoned on alcohol, pain-killers and barbiturates. Philip pleads with her to snap out of it, that he had forgiven her infidelity while endlessly apologizing for over-reacting to it.

About a month after my escape from prison, Sarah and I are sipping Irish whiskey and smoking some killer weed, and I ask her outright: "Why didn't you leave Philip after he beat you up?" She chuckles:

"Sure, why didn't I…I have a stack of reasons. Been over it a million times and the reasons keep piling up. No end in sight. Mostly, though, after I got out of the hospital I found myself lacking all incentive to do anything. My life had stopped. I wasn't blaming Philip. I knew him too well. He always had a short man's complex, and he was insanely jealous, something I had always taken as a compliment. He was the youngest of 12 children in a dirt-poor Mexican family, the only one of the boys who hadn't got lost in alcohol and violence. He was ambitious and determined to build a normal life with a normal wife who was as ambitious as he. When the urologist told him he couldn't bear children, he just bought into it, that appeal to authority thing we O'Briens never took seriously. But Philip did—way too seriously! The industry we were in called for lots of parties, and we had lots of them. And Philip's best friend, Adrian, had built up a magazine empire. And for some reason Adrian and I connected. I mean, he would come around a lot, and every time we would get lost in conversations about lots of things, mostly about history and paranormal phenomena, two subjects we both obsessed on. This would always annoy Philip, and when I became aware that he was being bothered, I made a conscious effort to include him in the conversations, but they never held his interest…not for long.

"You know, I would never cheat on Philip, but there were moments when I realized I was missing out on an important adventure, and talking with Adrian was mostly when those moments showed up. Yeah…and there was regret, but nothing that overwhelmed, you know? I just began to understand that what Philip and I shared most in common was an obsession with making money, lots of it. And after making lots of it we began to experience the emptiness of it. I mean, it took us nowhere, not really, but it was our obsession. That's when we started talking seriously about having children. Now I realize that part of Philip wanting children had to do with his jealousy, and specifically his jealousy concerning Adrian, that wanting a child for him was a remnant of that male obsession of keeping women barefoot and pregnant to keep them out of other men's beds. Adrian, who obviously had a lot more going on in his mind than building an empire and enjoying the perks that come with it, stopped coming around after I miscarried. And when mom had a nervous breakdown, stabbing the man she was living with and him refusing to press charges, him telling the police he had been drinking, and that during a fight he had fallen on a knife that *he* was holding, she left him, which was a shame because he really loved mom…would have done anything for her. I pleaded with Philip to let her stay with us, and he finally agreed only if we took immediate steps to have her committed for treatment. And part of the condition was that we not foot the bill for a private hospital. I remember Philip's words: 'If her boyfriend loves her so much, let him foot the bill!' That's when I wrote that letter to you in prison. Our lawyer advised it was necessary to get the entire family involved in the decision for commitment because there was no evidence that she was a danger to herself or others, unless the boyfriend changed his mind and told the truth."

288

"That's funny. In the letter I wrote back to you I said I'd rather see mom dead in the streets than see her in a state mental hospital, and she died in the street."

"I know, Sam…That's the first thing I thought of when I was told she was dead and how it happened."

"Do ya think mom read my letter?"

"I doubt it. I think it was the day after I received it that Philip tore it up. It pissed him off."

"I still don't get it. You were always so independent. How did ya get bogged down in how Philip treated you?"

"It's easy enough to understand. It's the curse. Don't you remember? You know, after the Fall: for her punishment Eve and her women offspring would be dominated by men, and they would never be powerful enough to undo that curse. They might dress it up, make it appear something other than what it is, or fight it only to lose, but they'll never undo it—the best they can do, what many modern women do, is hide from it by hiding from themselves, which is no life at all. It becomes a life of titillation, a life at the surface of life…But then, that does seem to be catching on with everyone, men and women. You see it everywhere. I accepted what happened not only as a curse, but as karma: I was involved in an industry that degraded women, actually promoting the curse, idealizing it, what would destroy my life in the end! Sex is the original addiction, and the toughest to kick. Porn just drags you deeper into the original shame of having willfully severed from every form of intimacy, but the titillation of it all is promoted on most every billboard and television show, even kids' shows, giving it an enticing and glamorous cover, a perennial neon-flashing fig leaf…When I finally left Philip I signed everything over to him. I didn't take a dime. You have to start somewhere. And that's when I found my way back to my calling, and why I am who I actually am after all those years of being misguided by greed. Yes, greed. I didn't see it that way at first. I saw it only as an escape from detestable poverty. And no regrets: all of it was my destiny."

"What about drug dealin'?"

"It's like I told you, Sam…drugs are neutral. Wherever you're traveling to when you take them, they'll just get you there a little faster, or slow you down a tat, or trap you for a time, maybe a long time, and from everything I've observed, there are people who want to stay trapped—it's their choice. I mean, if you try to encourage them to move on, they stop talking to you. It's just something you have to recognize and accept, if you think there's any value in sticking around. And if it's a pit you're traveling to, you'll get there with or without the drugs. But porn is always a diving into an endless pit with no bungee cord. You don't go anywhere but down. It corrupts in essence. And it doesn't matter how you decorate it. It's always Satan's shanty."

"You gettin' religious on me?"

Sarah laughs. "You ain't seen nothing yet!" And laughs again.

Chapter 20


After waving goodbye to Sarah at the airport I get the itch: the mushrooms. For me it's two things with drugs: wanting to part company with the sorrow of the real world as best I can, and every drug I've ever used achieves that in some degree, and curiosity, that perennial gnostic impulse to know, to know anything that might in any way alter the equation or open some door leading out of the matrix of life that in the end always delivers sorrow. My thought, based on what I had heard about psilocybin, was that I could experience the best of both worlds, for I had been told that hallucinogens are great painkillers as well as opening the mind.

When I got back to Sarah's house I went right to her stash in a small wooden chest at the side of her vanity table in her bedroom. There it was on top of the bagged-up ounces of marijuana and all the bottles of Quaaludes, microdot LSD, amphetamines and barbiturates: a plastic bag with about 15 long, purple-drenched dried psilocybin mushrooms. I pull the bag out and look at it for a minute trying to determine exactly what I am going to do. I could feel that pull on the one hand toward the titillation every drug has to offer, another form of escape from the world of repellant worldly sensations mysteriously rooted in some vague conspiracy against every manifestation of happiness, and on the other a desire to confront the horrors of existence with an abiding hope that I could find a way beyond them.

I sit on Sarah's plush bed meditating on the contents of the bag. Sarah had said to take three to experience what mushrooms are meant to provide. I go to the kitchen and make myself a cup of tea and then return to the bedroom and open the bag, removing the recommended three mushrooms, pushing all three in my mouth and start chewing, not as nasty tasting, gag-city, as I had imagined they would be, and then washing them down with the hot tea. Then I lay back on the bed, waiting on incipient sensations, which with most drugs occur first in my temples, a mild tingly sensation where the skin presses against the skull. I even get this when eating exceptionally good food, which leads me to suspect it is psychologically induced from somewhere inside my drug-addicted brain, a first sign that I had indeed found a substance that will bring me some degree of relief from the worldly onslaught.

I lay there with eyes closed for a good ten minutes, but feel nothing. Sarah said it would come on fairly quickly and build. I began to suspect that perhaps the mushroom had lost its potency, or had never had potency. I sit up and reach into the bag and grab three more, eat them, and lay back down, and after about 5 minutes I still feel nothing. Frustrated, I finish off the remaining nine and lay back down with eyes closed. Another 5 minutes. Still nothing.

At this point I would normally go grab some of the other drugs Sarah had in the chest, but it didn't even occur to me, probably because right in front of me, next to Sarah's bed, is a television on a stand, and television, after all, is my first obsession, the one I was always drawn to most consistently from childhood on. I turn it on and already in play is a Brian De Palma B-film-masterpiece, *The Fury*, with a host of great actors (Kirk Douglas, Amy Irving, Charles Durning, John Cassevetes and Carrie Snodgress), the kind of actors I can watch whether a film is good or not, a phenomenon centered in a fascination that overcomes me when I witness how a person can escape their surface personality (not edifying it as not-so-talented actors do) by hiding so well in the personality of an artist's creation, and to whatever degree an actor can accomplish this determines for me their greatness as an actor, not their awareness in the world, and why so many excellent actors disappoint when we hear them talk. This ability to hide inside the character of someone else where the real life of the character *and* the actor mysteriously reside,

292

for instance, in its own strange way, is the great plot device in an Alan Parker film, *Angel Heart*, where Mickey Rourke plays a man who has sold his soul to the devil, but when the devil comes to collect, the protagonist ingeniously finds a way to hide from the devil inside the body and soul of another man. This represents the magic of great acting. And in this film Rourke clearly displays his acting genius.

I settle in to watch *The Fury*, a film about a kid with telekinetic powers who is kidnapped by government bureaucrats who want to use the kid for their own malicious ends. At one point another kid with these same powers is holding a malevolent person's hand, and the pressure applied becomes abnormally intense, to the point that blood spurts out from the hand. And suddenly the action slows almost to a stop, a thin line of blood like an arrow shooting in slow motion straight across the screen accompanied by a metallic screeching sound inside my brain, and I feel my brain physically twist as I go into a kind of shock—no pain, but the effect is like a TKO. Then I smell something burning, and I turn the room upside down looking for something that might have caught fire, then realizing it is an effect of the drug (Sarah would later explain that it is a common effect when you take large doses of mushroom). I become fearful, terrorized in my aloneness and having no control over anything that might happen. I then remember that Sarah has a Persian carpet in the living room that has a large mandala design at its center, and it occurs to me that only there would I be safe, so I slowly make my way to the bedroom door, and when I get there the door's thick borders begin to screech with a metallic sound and bend in sharp angles, one border becoming longer than the other, like a building door from a German expressionistic film, and then a shaft of light crashes down in front of the door, passing through the floor. As scared as I am to move, I know with certainty the only safe place is the carpet, and so I walk through the light into the dining room, and once there I look off into the kitchen to the far left of the dining room at the walls that Sarah had painted red, and they are now thick walls of uniformly flowing blood, waterfalls of blood with no spray, the sections having no variation in depth or width, and no ground to crash into, just an endless flow into a bottomless void. I look farther left to the living room entrance and make my way as fast as I can, which is a trembling trudge, and when I walk through the entrance and look at the carpet, I know with certainty I will be safe if I just lay down in its center, and that's what I do, and when my back is firmly planted against the mandala with my arms at my side, that's what I experience: total security, a cosmic relief relaxing every molecule of my being…and then while drifting in this state, beneath me the floor opens up, like two long trap doors falling open, and I fall fast, down through the cellar floor and through the earth and out its other side and begin a journey far faster than the speed of light out to the edge of the universe, and on the way I see and hear in absolute clarity every second of my life that I had lived up to that point in reverse, vivid pictorials and sounds, with all the emphasis in each of those seconds on my interconnectedness and participation in the horrors of the world even before the dawning in me of what we describe as human consciousness, finally arriving in this journey to my first day of infancy where I enter the womb, which becomes the vast edge of the universe, something I cannot describe except to say it is an infinity of a slow, perfectly articulated  breathing of expansive, radically interconnected and undulating patterns, geometric in texture, but no sense of any straight lines, just vast curves moving in endless breathing with me at its center, suspended in its eternal calm.

And then I begin a journey back to the carpet: from the edge of the universe to the womb to the first day of infancy back to the eternal now, and in this return I again witness every second of my life in vivid pictorials and sounds, but this time the emphasis in every cosmic second is not on the horror contained in that second, but on its absolute humor, so much so that I can't stop laughing, a laughter that comes not from my gut, but from below my feet and up through my gut, heart and mind and exploding out the top of my head! And when I return I am in a peaceful place with a definitive sense that I will never again take any human willfulness seriously; but this sense would not last long.

*********

When Sarah returns and I tell her about the mushroom trip, she laughs and says "Actually, I was going to recommend you take the whole bag. I knew you were up to it. I mean, why waste time? You bypassed a lot of preliminary stuff. And I got plenty more. The next time we can journey together if you want."

And we do, the following week, but soon after ingesting the mushroom we part company, finding myself walking along a mountainous terrain with no sign of vegetation or other life form, where the weight of futility presses in on every molecule of my being, but I can't lay down to rest, for rest itself is futile, and besides, my eyes are fixed on a dark mountain in the far distance, like a silhouette against the horizon of a dark grey sky; it is an immeasurable distance, and I cling to a singular notion that perhaps if I get to the other side of that mountain something will be altered; if not the terrain, perhaps my state of mind. All I can do is trudge along with this very thin thread of hope, possessing no energy other than to place one foot in front of the other, and the only comfort I can muster is an image of myself spread out on the ground on my back with a steamroller approaching that will crush the bones of my life into oblivion. Then I see to one side of me three men in dark grey hooded garments who are one with their shadow lives, their heads bent down, looking into what could have been at one time a fire, but now just a pile of cold grey rocks. They don't move, not a tat, and I can't see their faces. They signify for me the uselessness of any false hope I might try to muster, but I continue to place one foot in front of the other.

When I return and tell Sarah where I had gone, she laughs heartily.

"I missed the punch line" I say. She keeps laughing. And then she says:

"I'm laughing *for* you Sam, not *at* you. You bore witness to the most important point. I've never met anyone else who has: there is no going forward except in going back, an honest grappling with a real past. Pressing forward, as one is wont to do, is almost always a vain distancing of oneself from the past, a distancing that always ends in emptiness and despair, what most of us are trapped in, and why we worship Progress as our great idol ("There's gotta be something up ahead!"), investing most every ounce of energy in constructing an ever-grander frame for this idol to stand tall, a technological habitat where Progress can at some point construct *itself* to ever-greater heights without our assistance, allowing us to finally lay back and relax and simply gaze in awe as it expands and continues reaching out in a masterful embrace of all that would oppose its ascendency—destroying the past to create the future as they say, for what past could in any way encumber this great project unless we permitted it? Everything past is now just an impediment that would obliterate every important advance in conquering the universe and granting us immortality. As Marshall McCluan revealed, technology is just an extension of who we are, and it is only through technology that we can become *Thee God!* And if we do not possess the sensibility to knowingly and openly destroy the past as ideologues do, discrediting it at every turn as irrelevant in continuing our advance, the only alternative is to *imagine* a past that will justify the construction of our final and lasting idol, for only technology can become immortal, living on even after the destruction of every life form. This would be a reconstituted, malleable past, an obliteration of the very real past in service to a malleable image of a future left to the genius of computers that will eventually think fast enough to dodge every assault from every impending disaster that man or the universe can dish out, undoing the curse of the Fall in grand fashion. It is only here that we in power can strive to defeat the awareness of the hooded ones, where we no longer have to trudge forward alongside an invisible wall in a cyclical maze, naively convincing ourselves of the possibility that we will at some point get to the other side of that dark mountain, and that once there some shred of hope might await us. This false hope is the ontological ground of every depression. I call it the land of ennui, but it can be called the land of weariness or the land of futility, but it is really only one thing: an awareness that how our every action, every investment of energy, is trapped in service to a denial of what actually has always existed since the Fall, a cyclical rut called futility, placing all our actions squarely in the realm of the absurd. Its most common expression is boredom, something every child is aware of. Our technological god called Progress will be *our* God in *our image and likeness*! And all that will be asked of us as sacrifice is our intimacy, something we learned long ago only creates division and the problems that go with it. You see, we now know that this longing for intimacy is what we have treasured most of all, what we have longed for deeper than anything, and in this longing there is the awareness of its fleeting nature and thus an entrenched desire to take possession of it, and in this possessive ontology there develops an oppositional self-imaging, a competition with endless others to possess it, forcing us to make accusations against those who would possess it in our stead, for they, like us, know that the desire goes deep, that it is infinite, and why in our heart of hearts we always carry a banner of death—death to those who oppose us, to those who would take possession of our possessions and leave us empty inside! Clinical cleanness is the only way, to be cured of our longings, and instead gaze eternally in awe on what we have achieved, immortality in a technology that is not afflicted with feeling, with longing. The longing for intimacy is the curse, the only enemy that opposes our standing our own ground as human beings liberated from all the gods of sorrow and grief. Do you see how intimacy drains us of the power to overcome? Even Jesus would be drained when someone touched his garment in intimate sorrow or grieving. My favorite gospel story is 'On the Road to Emmaus' where Jesus after his resurrection runs into two former disciples who have recommitted to a former cyclical impasse, a repetitious life that they had come to view as meaningless in comparison to what they imagined after meeting Jesus, but after his crucifixion and death they now view him and their hopeful imaginings as a lunacy that led them down an insane road to nowhere but torture and death; all they can do now is recommit to their original impasse, signified by them not even being able to recognize Jesus who had died only a few days before. Jesus knows he can't show them any way forward out of their impasse except by bringing them all the way back, much farther than they had ever honestly gone into their history which they are now denying, them not being aware that all of real history *is* their personal history, the singular story of how love is vanquished by lies in our willful ways. That's why all those who seek to liberate us from intimacy with our complicity must destroy the past, usually by altering it, reconfiguring it, making it conform to an intricate, seemingly complex design we create as an exit strategy from a cyclical journey that leads nowhere other than a campsite next to the Hooded Ones in secret anticipation of the final curtain being drawn and revealing the last illusion, the Grim Reaper, our singular comfort when looking on the Hooded Ones, what we long for more than anything, our fear of him only a masking of the real horror we live in and can't look at, a way of keeping him real for us, who will liberate us from what you witnessed in your mushroom vision: the truth of where most of us reside. Clinical cleanness or intimacy. Which is it? Don't answer yet. First, let's journey to the past and look at the depth of intimacy. It's best to know it before deciding to reject it. Clinical cleanness is easy to understand, and we know how to pursue it in this age of hyper-technology. But one should at least make an informed decision, don't you think? The Hooded Ones showed you a longing for Nothingness. Now you know what that is. And as far as I can tell, Sam, intimacy is the only avenue you haven't journeyed down yet."

"Where were you in that realm? I thought we were supposed to journey there together. I didn't see you anywhere."

"Of course not. But I was there. You just didn't see me, fixed as you were in your determination to trudge forward. And I experienced you wanting to die, to be crushed—it happens to everyone who goes there. If only death wasn't an illusion! And nothing reveals the power of this illusion like suicide. Your vision contained an awareness of this longing, too. But then, you've always known it, Sam. You told me about it years ago after you tried to kill yourself...remember?"

I remember the attempt, but not telling her, but I knew it was true. I always told Sarah everything, especially when I downed too many pills or drank too much alcohol. I knew it was wrong to tell her, her being so young and so radically impressionable, but I always found myself opening up to her, only her: she always got exactly what I was talking about. I could have told my brother anything, too, but more than likely he would shrug it off. He was focused on one thing only, making the world back off and anesthetizing his pain, and this was rooted in his idealization of dad. It just didn't make sense to tell him. A communication to be real has to be received on its own terms, whether one agrees with it or not—the recipient must at least be open to what is being said, to what is involved in what is being communicated. I knew, for example,

299

that when I would steal dad's car late at night when he was passed out drunk that if I told Tommy he wouldn't understand why it was so important to me, and he would only try to talk me out of it; so, to avoid that downward-spiral, I would instead go wake Sarah (I was 13 and she 9) and ask her if she wanted to go with me. She would always smile with eyes ablaze, shaking her head yes as fast as she could. And we would ride through the dark hillside and through empty city streets. She would always stay on the edge of the seat, leaning into the dashboard with arms propped up and crossed, just looking out the windshield to take everything in. Neither of us were talkers, so we never talked…just drove. And when as kids I was practicing my Eternity Man dive from the old cherry tree, she kept asking me to let her try. I wanted to, but couldn't risk it. Then I got an idea. I told her "It'll take a while to learn, but you first must learn how to fall on your back from a high place, and I know where!" I took the tire tubes and mattress from the hole and put them in the back of a long one-story tool shed that used to be a chicken coop in the far back yard. I then taught her how to do a flip off the roof and land on her back and bounce around. She would laugh and just keep saying "Again! Again!"


"Sam…I remember everything. You could call it another curse, for it is natural and even important to forget sometimes. Most mystics see it as one of the great gifts of eternity, eternal forgetfulness, and to see too much here is like seeing the face of God—it will destroy you because the brain can't hold up under an avalanche of truth. But I remember everything about my life, even before I was born, in mom's womb, and before that, in our bloodline. I talk to many of our ancestors, the ones committed to truth. I have just come to believe that a radical forgetting—a forgetting that includes what must be remembered if we are to advance beyond the stalemate that man and woman have reached, our point of alienation, what has become the norm—gets us nowhere in this world, but ironically helps us to survive our alienation inside our alienation!, helps us to embrace it, to even idealize it as autonomous living, but it is always a survival that's a living death, a prolonged suffocation. If there it is a beautiful memory that we have forgotten, it must involve something that would nudge us into a memory of suffering, and we prefer not to go there, and so we are robbed of the beauty that makes up our lives and reveals who we really are in our heart of hearts, and why we have been robbed of our identities, and why we're always manufacturing substitutes that disappoint us. Just look how in this age of the sexual revolution people are taking on sexual identities, and when that age dies, it will be something else. That's what I mean when I say one day we will journey to the land of real memories together. You recovered a memory of the dark world of alienation in your mushroom trip that no false identity can conquer, and why every false identity ends in despair, and in recovering that memory, that truth, you are given a license to recover a beautiful one, one that existed before you were born but no doubt exists in your personal history, in your DNA, one that has always existed in this eternal now that does *not* negate the past as the deluded ones would have you believe. And that's my hope, that one day you and I will journey to a land of light, a land you think you have no memory of, but you do…Remember how you told me you glimpsed it when you would knock yourself unconscious in the reformatory? I can take you to a place where you will remember that light. I'll be able to show it to you just like you used to show me things when I was little. I know you want to know what I've seen, and I can show you, Sam. And it will help you, I promise."

I knew she was right, but my mind flashed back to when I had my nervous breakdown in prison and how I couldn't find my way back. I didn't want to go there again even though I knew many important truths of my life were filed away there; my fear was of being taken that great distance into an endless maze, trapped with no markers pointing a way back to a consciousness that filters information and organizes a stable path to walk on; I was scared of a return to that steel-web of forgotten dark memories that I was now viewing as serving no real purpose other than to trap me in madness. Maybe I should have tried to keep possession of it, much more than I had, not allowed it to be warehoused out of reach, to have at least made an attempt to walk with those memories, but I chose to forget, to keep distant from that infinite abyss of changing forms and endless meanings that cancel each other out, where there is nothing to hold on to. Now my fear was that Sarah wanted to not only take me there again, but to go even further and deeper into forgotten realms before my birth. That thought was too frightening.

"So it's history, our history you're talking about" I say in an attempt to move the conversation into a higher realm of abstraction.

"Oh, no. No, no…Not history, Sam…not that history. In fact its opposite. What is history? It's the continual realignment of referenced events to build a justification for the next wild adventure we conceive of in willing anything to simply experience the thrill of willing on our own terms, an affirmation of our power as our only reality, and thus a sense of security, our minds imagining we are fighting for something like a greater good, trying to get an upper-hand in some battle to establish our virtuous reign over whatever territory we have mapped out to conquer in the big wide world or in our personal lives, especially emotional territory, even in what appears to be a laudable goal of willing a peaceful solution to any perceived problem, which, as you know, can so easily turn into a reign of terror: a civil war, a foreign invasion, a terrorist attack, or something quite personal and tragic as the sudden and unanticipated death of a beloved child through careless inattention, when from the outset our actions were subconsciously designed to fulfill a radical self interest, a willing for its own sake to garnish meaning on a relentless road to nowhere. It is what I call a sadomasochistic world where everyone is looking for an equal opportunity to oppress, to establish their structural truth that is nothing but the biggest lie of their lives to justify the expropriation of yet more territory to reign over, and those opportunities are designed with accumulated and properly arranged 'facts', 'facts of history', a platform for the changing of the guard in politics or personal relationships. This has nothing to do with remembering, but with arranging data for a purpose, for a *cause*. Remembering in those instances becomes the antithesis of genuine history, a search not for a revelation embodied in real facts that hold the truths of a real history, most especially our personal history (facts that could help free us from the histories we construct), but just another deceptive mechanism that hides the facts of real history—that's how powerful our denials are. Remembering too readily becomes an agent in our will to hide from our singular and most destructive desire: to will solely for the sake of willing, what gives us a false sense of being alive, rooted in a fear, a fear of finding out what the Hooded Ones know.

"It gets tricky, I know, because there are witnesses to honest, life-altering events, those rare individuals who record the absolute truth of their lives and the lives of others, what you might call confessions, or witness, what truly guides us and can be viewed as real segments of history, but how do we determine if they are true confessions, true witness? How are we to know? And even if they are, and the evidence is clear that they are, they are still in danger of being co-opted for someone's altering of events, someone's *cause*, manipulated to mean something other than the truth testified to. It's interesting…the original Greek word for 'martyr' means 'witness'. But what witness can you trust? For every true martyr never puts his life on the line for a cause, but only for the truth. Exactly why we love Socrates so much. If you die for a cause that is in opposition at any level to truth, you're a masochist who affirms his superiority in a meaningless sacrifice, what you might call an ultimate player in the game of false history alongside the sadist who stops at nothing to also feel superior to all around him, including the ultimate affirmation of destroying human life: to submit to or destroy the world reveals the heart of the sadomasochistic lie, its absence of any genuine concern for anyone outside of self. But why? Why play this game?... For one reason only: to escape the horrible truth of the trudge, to blind ourselves to the Hooded Ones, like teens that cut themselves to feel alive or an adult who unconsciously plans a car accident to shock himself out of an impending illumination, a terrible remembering of a truth that might destroy his false image of himself in an instant. It could be as insubstantial as an impending glimpse, a sense that behind a particular trembling something more devastating than the fear we are caught up in is about to rear its head. We can't wait to hurl ourselves back into the sadomasochistic matrix: the closer we get to embracing the illusion of death as real, the more enhanced our sense of the lies of history being true is established. Every great denial is always an extreme act of violence. Real remembering dismantles false history. And that's where I reside: in remembering I consort with a multitude of witnesses whose sorrow has no ground in false history but only in sorrow itself. A desire to win, to will for the sake of willing, is displaced by a compassionate surrender to that sorrow, for deep sorrow sees false history for what it is, the endless unraveling of needless pain and suffering rooted in our willfulness, in our power that seeks first to negate love that always humbles us: prayer is never revealed in tight grips or closed fists, but in hands extended, a welcoming in love, for love is

304

always an act of surrender, revealed best in an act of forgiveness. To abide in sorrow reveals love, to escape it reveals power and its river of blood. That's what real martyrs testify to."

*********

Sarah hadn't planned it. At least I don't think she had. Two of her regular customers, Sal and Betty, two hippie types, stopped by to buy some weed and LSD. Sal was about 22, a lot younger than Betty who appeared to be in her early 30s. Sal was short and muscular, Hawaiian/Spanish with long, thick wavy wild brown hair, always smiling, attuned to and appreciating the humor in everything. Betty was slender with artificially waved long light-brown hair, not in my view to imitate Sal's with an in-vogue unisex look. It was just a popular look for the hippie crowd, and Betty basked in everything hippie from tied-died clothes to growing her own spices and other organic foods.

It was customary for Sarah to make her clients feel at home. She would always make tea and chit-chat a while before getting them their drugs and turning them loose on their lives. I asked her one time, "I know you're neutral on all this, but don't you think maybe you're contributin' to somethin' that might go differently, maybe for the better if you didn't supply drugs?"

"Sam…it goes deeper than neutrality. It's destiny."

"Destiny? Like we have no freedom?"

"I didn't say that. History as lie is a process that records fragments that are used to alter our perception of destiny, and destiny is always at the heart of every real event, and every real event is irrevocably connected to destiny. We have this ludicrous innate sense that we can

305

oppose destiny, that we are captains of our own ship charting our own irrevocable course, constructing our own destiny; and we manufacture this lie to convince ourselves that we are in control, but the intended results of our efforts always elude us, eventually making clear that destiny is too powerful a force, and that if we persist in opposing this realization, we will either go mad or become zombies in the land of ennui. And the historical occurrences that harmonize with destiny, the ones not undermined by our willful restructuring of the facts and our enervating and futile efforts to stop destiny, accumulate over time and become real points of clarity, what you can call real history, a history that can show us where we are traveling to. Call it intersecting with God or Cosmic Mind or whatever, but there is this eternal memory that has logged this conglomerative record of genuine finite occurrences along with and in unison with the willed alternate false reconfigurings for our own imagined destinies from beginning to end before we even will any of it, leaving no stone unturned in the examination of our futile attempts at fulfilling a freedom that defeats destiny through personal power. You could say destiny, in how it mingles with our faulty power-oriented reasoning, has already passed sentence on itself in relation to us in its unity with us in our floundering, and simply leaves us to embrace its verdict as truth or lie, as light or darkness, or simply our own utter meaninglessness (the verdict is always in in how we choose to perceive it, and we choose the sentence). But what takes place in sorrow (not despair) and in love is absolute, no dichotomies, no dialectics if you will, a realm you could call God's personal and radically unique history that gloriously transcends our history in every second, and why we should be eternally grateful that he has taken our finite history, our endlessly staged dramas and satire, up into his history where it becomes meaning absent meaninglessness, where every verdict and sentence on life is overturned. There we would understand that we actually can choose freely, absolutely so, but only in love, never from power

306

that always places us in opposition, an opposition that turns us into slaves to every kind of war right down to the most innocent of relationships, between a loving parent and child. You are either in love or you are in power in any given second. There really is no middle ground, no dialectic, no matter how much you mix the seconds up…even in a grinder! Power is slavery and love is freedom, a love not in any way held captive to and corrupted by power. So it is that when my customers arrive to buy drugs I know I cannot alter destiny, but in our encounter perhaps they might in some way glimpse love in the realm of true freedom, for I am always open to it, and I'm open to it because I have no fear: only fear shuts the door on love. You see, my abiding sorrow that connects me to the sorrow of the world is what rips me to pieces in every second— for example, the loss of my baby, a sorrow that doesn't obscure the sorrow of others, but rather helps me focus more precisely on it. For me there is no escape. I tried every kind of drug, and I even hung out with the Hooded Ones for a time to avoid that sorrow (they, too, it turns out, are agents of denial), a time when I would walk blindly across major arterials hardly hearing the sounds of blaring horns. I didn't know any way out of that sorrow, and in fact there is none. But there is a more radical joy in not running from it. No one told me, and maybe I wouldn't have believed them if they did. I guess you could say I straddle a barbed-wire fence in dealing drugs, or I'm doing a clown-like juggling act, but the drugs I take have no effect on me, and it would be presumptuous of me to think my clients aren't capable of finding that place, too. I just embrace it as my calling and pray it resides in destiny. You know, you asked me once after you first arrived why when doing readings for people I use different mediums. For some it's Tarot Cards, for others tea leaves or crystals, and I told you I suit it to the person, what they like, what they most believe in. I didn't tell you that when they talk to me their destinies float around in front of my mind. It doesn't interfere in any way with us connecting, for all that stuff, after all, is not what

307

ultimately matters—it isn't my focus or interest. All I can do is encourage them to bear with it, not judge it, sometimes suggesting a book with genuine illuminations that speak to their experiences, or I simply encourage a person to persist in how they are traveling, knowing that I will not sway them otherwise, and so the best I can do is encourage them to continue the journey that holds their interest, what motivates them to put one foot in front of the other. Like Rebecca—you met her. She knows she is gorgeous but that all her relationships with men fail, and I could see her future involvement with a woman, something she had been preconsciously processing as an answer, and so on a particular encounter I tell her she should take a break, go to a lesbian club, and that I would go with her. She went, met a woman, and they ended up moving in together. Of course I had already known that illusion would end, and that eventually, many years later at a time she would be open to it, she would see her real dilemma, how her parents in obedience to the sadomasochistic matrix sentenced her to never be happy, their willful affirmation of their power over her that would be endless, even if they never saw her again; and then the first serious journey would begin for her to the other side of that dark mountain, which of course is no journey at all, but that impulse is the only place that opens a door to the real journey, the journey into love that frees us from our willfulness. I haven't met one person who early on is willing or able to let go of their fears in freedom, fears that reside in their addiction to power, and so I must bear with them—it is the charitable thing to do. It's prudent. Every person is like humanity as a whole: they have to exhaust all possibilities at attaining freedom on what they consider their own terms. I use the different mediums because that is what they are drawn to in the patterns of their willing, what gives them a sense of concretely making progress. I don't tell them that in the end all our willfulness will coalesce into one great illumination of how we have failed to love, and that only in love are we free, and that the life of every person since the dawning of time has only one meaning: to choose love, or be opposed to it, to be free or enslaved."

And here we sat in Sarah's living room: Sal, Betty, Sarah and I, expecting it to be like the other occasions when persons came to purchase drugs: smoke a joint, have a little conversation, finish the tea Sarah ritually served, and off they go. But Sarah took it to another level. She was selling Sal and Betty some weed and a fresh batch of LSD-25 that Sarah had just transferred to blotters, and after the transaction Sarah asked "You want to do some here?" Sal looked at Betty who shrugged her shoulders, and Sal looks back at Sarah: "Sure!"

Sarah hands each of us a hit of blotter that we swallow, and then she takes a small bottle with the remaining LSD liquid she hadn't transferred to blotter, looks at it and says "Might as well finish the rest." The rest was at least 25 hits of acid. That makes Sal laugh, and Betty says with a forced smile, "You're crazy." "Yeah," I agreed, "Crazy Sarah," forgetting they knew her as Julie.

"Can you put that Moody Blues album on, *Dark Side of the Moon?*" Betty asks.

"Sure" says Sarah as she gets up to put the album on, and the first track starts to play and lulls us all into a mellow mood as the colorful flower print in their interconnecting free-floating lines on the wall-paper take on what is obviously a simple, yet intricate geometric design similar to the one I saw out on the edge of the universe in my first mushroom trip, and our frivolous talk is heightened to a meaningful exchange. It always happens like this at Sarah's, her house the ultimate safe-zone in any drug-induced, perception-altering state. But this time an incomprehensible twist occurs: Sal and Betty, who are seated on a puffy love seat, both pass out, totally unconscious, and that just doesn't make sense. Who passes out on LSD? I am stunned.

And when I look at Sarah who is seated in her own cushy art-deco chair, she isn't there. Or rather, she had radically changed. She is older and dressed in Middle-Ages clothes, and behind her is a huge stone hearth. Her face is somewhat distorted, like a healed broken jaw that hadn't been properly set. And then I look back over at Sal and Betty, who are still fast asleep. Then it hits me: Sarah and I are in another region, what one might be able to accept from a massive dose of psilocybin, but *not* LSD, never LSD, which only *alters* or *heightens* perception, never *transports* you to regions outside of your environment.

Sarah is smiling and says "You're the first person who has ever seen me."

I had this eerie fear-based sense of the presence of someone other than Sarah, but it was her voice, and even in her altered appearance she still had marked features that were definitely hers.

"Sam...I sensed it was time for you to come here. This is where I am and where I traffic in gathering information from our relatives going back to the 13th century. This is where I learned how our women for hundreds of years were tortured, raped and murdered, where our fathers, brothers and sons fought hard to protect us, and how they failed us for so many centuries that they can no longer look at us, or any woman, without experiencing guilt. Sure, they, too, were tortured, sometimes for long periods of interrogation before being murdered. Remember how dad loved to repeat that an Irishman can sing with his tongue nailed to a tree? Well, our great, great grandfather had his tongue nailed to a tree after a British soldier heard him utter a word in a pub that was on an outlawed word list. Remember how you loved that song *Peggy Gordon* and how we thought it was about unrequited love? Well it is one of many encoded songs, and its meaning is that an Irish man is no longer able to have a contented relationship with a wife and children, that his centuries-old guilt and bitterness turned to a poison that is now

310

passed on genetically, and to remove himself from this guilt he must remove himself from who he has become, which is a more horrible death. He can only save himself by fighting. It is no longer associated with a cause. It's in his blood. If he can't find someone to fight, he'll fight himself, and no matter whose side he is on, he'll always lose.

"I know what you're thinking. It's me, Sam. It has nothing to do with the drug just like Tarot Cards and tea leaves have nothing to do with my visions. You see, with LSD you will at least be able to toss this experience up to an hallucination, and perhaps that is a choice you need to make right now. But you could have journeyed here without the drug. I can take you here anytime you want. You have the choice, to remember or forget. But everything remains the same for me in every moment, because I'm exactly where I really am in every moment, and the power of now is stronger than any place the mind would wander in abstraction, with or without drugs. The now I reside in encompasses past, present and future, and it's like I told you before—I'm not talking about textbook histories or prognostication, but a history that resides in a love founded in sorrow.

"Maybe I'm rushing it, but there's no harm in offering an invitation, is there? You want to come here, where I am? If you do, just walk through that light." And she looks to one side of me, and I turn and there is this 6-foot vortex of light slowly turning, not solid light, but like bubbles of flickering light that float around in a swirling pattern. And I know it's true: if I walk into that vortex I will arrive where Sarah is, but did I want to go there? And then suddenly I am gripped by terror and I become confused, and then a thought that if I walk into that vortex I will go mad like I did in prison and would never find my way back, and I decide *not* to enter, and in that instant we are back in Sarah's room, and Pink Floyd's words "the lunatic is on the grass" with the accompanying echo-laugh floating in the air, and Sal says "That's my favorite tune from the album." *Yes*, I thought. I made the right decision. And the next day I speculate that maybe it wasn't Sarah in her chair that I had seen, or it was her but she was possessed by some demon. Why would I be so frightened otherwise? And when I encounter Sarah I say: "I didn't know LSD can take you to these places."

"It can't. That's why I drank the bottle before beginning. A kind of proof for you that nothing changes for me when I take LSD because I'm in the place I'm actually in every second, meaning there is nowhere else to go; we are malcontents because we want things to be the way we imagine they should be, what we would will them to be if we had that power, but in fact, if that were so we would destroy ourselves quicker than anyone could imagine because willing always trumps being—it is the ground of how we perceive ourselves being free: destroying our essence is the only affirmation there is of having an existence independent of the one gifted to us, which of course is a negation, and exactly why nihilism becomes more and more attractive to us proportionate with our disillusionment, our discovering we have no real power at all to create anything of lasting value, how our Enlightenment is in fact our great Darkness. The glorious or frightening alteration of external perception is just another mask, a trademark of your average acid trip, which is nothing more than a way of hiding from where you actually reside, just a more interesting mask for the moment, with, of course, the delusion that with some chemical you become an alchemist who can conjure a rich interior life unbeknownst to the ignorant—all of this as a continuing escape from where you actually reside, something freely open to anyone, educated or not in 'academic' or 'mystical' knowledge. It's not about knowledge at all, but about being. And then of course the paradox that the denials themselves are important aspects of how you journey inside your destiny, the most fundamental reason I don't interfere with the denial systems people cling to. All I can do is help them recognize it, embrace it and come to terms

312

with it; it's simple enough: wherever a person resides in their mangled gestalt, that's exactly where they are supposed to be. For example, you don't see any of our ancestors, right? But they are with us all the time. There's seven of them with us right now…Sam, your life, how you imagined you died when you were sixteen, remember? In that dimension, as you suspected, the people you knew went to a funeral and mourned your death. And your continuing to live is real for them in their lives even though they imagine you are dead: your aliveness is being processed in their lives even though they buried you…I, too, am limited in what I see. Sure, I keep company with our ancestors going back hundreds of years, but in fact I am in relationship with every human person in their fullness who has ever walked the earth, and they with me. But it is enough to connect with family. Family is the microcosm and why for anyone to destroy another's family history is a way of destroying their lives. This was done to the Irish like never before or after. This gives us an edge if we embrace it. We are best equipped to understand it."

*********

Later in the week I ask Sarah about something that was bugging me. One of her customers, a dancer in a New York night club who lived on Staten Island had come by late one night. She was picking up some weed and some black beauties (amphetamine pills). Her name was Rachel, and not only was she the most beautiful of all Sarah's customers, she was the smartest and the most courteous, and at all times she wore an abiding and relaxed smile. I had asked Sarah about her background, and she said "She's really interesting. Comes from a fairly well-to-do family but wanted to be free from all that. She didn't want to go to college, what her parents insisted on, and her adamant refusal is what eventually sent her out the door, and she

313

came straight to New York from Indiana, and she loves it here. She uses her drugs moderately. She only takes the amphetamines on particularly grueling nights dancing."

Late one night Rachel had her car in the shop and had to take a bus to home, and Sarah asked me to give her a ride. And I did. And Rachel says to me on the way, "You want to stop and have a drink?"

"Sure."

I stop in one of my haunts, a hole-in-the-wall bar frequented by pool hustlers. We order a pitcher of beer, and I get to know a little more about her, and then she says "You know what my favorite thing to do is?"

"What?"

"Walk along South Beach late at night. Want to try it?"

"Sure."

While walking along the beach Rachel tells me about her plans. She works at night dancing in a club and goes to dance, singing and acting classes during the day.

"It's strange" she says. "I love everything I'm doing. But I don't know why: the persons I go to school with…we sometimes go out for drinks. But I don't make any connections. I feel like they talk around me, or rather just talk to be talking, no desire to connect. It's like an agreement that this is what we do until we become famous, and when famous we won't want to know each other anyway, so why start now? Does that make sense?"

"Actually, yeah."

"I don't feel that with Julie…or with you. Both of you are always present, really present. I know you don't talk much, but it's not like you're not there. I can see you listening, intently, and I want to know what you're thinking."

I smile. "I really don't have much on my mind. I've always found people fascinatin', and I love to hear what they got to say, but I pretty much stay to myself. I guess you could say I don't draw conclusions 'bout anythin'; mostly what I got on my mind is my plan to go to Europe."

"That's interesting."

I shrug, and I go to put my hands in my pockets and my right hand rubs against hers, and it stops, and the palm of her hand slides gently into mine, and I squeeze it gently and my whole mind and body melt. I'm back at that brutal realization that *this* is what I have always wanted more than anything. I knew it many years before in the park when I saw a kid I knew with his girlfriend walking by, and here it was happening, being lifted out of that fallen world I had adjusted to with drugs. There was no drug that could compare or compete with what I was now feeling. When we get back to the car we kiss, a gentle kiss, and I look at that confident smile of hers that promises everything that had long ago passed me by, and I melt even deeper into her whole being as my face leans gently into her neck, her flesh so soft with just a hint of perfume that sends my brain into total intoxication. Then I pull back. *What the hell am I doing?*

"You ok?" Rachel asks.

"Yeah...I should get back."

When we drive off Rachel says "That was fun, wasn't it?"

"Yeah."

"Maybe we can do it again sometime?"

"Yeah."

"You ok?"

"Yeah...Rachel...I don't know...It's just that...this was the best night of my life."

She is silent and puts her hand on my arm and leaves it there, both of us silent.

315

After I drop her off at home she says "Call me, OK? Julie has my number."

"Yeah." But I won't. I can't. I was getting a real good sense of what Sarah talked about when she talked about destiny. A psych would say in my commitment to drug use and crime I had arrived at an impasse. But now I was beginning to suspect something else might be going on. I just didn't know what. I did have this utter sense that I had somehow moved in a direction the furthest point from where I had always wanted to be, and now there was no way back, not even an inkling of how I might journey there. All I had was a tortured awareness that I could never see Rachel again, and whenever she called to let Sarah know she was stopping by, I always left and went to a local bar. And this is what I now wanted to know from Sarah: "Did you intentionally set it up that way, for me to take Rachel home?"

"Not really, Sam. It's like I always tell you—I don't get in the way…in no way try to alter where a person travels to. But it did occur to me that you wanted to spend some time with her. I could see it in the way you looked at her, that you longed for a minute with her. I helped that to happen because I knew that's what *you* wanted to do. Am I wrong?"

"No, you're not. Who in their right mind wouldn't? She's a sweetheart, the real deal. But you know my situation. You know it's impossible."

"Is it? You tell me: is there a radical right turn you can make? Is everything carved in stone for you the way you're looking at it? There's no harm in looking at other possibilities. There might be a road you're not looking at."

"Yeah…and it'd be nothin' but a detour."

"No other possibilities?"

"Why don't you tell me?"

"Oh, Sam…I can't do that."

316

"Sure you can! Do the cards, read my palm. It's all the same for me, too. I just wanna know."

"Sam...I don't read for family. Never have. Never will. It's out of the question."

Chapter 21


I hadn't seen Kris in weeks. He was supposed to be finding us a job so we could get IDs

and tickets to Amsterdam, what we had obsessed on for years. He finally shows up with some

excellent news:

"Thought I forgot about you?"

"No…Thought you got busted for boostin' Tootsie Rolls."

"That's funny, man, except I don't eat that shit anymore. I'm gettin' in shape for Europe.

You know…that Continental thang! It's right up my alley."

"So you got somethin' good?"

"Better than good, bro! We're talkin' drop point for numbers people."

"Mob money?"

"Not exactly. Some independents tryin' to work their way up. They're destined to crash,

and we may as well collect before it goes down."

"Who're we talkin' about?"

"Like I said, an independent—Italian with big dreams and a chipper. I'm his connection

for scag. Doesn't want to cop from any of his people—doesn't want it to get back to the bosses.

They gave 'im an opportunity to get off the scag, but, you know—why give up a good thing? His

chipper's turnin' into a full-blown habit, and he don't make enough scratch runnin' errands. I

know he's for real on this. It's a main numbers drop, man, a country club, where they distribute

money to launder, a big piece of it laundered right through the country club itself. Hard

318

untraceable cash, man. I'm tellin' ya, we ain't gonna find a better score, not even a bank, and there's no weapons involved."

"You sure he ain't givin' you a line of shit?"

"It's legit, man. He was ridin' 'round class A back in the day. He came to me when he got leery about the bosses findin' out. I'm the only person he trusts. And he knows I'll be doin' it with you. I'm tellin' you—he's really strung out and hungry. It's our best shot, man. No guns. Clean break in. No alarms at the roof. We can go through the vent."

"Why'd you tell him I was in on it?"

"He wanted to know. He knows I can't crack a safe, and he wanted to know. What was I supposed to tell 'im? Don't you get it? If it wasn't legit he wouldn't be so concerned, strung out and all. I mean, if he was makin' it up, he could give a shit who I was goin' with. He knows he's puttin' his life on the line here, and if he wasn't strung out he wouldn't be doin' it, trust me. Guaranteed $50,000, and he's certain there'll be a lot more. He wants 20%."

"You tell 'im we'll give 'im 20% if it's 50 grand or more, but if it's under, he gets 5%."

"Yeah—I'll tell 'im. And the guy workin' on the IDs. They'll be ready in two weeks. A thousand for both sets. We'll have to get the passports ourselves, but the social security will check out, no problem. They're not dead guys, either, but walkin' and breathin' ones. It's like we'll be their doubles! You heard about that shit, right? Dopegangers or somethin'? You know, like everyone out there has a dope addict double?"

"What the fuck you talkin' about?"

"Forget it, man. Just want you to know it's all fallin' in place. Got all the tools to do the safe. Everythin's good to go. This is the big one, what we always dreamed of, right? I mean, it's like destiny, man, like everythin' was leadin' to this, ya know?"

319

"Yeah. But let's keep it tied to the plan, OK?"

"Yeah, man. You got it. It's good, man. It's all good."

"I figure after we get to Amsterdam we'll feel our way around Europe and figure out where we want to settle and then find someone to get us some new IDs. You better say your goodbyes. We won't be back."

"Goodbye who? You're fuckin' kiddin', right? How 'bout Goodbye New Jersey, Hello fuckin' unlimited drugs in Amsterdam without a pig breathin' down my neck!"

"Yeah. Exactly." But I was thinking more along the lines of letting the drugs go, finding a way to settle in as far away as I could get. I figured adapting to a radically different culture would be the best way for me to make it out the other side of this loop I couldn't kick. I knew Kris would either do the same or eventually head back to the States.

\*\*\*\*\*\*\*\*\*

It was a country club in New Jersey. Getting through the roof vent was easy enough, and we tipped through the dining room and into the main office. It was my basic paranoia about alarms. Once inside the office, I go right to another door behind a big oak desk and pick the lock, taking us to a smaller back room where the safe is. I have everything I need. I would use Tommy's tried and true method of drilling a ½ inch hole to one side of the combination lock and then tape the stethoscope to the hole, giving a clear echo when the tumblers fall, and if that fails, on to the laborious task of peeling with a portable hammer-jack chisel, a two-hour job. The most important thing I have is certainty: I know I will get inside the safe, and the money will be our ticket out of every environment I had ever known. For me it was a recurring belief in geography: changing locations *can* change your life, and I was looking at radical change. Simple as that.

I took a deep breath and got ready to work, but as soon as I laid my bag down I hear sirens, which sets off an alarm in my head. I look at Kris:

"Did you trick an alarm?"

"What the fuck you talkin' 'bout? There ain't no alarms inside. Only on the windows."

I look around and don't see any beams of light. "That's the cops, man! We gotta get the fuck outta here!"

"Fuck no, man! Let's hide. They won't detect anythin'. We came through the fuckin' roof, man! They'll mull around, look for shit...and they won't find it. Let's just cool it, OK? Hide somewhere till they leave. We got time."

"Fuck that! They'll find us...We gotta get the fuck outta here!"

"It's the third floor, man. Where the fuck we goin'?"

"Out the *fuckin'* window...what the *fuck* you think?"

"You're *fuckin'* nuts, man...I'm hidin'. No way in hell can we make that drop."

"Well, *fuck it*, then...I love you, man, but I gotta go."

I go to the window and open it. An image of returning to Denville crosses my mind, and I know that ain't no option. I look down. It's a grass lawn. And I slip into that place with Sarah when we were kids, in the cherry tree looking down at her smiling in awe and great anticipation, waiting for the jump. I knew she would applaud, that she would understand, and that knowing helped move me outside to the small ledge. I am holding onto the side of the window frame looking down, and just like when I shot up the seven bags of heroin years before, there was no thought of death—just a clear view of the lawn and Sarah smiling. I graciously leap out from the window ledge in my swan dive, doing my perfectly orchestrated turn mid-flight, but this time I do not grasp my legs and turn in on myself in a fetal position, but instead stay outstretched for a quick glimpse at the multitude of stars above me before crashing into a ground that offers no bounce—only an instant journey into darkness.

Chapter 22

I hear the ventilator. I hear doctors, nurses and visiting police officers. None of it connects. It is like their words are floating in space and me not having a tat of energy or desire to reach out and claim any one of those words as something of interest. I am immersed in the peace of where I am. After all, there are monks and gurus who invest a lifetime developing disinterest, what they call spiritual indifference, a way of being unplugged to the endless sadomasochistic games and chatter that keep an absurd life interesting, keeping one on one's toes so as not to turn and look into the gaping abyss. Many acolytes fail, as do others who persist even into old age without ever achieving this distance that I had arrived at. Here I am in that place they struggle so hard to reach. Why would I want to give it up? The miracle is mine without investing a second of my life to transcend anything.

It is like floating in an anti-gravity chamber, no pressure on any molecule of my existence, every current in the flow of voices, other sounds and visiting memories instantaneously vaporize upon reception, much like a television image of little or no interest that moves in and fades out, an image powerful enough only to mildly in a miniscule fashion fascinate one's abiding indifference. The one recurring thought is *Why invest energy in anything? For what purpose? It all ends in the same place, a grave or a crematorium. There is no punishment or reward at the end of the line. There is just an end of the line, and I am at the end of that line but still conscious…I like this place…Why go anywhere else? I can be alive but not sucked into any of life's games. There really is no better place.*

I don't know how many days pass. I really have no sense of time. I am a spectator in some type of eternity, for what is time other than a ticking clock we install inside a willed action as a kind of metronome to lend musical sense to a meaningless act? And because I no longer possess a desire for meaning, I have no use for time. And I love my position, registering all the conversations without any consideration of their import, an open and unprejudiced witness to the construction of thoughts and emotions generated for no reason of substance other than to simply occupy interior space as a means, once again, of avoiding that glimpse into the endless abyss of meaninglessness. And this places me in a superior position. I recall with ethereal delight the French film, *The Trout*, the heroine played by the incomparable Isabelle Huppert, a character who as a child, through a series of circumstances involving the stupidity of adults inside their wanton desires, perceives clearly their sadomasochistic games, and chooses in self defense to become a master of those games—and she takes what little comfort is available in whatever space that arrives outside these games to affirm her unique position of being one of the few who are aware that it is only games being played inside the futility of a universe where humans seek only to entertain themselves, the best equipped form of denial, and through the years she finds only one accomplice, a true compadre, an elderly Japanese business man, and in the affirmation of true friendship she discovers the vagaries of inner-spaces of love where whatever is genuine surprisingly shows up and quickly disappears...or is shooed away. But she learns to capture and treasure these moments like rare stones. I had always thought that her character is the only artistic depiction of a person who not only knows beyond the knowing we know, but is clever enough in her maneuverings to find a place for herself outside of the sadomasochistic matrix while still joyfully, impish like, participating in it, and those taking an interest in her, trying to suck her into what they view as their uniquely devised games, become like little children trying to catch a pigeon. And it occurs to me that where I am is an even higher place than where this ultimate heroine had arrived. So what could anyone offer to convince me to depart?

Chapter 23

Sarah obviously had other plans for me, or, as she would have it, she was fulfilling her destined role as an agent in my personal destiny. The State was making plans to have me moved to the prison hospital where I would lounge without interruption in my ultimate comfort zone, and the move was to take place the next morning. Although I was incapable of escaping, they still, as a precaution, had a police officer sitting outside my door. Kris and Sarah arrive—Kris in a theatrical disguise, something both he and I had mastered during our shoplifting escapades, and Sarah with a wheel chair. Kris creates a commotion, yelling at and threatening a male nurse:

"Calm down, sir!"

"Fuck you! I'm not gonna calm down—I'm gonna punch your fuckin' lights out, mother*fuck*er!"

The police officer gets up from his chair and starts moving towards Kris. Kris looks at him and yells "Oh shit!" and starts running through the hall, the officer running after him, and as Kris reaches the other side of the hospital floor, he goes through an exit door, the officer right behind him. And Sarah is already at my bedside pulling the long feeding tube from my nostrils and esophagus and the IV from my arm and then pulling me down off the bed into the wheelchair, putting a blanket over me and taking me to the elevator and down to the garage where her royal blue '68 LeMans convertible, the top already down, is waiting. It takes her only a good minute to pull, push and pull me into the passenger seat, and then leans the seat back. She folds up the wheel chair and throws it in the back seat, placing a blanket over it and tucking it securely under the chair. She then places a pillow to the door side of my head and leans me into it. After pulling out of the garage she turns on the music, and every song has a particular clarity that I had never heard in music before; yet, like the conversations I had heard in the hospital, I wasn't moved in any way by them emotionally or intellectually. What was different, though, is that when the music floats out of the speakers and into space, they don't just hover for a second and dissipate. They are more like waves that pass through me with no sensation other than an awareness they are passing through me in a kind of aesthetic delight, and once departing from my body they are carried off into the wild wind that is blowing all around us.

Sarah drives the entire night, keeping the top down and the heat on. She must have gone through at least three states, only stopping for gas. She doesn't talk much, and when she does it's like declarations:

"Sam, I know how peaceful it was back there, but that's not your destiny. This is your destiny."

"Sam, when I was five years old I overheard mom speaking about us to a friend she had over for tea. And when she was talking about you she said 'He's the one. I knew it all those days I kept him alive.' I never knew what that meant, and still don't. I don't see anything in the cards either. But I do know that whatever mom saw, it has nothing to do with wasting away in a prison hospital ward."

"Sam, when I showed you that vortex of light, I know you got scared and thought I might be possessed, but that was your reluctance to know the truth. I wanted to introduce you to our

327

clan in Ireland going back 800 years. They were inside that light, and they were anxious to greet you. You see, we never left…we're still there working it all out with them, and they're working it out with the rest of humanity. Nothing's changed, not really, and they're with us now, rooting for us. We can't do anything separate from them. That's the real reason you can't get away from dad. It's not what you think. You have to stop running from him. It's not about *becoming* him like Tommy tried to do. That's as silly as running from him. It's just recognizing that you will never arrive at who you are if you reject dad or any of us."

"Sam, where I'm taking you is a place I have known for a long time, a place I knew I had to take you to the first time I saw it. I was on the road, just passing through after I left California. I looked at the horizon and had an urge to pull over, and I did, down this dirt road, and when I pulled down that road I felt you ever so close, closer than we had ever been in life. I could feel you breathing next to me. And I knew I had to take you here one day, and every once in a while I would feel a tinge of regret that I hadn't, especially when you told me you would be leaving the country and that I might never see you again. But now I know this is the time for you to go there, that this has always been the time. Not any other time, not in the past or future."

Sarah turns up the radio as we move along the highway, no doubt mindful that I had always preferred the closeness of others in a car listening to music: one can catch every note in all its clarity in that confined inner-space while being in motion, how it should be with music for anyone with American blood coursing through their veins, *always* in motion—not to get anywhere, but a refusal to sit still, what music demands of every malcontent. Duke Ellington's

"Take the A Train" is playing, the perfect invite to Harlem not for its landscape of sorrow, but every imaginable celebration of life distant from it without denying it, from the many vibrant churches to the jammin' nightclubs and acappella street performers on to the 100-year-old ginseng root and every other mind-altering fix at one's fingertips that take on a rich alchemical property when mixed with music and dancing. The Duke's piano conjures amusing images from my days running the streets in New York, hustling in Midtown to get enough money to head up into Harlem to cop some dope. I recall the time I copped ten bags at the 105th street Projects and headed straight for a basement inside the Projects, a shooting gallery, a large bare-cement and cinder-block area with two industrial wash tubs. Seven blacks stoned on heroin sitting up against the walls and three standing in slow rhythmic nods and slurred speech as cigarettes burn between their fingers. I sit on the floor, pull out my gimmicks and empty five bags into the bottle-cap. And then something strange happens. Five bags would get me twisted, but I got this urge to put the other five bags in the cap, and I just follow through on that impulse, and with the works draw up some water and squeeze it into the bottle-cap, bringing it to a boil and then drawing up the liquid. I tie up with my belt and then shoot the liquid into an easily accessible vein. I go into a nod and feel the pull of unconsciousness. And it hit me: I was dressed to the max: top-of-the-line Italian knit shirt, silk-mohair pants, alligator shoes and a full-length leather jacket, all recently stolen. Out of the corner of my eye I can see one of the blacks side-glance me going into a serious nod, and I know if I OD not only would I be ripped off for the little money I had, but my clothes, too; and I wasn't wearing underwear!, which meant if I didn't die from an overdose I would be a white boy stuck up in Harlem naked! This fear of humiliation was a jolt, like an adrenaline shot to the heart. I jump up and stagger over to the wash-tub. I can feel my knees buckling, but persist with exacting concentration, like a zombie determined to place one foot in front of the other, and when I get to the tub my left hand reaches out to the rim of the tub to stop myself from crumbling to the floor, and holding onto it tight to support my frame, my right hand reaches for the cold-water faucet, and I turn it on full blast. I begin cupping cold water into my right hand splashing it into my face again and again and again. I stumble out of the basement, leaving my belt and works behind. The memory is a reminder how cowardly I was, but that I feared humiliation far more than death, for the thought of dying didn't even enter my mind when I knew I shot up too much dope, and it occurred to me that this spoke the essence of my being human—not my intelligence, imagination, memory and will, what we hail as differentiating us from other animals; it was something far more fundamental and exclusive: the fear of my shame being revealed, and I understood immediately why Adam and Eve's first task after awakening to full consciousness was to sew fig leaves together to hide their shame, for *that* was the first thing that radically distinguished them from all other forms of life.

We had been on the highway for many hours. Sarah with her right index finger is punching chrome buttons to pull in different radio stations, and then stops when she hears Dionne Warwick singing a Salsa version of her "Do You Know the Way to San Jose", a perfect bubbly lull for a pre-dawn glow I can't see but can smell, hear and feel in the air all around us. Warwick's voice has the clarity of a gentle romantic knowing mostly lost for me while doing prison time, a knowing that can gently glide through the deeper realms of sorrow while simultaneously, with the ethereal magic of her voice, tap into the perennial joy at the hub of every soul. And after the second verse of the song, subtle waves from the complex intonations of her words ripple with a hint of sensation along the corridors of my bloodstream, similar to what I had experienced at age 8 when I chose not to cry and my dad in sadistic delight beat me with his

330

construction belt into what he determined would be my death, and how I had an out-of-body experience, floating high above him and my body, and then experiencing a soft but powerful ripple passing through my body that communicated a fear of death, but this similar ripple I was experiencing now is not associated with any fear at all. I can only describe it as a wave, a soft current absent any semblance of force, a cushioned interior movement that modestly stirs an interest in the world outside my peaceful void.

It is enough of a sensation to barely lift my eyelids half open. As the concluding verse of the song plays on I can see farmland and old fences and an occasional home high on a distant hill, a pleasant sight, and then I become aware that there is a thick doubled-overed towel under my chin that I am drooling into, the ends thrown over my right shoulder to ease the pressure of it against the door, and I make an effort to lift my head but it won't move, and that single effort exhausts me. And then the sunlight begins to creep over the edge of a distant mountain, its arrival celebrated by Warwick's refrain: "I'm going back to find, some peace of mind in San Jose."

When the tune ends, Sarah turns the radio off, and we journey for a few minutes more inside the sound of car tires grinding minuscule pieces of asphalt torn from the road into dust.

"Here it is" she says, slowing down and pulling into a dirt road, driving on for another minute, and then coming to a halt. We are atop a wide grassy mound looking down on a vast cherry orchard that is in full bloom. To the right is an old musty wooden shack barely hanging together, perhaps once used as a tool shed, or maybe an outhouse.

Sarah pulls the wheelchair from the back seat and then pulls me from the car into it. She throws the blanket over my legs and tucks it into all the surrounding metal and then wheels me up to a grassy mound at the top of a hill overlooking the cherry orchard. She then sits down on the ground next to me with her arms folded around and chin pressed into her knees, the creeping incursion of sun's morning light now clearly visible in the jagged outline of a mountainous horizon, its gentle rays now dispersing an all-encompassing shadow and illuminating the full dimensions, colors and elaborate design of the cherry trees in their perfectly symmetrical placement. The sun continues its glorious ascent with a presence so powerful its light seems to set fire to the trees, and when it is fully seated in its glory and its rays graciously received and absorbed by every moist molecule of every soft leaf in every cherry blossom in every direction, everything is set on fire, including the old wooden shack that now appears more majestic than the Taj Mahal, and while gazing on the old shack a profound insight takes possession of me, how human beings in this place had long ago gathered together with wood, saws, hammers and nails and with confident precision put together this work of art, clearly revealing the creative impulse so radically alive and operative in every second throughout the universe, and every attempt to thwart it only gets caught up in and consumed by that force, incorporating even the moments of degeneration and death itself into the ongoing glorious act of creation. In the blazing light all around me that burns away every vestige of time, I am barely able to utter a sound as joyful tears pour down my face, having only enough energy and desire to whisper to Sarah, "Am I dead?"

Sarah chuckles. "Come on, Sam...You know you're never going to die."


The End

Made in the USA
Columbia, SC
12 October 2018